THIS SENSATIONAL NEW NOVEL
GOES BEHIND THE HEADLINES
TO TELL A STARTLING STORY
ABOUT THE MAFIA'S
STRANGE POWER TO CORRUPT
BIG BUSINESS AND GOVERNMENT!

ROBIN MOORE'S
THE FIFTH ESTATE
has all the stunning impact of his thriller
The French Connection—yet is much more
far-reaching in its frightening implications!

IT'S A SHOCKING, SUSPENSEFUL
BESTSELLER THAT MIRRORS
A VIOLENT, TROUBLED
AND EXCITING TIME!

D0818542

"IN FIVE YEARS, THE FIFTH ESTATE WILL ELECT A PRESIDENT OF THE UNITED STATES."

That's the shocking promise made to Brad Kendall by one of the top men in The Syndicate—also known as The Fifth Estate.

The Fifth Estate has a fascinating scenario planned for the United States of America—a paramilitary take-over bringing iron law and order, and the deletion of undesirables.

In *The Fifth Estate*, Robin Moore has gone far beyond the violent street world of Popeye Egan, which he portrayed so vividly in *The French Connection*, to write about the world of the giant criminal conglomerates, where the real power lies.

In their plush executive suites—to extend their power even further—The Syndicate—The Fifth Estate—is already working on some major new acquisitions—all the prospective presidential candidates for 1976.

THE FIFTH ESTATE
BY ROBIN MOORE

FAR-REACHING IN ITS
FRIGHTENING IMPLICATIONS

THE
FIFTH
ESTATE

ROBIN MOORE

BANTAM BOOKS · TORONTO · NEW YORK · LONDON

All of the characters in this book are
fictitious, and any resemblance to
actual persons, living or dead, is
purely coincidental.

*This low-priced Bantam Book
has been completely reset in a type face
designed for easy reading, and was printed
from new plates. It contains the complete
text of the original hard-cover edition.*
NOT ONE WORD HAS BEEN OMITTED.

🛇

THE FIFTH ESTATE
*A Bantam Book / published by arrangement with
Doubleday & Company, Inc.*

PRINTING HISTORY
*Doubleday edition published May 1973
Bantam edition published May 1974*

*Bantam Books are published by Bantam Books, Inc. Its trade-
mark, consisting of the words "Bantam Books" and the por-
trayal of a bantam, is registered in the United States Patent
Office and in other countries. Marca Registrada. Bantam
Books, Inc., 666 Fifth Avenue, New York, New York 10019.*

PRINTED IN THE UNITED STATES OF AMERICA

During the four long, frequently discouraging years this book was in the works, a small group kept me writing and helped me over many rough spots with time and encouragement when needed. To them this book is dedicated: My parents, Robert and Eleanor Moore, Jack H. Klein, Martin and Sylvia Heller, John Starr, Lisa Drew, Ken McCormick, Louise Webb, Dorothy Hess, Oscar Dystel, Marc Jaffe, Eugene Weissman, Frances Kramer, Paul Rosen, Anthony Quinn and my brother, John Moore.

CHAPTER ONE

He loitered inconspicuously in front of the airline seat-selection counter at London Airport. He had been the first passenger to check his suitcases onto the New York flight. The young male clerk was methodically tagging the tickets of the other passengers with the seat number of their choice.

The sight of a beautiful young woman coming toward him diverted his mind from the icy fingers of apprehension that clutched at his entrails. She looked to be in her early thirties. Inwardly he registered approval of the svelte, tailored figure, the long black hair falling in waves almost to her shoulders. A practical-looking brown leather bag, tickets and travel documents protruding from a pocket in its side, hung from her right shoulder and she carried a square cosmetics case in her left hand.

As she approached to select a seat assignment the handsome, graying man fell into step behind her. For this girl, the man said to himself as she reached the counter, I'll change to economy class if I have to. He held his breath a moment as she studied the seating diagram. She certainly looks the first-class type, he thought.

"Five A, please," the young woman said in a British accent curiously tempered from the usual English crispness. First class it was.

1

The clerk detached a blue sticker from the diagram labeled 5 A and pressed it to her proffered ticket. She walked away from the counter without a backward glance.

"Five B," the man said without hesitation. The clerk stuck the 5 B tag to the ticket, a conspiratorial grin on his face. The man ignored the implication.

The boarding of the flight still had not been announced so, with his ticket in order to his satisfaction, he walked through the ticket lobby and up the stairs to the VIP lounge. He pushed the button and a pretty honey blonde opened the door. Her set smile suddenly became wide and bright. The severe blue uniform only exaggerated her attributes.

"Brad! Where have you been? Where are you going? I thought I might have heard from you before now."

"Hi, Karen. I'm en route from Beirut to New York." His hand took hers a moment. "I'd hoped to lay over in London for a night but I got this urgent cable from home office. I have a meeting in New York this afternoon."

Karen pouted as she let the door close behind him. "I'm disappointed. You've been neglecting us here."

"Sorry, my dear. I'll make up for it next trip."

"I say, Brad. I've got a long weekend coming up. I thought I'd hop over to New York. Would you be free to see me?"

"Probably, but I can't promise."

"Can I call you from London just before I leave? We've never been in New York together."

"Of course. I'd love to take you out in the big city." For an instant the image of his seat companion on the coming flight crossed his mind. Who could tell what might develop there? To Karen he said, "Call me at the Ascot Towers. Whatever happens I'll see to it the hotel has a room for you—complimentary."

"Thanks, Brad. Try to be available."

He nodded. "I'll be at the bar," he said as the door buzzer rang and Karen turned to open it. "Check Flight 501 for me?"

Coolly he waited for the second call to board before

walking out to the departure gate. Inside the first-class cabin he spotted the seatmate he had contrived to be with for the trip. She was looking out her window. Across the aisle a gentleman traveler was staring fixedly at the empty seat next to the lovely young woman, a positively hungry look about the eyes, Brad thought. A tongue licked at the moisture about the corners of his mouth below a droopy, ginger mustache. He seemed on the verge of heaving himself out of his seat into the one beside the girl. Brad showed his ticket to the stewardess and strode up the aisle, gracefully sliding into the seat. He winked at the suddenly crushed-looking individual. "Sorry, chum!"

As he buckled his seat belt the girl looked away from the window and smiled tentatively. His spirits rose though he was still conscious of that metallic knot of anxiety in the pit of his stomach. He glanced at her left hand which was holding a copy of *Vogue* magazine and noticed that she was wearing a handsome ruby ring, but nothing that looked like a wedding band or even an engagement ring. She seemed to become suddenly interested in her magazine so Brad sat back. There was plenty of time. No point killing something that could be beautiful by being prematurely forward.

His thoughts turned to the precipitous recall to New York he had received. He had been close to hammering out a deal with the Lebanese Government and certain Beirut banking interests to finance another international Ascot Hotel when the cable had arrived. It had been succinct but left no doubt that either he personally was in trouble, the Ascot Hotel chain was in trouble, or both of them had big problems.

For more than fifteen years he had devoted his life to serving the fast expanding company, any meaningful private life long since subordinated to the acquisitions and mergers which had made Ascot the tremendous force it was today in the world of international real estate. Was there really a monolith mushrooming in the financial community capable of buying and digesting Ascot? The information he had been able to gather in Beirut was sketchy at best. Merely that Rafe Leighton, chief executive officer and founder of Ascot, had completed negotiations with Charles Lawrence Ciano, whoever he was, to sell Ascot to Whitehall Development, Ltd., whatever that was.

In the brief few hours before leaving Beirut, after receipt of the cable, Brad had stopped by Intra Bank and talked to his friends there. They knew little about Whitehall. Its operations were clouded in mystery and it never released financial statements. The company was only ten years old and said to be the owner of close to a billion dollars of real estate. The company's stock was owned by Ciano and his partner, Hyman Steinert.

Among other impressive properties Whitehall owned the famed Spire Building, one of New York City's tallest skyscrapers, and the company offices were located on the top several floors. When Brad questioned the knowledgeable Lebanese bankers about the source of funds enabling Whitehall to build to such proportions in just ten years they shrugged their shoulders, rolled their eyes and murmured about the substantiality of the company and its seemingly limitless sources of financing.

The jet was airborne now and the seat-belt signs had flashed off. The steward and two hostesses were preparing to roll the tray of drinks down the aisle of the first-class cabin.

Ever since the days of the slow, lumbering old Boeing stratocruisers when Brad had first begun to travel extensively and continuing with today's elongated Boeing 707s and giant 747s he had made a study of soliciting female companionship along the airways. In the old days one could take a leisurely approach, but now to keep up with the short jet-age flight times, a sort of jet-powered communication had to be set up early in the flight if upon landing a relationship with real and immediate possibilities were to be established. It used to be that he could count on making a liaison with one of the air hostesses but now they were so busy, except when a flight was especially uncrowded, that it was almost impossible to make a post-debarkation engagement.

Just before the stewardess reached his seat Brad turned to the girl beside him. "Can I order you a bloody mary or something?"

Again the fleeting smile. "It's a bit early for me, I think."

"Never too early when you're flying."

The girl redirected her attention at the magazine. The cart of drinks came abreast of them. The walrus-mustachioed gent in the tweediest and baggiest of suits had watched Brad's first ploy with intense interest. It seemed to please him when the girl rebuffed her seatmate. He ordered a brandy and soda.

"Let me have a bloody mary," Brad said to the stewardess. Then to the girl, "Sure you don't want something? Orange juice and vodka, get your vitamins and spirits at the same time."

She chuckled. "Oh, I suppose it's all right. Yes, I'll try one of your screwdrivers."

"Screwdriver," Brad ordered. He watched its manufacture, flashed a triumphant glance at the mustache, took the drink and handed it to the girl. Then he held his bloody mary up to her.

"To a pleasant flight."

She nodded and held her glass up. "Let nothing go wrong." They sipped their drinks a few moments in silence.

"You're not worried?" Brad asked. "You look like a seasoned jetter."

"I do fly a great deal, but I always worry. Landings are the worst really, though takeoffs terrify me."

She sipped silently on her drink again. After a few more moments had passed, Brad asked, "Are you staying in New York or going farther on?"

"I'll be in New York about a fortnight, I should think."

"Do you know the city?"

"I've visited New York. I don't really know it."

"I've been living away from the United States for three years. I'm not sure I know New York any more either."

After a long pause Brad decided introductions were

in order. "By the way, I'm Bradford Kendall. I'm in the hotel business."

The young woman laughed. "You Americans always state your business affiliation when you introduce yourselves."

Brad smiled. "It does get to be a habit."

"Well, my name is Luciana" (she pronounced it Lu CHA na) "Blore."

Immediately Brad recognized the last name but decided not to ask if she was any relation to Barkley Blore, the British financier, who had risen from humble beginnings through many dubious business dealings to his present state of affluence and influence. In fact, Brad had intended to contact Blore about financing an Ascot Hotel in London and in Paris.

"Luciana," Brad repeated. "The way you say it sounds Italian."

"My father was Italian, my mother is English. I grew up in both Italy and England."

"That's the reason for the pleasing softness of your British accent."

"The British don't have an accent. They talk English. It's the Americans who have the quaint way of talking."

Brad laughed. "OK. Touché. But I must say Blore doesn't sound Italian."

"My husband's name is Blore."

"Oh?"

After a pause. "My ex-husband, I suppose I should say. It's all so new being an unmarried woman. Thank God, my father didn't live to see his daughter divorced. Italians don't have divorces, you know." She stared at her empty glass. "I don't know what's wrong with me talking so much. I'm just not used to drink, I guess."

"Have another," Brad suggested. "It'll relax you, take the flight anxiety away."

"I think it's gone now." Luciana smiled. "I'll wait for the wine with lunch I think."

A hundred questions rushed to Brad's mind but he avoided asking any of them. He would find out about this charming divorcée in due course. There was almost one hour behind them, five more to go, he calculated. And then, maybe, they'd have a delay over Kennedy Airport. For once it would be welcomed. Of course that would drive old Rafe Leighton mad but nobody could blame Brad Kendall. He wasn't so anxious to find out his corporate fate that very evening anyway.

If he had to go out job hunting it would be the first time in his life. He had graduated from Princeton right into a Marine Corps commission during the closing days of World War II. Fighting the last few island campaigns of the war he returned to New York and stepped directly into a good job in the Wall Street investment banking firm with which his father had been connected before an early heart attack had taken him. Brad was just becoming bored with the business of dealing in pure money rather than in an industrial or service company when his Marine reserve unit was called up. He was also beginning to realize he had made a big mistake in marrying Gwen. He made no protest at being sent back to war, this time in Korea.

Somehow he had survived the Korean conflict, a far more vicious war than he had seen in the last days of the Pacific campaign, and as a result of the death of Rafe Leighton, Jr., he had gone to visit the youth's parents in Fort Worth, Texas, and ended up working for Leighton, Senior, the owner and founder of the Ascot Hotel chain.

Over white wine and the fish course Luciana explained that her name had been Luciana Paolazzi. Her mother and father were both from banking families, her father's bank was in Milan, her mother's family bank a small one in London. Her father had frankly prospered under Mussolini but by the time she had been born, Brad calculated the year must have been 1939, her father had fallen out with the fascists and allied all his holdings with her mother's family institution in London. After the war he had reopened his bank in Milan and built it up again. She and her mother had returned to Italy where they remained until her father died and then returned to London when she was twenty.

"When I think of the time I spent in London trying to put an Ascot Hotel in Portman Square and never once met you, I am desolate," Brad exclaimed.

"Well, I was married about two years after we returned to London. Perhaps you might have met my husband, Barkley Blore."

"Your husband? But he's . . ." Brad paused and Luciana interrupted.

"Yes, he's older than I am."

"To understate," Brad remarked dryly.

"We were quite happy the first few years. It wasn't so much the age difference—I prefer older men—it was just he was so busy after a while. And other things . . ." She looked down at the seafood cocktail, speared a shrimp with her fork and ate it and sipped her wine.

"Anyway," she smiled brightly, "all the dreary final arrangements are finished, the newspapers have had their go at the divorce story, and I decided to get out of London for a while."

"I suppose you have friends in New York?"

"Oh, yes. It will be interesting to find out which are Barkley's friends and which mine."

"Well, I never met your husband, so count on one friend all your own in New York."

"Thank you, Brad. I do have some relatives on my father's side in America. An uncle in investment banking in New York, and a cousin of sorts in business in Chicago."

As they finished the filet mignon and red wine Luciana said, "Now that you know all about me, what do you do besides make hotel deals all over the world? Doesn't your wife miss you being away so much? I'll bet like all Americans you have a billfold full of pictures of your family."

"I've been divorced for twelve years."

"Do you have any children?"

"A daughter, almost nineteen."

"A lovely age. Have you a picture?"

Brad shook his head. "I'm not that kind of American. Maybe if you're interested you'll let me introduce you to her. Among other things she's mad to go live in Europe for a year."

"She should. She'd learn so much."

The stewardess took their trays, leaving them their almost full wine glasses. They sat back silently for a while. Brad thought of Gwen, never a happy reminiscence. At least she had remarried, but financially it hadn't changed things for him greatly. Unfortunately, he chuckled to himself bitterly, Gwen Kendall and Ed Connor had each sold the other a bill of goods about their personal worth, and after the marriage each found the other was far from the financially substantial partner they thought they were getting.

It was always painful to think about Gwen and he turned back to Luciana and asked her about growing up in Italy.

It was a surprise and a shock to Brad when the pilot announced that in forty-five minutes they would be on the ground at Kennedy International Airport. Never had a flight slid by so fast. By this time, Brad learned that Luciana was staying at the St. Regis Hotel for at least her first week before paying any visits.

As the seat-belt sign flashed on, Brad asked, "By the way, is anyone meeting you at the airport? The company should be sending a limo for me. I'd be happy to drop you off at the St. Regis."

"Actually I'd planned to just hail a taxi," she replied. "But it would be lovely to arrive at the hotel in style. Maybe it will impress the concierge and he'll get me better theatre tickets."

"I'm going to try and catch up on theatregoing myself." Brad felt a delightful empathy between them. "Let's go together."

"You know where to call me."

"How about dinner tonight?"

"After all that food they've fed us?"

"Well, we'll just wander around New York, maybe stop in for a drink at a couple of fun places. It's nice out in the city this time of year. Maybe you'd like to take a horse-and-buggy ride through Central Park?"

"Sounds like fun." Her eyes sparkled and he thought how subdued she had been when he first had tried to talk to her, just a few hours ago. She had done something for him, too. Instead of dreading this return he was now happy and looking forward to dealing with come what may. And he was already planning how he would make Luciana's stay in New York a delight for both of them. In fact, he was thinking even further ahead. Somehow he would convince her to stay in New York until his next trip and then travel with him—if he had a job. If not—well, he was one of the best-known hotel executives in the industry. There were many top-management situations into which he could fit.

The way she entwined her arm through his and interlaced her fingers in his as they began the landing descent exhilarated him. "I'm sorry," she apologized. "Landings terrorize me."

"Hang on, Luciana," he soothed. "Won't be long." I'm sorry to say, he added to himself, feeling her firm, strong thighs pressing against the back of his hand and fingers as she gripped them.

As the plane taxied toward the debarkation ramp, she slowly released his hand. Her face flushed as she realized how intimately she had been pressing his hand to her.

Brad helped Luciana clear customs and immigration and they followed their baggage out to the limousine stand. A driver came up to him. "Hi ya, Mr. Kendall, you don't look a bit different in three years."

Brad was ashamed that he had forgotten the name of the driver who usually drove the Ascot Hotel executives, but covered it up with a cheerful "hello," explaining that the first stop would be the St. Regis Hotel.

"I just can't believe it's only midafternoon here," Luciana exclaimed in pleased surprise. "In London, they're just finishing dinner."

The chauffeur opened the door and Brad helped Luciana in. Forty minutes later, the limousine pulled up in front of the St. Regis-Sheraton Hotel and as Brad helped her to the sidewalk, her suitcases were carried from the trunk into the hotel lobby. Brad walked inside with her, asking the driver to wait.

"They won't let me stand here, Mr. Kendall. I'll hafta drive around the block."

"No. Tell you what. Just take my gear over to the Ascot Towers and tell them to send it up to my suite. I'll take a cab direct to the office."

"No, really, you mustn't go to all this trouble, please," Luciana protested.

"No trouble. I know the entire staff here. Just in case there's a problem, I might be able to help."

Luciana walked to the desk. Discreetly Brad stood aside listening as she checked in.

"Yes, Mrs. Blore, we have been expecting you," the room clerk welcomed her.

This really was Luciana Blore, Barkley Blore's ex-wife. He was ashamed of himself for ever having doubted anything about the girl. But after old Rafe Leighton's disaster, one never knew completely.

"I'll call you about this evening, Luciana," Brad said at the elevators.

"Thank you for everything, Brad. If I should make contact with friends and go out, I'll leave word."

Brad watched her turn and walk into the elevator. She was exquisite from the rear too, the travel creases in her skirt accenting the slight twitch of buttocks. Then she turned and smiled again.

Once more old Brad Kendall is overboard for a dame, he thought. At forty-five, wasn't he a little old for this? Hell, she said she liked older men, and he estimated he was ten to fifteen years nearer her age than her first husband had been.

CHAPTER TWO

The main offices of the Ascot Hotel chain took up two full floors of one of the large new office buildings on Avenue of the Americas. Miss Lehman, Rafe Leighton's redoubtable old executive secretary, greeted Brad Kendall with a stricken look, trying unsuccessfully for a cheerful smile. "He's been waiting for you all day," she said in hushed tones.

"Everyone knew what flight I was on," Brad replied, defensive in spite of himself. "The limo was there."

"I know, Mr. Kendall. He just isn't himself these days."

"What's been happening?"

"So much," she sighed. "He'll tell you, probably much more than he's told anyone else. Oh, by the way, Mrs. Connor has been trying to reach you. She says it is very important, something about your daughter, Andrea. Do you want me to get her before you go in?"

What could be wrong with Andrea, he wondered. Undoubtedly the same old thing, money. Gwen and her husband seemed to live on the edge of financial disaster. Ed Connor just didn't know how to make money. A professional golfer, he appeared to be always well-heeled and seen with the right people, but in business he was a dead loss. One of the good things about living abroad, as far as Brad was concerned, was it made it harder for Gwen to tap him for more money.

Brad smiled at Miss Lehman. "I'm sure it can wait. It sounds as though Mr. Leighton needs to see me immediately."

"I'm sure he'd understand—your daughter and all."

Brad shook his head and walked toward the closed door to Leighton's office.

Miss Lehman announced Brad's arrival on the intercom and then the door mysteriously opened as she pressed a button. Brad walked into the bright, richly decorated corner office and the heavy door silently closed behind his back.

Already an intimately autographed picture of the current President of the United States had joined the four other presidential likenesses, similarly autographed, hanging in silver frames on the wall behind his desk. Briskly, Kendall strode across the carpeted floor. He was appalled at the change in the old man's face and bearing since the last time they had met. When—only a few short months ago? Brad tried to cover his shock with an extra broad smile.

Leighton's eyes were haggard and sunken, new lines cut deeply into a sallow puffy face, his shoulders seemed stooped, and the white mane of hair somehow seemed thinner and less groomed.

"I came as soon as I got your cable." Brad could think of nothing more appropriate to say.

"Sit down, my boy." Even his voice was weak and trembling. Leighton indicated the chair beside his desk. "I'm glad you're here."

Kendall took the chair and waited for Leighton to start the conversation. Glancing at the ship's clock that tinkled the time in bells every half hour, Brad wondered when he would be free to call Luciana.

"Big changes," Leighton said huskily.

"Yes, so I gather."

After a pause, Leighton said, "You've done a fine job in the International Division—with hellacious little working capital from here."

Kendall nodded, but said nothing, wondering what direction his chief was trying to take this discussion. Leighton leaned back and stared out the window looking north up to Central Park. "Sorry I moved the home office to New York. Big mistake. Everything was fine until we left Fort Worth."

"Your high-priced directors put a hell of a lot of pressure on you to make the step," Kendall recalled.

"Never should have done it. Oh, you get to thinking big in New York." He nodded grimly. "So big you bust your britches and then your ass starts to showing." There was another long silence. "Ever heard of White-hall Development"—he paused—"Limited, if you please."

"Not much. Privately owned. No balance sheets or annual reports. Well financed."

"They got plenty money, I can tell you. And none of it's oil money. They own more real estate in New York City than the Catholic Church, and that's going some. Now they want to get into hotels. They bought hotels wherever they could, but the good ones are owned by us, or Sheraton, or Hilton or the other chains."

"I can see that Ascot would be a good acquisition for them," Kendall prompted.

"It took them a long time, four years or more. Started when we came to New York. Ascot Towers did it," he said bitterly. "Remember when we decided to build that house?"

Well did Brad remember. A suave new director of Ascot, Bryant Beddington, had persuaded Leighton to go into the deal. Beddington was the prestigious chairman of the Conference of National Leadership. The organization was made up of the top leaders in all fields of national endeavor. Shortly after old Rafe Leighton had been asked to join the Conference he invited Beddington to sit on his board. Beddington was a professional company director and considered a catch for even the largest corporations.

In all honesty Brad had to admit to a touch of professional jealousy. Yet there was something about this impeccably financed businessman, just Brad's age, that had caused Brad to warn Leighton from going into any deal with him, especially the Ascot Towers project.

"Anyway, Brad, you're going to be working for Whitehall in a few weeks. Assuming, of course, you stay with the—" Brad sensed the pain in the old man's tone "—Ascot Division of Whitehall, Limited."

"I'll do whatever you want me to, sir," Brad replied. In his seventeen years with Ascot, he had never called Rafe Leighton by his first name.

"I'm afraid you'll have to make up your mind on that yourself. Whitehall is a big organization. Digesting Ascot will increase its total size by no more than 5 per cent."

"The deal is definite then?" Brad asked.

Leighton nodded. "I'm afraid so." He paused, then, "No. That's not fair to say. I'm glad Ascot will continue as a corporate entity, growing and prospering, holding the properties and employees together." He smiled sadly. "And I can't really complain too much about my personal financial arrangements."

"What happens from here?" Brad asked.

Leighton looked at him wearily, and putting his hands on the desk in front of him, pushed himself to his feet. "I promised C. L. Ciano, president of Whitehall, that I'd bring you over to his office when you came in. I think he wants you to take over as president of Ascot under Whitehall. I will be retired in a few days. Don't ask me what I'll do with my time."

CHAPTER THREE

The company limousine was waiting at the curb outside the office building when Rafe Leighton and Brad Kendall emerged. The driver stepped out and opened the rear door for them.

"I took your luggage over to the hotel, Mr. Kendall," the driver said. "They'll have it up in your suite, waiting."

"Thanks," Brad acknowledged.

They sat silently as the car pulled away up Sixth Avenue; Brad could never get used to calling it Avenue of the Americas. He could sense Leighton's real despair over the loss of his company. It had taken a lifetime of hard work, shrewd maneuvering and building a reputation of honesty and square dealing to create Ascot Hotels.

After a few minutes, Leighton turned to the younger man. "I don't know what's going to come up at this meeting, but remember, I'm behind you all the way, whatever you decide. Hell, I'm through anyway and even if you are offered the presidency, I don't think they're going to let you do just anything you want."

"I appreciate your feelings, chief. We'll see what this Ciano has to say. What's he like?"

"You be the judge of that. He graduated from college and business school. Keeps the diplomas on the wall of his office. Maybe he wants to impress all us country boys who made it through State Teachers College or whatever."

Leighton fell silent, staring out dourly at the mass of cars on the streets. Finally they reached Park Avenue and turned downtown. In the distance he could see the top of the Spire Building. Ten minutes later, the company car drew to a halt in front of the famous office building, and Kendall jumped out, Leighton heaving and pulling himself from the limousine behind the younger executive. Wordlessly the two men entered the building and walked to the bank of elevators running to the top five floors.

On the sixtieth floor, Leighton led the way from the elevator into a carpeted foyer with a view down over New York City that made Kendall catch his breath. A man in uniform sat behind the desk marked "Reception." Leighton told him who they were and the announcement was made. They waited until a reply came over the interphone. The guard—there was no other way of describing the man—motioned toward a door and they approached it just as another smartly uniformed, powerful-looking young man opened it from the inside and asked them to follow him. Walking down the corridor Brad noticed that all the office doors were closed. No name plates of any sort identified the occupants of the various offices.

The north end of the floor was closed off into one large suite, to which the second guard admitted them through a sliding door.

"At last, a real girl-type secretary." Brad grinned at the girl sitting at a desk. "I was beginning to wonder if this was an office or some kind of a vault."

The girl, a pretty and young brunette with oval-shaped brown eyes and an olive complexion, stood up and walked to them. "Mr. Ciano is looking forward to meeting you. Please follow me." She led the way to yet another sliding door, pressed a hidden switch and the door silently glided open. Brad followed the chief into the richly carpeted, spacious office. All of New York City north of the Spire Building spread out under the large, wall-sized windows in front of which, at a wide desk, clean but for one file folder, stood a swarthy-complexioned, lean-faced man of middle height. His hair was jet black with thick tight curls close to the scalp and his dark eyes seemed a trifle hooded behind rimless spectacles. He wore an impeccable dark-gray flannel suit, button-down blue oxford shirt and a regimental striped tie. It was hard for Brad to actually make out the facial expression, so bright was the north light behind him.

Charles Lawrence Ciano came toward them and shook hands with Leighton and then with Brad. It was a firm handshake; the hand was surprisingly hard for a man who worked out of such an office. Unconsciously Brad looked about for the diplomas Leighton had mentioned and saw them on the wall opposite the desk.

"I appreciate your coming up to see me, Mr. Leighton." He looked to Brad and a tight-lipped smile appeared. "And I am very grateful that you were able to bring Mr. Kendall." He gestured toward an arrangement of a leather sofa and two deep leather easy chairs. They walked over and sat down, Ciano in one chair, Brad on the sofa, and Leighton slumped back in the other easy chair.

"Well, Mr. Kendall, I'm sorry we brought you back from Lebanon before you were able to complete your negotiations, but we felt that your presence here was more important right now." He speared Brad with a long stare, his black eyes glittering.

"We intend that Ascot go on to become the most powerful hotel chain in the world. We are particularly interested in international development, your specialty. We want you to develop large luxury hotels in Turkey, Syria, Lebanon, Sicily, Marseilles, and Montreal—all areas in which you have been trying to make deals."

"That's right, Mr. Ciano," Brad broke in, excitement already gripping him. "But in every case I've had difficulty raising sufficient capital locally."

Now Rafe Leighton leaned forward. "Brad has done his best, but we just didn't have the working capital. Every deal he's made overseas, and there've been some damned good ones, we've never put in more than fifty thousand dollars. The Caracas deal Brad made is worth half a million a year to us."

"How much cash would you need to insure making the Middle East deals?" Ciano asked.

"If I had ten million dollars I could deliver every location you mentioned," Brad replied. "I've worked it out a hundred times. And each hotel would be at least a six- to eight-million-dollar structure."

"You'll have your ten million when you call for it. Now one other thing." Ciano flashed a significant look at Leighton. "You've talked to him about taking over as president?" The old man nodded and Ciano continued. "We've checked you out thoroughly, Mr. Kendall. Hy Steinert, my partner, agrees with me that you have all the qualifications to be the new president of Ascot Hotels. We are expecting you to expand dramatically both in the United States and throughout the world."

Brad nodded thoughtfully. "I appreciate your confidence, Mr. Ciano." He paused and then added, "Of course, I would like to know more about Whitehall, too." He caught a surprised look from Leighton. "I've been operating abroad for the past three years, you realize."

Ciano seemed surprised, but he quickly picked up the conversation. "We are a very diverse group of corporations within the single holding company known as Whitehall. Since our ownership is severely restricted, so is the general information we release. I'm sure Mr. Leighton can tell you about us. We have a strong regard for the Ascot Hotel chain and we are most anxious to preserve its continuity of direction and its standing in the hotel industry. We could conceive of no better way of doing this than by asking you, who are so closely identified with the company, to become president."

"I certainly would like to see Ascot realize its international potential," Brad fenced.

"You would probably have to make New York your headquarters from now on. We'll send you a new international man, a most experienced individual. You can teach him the art of hotel acquisition."

"Most of my deals are the result of personal contacts," Brad protested.

"I'm sure you can transfer them to your new international man. You are a well-known, a famous hotel executive. We will need you always available. By the way, I suggest you join a country club. With your handicap, it would be a shame not to keep up your golf."

They have been checking on me, Brad thought. "The good ones all have pretty long waiting lists," he hedged.

"I had Copper Rock in mind for you. Your name is number one on the list at the moment." He nodded to Leighton. "Our Ascot director, Bryant Beddington, has arranged it."

Then Ciano seemed to lean back in his chair and Brad felt a sudden release of pressure. This was a powerful, intense man. Brad wondered if he shouldn't just extricate himself from the whole Whitehall-Ascot situation right now, while there was still time to do it gracefully. Yet somehow he seemed unable to resist the mysterious compulsion of this Charles Lawrence Ciano.

"I suppose we are covering a great deal of ground in a hurry." A sympathetic smile appeared on Ciano's face. "But it has been fast, decisive moves that have enabled us here at Whitehall to expand."

Rafe Leighton had never ceased to be impressed by C. L. Ciano. Perhaps fascinated would better describe what he felt in the financier's presence. Watching Ciano manipulate Brad Kendall, Rafe as always speculated on how much of the circumstances which culminated in his sale of Ascot had been manipulated by this shrewd, smooth man of Italian origin. To all outward appearances, it had been a last-minute move when Ascot had been in serious trouble.

Rafe would never forget the day in his own elaborate offices, when the mayor of New York, his commissioner of special projects and Bryant Beddington had convinced him to take the plunge and pledge the collateral of the entire chain behind the financing of what would be New York City's newest, most luxurious and largest hotel.

Changing the tempo of the conversation, Ciano said, "I guess we have thrown a lot at you in a short time. You've been doing a great deal of traveling and this has been a long day for you. Why don't we plan to meet here again in twenty-four hours? That will give you a chance to make up your mind."

Brad nodded. "Thanks. It sounds like a great opportunity. I'll look forward to seeing you tomorrow afternoon, sir."

"We do want you with us," Ciano said, concluding the meeting. "I'm sure you'll find the salary and benefits more attractive than anywhere else in the industry."

Through the long ushering-out process, Brad's mind darted from one consideration to another as first the pretty secretary and then the two male receptionists conveyed him and Leighton toward the elevators.

Once in the limousine, Brad turned to his chief— his ex-chief now. "Did you ask for the job for me?"

Leighton shook his head. "I don't even know if you should take it."

"I could give it a try. I can always resign later."

After a long silence, Leighton said, "Maybe, but I have a feeling in my bones that once you join those fellows it's for life."

"Are you implying that Whitehall is some kind of quasi-legal criminal syndicate?"

Leighton ignored the remark, sitting impassively as the limo struggled through the late afternoon traffic. Finally he said, "Whatever Whitehall is, there wasn't one complaint from the stockholders. After all, they had their choice of selling out for something or owning shares in a bankrupt company. And I couldn't complain. Ciano made a side deal with me to pay a premium for my shares. I'm just sorry you didn't get a better price for your stock. It was up to twenty for a while." He sighed. "The hole we were in, we were lucky to get Whitehall's ten dollars a share."

Brad Kendall nodded somberly but he did not tell Leighton that he had given half of his stock to Gwen as part of the divorce settlement and sold considerably more as Gwen's demands, allegedly on behalf of their daughter, had increased. At one time, just because he loved Andrea, he had been supporting Gwen, her husband and their own young son, Edwin, Jr., Andrea's half brother. At least he had sold it at the top of the market, he thought.

Finally, the black limousine pulled up in front of the office and Leighton, followed by Brad, stepped out on the curb. After the visit to the Spire Building, the Ascot offices looked a little less imposing as Brad followed Leighton back to his office.

"If you take the job, I'll get my things out of here this week, Brad."

"Why don't you stay for a while," Brad suggested. "I can work out of one of the smaller offices."

Leighton shook his head. "No, my boy, it's yours, if you want it. The sooner I'm completely removed the better it's going to be for both of us. I'll just take my money and go back to Texas. I've taught you all I know and you've gone way beyond my competence anyway. How about a drink? By the way, isn't there anyone you want to call?"

Brad thought longingly of Luciana. He was way overdue calling her, but he didn't want to make the call in front of Leighton. As if reading his mind, the old man said, "I'm going into the can for a minute. Make yourself at home in your new office. The red phone does not go through the switchboard," he added. The bulky Texan disappeared.

Brad picked up the red phone, and dialed the St. Regis. Luciana's line was busy. He held on until Leighton emerged from his private bathroom and made for the cabinet he used for a bar. As he dropped ice cubes into two glasses and then poured an Old Fitzgerald Bourbon over the ice and added soda, he asked Brad, his back to him, "Have you got a little time now, or do you have an appointment?"

"I've got all the time you want with me, chief." He hoped his desire to be somewhere else didn't show.

Leighton turned and came toward him, a glass held

out. Brad took it and both men sat in chairs on the same side of the executive desk. The old man raised his glass. "Here's to your future, wherever it may lie." They both took long swallows and then Leighton made another pronouncement. "May you soon figure the right trail to follow."

They sipped the drinks quietly and then Brad broke the silence. "What really did happen?"

"That's a long and painful story."

"Might help me to know."

Leighton nodded. "Yep. It sure might. Just that a man hates to tell what a damned old fool he's been."

"You never were that, sir."

After a long silence, Leighton nodded to himself. "No matter how smart you are, no matter how many connections, no matter how much money you can call on, there's always someone got you beat. And that someone is always the fellow you least figure on to be able to take you. Otherwise you'd be prepared against him."

Brad leaned back and waited for his old mentor to go ahead with the story. Finally, after they were into a second drink, the story came out.

CHAPTER FOUR

By 1958, Rafe Leighton had no longer been able to convince his directors that Fort Worth, Texas, was the right home city for the burgeoning Ascot Hotel chain. Even the Texas members of the board, the oil interests who had invested with Rafe in real estate, pressured for a Chicago- or New York-based operation. When Bryant Beddington, long before he had become a director, had brought Ascot the deal to buy a group of fifteen hotels in important eastern cities, an area in which Ascot was weak, Leighton reluctantly acceded to the wishes of the directors.

At first, Rafe had established headquarters in their large but by any standards second-class hotel, the Park West. Soon Rafe found himself with a growing marketing and operations staff and then vice presidents began surfacing all over the organization. Until the New York move there had been only one vice president, but by the mid-sixties, with over seventy owned and franchised hotels and motels in the chain, he had vice presidents and second vice presidents all over the place.

Beddington made clear to Leighton soon after the New York move that he had to achieve a corporate image, that Leighton himself must be discreetly publicized as one of America's important corporation presidents. He succumbed and a powerful public relations agency was retained to build up Ascot and Leighton in both the financial community and to the public at large. Leighton became a member of the Conference of National Leadership.

In 1965, the first serious offers were made to him to sell out his interest in Ascot. But life without his company wouldn't have been worth living and he curtly refused all potential buyers. At one time he had been building his business for his only son, Rafe, Junior, but when he had been killed in Korea during the so-called peace negotiations, Leighton had all but lost his drive to make his hotel chain the most powerful in the world. And then Brad Kendall, his son's Marine battalion commander, had come to Fort Worth to express his condolences. As was the case with young Captain Leighton, Major Kendall was a reserve Marine officer, called unexpectedly to active duty.

It took all his powers of persuasion, but Leighton convinced Kendall, once more a civilian, to leave his waiting job in an old-line Wall Street investment banking house and move to Fort Worth and become the vice president of Ascot Hotels.

With the arrival of Brad Kendall, his wife and three-year-old daughter in Fort Worth, the whole tenor of Ascot Hotels changed; an aggressive acquisition and building program was launched, combined with a hard-driving sales force. Operations were streamlined and every year Ascot announced dramatic sales gains over the previous year with correspondingly increasing value in the company's common stock. It was only when Brad joined forces with the other directors urging the company to move its headquarters to New York that old Rafe finally gave in. Perhaps Brad was influenced more by his restless wife, Gwen, who hated the Southwest, than by business judgment, but the move to New York was made.

Simultaneously with the sudden persistent efforts to purchase Ascot, Bryant Beddington had brought a dramatic proposal to the attention of the board members of Ascot at a special meeting. His investment banking company was in the process of completing the assembly of a prime block close to the United Nations Build-

ing and was interested in arranging the financing for a
new Ascot Hotel on this land. It would be the most
important hotel in New York. Beddington's presentation had electrified the directors and even Leighton himself had been profoundly impressed when Beddington
went out into the hall and ushered back into the meeting the mayor of New York and his commissioner of
special projects. The mayor left soon after he was introduced and had given a short, forceful speech on the
need for this hotel to the city and hinted that the city
was willing to make many valuable concessions to get
the hotel built. He left the commissioner at the meeting to answer further questions.

Months later, as negotiations progressed on securing
the financing, Brad Kendall began opposing the project. This one hotel, he reasoned, would tie up all other
company expansion for several years if Leighton
pledged the collateral of the entire Ascot chain behind
the project. There just wouldn't be any leverage left to
borrow money or otherwise finance the international Ascot Hotels which had become Kendall's most consuming
project. For this one hotel in New York, albeit one of
the world's most prestigious, foreign development would
be severely crippled. Putting the company behind the
hotel was taking the risk of bleeding the entire Ascot
chain to death through this one vulnerable artery, he
argued.

Bryant Beddington had won out over Brad Kendall,
though not without formidable assistance. Lilli Darlene, the fiery French woman who had come into Leighton's life, used every subtle form of influence at her
command to persuade her Rafe to go ahead with the
project. She reinforced her campaign with attacks of
vituperation against Brad Kendall, both personally and
as businessman, to discredit his arguments against
pledging the credit of the entire company behind this
one deal. Attacked on all sides, by Beddington and the
directors who favored the Ascot Towers project, and
the mistress of his chief, Brad elected to specialize in
international development even with the limited resources at his command.

"Lilli Darlene." Leighton sighed and stood up, walking heavily to the bar to pour himself a third Bourbon. Brad shook his head at the suggestion of another and watched sadly the once-vital and powerful businessman taking a long gulp of the drink. "I owe you plenty for what I let happen to you, Brad."

The younger man shook his head. "I did all right, chief."

"I'd still like to know whether Lilli and I just happened, or if it was all part of the big plan, maybe Ciano's big plan. I don't know." He shook his head helplessly. Brad knew the story, but let the old man tell it again anyway; perhaps it would be a good catharsis for him.

Lilli Darlene was everything Rafe had imagined a beautiful young French woman, a wealthy widow, should be. She was blond, tantalizingly bosomy, with a slender figure, and just thirty years old. She made Rafe feel thirty years younger before the reception she was giving in her lavish duplex apartment on Park Avenue was half over. Madame Darlene was one of the chief patronesses of the Paris in Spring Ball being given to benefit a fashionable charity that Ascot's public relations firm said Leighton should be interested in. As a major donor and patron, Rafe was one of the select members of the committee invited to Madame Darlene's soiree.

To Rafe's surprise and delight, when the reception was over at eight o'clock, she asked if he would stay later, perhaps have supper with her, she was so interested in the hotel business and would like to learn more of it. In fact, she was thinking of investing some of the fortune her husband left her, she said, in the hotel business. When Rafe Leighton left Madame Darlene just before midnight, he had gone soft as a marshmallow, as he put it, and that was the end of truly rational thought on his part for over a year.

Mrs. Rafe Leighton, the same age as her husband, had not aged nearly as well. Rafe had been just sixty when he met Lilli and was leading the bachelor life by dint of keeping his wife in the care of attendants, at their home in Fort Worth. Their marriage had been a good one, except that they had been able to have only one child. Hester Leighton had been failing, her mind wandering for years, and when the reality of her boy's death penetrated to her, she moved into a world of permanent fantasy, never to emerge and face harsh realities again.

What had captured Rafe Leighton so completely about Lilli was the fact that she was a wealthy woman who neither needed nor wanted anything from him beyond advice, which he was flattered to be asked for, and companionship which he yearned to give her. How attentively she had hung on his every word and how easily and naturally the romance had developed between them. It had to be the real inner Rafe Leighton she was interested in. Indeed, on the financial end, Lilli seemed to try and outdo him in bestowing gifts. She had asked him to be her escort at the ball, a fact which delighted the public relations men, and she had given him a set of platinum cuff links set with diamonds to commemorate the occasion. He tried to match her imagination and generosity but Lilli outclassed him.

Leighton had always kept himself in good physical shape, but after the first meeting with Lilli he almost completely gave up drinking and smoking and did calisthenics three to four times a week at the New York Athletic Club, and then swam five or six laps of the pool.

The first time they had made love was a month or more after they met. In anticipation of the event, he had been taking special hormone pills prescribed by his physician. He needn't have bothered, as it turned out. So accomplished, so erotic was Lilli, her long fingernails scratching just so under his scrotum as she hungrily used tongue, lips and the inside of her mouth to produce the most exquisite sensations the old man had ever known in his rather sexually barren existence, that he found himself performing with the frequency and ardor of a young man. She was everything Rafe wanted. He set in motion the expensive legal proceedings to divorce his balmy wife.

To Rafe's amazement, Lilli was highly informed on business, particularly the hotel business. He found himself telling her the most intimate business details of Ascot Hotel Corporation financing. Finally he began seeking her advice, instead of the other way around, on matters involving the daily operations and finance.

Lilli's chief interest was in the Ascot Towers project. "What a great hotel opening you and I could give," she would enthuse. When he told her of Brad Kendall's objections to the project, she appeared to give them great thought and deliberation before finally telling Leighton that the young man had no feeling for big business, the company had outgrown him. Soon there was never an evening together without Lilli urging Rafe to put everything into the Ascot Towers deal. She would pledge her own fortune behind the project, she declared. "Do it for me, Rafe." Her eyes were bright with excitement. "For us, darling."

At a large closing the Ascot Towers construction project was signed. Beddington's firm was underwriting the construction bond issue and Rafe Leighton pledged his entire chain behind the bonds and mortgages to pay for the construction and equipment and furnishings of the thirty-eight-million-dollar project.

Lilli had been standing beside Rafe as he turned over the first shovelful of dirt with the company's gold ceremonial shovel, and construction had begun.

At this point, with both Lilli and the directors pressuring him to move Brad Kendall out of the picture, Rafe encouraged his protégé to pick a foreign city for a headquarters and spend full time on foreign development.

If, now that the hotel was actually under construction, Lilli seemed a bit distant, if she was unable to see him anywhere near as often as formerly, if her ardor had cooled and their love-making became a thing of the past, Leighton made no mention of this to friends or associates.

His first meeting with C. L. Ciano had occurred while financing was still being arranged for the Ascot Towers. Ciano's Whitehall Development Company offered to purchase half interest in the Ascot chain if this money would be used to build the new hotel. Rafe Leighton turned the offer down, telling Ciano that as long as he was alive no stockholder would ever be in a position to press demands on Ascot management.

The financing, through Beddington, was arranged and Leighton pledged the credit and security of his entire hotel chain to guarantee the construction loans and the bond issue which was quickly oversubscribed. Commissioner of Special Projects Dave Colten was constantly at Leighton's side during the planning of the hotel and highly recommended a certain construction company which did a great deal of work for the city. At one of Lilli's soirees, Commissioner Colten and Thomas Abrizzi, president of the construction company, spent half the evening discussing building the hotel, and it seemed that Lilli was a friend of Abrizzi and his wife. A month later, even though Abrizzi was not the lower bidder, he was awarded the contract and construction was under way with great fanfare. An entire section of the New York *Times* was devoted to the new hotel under construction and the other hotels of the Ascot chain.

And then the trouble started. Although Ascot had always enjoyed good relations with labor, unjustified strikes began to break out at the profitable hotels around the country. One of the most profitable had always been the Ascot in Pittsburgh. Suddenly, a labor leader called a strike and shut the hotel down. The strike went on month after month without settlement. In Chicago, the Ascot Hotel restaurant served a dinner to the elite of a large convention. All came down with food poisoning and sued the hotel. Each suit had to be settled at great cost, but the worst result was that subsequent conventioners as well as the local populace shunned the Ascot restaurant and only stayed at the hotel when rooms could not be obtained elsewhere.

It seemed to Rafe Leighton that during the construction of the new hotel he was constantly solving crises. And then what Commissioner Colten had told him was impossible happened. A strike was called by the construction workers of the Abrizzi Company working on the Ascot Towers Hotel. Despite the efforts of city mediators, Ascot's labor negotiators and Abrizzi himself, the strike went on for four crippling months.

The banks who had supplied the construction loans became restive as it appeared obvious that the hotel would open at least six months and possibly a year later than scheduled. Meanwhile, strikes, mysterious fires, accidents leading to litigation, and key personnel quitting plagued the structure of the company.

Rafe Leighton had nowhere to turn for comfort. Lilli Darlene had mysteriously disappeared from the city. Suddenly, no one knew anything at all about her. The first inkling Leighton had of the true source of his problems came from an Ascot investigator he had assigned the job of locating Lilli. The apartment building in which she had lived so lavishly was owned by a subsidiary of Whitehall Development. Also the investigator discovered that a public relations firm which handled certain business for Whitehall had also been retained to make a society figure of a French woman named Lilli Darlene.

When the hotel finally opened one year late, the entire Ascot chain was in serious trouble. The banks were worried at the plummeting profit figures of the company. For the first time since Leighton had founded the company, it showed two consecutive quarters in the red. Bankers began foreclosing on their loans. Leighton was in the middle of the most debilitating financial struggle of his life. Strangely, the only division of his chain reporting no troubles and sending back consistently increasing profits was the international division. Whenever Brad Kendall came back to New York, Leighton felt his spirits rise. Kendall was acclaimed in the hotel trade papers as one of the most accomplished international directors in the industry. But the profits of the international division notwithstanding, Ascot was slipping at an ever-increasing rate toward bankruptcy. The entire chain was on the verge of being dismantled one hotel at a time to be sold to pay off loans and make the guaranteed payments on the bonds, when Leighton received the phone call from C. L. Ciano asking him to attend a meeting at his office.

"Well, Brad, you have the entire picture now, I expect."

Brad nodded silently and stole a glance at his watch. Maybe he should try another call to Luciana. But he didn't want to remove his presence as long as the old man needed him around.

"Pour yourself another drink, my boy," Leighton invited. Brad stood up and walked over to the bar and poured himself a light highball to keep Leighton company. He turned to his former boss.

"OK, Mr. Leighton. Tell me what you think this Whitehall Development, Ltd., really is? You've been hinting all over the place."

"I guess I don't have to tell you what I think," Leighton replied uncomfortably.

"Well, I'll tell you what I think then. Whitehall is using the money and muscle of organized crime to infiltrate legal businesses in the country."

"You may be right, Brad. Well, I'm too old and tired to worry about it now. I didn't know a man could go through such hell and still think and talk like other men. When you know that you have only yourself to blame, it's damned hard living. I guess I'm lucky those fellers at Whitehall let me go home with as much as they did. Of course, I could have made it a lot harder for them if I'd wanted to fight it out, put the company into Chapter Eleven of Bankruptcy. But they'd have won anyway."

Leighton swallowed the rest of his drink. "All right, Brad. I'll let you go now. I guess you want to check with Gwen about Andrea. They've both been calling to find out when you'd be home." Leighton winked. "Of course, I didn't tell them for sure you'd be in today. So if you want to put it off till tomorrow they won't know you didn't call the minute you arrived."

"Thanks, chief," Brad said gratefully. He knew that tonight he couldn't take Gwen's histrionics.

"Not chief any more, Brad." The lines and jowls of

his face set in a look so sad that Brad couldn't bear to look at him. He stood up.

"See you tomorrow."

"Good. You've got a lot of thinking to do about the offer."

Brad Kendall shook his head. "Nothing to think about. I guess I'll just try to find a job somewhere."

CHAPTER FIVE

As often was the case when he traveled, Brad Kendall couldn't remember where he was when he woke up in the bedroom of his hotel suite. He had a slight suggestion of a hangover, which was not unusual. He also woke with the realization that he needed to be waking up with a woman but wasn't. Then he remembered. New York, the Ascot Towers. He smiled. It had been a beautiful evening with Luciana. Women were usually tired after a long jet trip, but not Luciana. As she pointed out when he finally took her back to the St. Regis in a horse and carriage after a ride through the park, it was eight in the morning by the time she was used to. The kisses as the horse clopped along had been the sweetest he had known in years, undoubtedly aggravating the present condition in his loins. But they would be together again tonight, she had promised. She had deliberately refrained from making any engagement last night in hopes he would ask her out, she admitted between kisses in the carriage.

Briskly he jumped out of bed and made for the shower. By the time he had shaved all was under control and he dressed to face the day. Although because of the five-hour-time difference he had not had much sleep he felt rested and alert. There were many decisions to be made. He would have to tell Ciano to look elsewhere for a president of Ascot Hotels and then start actively looking for a new position. To find what he wanted wouldn't be easy. There just weren't that many large hotel chains that were in need of an international director.

He thought of the necessity to see Gwen and grimaced. It was 9 A.M. A good time to call. Gwen never rose before ten-thirty or eleven in the morning. Maybe Andrea would answer and they could meet without his having to talk to Gwen and listen to a long rehearsal of the financial problems he was not facing up to, according to her. He dialed the number. On the fourth ring, just as he was about to hang up in relief, Andrea answered.

"Hi, it's Brad," he said cheerfully. She had always called him by his first name. She called her stepfather "Daddy." "Back from foreign shores."

"Hello, Brad. We've been wondering where you were. When did you get in?"

"Too late last night to call. How's everything?"

"All right. Do you want to speak to Mother?"

"Not particularly. I called to see when we could get together."

"Mother wants to see you."

The old game that had been going on since Andrea had been old enough to talk on the phone. He thought, had hoped, that when she reached college age she'd be thinking for herself and not merely team up with her mother in a whipsaw operation to extort money from him.

"I'll arrange to get together with her when I can. Looks like I'm going to be pretty busy the next few days."

"When am I going to see you?" She was so good at getting to him, Brad thought ruefully. She sounded as though in her whole life nothing was more important to her than being with her father. But once together the wheedling would start. Gwen never let go of the myth that Brad Kendall was a very wealthy man in his own right and from a wealthy family. Actually, his father had left Brad and his mother sufficient money to live on and for Brad to go to college, and when his mother died the entire estate went to him. As a result, Andrea sincerely believed that it was just meanness on his part when he refused expensive requests.

After a pause Brad answered his daughter's question. "Whenever we can find a time good for both of us."

"Like when?"

He thought of all he had to do, immediate contacts toward securing a new job, gracefully declining the job with Whitehall in such a way that the boys with the baseball bats wouldn't be around to break his legs.

"I'll have to let you know," he replied lamely.

"Can we have lunch, Brad? Please. I've missed you. You haven't seen me for a year."

"Has it really been that long?" he asked wonderingly. It had, he realized. The last time was the quick flight up from Caracas to get final approval on the hotel there.

"Yes," she replied petulantly.

"All right. Lunch it is."

"Will you come up early and get me? I know Mama wants to see you."

Mousetrapped! he thought. Well, he had to do it sometime, why not now. "All right. But it will have to be a short chat." There was a long silence on the other end. Brad decided to throw out a little preparatory softening. "Yes," he went on. "I'm really going to be in a scramble for a while. I've got to find a job."

"A job?" came the cry from the other end. "But you are part of Ascot Hotels."

"Not any more."

"What happened?"

"Tell you when I see you. Let me go now. I'll be up at a quarter of twelve. So long until then." He hung up.

Now, he thought, where do I start looking? Sheraton? Hilton? Loew's? Holiday Inns? There just isn't my type of job around. Well, coffee and orange juice first.

As he looked around the ornate lobby of the hotel, the luxury of wasted space and high ceilings and old world chandeliers, the discreet shops, the rich carpeting, the glass walls that gave out on the United Nations Mall and the East River, he was impressed by the fact that the Ascot Towers was indeed the finest and most luxurious hotel in the world. Hotels just weren't built this way any more. Lilli Darlene, reflecting some higher authority, Brad was convinced, had influenced many of the inefficient though luxurious aspects of the hotel which had helped serve to explode costs of construction and decorating beyond all proportions. No wonder this hotel had broken the chain.

"Brad Kendall!" He turned to see Knute Bjorgund, in striped pants and morning coat, coming across the lobby toward him. Knute was the general manager of the hotel, picked by Rafe Leighton from all the managers in the chain to take over the company's flagship. Knute had been wearing a permanent expression of elation when last Brad had seen him. Now he looked tired and haggard, his blond hair turning gray. He definitely did not look like a man who slept well at night.

"Hello, Knute," Brad greeted him, "how goes the battle?"

The hotel manager shook his head silently. Then, "I'm very glad to see you back, Brad. We all hope the rumor we've heard is true?" Brad had always liked Knute's soft Scandinavian accent.

"What's that?" he asked.

"Oh, come on, Brad. Everyone knows you are like the old man's son. And a few of us, you know, gotta eat some crow about getting into this deal. You were right."

Brad smiled at Knute's persistent efforts to use American slang. "Truly, Knute, what rumor?"

"The old man's going to step down and you are going to be president of Ascot."

Brad was startled. "Where did you hear that?"

"It's all over the chain. I tried to call you about it last night but I couldn't get you."

Brad smiled. "I was out late last night."

Knute laughed richly and for a moment the tired

lines of strain disappeared. "Same old boy, eh? Good, good. I tell you I wish I could be the same way, but my wife, she watches everything."

The smile left Brad's face. "What way, Knute?"

"Aw, you know. I was just kidding, Brad. Seriously, we need you. Nobody, nobody but you can save Ascot."

"It may be too late already."

"Not with you in the picture. Well, I gotta go. Can I take you to lunch today?"

"Like to, Knute, but I just made a date with my daughter."

"She must be a real young lady now. How old is she?"

"Close to nineteen. It's been a year since I've seen her."

"Why don't you bring her up to the Star Club for lunch? I'll bet she would like that."

"Good idea, Knute. I'll do it. Stop by for a coffee with us."

"Yes, I will. See you." The worried expression back on his face, Knute hurried off.

Brad Kendall left the hotel and walked crosstown toward Park contemplating his future course of action. Knute's words stayed with him. Did the managers and executives of Ascot really think he could save the company? He began to wonder if perhaps he was not jumping to conclusions in reaching the impression that Whitehall might have some sinister connections. He decided to take a chance on Harry Wattling being in his office. Harry was his counterpart at Sheraton, but unlike himself, Harry was firmly ensconced in the home office and dispatched his assistants to the far corners of the globe to make deals. Brad and Harry had always been friends, although they had frequently competed on deals and each had won out over the other. Lately Harry had won more because Brad had so little capital to work with.

Brad was awestruck at the offices of the mighty conglomerate that had taken over Sheraton. Up until recently, Harry Wattling had managed to keep his own office in one of the Sheraton Hotels. Now he was right in the center of all operations of the international monolith, of which the one-hundred-hotel chain was one small part.

Harry was affable and prosperous-looking, Brad thought. He had never seen his friendly rival so outgoing. He had walked through two large offices apparently devoted to nothing but the study of hotel plans from all over the world.

Brad gestured to a long sofa with a coffee table in front of it, blueprints littering it. They talked for some time before Brad casually asked what the chances were for foreign development executives.

"I forget how long you have lived abroad," Harry replied. "Well, to answer your question, I watch my health carefully. There are more of us on our level than there are places. If I was sick for a week, one of the bright young men who have studied foreign development at college and business school and have degrees in what it has taken you and I twenty years of experience to learn would be in my place in a moment."

"Nothing takes the place of personal experience and long-standing contacts," Brad countered.

"Don't think that these kids can't do anything we can do, given a year or even less in our jobs. Believe me, Brad, I never miss an opportunity to impress on top-level men in this frightening amassment of businesses," he pointed up toward the floors above, "that I am unique and would be hard to replace. I win a few points, but quite honestly, this place is run by computers. When we were taken over, every one of us was studied, computerized," he paused, "dehumanized and then those of us who were lucky were placed back in slots electronically determined. I was one of the lucky ones. I ended up in my old job. But I never know when some machine I can't talk back to is going to spit my termination card out of its metallic little mouth."

Harry offered a cigarette, which Brad refused. He lit his own up, leaning back. "You're lucky, Brad. You can still work the way we used to, by instinct and experience. My God, this company even manufactures computer components. No wonder we're all so electronicized." He inhaled deeply and let out another long stream of smoke, looking at Brad quizzically.

"I hear through the jungle drums in the trade that old man Leighton is stepping down and you are it for president."

"I heard that rumor for the first time this morning," Brad replied cautiously.

"As president you won't have time to be out making international deals any more," he said suggestively.

Brad chuckled. "Tell me, Harry, isn't it nice to have all that money behind you when it comes to making a new deal? Helps, doesn't it? Remember the deal we were bucking heads on in Brasília? You won it because you were able to put more cold cash up front where it counts."

Harry smiled and nodded. "Sure, but you had me in three other situations because you could come in and talk for your company. By the time all the computers had gone over the thing and their results fed into other computers and then the boys on top pledged the cash, it was too late."

"What's the answer, Harry?"

"Simple. Have the big boys and the money behind you. But be permitted to make the deals in your own way with no interference."

"There aren't many opportunities like that around," Brad commented.

Wattling shook his head. "No, there sure aren't. But given such a situation, you or I or any experienced man in our game could own the world through luxury hotels. Can you imagine if we had a big luxury hotel in Saigon? I suggested it here and the computers said no. I had an all-day meeting with one of the top experts in limited warfare in the Pentagon. He showed me, country by country, capital city after capital city, where limited wars would be fought around the world. CIA has the communist timetable of so-called wars of national liberation. If we could build a big, luxury hotel in each capital where such a war will be fought, we'd have the money-makingest chain of hotels in the world."

Brad shook his head in admiration. "Goddamn. You were always the most imaginative international man in the field."

Harry shrugged. "What good is imagination with King Computer?"

"Well, Harry," Brad said, standing up, "let's get together for lunch. Looks like I'm going to be around for a while."

Wattling stood up and clapped a hand on Brad's shoulder. "Remember, when you take over Ascot and are looking to fill the slot you're leaving, a man with imagination and some money can beat the hell out of big money with only machines, whether they be electronic or flesh and blood, to spend it."

Brad smiled grimly. Here he'd come to feel out job possibilities and Harry was obliquely asking him for a job.

Back on the street, a discouraged Brad Kendall slowly walked uptown. He had half an hour before time to pick up his daughter. Gwen would just love to have him come early, give her more time to hit him for more money. He passed a Longchamps and decided to nip in for a fast bloody mary and try to think things out. Although the bar was almost empty, the calm before the van of the luncheon martini drinkers overran the place, its warmth and the polished mahogany and red brocade walls seemed to embrace him.

Halfway through the drink he remembered an old friend for whom he'd done some exceptional favors. Last he knew the man worked for Dun and Bradstreet. Brad laid a five on the bar to hold the rest of his drink while he went to the phone. He returned after the conversation, finished his drink, scooped up the change, leaving a half-dollar tip, and out on the street he headed uptown.

CHAPTER SIX

Andrea answered the door. For a moment Brad was stunned. A year ago she had shown promise of being a lovely girl, but he was hardly prepared for the beautiful young woman who invited him in. She kissed him on the cheek and he was aware of her perfume, subtle yet suggestive.

"My God, you've become beautiful." The words came from him almost unconsciously.

"Why, thank you, Brad. You're looking well—as handsome as ever, I see." Gracefully she led him to the living room of the apartment in the fashionable building in which Gwen and Ed had lived for the last ten years. Most of the furniture had been in the house Gwen and Brad had shared when they were married. The old leather easy chair was cracked. The television set was sixteen years old, a tribute to RCA's early models. The carpeting was threadbare. Still Gwen somehow made the dining alcove look cheerful with the porcelain and pottery she had collected when married to Brad. Nothing had changed in the past few years since he had visited there, coming as seldom as possi~~

~~ stood in the living room, Gwen swept out
~~room in the bundle of lace, silk and ruffles
~~en her bed jacket for so many years. All
~~e had poured into them these past years,

he thought, and so much had to go to pay the rent that they still couldn't afford to fix the place up. Of course, they had all literally existed on the money he contributed for his daughter's support, and Andrea received very few special things for herself so badly was the money needed for the family's survival. Despite all he did to help Ed and Gwen out they still had tried to turn Andrea against him at every opportunity.

Brad realized he had made a mistake when he had been so anxious to extricate himself from the marriage to Gwen that in order to get the divorce he had given her full custody of Andrea. Even all visitation rights were at her discretion. Andrea hadn't been allowed to visit him for the past three years, such headway had he made capturing her love and affection that one month she had visited his home in Venezuela. The fact that a lovely Latin lady who served as secretary, Spanish teacher and girl Friday had her own room in his establishment had been Gwen's excuse for disallowing further visits. Probably the fact that fifteen-year-old Andrea had developed an adolescent crush on the beauteous Eugenia had added to Gwen's wrath at her daughter's temporary mental emancipation from her mother's narrow world.

"Well, welcome home, traveler," Gwen greeted him with a smile and tone so false that he almost shuddered. "Sit down." She pointed to one of the pair of Princeton chairs that had been his but which she had insisted on keeping at the time of the divorce. It used to irk him that Ed Connor and his friends, most of whom had been lucky if they graduated from CCNY, sat their butts in these symbols of an Ivy League past. But, as he grew older and worked harder, such snobbishness as might once have influenced his thinking evaporated completely.

After ten minutes of meaningless small talk, Gwen came to the point. "We've entered her in Hunter College for next fall so she can continue to live at home."

"Don't you think it's time she got away to college where she could be on her own?" Brad asked.

"Andrea has a lovely home and she's happy here with her daddy Ed and her mother and her brother."

"As I've said many times, Gwen," Brad's tone was already weary, "she's too old to share a room with her brother. What is he, thirteen? It's all wrong."

"Well, you refused to do anything about it. There was the three-room apartment upstairs but you refused to face your responsibility."

"That's ridiculous. I offered to send Andrea to boarding school, any boarding school you chose, but you refused."

"Andrea didn't want to go to boarding school."

Recalling how Andrea had begged him to send her to a boarding school after the summer in Venezuela, and Gwen's refusal to have her daughter leave the small apartment, Brad had to fight himself, as always, not to contradict. And, he supposed, even now, Gwen would take it out on Andrea if he mentioned this again.

"I think Andrea and I had better go. I have an early appointment this afternoon."

"There are a few other things we have to go over." The hard lines in her face, concealed at first by her attempt at conviviality, and the glittering eyes told him he would have to listen to the harangue awhile longer.

"Andrea needs a whole new wardrobe. And you haven't paid the tuition bill at her school. And there are the doctors' bills that haven't been paid. And Andrea wants to go to Europe next summer."

Brad glanced over at Andrea, coolly listening to her mother's catalogue of expenses. And she wonders why I so seldom come to see her, he thought. Since Gwen was obviously trying to demean him in front of his daughter, he had to answer back, which he disliked doing.

"A year ago you gave me a list of all the expenses you anticipated for Andrea. Because I never know when I am going to be, I gave you a check for all of it, including her tuition, clothes and a trip last summer to Europe, which apparently didn't materialize, until now September. This was in addition to the regular monthly support payments. Apparently, that money was used for other things."

Gwen shook her head, her face assuming a patient, patronizing look of pity. Then she turned to Andrea. "You see, your father leads such an insulated life with all his expenses paid and an income so high that he doesn't have to face realities." Then she turned to Brad. "You don't know about the rising cost of living. Do you know how much it costs to feed Andrea? And there is her share of the rent . . ."

"Half the room and bathroom she shares with her brother?" he snapped impatiently. Then, "All right, let me have the bills right here and now." He stood up from the chair and walked over to the desk. A smile of triumph on her face, Gwen also stood up and went over to the desk. She pointed to a pile of envelopes. Brad picked the pile up and started going through them. He took out his pen and on the back of one of the envelopes began writing a column of numbers. After five minutes he looked up.

"OK, I see thirty-eight hundred dollars' worth of bills here. From the school, from shops, department stores, doctors, drug stores—everything I gave you a check before this summer started to cover for the coming year." He reached into his pocketbook and pulled out a checkbook. Slowly, meticulously, to cover his agitation and anger, he wrote out a check for the amount. It was a good thing he had another paycheck coming to him the end of the week, he thought. This just about cleaned him out of cash.

Brad stood up. "OK." He turned to Andrea. "You see, dear, all paid for, a second time. Satisfied?" She nodded.

"I told you, Brad." Gwen's tones were brittle hard. "It's very expensive living in the city. Just because you haven't"—her voice lilted mockingly—"a care in the world doesn't mean that Ed and I don't have to take care of your daughter."

Brad knew the futility of getting mad. The only answer was to stay away from all of them. But he d love his daughter and wanted the best for her. He turned to Andrea. "Come on, dear. Let's go."

Andrea stood up. Gwen looked out the window. "What's the temperature out? Do you think Andrea should wear a coat? She needs a fall coat. Maybe you could get her one."

Brad distinctly remembered a coat on one of the department-store bills, but said nothing beyond "It's nice out."

"Put on a coat, Andrea," Gwen commanded.

Out on the street, Brad took several deep breaths of air and resolved that they'd never get him into that dreary apartment again. For Andrea's sake, he could say nothing in return to Gwen. As he knew only too well, Gwen took her frustrations out on Andrea anyway and after a fight with Brad, life for Andrea was made truly miserable.

"Where are we going, Brad?" Andrea asked cheerfully.

"How about the Star Club Room on top of the Ascot Towers?"

Andrea wrinkled up her nose. "Why do we always have to go to one of your hotels?"

"I haven't been up there since the hotel opened last year. I'd like to see it."

"All right. Whatever you say."

The headwaiter at the Star Club bowed to Brad and Andrea. At a table looking over the East River, Brad asked for a martini. Andrea ordered sherry and they sat back, staring out the window in awkward silence, until the drinks arrived. Brad held his up to Andrea and then took a long sip. "Well, so you're going to Europe next summer? What happened this summer? Your mother spent the money on something else?" Andrea shrugged noncommittally.

"I'd like to go next year if it's OK with you."

" ure, I think a trip to Europe would be great   Where do you think you'll spend most of your

    e a group going to Italy. Then I'd like to

"What about college next fall? Wouldn't you like to go away? I mean it couldn't be too much fun the way things are at home."

"We have a very happy home."

Brad gulped the last of his martini at this parroting of Gwen's phrase. He held up his hand for a refill.

"Another sherry?" Brad asked.

Andrea shook her head. "I wish there was something I liked or was interested in that would make confusion go away. How nice if you could just take a pill and everything would be all right."

Brad gave his daughter a worried glance. "You really do have a few things on your mind, don't you?"

"It's just," she hesitated, "I wish you saw me more often."

"So do I, dear. I wish your mother would let you visit. Actually, you're old enough to put your foot down and do what you want to do."

"Why didn't you want me to be with you enough to have it written in your divorce agreement?"

"You've asked me that before. At the time, it was the only way to break a very difficult deadlock. Now, let's talk about the future. You have one more year of high school. Then wouldn't you really like to go off to college?"

"Mama would never go for it."

"Damnit, Andrea, you're a big girl. You damn well demand it."

"Could I have a car, a new one, not some second-hand job?"

"That's your price for going away to college?"

"One has nothing to do with the other."

"Well, a car is nothing but a nuisance and expense in New York. And you know it. If you were going away, that would be something else." He reflected on the expense of an eighteen-year-old daughter. She was a year older than her classmates because of an illness which caused her to lose a year at school. And it would only get worse, he knew. At least he didn't have to give a debutante party for her. The circles that Gwen Ed moved in didn't know what one was. Since a Catholic, Andrea had also been brought up Catholic and Gwen had converted. Of this Brad approved. At Andrea's Catholic school, the sisters didn't bother the girls' heads with society nonsense. But he wanted to do what was right for his daughter in every way.

He suddenly remembered that he was about to become unemployed and that his total resources amounted to about fifty thousand dollars in no-cost Ascot stocks. When he received the check for the purchase of this stock from Whitehall, he would have to pay 25 per cent of it in capital gains taxes. Thus, all he had to show for his seventeen years of service with Ascot was thirty-seven thousand five hundred dollars in the bank.

"Well, let's play the car part by ear," Andrea said brightly and picked up the menu. "I'm hungry."

CHAPTER SEVEN

After lunch, Brad put Andrea in a cab, handed her ten dollars and then took another cab downtown. At the Dun and Bradstreet building, he found the office of Les Schrieber, who had once interviewed him at length and written an extensive and penetrating story for the *Wall Street Journal* on the hotel industry.

"After our phone conversation this morning, Brad, I dug up everything I could on Whitehall. Everybody has investigated them. The New York *Times* spent six months looking into the company and was never able to prove any connection between either Whitehall or its principal officers and any criminal activity."

Brad nodded. "Possibly both old Rafe Leighton and others like myself who have seen their companies taken over by Whitehall tend to leap to conclusions. For that matter, any of these conglomerates could be viewed in a sinister light."

"Of course," Schrieber interjected, "it is unusual for a company starting from nothing to be worth seven billion in ten years. That is a figure we gues impossible to judge the company's worth acc He held out a mimeographed sheaf of pape together. "Here's the Dun and Bradstreet rep company. Not much to go on. The only fina ment ever seen was an unaudited statement 31, 1966; that's five years ago. The compa to owning $251,000,000 of property at market value with $170,000,000 in first mortgages. They probably had twice that amount of property concealed in subsidiaries. You can see how they have used the property as leverage, mortgaging to the hilt to acquire other property. But it still seems impossible for Whitehall to have become so gigantic in just ten years."

"What does the financial community think of C. L. Ciano and his partner, Hyman Steinert?"

"Nobody knows Steinert. Ciano gets around pretty good, though. He's at the head table at the top political dinners. In Washington, you see him with the most important senators and representatives. He's been to the White House for luncheon at least twice we know of, and was a guest at a couple of white-tie dinners the President gave. He golfs with the highest business executives and bankers. They may all suspect his base of power and money is organized crime, but you can bet they never say it. We feel he may be quietly providing financing for a number of big corporations. Whitehall may even control one of the country's leading banks, but nobody can say for sure. It's just plain impossible for a journalist to contact the management."

Schrieber paused and gave Brad a shrewd look. "I guess your interest confirms what we've heard about Whitehall taking over Ascot Hotels."

"You've been a big help to me, Les. Thanks."

"I don't know how. There's nothing to tell. Now what about this acquisition?"

Brad nodded. "It's true. But don't break the story. Let Ciano and Leighton make the announcement when they're ready."

"Ow," Schrieber groaned in mock distress. "To have such a story and keep quiet? Tell me one thing. Is it an exchange of stock?"

"Think, Les? Is there such a thing as a fund? Right on your D & B it says fifty-fifty by Ciano and Steinert."

"The whole company? For cash?"

"don't quote me—yet."

"Then they really can lay their hands on big cash when it's needed."

"You bet your ass."

"Well, money talks," Schrieber said philosophically. "I know that nobody wants Ciano for an enemy. Even the papers have suddenly laid off investigating White-hall."

It was 3 P.M. when Brad left Wall Street, heading uptown to the Ascot Towers. At the hotel he checked his box and found a handful of messages. He went up to his suite, beautifully decorated in Swedish modern, and looked through the pink slips. Gwen, of course. Mr. Leighton. The old man wants to know what I've decided, he thought. Knute, apologizing for not joining him at lunch, important meeting suddenly came up. Mr. Ciano's office confirming the five o'clock meeting. Mrs. Blore called; please call at six. Well, he'd be out of Ciano's office seconds after he refused to take the job. He picked up the phone and called Leighton's office. Miss Lehman thanked God he'd called and put the old man directly on the phone.

"Brad, I'm glad I caught you." There was a note of urgency, perhaps even fear, in his voice. "Don't be hasty in deciding about the Whitehall deal, my boy."

"I've been thinking of nothing else all day, chief."

"I want to talk to you before you go to that five o'clock meeting. I know what we were saying last night, but I was tired, I guess pretty damned bitter, and I was pouring the Old Fitz heavy. You haven't talked to Ciano today?" he asked anxiously.

"No. Just got a message that the meeting was still on for five. I'll be there."

"I'll meet you in the limo in front of the hotel and drive you to the Spire Building. Give us a chance to talk some."

"OK. I sure appreciate your concern, sir."

"I'll be there at four-fifteen. We can drive around a little and talk."

"I'll be out in front." He hung up and paced about the luxurious suite. Maybe tonight he would get Lu-

ciana up here for a drink after the theatre. Since he
would be out of Ascot, it didn't matter if Knute saw on
the house officer's report the next day that Brad had
entertained a young woman in his suite overnight. Hey,
he was getting ahead of himself. On only the second
date? There was nothing like being at the head of a
large hotel chain to amass information on the personal
lives of men and women, large and small in importance. He remembered trying to cover up for a special
assistant to the President of the United States. The congressional investigation would have nailed his hide to
the Capitol dome if Brad hadn't sent out a flying squad
to all the hotels involved to find and destroy all the
records of the suites the man had occupied, with whom
he had shared them, and who had paid for them.

CHAPTER EIGHT

Rafe Leighton was in front of the hotel sharply at four-fifteen with his limousine and Brad climbed into the back beside him. Leighton turned up the glass separating the chauffeur from them and then turned to Brad urgently.

"I'll make this short, Brad. I think you ought to seriously consider taking the Whitehall deal. I don't have to tell you business is bad. In its fight to curb inflation, the Administration is curbing business expansion everywhere. There has never been a better opportunity to put cash to work if you happen to have it. Whitehall has it.

"Listen to me, boy. I want to see you command the respect and financial resources due you. I owe it to you. Now look, I had a long talk with Ciano today. I took the liberty of doing a little negotiating for you. The way Whitehall works, there's no way you can acquire stock in the company or any of their subsidiaries. They'll pay you a high salary, but taxes will cut that down. They'll give you an unlimited expense account, but that doesn't build an estate. They want you bad, Brad. The fine public relations you have always enjoyed in not only the hotel industry but the business community is going to pay off for you. They need you badly as a working front man who can make Ascot the world's most powerful hotel chain."

"But we both suspect that Whitehall may have some connections with organized crime in America."

"Crime is a much used and little defined word, Brad."

Brad laughed bitterly. "I suppose we could paraphrase that cynical German military authority Clausewitz when he said war is carrying out diplomacy in a different way. Whitehall is merely doing big business in a different way."

Leighton chuckled. "I guess so. You know, when the offers to buy Ascot started coming in, one would-be buyer who had studied me to find a weakness came up with a novel approach. He asked me how I'd like to read in the papers that my wife had had her head kicked in. I laughed at the hood. I told him, go ahead, she's insane and he'd be doing both my wife and me a big favor. Of course, if Rafe, Jr., had lived and had a wife and given me grandchildren I can see that I might have looked at things differently."

"And you think I'd be comfortable working for an operation that used that kind of methodology?"

"You'd become a very rich man in a very short length of time and if you don't take it some other respectable gentleman will. Do you know that no less a personage than one of the most powerful presidential advisers of a recent administration is setting up a very legitimate series of mutual funds offshore and domestic, financed by Whitehall?" Leighton laughed. "Besides, Ciano and his people have long since graduated from strong-arm methods. They don't need them."

"Mr. Leighton, why are you giving me this pitch?" Brad asked.

"Because I owe you a great deal, and I let you down when I shouldn't have and if I'd followed your advice I wouldn't have had to sell Ascot."

"Would you have advised Rafe, Jr., to take this deal?"

Leighton looked at Brad for a long moment. Then, "Under the circumstances I think I would. If you can't lick 'em, join 'em. I don't see the United States Government, the Supreme Court, or any of the law-making or enforcing departments of the U. S. Government doing anything but helping Whitehall to thrive and become bigger. There is no government protection for legitimate big business; its sole function is harassment. But does Whitehall get harassed? Not anywhere that would tend to weaken it. Legitimate conglomerates are restricted on every side, and legitimate businessmen pay taxes on every hard-earned dollar they put into expansion or new business."

"I get your message, Mr. Leighton. I don't think I like it but maybe I can't afford not to like it."

"Ciano's offering you a good thing. And I wrung one more concession from him for you so you can become a millionaire. You know how you become a millionaire, a multimillionaire today? Only one way. You own the majority of the stock in a highly successful corporation, you go public and your shares become worth millions. So many millions that even when you sell out at the top and pay a capital gains tax of 35 per cent you've got millions left. Or you keep the stock and use it as collateral to make big loans which you invest in other businesses or stock on the New York Stock Exchange."

"Just one problem. I don't own the majority of the shares in anything, much less a successful company."

"You will. Form a company, say a company to process beef. The meat packers who buy your beef suddenly find they have the entire Ascot Hotel chain market as long as they buy your beef. They also find they are selling chain stores they never got into before. Pretty soon you take over the meat packer too. Now, your shares are worth millions."

Brad wondered if Leighton had gone a little off mentally since the evening before. "I haven't the resources to start such an operation," he protested.

"Ciano will do it for you."

"Ciano looks like the type who would do it for himself and Whitehall. But why the hell would he do it for me?"

Leighton chuckled and then began to laugh in great belly-whooping spasms. Brad looked at him worriedly.

He waited until the huge guffaws subsided, "Because, Brad," and he sputtered and started to laugh again. He coughed and choked on the smoke from his cigarette. "Because wops need WASPs. Prominent, Ivy League WASPs with a distinguished business career both behind them and before them. You fit the bill, my boy."

Finally, Leighton stopped laughing and sputtering. He leaned forward toward the bar behind the front seat, took out a glass with ice already in it from a small refrigerator, filled the glass with Bourbon from a bottle in a rack behind a panel he slid open and then sat back with his drink.

"OK, Brad, you can lead a horse to water. I've done that. It's up to you. I won't offer you a drink. You'll need your wits about you if you have enough wit not to say no until you hear Ciano's proposition out."

"I'll listen. But I have an important date at six."

"You'll make it easily. Ciano does business very, very fast. Or he doesn't do business."

The limousine pulled up in front of the Spire Building.

"Do you want the limo tonight, Brad?" the old man asked him solicitously. "I'm going right home and I won't be going out tonight. If you handle things right, it will be yours tomorrow anyway."

Brad's first reaction was to say no, he didn't think he wanted any part of the limo or Ascot or Whitehall. But to his surprise he found himself smiling. "Thanks, chief. Ask him to be at the St. Regis tonight at seven. I'm taking a beautiful lady to the theatre."

Brad Kendall walked through the lobby of the Spire Building to the bank of elevators which ascended to the top five floors, those occupied by Whitehall Development, Ltd.

As had been the case the evening before, he was ushered from minion to minion until he was finally delivered into Ciano's presence. The first thing that struck Brad's eye was a model of a Grumman Gulfstream executive jet airplane on the round table in front of the brown leather couch. In neat letters on

the side of the plane was painted "Ascot Hotels."
Above a gleaming mahogany mantelpiece was a large
map of the world spangled with multihued pinheads.

Ciano shook hands with Brad and gestured toward
one of the two leather easy chairs facing each other
across the round table. The model of the jet was between them.

"I gather, Brad, may I call you by your first name?"
Brad nodded. "I gather that you have been spending
the day trying to decide whether, indeed, you feel your
future is with the new version of the Ascot Hotel
chain."

Brad nodded and smiled. "That's right, sir."

"I suppose you've heard a lot of rumors about us.
You will about any of the conglomerates, but we seem
to be a particular target of the rumor mills down on
the street—all over, for that matter. But such is the
price of success."

"You can hear anything you want to hear about
anybody, I suppose," Brad agreed.

"Right. Well, we have grown fast. You and I are
about the same age. You may wonder if I had some
particular edge or the help of some alliance to have
been able to create what is Whitehall today." Brad
showed no reaction. "The fact is that my partner and
I have worked hard. Long hours every day for many
years. We've been lucky. But I can guarantee you
that Whitehall has a cleaner record than most of the
conglomerates today. Certainly there has been no il-
legal or unlawful corporate move made by the company or any of its officers since the day this company
was founded."

Ciano stood up and walked toward the window facing north. He was silent a moment and then turned to
Brad. "Yes, we have required large amounts of financing to build as fast as we have. We have not asked
those who have invested money with us where their
money came from. They were content to get in, take
a profit and get out. Large profits, I might add. As
you know, my partner and I own all the shares in
Whitehall, but there are hundreds of legal ways in

which those who turn their money over to us can take back their profits, whether over a long term or short term."

Brad watched Ciano walk about the large office, almost as though talking to himself. The man had the grace and beneath the impeccably tailored suit the muscular build of a professional athlete.

"What we do is invest huge amounts of money into business enterprises all over the world. Right now, we want to build the most powerful and profitable hotel chain in the world. We will put up whatever it costs to do this. We want you to head up this hotel chain working under our direction, of course, but in effect telling us how to direct your efforts. You will have more authority and resources behind you than any other single individual in the industry. Your word will be law—" Ciano smiled. "Just give us a phone call before you commit us to, say, over two or three million dollars." As he had the previous evening, Brad felt himself falling into some sort of hypnotic spell as Ciano talked. And, try as he would, he couldn't help glancing at the model jet.

"Actually," and Ciano smiled almost sadly, "there is really no reason for you not to jump at this job except for one thing. To put it right out on the table, you are worried about our financing connections. I am of Italian background, or ethnic origin, which may add to your concern. Now, so that there will be no misunderstanding whatsoever between us, let me tell you what our philosophy is here."

Ciano, who had been holding the back of the empty chair, walked around it and sat down, leaning intently toward Brad. "One of the country's most respected and successful lawyers, who frequently represents alleged felons, has said that he never asks his clients whether they are guilty or innocent. He merely wants to know all the circumstances about the case before he takes it to trial. We here at Whitehall feel the same way. We are professional money investors. We do not ask whether money is, as they say, 'hot.' Quite frankly, there are times when we suspect that a satchel of a million dollars in cash might not stand too much scrutiny, so we try to turn it into some worthwhile venture immediately. Perhaps, for instance, our share of working capital in a ten-to-twelve-million-dollar hotel financed by a foreign government and turned over to Ascot to operate on a typical one third of the profits to us and two thirds to the government. Now, we regard this as putting what might be bad money to good use. We help build the economy of this foreign country, provide first-class hotel space, and expand the United States role in world business."

Brad was dazed at the glib way Ciano explained away the use of what had to be gangster-derived money. Yet Ciano's logic made sense to Brad as he listened.

Ciano pointed at the map of the world. "Those one hundred redheaded pins represent Ascot owned or franchised hotels. The silver pins represent cities in the United States and Canada where I want hotels under construction within the next three years. There's twenty-eight of those. Now the black pins, you'll observe, are all in foreign countries in this hemisphere. There are eleven locations in the Caribbean, Central and South America."

Brad Kendall was finding it difficult to retain a sense of reality as Ciano went on. "The gold pins, you will notice, denote cities in Europe where Ascot should be. You'll observe that we have included Moscow, Belgrade and Prague among the cities. The communist countries are becoming increasingly wealthy."

Ciano continued, pointing to the various continents, explaining why one city or another was an important one for a new hotel. Almost every location, including Moscow, had been brought to Brad's attention but he marveled at the orderly, businesslike way Ciano had gone about planning his hotel empire.

"This expansion program," Ciano continued, "will require many skilled men and they will have to do a great deal of traveling. If you accept the presidency, you will build up the executive talent to work with certain of our people to accomplish this program. In order to conserve the time of these valuable men I have ordered two executive jet airplanes for the Ascot Hotel chain." He pointed at the model. "Each will be equipped with the latest communications devices so that while airborne you or your executives can communicate with any city in the world, and, of course, a twenty-four-hour-a-day communications center here in New York."

Brad could no longer restrain himself. He jumped to his feet staring at the map. "That's the boldest plan of action I've ever heard of outside of the Joint Chiefs of Staff planning a war on Russia."

"Please." Ciano made a gesture of pain. "War we don't want. We don't need. Not that we wouldn't make money in war, too, but our planning is based on general peace with the inevitable small wars that will always be going on in this world."

"There is one thing I'd like to ask, Mr. Ciano."

"Go ahead."

"Do you believe in widespread use of computers in making business decisions?"

Ciano thought about this and shrugged. "If you want a computer you can have a computer. In the years we have been developing Whitehall I always found a man could make a better decision and implement it faster than a machine. But don't let that stop you if you figure you can work better with one."

"No, not at all. A computer can be useful, but in many companies it's taking the place of experienced men."

"We never used one."

Ciano paused. Then, "Well, Mr. Kendall, do you accept the position or not?"

Brad hesitated, the old doubts coming back to him. Ciano noticed the hesitation. "We haven't discussed remuneration, of course. My thinking was a salary of $200,000 a year, unlimited expenses of course, and as I'm sure Mr. Leighton explained to you, he *is* a shrewd negotiator I'll have to say, we will start a mutually agreed upon company for you which we will make worth several million dollars in the next few years. You will own 51 per cent and Whitehall through a straw will own 49. That way, no matter what happens, even if you decide to leave us, which I'm sure you'll be much too happy to do, you will be worth a few million that the government can't touch."

Ciano watched Brad warily. Brad knew that the time had come to take it or leave it. He didn't want to leave it, and yet some tiny voice deep inside him was trying against overwhelming odds to tell him not to take it. He thought of his immediate expenses, what a great thing it would be to take Andrea around Europe in a company jet, and he thought of Luciana and he thought of the impact he could make on his industry. He could hire Harry Wattling away from one conglomerate to work for a bigger one.

Ciano glanced discreetly at his watch and moved over to his desk. He sat down, the early fall afternoon light behind him making it hard for Brad to look at him. "Unfortunately, I was unable to avoid accepting an appointment at five-thirty," he said significantly.

Had so much happened in half an hour? The scope of the project which had been outlined in that time appalled and elated him. "When do you want me to start, Mr. Ciano?"

Ciano smiled broadly. "Right now. By tomorrow I want a preliminary plan of action. We'll take it from there. And by the way, most of my closer associates call me by my initials, C.L."

"OK, C.L. I'll be in the office first thing in the morning."

"While you're at it, work out a plan to get the entire Ascot Hotel company moved into the Spire Building as soon as possible. The space is available here. Make whatever arrangements have to be made with the old building."

"Check."

"And, Brad?" Ciano gave him a questioning look. "No reservations? No doubts about being part of us?"

After the barest hesitation he heard himself say, "No, C.L."

Ciano nodded. "Just don't ever forget that to do

what we plan, to do what we have done, requires a somewhat unorthodox approach to business. You understand me?"

Brad nodded.

"OK. You're part of what I call the fifth estate now."

"The fifth estate?" Brad asked.

"It's a phrase I coined. The so-called estates of American life are business, government, the church and academe. Press and communications media are known as the fourth estate."

"And the fifth?"

"That's us and when we're through we'll be more powerful than the other four put together." Brad was almost frightened at the gleam of intensity that burned in Ciano's black eyes. "And, Brad," his voice cut through the room, "in five years the fifth estate will elect the President of the United States." Ciano stood up from behind his desk and walked Brad to the door. "By the way, read up on our congressman from this district, William Fortune Adams. You'll be meeting him soon."

Then, as an afterthought, "Maybe you'd like to have a suite in the Ascot Towers especially decorated for your personal use, Brad."

Brad shook his head. "Thanks, but I don't like the whole chain knowing what the president does in his off hours. I'll rent an apartment."

"Don't be foolish. Ascot will buy you a co-op apartment in one of our newest buildings. I'll have diagrams sent to you tomorrow."

Brad left the Ciano presence with mixed feelings of elation and a slight gnawing of doubt in his gut. But it was too late now. He had come up to see Ciano, thank him and refuse the job. But this day had changed him. Probably this day was that irrevocable turning point in a life from which there can be no return. He thought of the executive jets and all those pins on the map. Wow! Never in a lifetime would he have believed this possible. The enormity of what he had done could only be contemplated in solitude over a dry tanqueray martini at the New York Athletic Club bar followed by a steam bath. He had just time for this program before meeting Luciana at the St. Regis. Now the only problem was to get a taxi. A serious one, but a problem that beginning in the morning he would never face again. Tomorrow he would take over the limousine.

CHAPTER NINE

Brad Kendall and Luciana Blore reclined in the comfort of the company limousine. Brad at last had learned the name of the driver, Williams, and a little bit about his family. In the past two days, he had developed the comfortable proprietary interest in his car and chauffeur of an executive or government official entitled to this luxury perquisite. Luciana, in her white fox stole and black sheath, seemed created to be escorted in style. Looking ahead out the windshield as they turned into Sixty-eighth Street from Park, he saw the array of limousines depositing their fashionable passengers at Charles Lawrence Ciano's town house halfway down the street on the right.

"I can't tell you just how long we'll be, Williams. But I suggest you get yourself some supper and be back in a couple of hours." He turned to Luciana, squeezing her hand. "I expect we can escape after that. But this is a sort of command performance."

"Whatever you say, Brad. I'm happy." He leaned toward her and kissed her on the lips. "Mind." She laughed. "It wouldn't do to go to such a posh bash with my lipstick crooked."

"Just make the men in the crowd jealous." He opened the door as the limousine pulled up in front and stepping out onto the street reached for Luciana's hand. She stepped out daintily, he closed the door, and they gained the sidewalk.

"I wouldn't be surprised if you had a chance to speak Italian tonight," he whispered as they approached the entrance. Ciano's city residence had been created on the site of two former brownstone houses, Brad noticed as they entered.

A man dressed as a butler, but looking too young and too physically impressive for the part, politely asked them their names. "Yes, Mr. Kendall, Mr. Ciano is expecting you." He bowed to Luciana. "Go right upstairs, please."

The living room took up the entire second floor of the house, a row of french windows giving onto the street, another row looking out on a manicured garden behind the house. Stairways led up to the third floor at each end of the room. As they entered the gracious main salon, Ciano walked over to them. Brad introduced Luciana to their host. Ciano bowed over her hand, repeating her name. "It sounds Italian."

"My father was Italian, from Milano."

"Ah, Milano." Ciano wus charmed with her and went on in Italian. "My grandfather was Neapolitan. He came to America as a young man but he never forgot the old country. Always we grandchildren had to listen to him tell of Italy. And he made my father and my uncles and aunts and all their children speak Italian." He turned to Brad apologetically. "Forgive us for speaking in a foreign tongue. The opportunity so rarely arises at these parties." Then, *sotto voce* to Brad, "She's charming, beautiful. Where did you find her? You won't think me grasping if I monopolize her somewhat this evening? It happens that I have invited several important Italian guests tonight, including the Italian consul general in New York and two very successful financiers, both of whom want to finance Ascot Hotels in Italy." Ciano smiled. "I see your reputation as a business diplomat was not in the slightest exaggerated."

"By all means, C.L., do introduce her around. I am

trying very hard to persuade her to stay in New York."

"Oh, she must, she must. We will see to it."

Ciano, with Luciana's arm in his, started off. Then he paused. "How's the Tropic Plaza deal coming in Miami?" he asked.

Brad shook his head. "No go. Unger won't sell, even though his partners are ready to make a deal. Sorry, C.L."

"Don't worry about Morrie Unger, Brad." Ciano put a hand on Brad's arm. "By the way, there's Bill Adams. Get acquainted with him. We're backing him in the senatorial race."

Ciano, with Luciana at his side, started making the rounds of the guests. Brad, realizing he had made the hit of the evening by bringing Luciana with him, moved across the room toward Representative William Fortune Adams. He reviewed in his mind the research he had done on the congressman at Ciano's suggestion. Adams was the congressman from midtown Manhattan, the so-called Silk-stocking District, and his constituents were some of the wealthiest individuals and corporations in the world. Under ordinary circumstances this ruggedly handsome forty-three-year-old WASP would not be considered material for higher office comprising a more broad-based constituency. But Adams had achieved acclaim among blue-collar workers throughout the nation for the uncompromising stand he had taken over the past four years on street crime. He had authored a bill, still to be passed, giving city, state and federal law-enforcement authorities much broader powers in dealing with street crime. It would be unnecessary to have a search warrant to get a conviction if incriminating evidence was found on a suspect or in his home. Stop and toss procedure would be nationally legal. Controversial as these provisions were, Adams advocated holding in jail indefinitely without bail at the discretion of the police chief or commissioner any suspect deemed likely to repeat the crime for which he was arrested.

Obviously, Brad thought, Adams would lose the

black and Puerto Rican vote since all crime preventive measures were considered direct anti-minority group action. In his own district, made up almost entirely of the people who favored all aspects of establishment-oriented legislation and feared street crime as a direct personal threat, Adams could continue to be re-elected as long as he chose to remain in Congress. Under ordinary circumstances, the liberal intellectuals of New York City who exercised such power over the academic and communications community would have hounded Adams out of office. But with the shocking daily accounts of murders, thefts, robberies, rapes, gratuitous indignities and generally anti-white incidents occurring in the city, the Adams position grew stronger every week.

What puzzled Brad was how Adams had so quickly achieved such a powerful position on the House Crime Committee. It was an obvious steppingstone to recognition for conservative congressmen. Even though Adams was from an old-line political family, it was highly unusual for a second-term representative to be appointed to the committee and made deputy chairman. Clearly Adams enjoyed powerful backing among the real leaders in Congress. Yet nothing Brad had been able to find in Adams' political history indicated why this should be so. His father had died ten years ago after failing to achieve re-election as a Connecticut senator and his uncle had retired from active politics. Surely, Brad asked himself, just because Adams was youthful, attractive, a solid family man with the handsome type of wife with whom the women of America wished to identify, the seniority-prone, highly political committee assignment system wouldn't have given such a plum to second-term Bill Adams.

Brad introduced himself to Adams who detached himself from the people around him.

"So you are the new president of Ascot," Adams began. "Believe me, I'm happy to meet you. I especially requested C.L. to arrange for us to get together. Your unbelievably fabulous hotel is in my district, you know."

"Of course. Not only am I a corporate constituent, so to speak, but also about to be a personal one. I am buying a co-op in the new Etoile Apartments."

"That's good to hear. As a matter of fact, I am too. C.L. insisted and when he insists, it is very difficult to refuse him."

"So I've discovered." Brad studied the youthful congressman with interest. He certainly was the epitome, as had been pointed out repeatedly in the newspapers and newsmagazines, of the eastern establishmentarian gentleman, even to his Harvard Club tie and neat short haircut. One would think in this day and age that such Ivy League nonsense was a thing of the past and could only hurt a political candidate. But recently a number of candidates from John F. Kennedy to John V. Lindsay had proved otherwise.

"C.L. said you flew up from Washington especially for this party." Brad tried to be flippant. "I hope it turns out to be worth it."

"C.L. is easily disappointed and he was expecting me."

A willowy, tall blond woman, in her mid-thirties, Brad judged, came up to them.

"Meet Terry Adams, my wife," the congressman said. Mrs. Adams immediately began chatting about hotels, one of her favorite subjects, it seemed.

"It must be very hard to keep your eye on so many hotels," Mrs. Adams gushed. "I mean, when the cat's away, the mice will play sort of thing."

"As a matter of fact, Mr. Ciano has ordered two jet executive aircraft to make the job a little easier," Brad replied.

Adams immediately became interested and started asking questions about the jets. Mindful of Ciano's interest in the legislator, Brad answered as many questions about the jet as he could. "You could really cover the state in a campaign with one of those babies," Brad enthused.

"Just what I was thinking." A wistful look came over Adams' face.

Brad decided he had better let C.L. make any offers

to politicians to use the plane. However, he could not resist a few minutes of political chatter with Adams, pointing out that he himself had worked on several national political campaigns in his time. "Perhaps C.L. would let you give me some time if I expand my horizons," Adams suggested.

"I'll sure ask him," Brad promised.

Terry Adams left them to join another group when a short, wiry, swarthy man, with a shock of black hair and as wide and friendly a grin on his face as Brad had seen, walked over to them and looked up at Adams, who at six foot one or two towered over him. Adams put his hand out and shook hands with the newcomer. "Hey, Fred," he greeted him affably. "Meet Brad Kendall, new president of the Ascot Hotel chain. Brad, this is my congressional colleague, Fred Black, from the Twenty-first District out in Brooklyn."

"Good to meet you, Brad." The cheerful little man gripped Brad's hand in a crushing grip.

"Glad to meet you, Fred," Brad returned, taken aback at so strong a grip on one so diminutive. "Where is your district? Forgive my ignorance, but I'm just getting used to being a New Yorker again after three years abroad."

"I've got a corner of Bedford-Stuyvesant, the rest is closer to Manhattan." He grinned up at Adams. "Little different bunch I represent. About one third of my constituents are colored, another third, Puerto Rican, the rest, Italian and some Irish." He laughed. "I'm a guinea with the name Black, so most of my people identify with me."

Brad listened as Adams and Black discussed their mutual coming campaign problems. At the far end of the room he saw Luciana, Ciano beside her, talking to a group of people. She looked up, caught his eye and smiled. He felt it would be superfluous to join the group. Ciano seemed to be enjoying introducing her to his friends. He turned back to Adams.

"I haven't met Mrs. Ciano. Do you suppose you could point her out to me?"

"She's not here," Black said. "She sticks at home

with the kids. They have quite a place up in Westchester."

William Fortune Adams seemed to be quite a drawing card at Ciano's party. By staying close to him, Brad met a State Supreme Court judge, a Kings County judge who had gravitated toward Black, a Manhattan assistant district attorney with political ambitions, the president of one of the nation's largest liquor companies, a famous motion picture producer and his latest protégée. The actress only succeeded in making Luciana look like the movie queen at the party and was petulantly aware of this. He talked at some length to a top editor of the New York *Times*. Brad's ego was considerably raised when all the celebrities and important people displayed considerable interest in getting to know him. One thing about being a top executive in a hotel chain, Brad had discovered early in the game, everyone of any importance needs a friendly, accommodating, discreet hotelman on his side in every major city of the United States. Brad Kendall as an individual answered this need more thoroughly than all but two or three men in the world, but at the mandate of Charles Lawrence Ciano, he reminded himself wryly.

"Brad." C. L. Ciano seemed to materialize out of a knot of chatting people. "I want you to meet General Alton MacFarland."

Brad stared into the snapping blue eyes of the tall, erect man standing beside his employer. The general could definitely be characterized as having a military bearing.

"Al," Ciano said, "meet the new president of the Ascot Hotel chain, Brad Kendall." Brad and the general shook hands.

"General MacFarland is deputy chief of staff," Ciano went on proudly.

Brad knew little about the military establishment but he managed to carry a short conversation with MacFarland about military attachés in foreign countries. The general was soon swept away in the drifting current of people trying to talk to everybody at the party.

Within moments Ciano was back at his side with a square-jawed, young-looking man with a shock of sandy hair that spilled over his forehead.

"Meet Representative Everett Jamison from McAllen, Texas," Ciano was saying. "We may build a new hotel in his district."

"We could use one," Jamison replied. "The sooner the better."

Jamison had looked familiar to Brad and now he realized who he was. A liberal Republican who was opposing his Republican President, threatening to run for President himself over the Vietnam war issue and other popular liberal causes that appealed to youth in particular. Brad chuckled to himself at the way Ciano balanced out his political support. Here was the candidate of youth, liberalism, anti-war sentiment, popular with Negroes, Mexican-Americans and other minority groups who by rights should have been a Democrat, and on the other side of the room was the conservative Adams who really seemed to be a Republican at heart.

"I want you to take a good look at the valley area on your next trip to Texas, Brad," Ciano said earnestly. "It's really growing."

"It will be my pleasure to show you my territory, Mr. Kendall," Jamison added.

"I'll look forward to it," Brad replied. "I'm sure Mr. Ciano has a lot of Texas business for me to handle." Smiling, Ciano nodded. Luciana came up to them and Ciano, with much gallantry, introduced her to Jamison, mentioning that the Texas congressman was in New York alone and they must show him around the town before the weekend was over.

Leaving Jamison and Luciana in animated conversation, Ciano took Brad by the arm and steered him toward a short, swarthy, black-haired man, possessively watching a striking-looking blond girl who was the center of attention in a knot of men.

"Brad, this is Señor Jorge Ramirez," Ciano said. "He is the chief delegate to the United Nations from Santo Morango, you know? In Central America?"

"Certainly, I know the country. I visited there about a year ago to see about a hotel in the capital."

"Talk to Jorge about it some more," Ciano urged. "Jorge has excellent contacts in government circles all through Latin America. And no one in the UN gives parties like Jorge."

As abruptly as he had appeared, Ciano faded back into the crowd. Brad and Señor Ramirez chatted amiably at length, found they had friends in common in several Latin-American countries, and Ramirez introduced Brad to the blonde who had by now extricated herself from the crowd of men and returned to his side.

Brad knew there was a definite reason why Ciano wanted him to meet everyone to whom he had especially introduced his new hotel chief. He tried to figure out in each case what that reason was. He couldn't help having a nagging intuitive feeling that everyone he met knew something, or many things that he didn't know, and was wondering how much he knew about the organization he now worked for, Whitehall Development.

It was a relief to Brad when the guests began wandering into the dining room and surrounded the buffet. He squeezed himself into the group around Luciana. Ciano smiled at him. "You have been very patient, Brad. I think it is time you had a chance to talk to your lovely lady."

Nevertheless, Brad and Luciana became a center of attention when they sat down at one of the tables with their plates. Another table was pulled up next to them and Luciana enjoyed a multilingual conversation throughout dinner. One of the few important syndicated columnists left in business spent some time with Brad asking whether the take-over by Whitehall would change the policies of Ascot. Brad answered evasively and the columnist turned to Luciana, asking about her plans. He knew her former husband, it seemed.

Not two, but four hours after they had arrived, Brad and Luciana were permitted to leave the party by Ciano. "Now over the weekend, Brad," he turned to the woman with whom he had been entranced all evening, "Luciana, I am having a quiet Saturday afternoon at home. Why don't you plan to come out for lunch? We'll relax. Maybe I'll even play the piano."

"You are a musician?" Luciana asked.

"All Italians love music," Ciano replied. "Now, can I expect you?"

"I had planned to see my daughter on Saturday, C.L.," Brad protested feebly.

"How old is she?"

"Eighteen, almost nineteen."

"My daughter is twenty-two," Ciano replied delightedly. "You must bring her. She and Elda can get to know each other. And you and I have some things to talk about too."

Brad knew it was a command performance again. He looked helplessly at Luciana. "Can you make it?"

Luciana gave Ciano a warm smile. "Of course I can. I'll put my uncle off until Sunday."

"Marvelous," Ciano sang. "About one o'clock Saturday then."

"We'll be with you, C.L.," Brad confirmed, wondering if he would ever be free to manage the social end of his life again.

Luciana, radiant at her brilliant success, left the party holding tightly to Brad's arm.

Relaxed, holding hands in the back of the limousine, Brad leaned over and kissed her neck. "Anyplace you'd like to go from here?"

"Anything you say, Brad."

"Ascot Towers, Williams."

As the limousine carried them toward their destination, Brad slid his hand over hers. "Given any more thought to moving over to the Ascot Towers? We'd love you to be our guest, you know."

"Mr. Ciano said the same thing tonight," Luciana replied.

"I wish you would. We have some beautiful suites."

"I don't know how long I'll be staying in New York."

"All the more reason for you to move to a friendly hotel."

"Before too long, I'll have to find a job. I'm not sure I could get a work permit for the United States."

"I'm sure we could find something interesting for you at Ascot, perhaps in the international department."

There was a sparkle in her eyes. "Have you and C.L. been talking about me? He said the same thing."

"Hey, just because he bought my company doesn't mean he gets my girl too."

"Oh, it was nothing like that. I think he really thought I could be useful. But I don't know why we're talking like this. I really have no intentions of staying in New York anyway."

The limousine pulled up in front of the hotel and Brad helped Luciana out and then walked toward the door. The gold-braided doorman touched the bill of his cap and opened the door. "Evening, Mr. Kendall."

They took the express elevator to the Star Club room and were immediately led to one of the more secluded tables with a spectacular view of the city. Luciana described her impressions of the party, mentioning especially how many Italians or Americans of Italian background she had met and talked to.

"But you know, Brad, the gentleman I most enjoyed was that nice politician from Texas."

"Ev Jamison?"

"Yes. Such a nice, straightforward man. He doesn't really talk like a Texan. I understand he is dueling with the President who is of his own party."

"That's right."

"Must take a lot of courage."

"Or a lot of political savvy. If Jamison really wants to run for President as a Republican he wouldn't stand a chance in '72 but four years later the only Republican that could make it would be one who was against the President. That's the way things work. We never elect Vice Presidents to succeed the President they served under."

"I think you're an old cynic." Luciana laughed.

"Maybe. That's why I understand C.L.'s political thinking."

"Anyway, I liked Ev and if I'm in New York the next time he comes back I'll be looking forward to seeing him."

"He's married and has five children."

"He told me. Straightaway. That's another reason I liked him."

"My God. There's no future in being an honest unmarried man," Brad groaned. "When are you going to give me a chance?"

Luciana laughed and took Brad's suggestion of a brandy and soda. After holding hands under the table until a second drink arrived, Brad suggested that he show her his suite. He could get one just like it for her if she wanted to move to the Ascot Towers, he promised.

"I'd love to see your suite, Brad, whether or not I ever move over here. How about tomorrow, though? I'm really tired now. It's been a long day for me."

She made a pretense of sipping on her second drink and then asked to be taken home. Brad escorted her from the room after signing the check and tipping the waiter and the headwaiter. He had debated on whether to keep the limousine or send it home. Fortunately, now he had kept it. One can never take anything for granted.

In the security of the St. Regis-bound limousine, Luciana turned warmly to Brad and ardently returned his kisses. At the hotel, Brad saw her up to her room in the elevator. She allowed him a peek inside; it was all very feminine. He wondered how women could so quickly give a hotel room personality and allure when they wanted to.

He kissed her and then she said, "I'll see you tomorrow, Brad. Just us. No party or anything."

"Right, darling. And we'll see if we can't possibly woo you away from here. It just won't do, here you are being escorted by the president of the Ascot chain and you're staying at a Sheraton Hotel."

"Well, we can't have anything as incongruous as that, can we? Until tomorrow, lovey." A last kiss and then he knew he must leave her.

All the way back to the Ascot Towers he plotted the scenario for the next night.

CHAPTER TEN

There were still a number of guests at the party when C. L. Ciano, with a nod to Fred Black, a significant head movement to another guest, quietly slipped away down the back staircase to the garden outside. He walked through the garden to the wall separating it from the rear of the property fronting on Sixty-seventh Street. At the corner, behind a tool house, he pressed a catch and a door slid open which he walked through. It slid to behind him. Now he was in a dark corridor running down the wall separating the two lots adjacent lengthwise to the street. He reached in his pocket, pulled out a small flashlight, snapped it on and followed the corridor which led into the back of the house on Sixty-seventh Street.

Another corridor ran to a door which opened on the street. He pushed the door open, gaining the sidewalk. He walked half a block toward Lexington Avenue until a parked limousine switched on its lights and rolled west on Sixty-seventh Street toward him. It stopped and the rear door opened. Ciano stepped in.

"How are ya, Charlie?" a hoarse voice asked.

"Good, Sal. You?"

"OK." Ciano did not reach out to shake Salvatore Di Siccerone's massive hand. His nickname wasn't Sal the Hand for nothing. Many years ago when Sal, a huge, though trim two hundred and thirty pounder

77

standing six foot three, graduated from high school with three years of all-state tackle behind him, he had immediately been made an enforcer in his uncle's powerful Cosa Nostra family. His specialty had been the quiet garroting with his huge right hand of rebellious family members even as they were attending a family meeting or funeral, unsuspecting of the fate awaiting them. This activity had earned him his sobriquet, Sal the Hand. Sal's education (there were few high school graduates in the family thirty-five years ago) and his native shrewdness, combined with the blood relationship to the family boss, made for fast promotion within the family. At the relatively early age of thirty-five, he had risen to the all-important post of family *consigliere*. When his uncle was forced to retire after a heart attack, no member of the family disputed his right to take over as boss. The commission of family bosses approved the appointment and at age forty, Sal the Hand became one of the most powerful and respected members of the commission as he ruled New York's mightiest army in the nation's crime consortium.

Sal the Hand's limousine rolled ahead, turned up Park and would continue to wend its way about the streets of New York until the driver received new instructions. Sal pressed a button on a small console beside him and a slight humming reverberated through the interior of the limousine.

"Something new?" Ciano asked.

"My bug man figured it out," Sal replied. "He goes over this car every day to make sure nobody planted any bug. But the feds now, they got stuff you'd never believe. They can bug without even putting anything in a room or a car. But this anti-bug thing you hear, nobody can use anything electronic and hear anything."

"Good precaution. My God, anybody who can read can know more about you and the other families than you knew yourself ten years ago. A lot of carelessness went on."

"Yeah," Sal growled. "They knew everything there for a while. I was shocked, I can tell you, Charlie. It's the worst thing ever hit us. They know every outside guy we had." Sal swore in Italian. "That judge, they kicked him off the bench, out of the law. The prosecutor we had, out. Maybe he'll get sent up. My state Democratic Party chairman, he's indicted. And my Republican national committeeman, he's hiding out somewhere. And there's more, more going to be exposed. We gotta get those laws tightened up so the feds can't invade our privacy like that."

In the dark interior Ciano smiled wryly to himself. The families had always needed him. Now he operated on a level above the boss of bosses, which he suspected was Sal the Hand's present status.

"You just better impress on the families not to talk, not even in the privacy of their homes and offices," Ciano warned sternly.

"They know, I can tell ya. We made those examples. Every one of those guys quoted in that *Life* magazine —hit!"

Ciano did not bring up the delicate matter of Sal himself being quoted extensively from wiretaps and electronic surveillance devices. However, he did say discreetly, "I'm glad you never mentioned me or Whitehall. That could be seriously damaging."

Sal swore in Italian. Then, "Never, never, Charlie. You should know better. Nobody, nobody in Salvatore Di Siccerone's family ever heard of you. Nobody in any family ever heard of you. Only me. Not even one family *consigliere* knows about you. You better learn you can trust us. The name Ciano has never been uttered, even in commission meetings."

"OK, Sal," Ciano said placatingly. "It's just you can't be too careful these days."

"Yeah. I can't get outside help any more. The judges, politicians, even little state representatives are scared. We never had such heat since I can remember. I'm trying to build up again, but everybody is scared. My chief corrupter can't get near anyone. Money? Don't mean anything, they're so scared. I gotta go out and try to buy our beards myself."

"Sal, Sal," Ciano began soothingly, "it's a whole new ball game. I've been trying to tell you for three years, but you don't listen to me. It's not like when Vito was running things. The United States Government has declared war on you. Understand? And they aren't kidding this time. You guys are going to be dead unless you modernize. Think seventies, not thirties and forties and fifties."

"What does that mean, Charlie?" There was a recognizable tremor in the harsh tones.

"When the United States Government declares war, you have to react scientifically. The old ways can only kill you if you don't bring them up-to-date."

"I don't know what you're talking about."

"OK. So against my advice you put your nephew in the soft ice-cream business in Brooklyn. That kid doesn't know about business. He never even graduated from high school."

"The kid's father put me in business. So what?"

"So he makes a loss. What does he do? He blames it on his competitors. What do you do? You send a couple of enforcers to the competition. They break up the machinery on thirty or forty trucks. Your kid is back in business—for a week. But all of a sudden the world realizes you are out to get legitimate business. And they are scared. They elect men who wouldn't have stood a chance four years ago. All they have to say to get elected is 'law and order.' Even the blacks are voting for law and order. The President knocks off our edge in the Supreme Court, the Attorney General comes right out and tells the people he's going to use every weapon he's got to destroy you, Sal, and the rest of the families. And the people cheer, because you've gone too far, you are now a visible threat to the small men. It used to be you only provided them services they wanted. Gambling, prostitution, labor fixing, they didn't even kick at paying for protection, and you control all the narcotics traffic. The average guy wasn't too concerned about narcotics until the average nice kids were getting hooked. Suddenly it isn't just blacks and Puerto Ricans and slum teen-agers getting on dope. Now the nice people are getting worried. And that's when the government could get away with something it hasn't tried since George Washington was inaugurated." Ciano paused.

Sal the Hand's breath was coming in short, heavy grunts as he listened in growing agitation. He waited for Ciano to continue. Sal knew Ciano was so far ahead of any member of the commission, including himself, in understanding the ultimate power of crime and its use as well as its vulnerability, that this was the only man in the world he was afraid of, though he fought never to show this. Finally he asked, in spite of himself, "What's that, Charlie?"

"Suspension of democratic processes."

"What does that mean?"

"It means that the feds know all about you, but they can't use electronic evidence—bugging—to get a conviction. But they pick you up anyway."

"My mouthpiece would be all over them so fast they wouldn't know what hit 'em." Sal heaved out the words.

"When your mouthpiece arrives, he goes into some cell right beside you. And nobody sees either of you again. And someone comes looking, and he disappears. Then it comes out that Salvatore Di Siccerone died of a heart attack in detention. And that mouthpiece, when he finally walks out, if he does, gives up criminal practice."

"Oh, cut the crap, Charlie, why you trying to frighten me? In case you didn't know, I'm *capo* of *capos,* boss of bosses. And this is a free country. We got laws, a Bill of Rights. Not like Mussolini."

"Just trying to let you know what can and likely will happen. If that's what the nice, average people want, they'll get it."

In spite of his bluster, Sal the Hand was obviously shaken. Finally he asked quietly, "What do we do?"

"This heat's going to last until they destroy you or at least get you under control. Best thing is to look like you're under control. Keep out of corrupting and destroying legitimate business. Leave that to me, and to me alone. And keep away from trying to bribe public officials. Leave that to me, too. You have no way of knowing what the personal interests of a congressman are. I have an entire staff in Washington doing nothing but finding out how to get to a man. And then you don't bribe him. You find a reason to use his law firm, you contribute to campaign expenses, but at the right time through the right go-between."

"We can't operate without buying protection."

"Well, keep off the higher levels. I'll handle that. Stick to police corruption. And stop every member of every family from even talking to each other."

"The commission drew up a whole new security policy. Like you say, we don't even know what the hell kind of supersonic stuff the feds got, or whatever the hell they're using. But we drew up the whole new procedure, see. There'll never be any kind of wholesale leaks again."

"In the meantime, the commission and the whole structure are on charts in the federal offices, most of your soldiers and *caporegimins,* even names, dates were made. The works."

There was no answer Sal could make and Ciano decided to lighten the tone of this discussion a bit. "OK, Sal, I'm proceeding on all fronts at my end. You enjoying that nice clean money coming back to you?"

"Of course, Charlie. You're a genius. And you're lucky, you know. We need you more than anyone else, including each other. With those computers and all the Revenue Service got, it's hell to try and live on anything but clean money."

"How much you got to be cleaned this month?"

"Can you take fifteen million?"

"Of course. I bought one of the world's biggest hotel chains. Don't you read the financial news?"

"Not much. I leave that to you."

"Where's the cash?"

Sal reached into his pocket and pulled out three safe-deposit box keys. "It's in these safe-deposit boxes at your bank in Queens. Must be nice to own a bank. It took three of the big boxes to get it all in."

"Fifteen million, eh? Small bills mostly, I suppose."

"Everything."

"OK, Sal, now so that we understand each other perfectly since we don't find written agreements a very secure way of operating, let me go over the rules. Right?"

"Sure. I know them."

"Nothing safer than a refresher course, so no misunderstandings. Yes?" Sal nodded.

"First, tomorrow I go to the bank and hand these keys to my president. He has the money taken out of the boxes, counted, and then he changes it into one- and ten-thousand-dollar bills and tells me how much he changed. A memorandum comes to you with the figure. Whatever that figure, you accept it."

"Of course, Charlie. It's always been that way."

"Now, I divide the money up into ten attaché cases and send a million and a half dollars in each case to my bank in Switzerland with a courier who enjoys diplomatic immunity."

"Yeah. That's pretty clever."

"Why do you think I take such an interest in the United Nations? Nice to have such a secure service right on your doorstep." He paused as a car passed the limousine and watched it until it sped two blocks ahead. Sal's driver immediately turned off into a side street.

"OK. I send ten to Switzerland over the next week. I know all the men are good, we haven't lost a shipment yet. But there is always that chance. So out of fifteen maybe you lose one and a half, or even three million."

"Yeah, I understand, Charlie. We lose, we take the loss. I told you, we trust you."

"Right, Sal. Even if you lost three million out of fifteen you're still way the hell ahead of the game. If you had to pay U.S. taxes on that money before you could invest it, you'd have less than half to invest."

"Yeah, we know all that."

"Whatever amount gets to my bank in Zurich, that's the amount we borrow to invest in fast turnover business or real estate. Now we have a big hotel chain to put the money in. Your checks will keep coming back, nice clean dividend checks, and capital gains deals. You pay your one-third capital gains tax, but what an edge when you invest big money without paying taxes on it before it goes into a deal."

"The commission is all behind you, Charlie. You talk to me, you talk to the whole commission."

"Good. Now, anything you need from me?"

"Yeah. I read, my *consigliere* read," he amended, "that down there"—Ciano knew he was referring to that nebulous area of enemy territory commonly known as Washington, D.C.—"they're doing something to change the welfare laws. Making it tougher to get on welfare or to spend it freely. I don't know. You better throw all your people with muscle down there to getting more welfare for these people. You know how much of that fifteen you're going to pick up came out of welfare checks around the country the past two months? Goddamned near half."

"I'll work on it, Sal."

"When you getting in the next load from over there?"

This was Sal the Hand's way of referring to a heroin shipment from France.

"Let you know next meet. Like I say, we've got to be ready to get out, so make all you can while you can."

"We were figuring to make a panic, drive the price up. We're getting short anyway. Every month we get about five thousand new customers from Los Angeles to Brooklyn. Gotta keep 'em supplied. It's, I look at it like it's kind of a sacred trust. What are they going to do if we can't supply them after getting them started?"

"I'll have three hundred and fifty kilos for you to pick up in the next two weeks."

"Yeah, good, Charlie. That'll do it for a while."

"Goddamned well should. That's a hundred million dollars' worth, when it's cut and pushed on the street."

"That reminds me. There's a cop in Bed-Stuy, one of our best areas, getting out of line. Tomorrow's the fifteenth of the month, the day the welfare checks hit the street, see? The boss nigger out there does a quarter of a million in H, policy and check cashing in just that one day. But this cop is giving him and his boys a bad time. Can you handle him?"

"In 1969 I broke up the New York Narcotics Bureau for the New York families. And you're worrying about one cop? Who is it, Kenney? The big hero of the new cop book?"

"Yeah. It's small potatoes, but it doesn't look good we can't protect our guys in such a lush district. You know? Not one other cop in all the good areas in this city gives us that kind of trouble. Like I said, it's small but it makes us look bad. He's famous, that book about him and all, gone to his head. We gotta teach him a lesson."

"OK, Sal. I'll figure something to get Kenney out of your way."

"Yeah, do that for me, Charlie. Something that won't bring any heat on us, though."

C. L. Ciano chuckled to himself. "Don't worry. I know just what to do with Mr. Kenney, and in a few days you won't have any more trouble in that area again. Anything else you need?"

Sal the Hand hesitated as though embarrassed. Ciano looked at him slightly amused. "You don't have to be afraid to ask me anything, Sal." His voice was soft and warm. "You know I'll do anything I can."

"It's the tough one, Charlie."

"The Stick?"

"Yeah. He's been up there three years now. He's eligible for parole hearings but they'll never give it to him. If we leave him serve the whole twelve years we lose a lot of confidence."

"Sam DeCalvo, Sam the Stick," Ciano said thoughtfully. "What was it? Stolen stock certificates?"

"Yeah. Five million worth he got out of that bigname Wall Street place. If you can do anything it will help me big at the commission."

"I've got the file on Sam. I'll go over it and see what we can do."

"Sam was responsible for a lot of the cash and bank paper I was handing over to you five years ago, you know."

Ciano raised his eyebrows. "No, I didn't know. I didn't want to know."

"That's right, Charlie. You know now. That's the biggest thing you can do for me now. Spring Sam."

"It's asking a lot."

"I know. It's the big one. See what you can do. If you can't help I'll understand. The governor, the D.A., the newspapers all want him to do every minute of his time."

"Anything else, Sal?" Ciano asked wearily.

"No. Just the welfare and the cop Kenney. And fight them legalizing gambling and pot."

Ciano laughed again. "I have financed a council of interdenominational church leaders who are fighting it all over the country."

"Yeah, even the New York State Lottery is hurting us."

"OK, Sal. Now, I've got a problem for you to handle. I need a lot of trouble and a strike at the Tropic Plaza Hotel in Miami and then I need a guy named Morrie Unger, a director and the big stockholder, to agree to vote to sell the shares in the Tropic Hotel Company to a guy whose name I'll give you. A straw for Ascot."

"I thought you said that stuff don't go no more."

"In this case, Mr. Unger is hardly a legitimate businessman. He's got many reasons not to want to contact the law."

"How far do you want me to go?"

"I need those shares."

"You got 'em, Charlie."

"One more thing, Sal."

"Yeah?"

"You know where to find Augie Falconi? There's a kid seeing my daughter Elda. He calls himself Tony Falcon. I think he's Augie's kid."

"What d'ya want me to do, Charlie?"

"Let Augie know he shouldn't let his boy see my daughter any more. He's coming to the house tomorrow to see her. I want him to say a nice good-by and never see her again."

"Kid's no good, huh? Augie was always a stand-up guy."

"The kid might be OK, I don't know. I just don't want him around my daughter." Ciano's tone softened. "Look, Sal, what I mean is I don't want my family in any way connected with your thing, you know? It could hurt all of us in what we're doing. Maybe this Tony Falconi or whatever his name is only went after my daughter figuring to get in with a rich kid and her friends and improve his life style. But he's a smooth, good-looking kid and I want him out of Elda's life before she falls for him."

"The kid says bye-bye tomorrow," Sal replied forcefully.

"Good. And Kenney says good-by to Bed-Stuy. Now take me back and I'll set the next meet the usual way."

CHAPTER ELEVEN

Detective First Grade Pat Kenney finished buckling the leather holster strap around his right ankle and pulled his sock up over the .38 revolver. He stood up and pulled his pants leg down and was ready to face this day, one of the month's two most active and depressing days, at the Eighty-first Precinct in Brooklyn's teeming Bedford-Stuyvesant district. He had gone to bed early the night before, as did all the detectives, to be rested and ready for the grueling hours ahead, which might stretch out to twenty-four hours straight with day court, night court and day court again. For this was Mother's Day, the day twice a month when the welfare checks came in and criminal activity reached a peak.

Prepared for battle, Kenney walked out into the living room of the large, fashionably located apartment he shared with Tom Henry, the journalist and writer who had recently written a book about Kenney's exploits as one of the top cops of the New York Narcotics Bureau. Even before the book had come out, there had been a mysterious shake-up in the bureau. Pat's old boss, the chief of the Bureau, had been transferred to an obscure precinct in Queens, and one by one the most effective men had been transferred until there was nothing left of the Bureau but untrained and inexperienced men, who wouldn't know the difference between a five-dollar pop and a sugar bag.

"The Mafia never had it better. Everybody's in junk now," Kenney had told his roommate, who unaccountably had been unable to get a story published anywhere on the destruction and dissolution of the Narcotics Bureau.

Kenney made himself a cup of instant coffee and ate a bowl of dry cereal. The kitchen was a mess from a party Tom had given for some other writers the night before. Kenney's thoughts shifted to the necessity of finding himself his own pad. When he had left his wife after finding out she was screwing an Italian who he knew damned well was a mafioso, Tom had invited Pat to stay with him until he could get settled. That had been six months ago. He knew he'd never find a place he could afford, as convenient and comfortable, what with the payments he had to make for his two kids, so he had delayed looking elsewhere. At least he had been able to put Tom onto the track of some good stories.

The detective spent ten minutes cleaning up the kitchen and then left the apartment.

Out on the street he unlocked his car and took the metal identification plate out of the windshield. Not that it did any good; his car had once been towed away, plate and all. He slid his car into the traffic and made for the East River Drive. It was a half hour's drive from the pleasant neighborhood of Tom Henry's apartment to the squalor and deprivation of Bed-Stuy. He hated going to work these days at the precinct, so different from when he and his partner Vic Gatto had worked in their free-swinging style all over New York City, free to operate in any of the five boroughs as their quarries led them. Those had been the days. Now he was just serving time until he could retire with a pension. He and Vic had sometimes worked forty-eight hours straight to make an important narcotics arrest. He led not only the New York Police Department but, as far as could be ascertained, every police department in the world in arrests leading to convictions. It was still impossible for him to understand how this could have happened to him. One day super-cop, as the newspapers had called him, the subject of one of the hottest books by one of the country's most noted authors; the next day, assigned to the most degrading work an officer of his rank and experience could be given. And Vic. Where was he? Riding up at the two-eight in Harlem.

Today he would live at firsthand through the real tragedy being brought on by the destruction of the Narcotics Bureau. How many overdose deaths would today bring? Youths dead, the needles still in their arms. With all the experienced narcotics detectives replaced by rank beginners, the sale of narcotics began to take on a different cast. The informers who had attached themselves to the old officers melted from the streets. The new men had no information to go on. They didn't know how to make arrests. Now everybody was in junk. Punks who had been mere delivery boys or users were now buying heroin, packaging it and selling it at great profit. Unfortunately, they did not know their business, and in cutting the pure stuff they either used impure ingredients or sold bags that were too pure for the addict to inject into the bloodstream. Thus, almost instant death by overdose or the slower death by infection and poison.

As he entered Bed-Stuy, the eight-fifty local news came over the radio. Already one death from an overdose. Bitterly he relived the morning he was transferred out of the Bureau, along with so many other officers.

Kenney pulled up in front of the ancient, dilapidated precinct station and parked. In a fury, cursing the powers that saw fit to break up the Narcotics Bureau, he entered the Eighty-first Precinct. It was just nine o'clock. The mailmen would already be making their rounds. In the detectives' room he waited for his partner to show up. Carlos was a damned good man, a Puerto Rican, and since he had been driving with Pat Kenney he had become an accomplished detective third grade. Pat had already recommended him for promotion to detective second. Carlos Rivera even had a year of college behind him and he was a much bigger man physically than the Puerto Ricans they picked up day after day, sometimes in a trance, the works still hanging out of their arms. The best thing about today, Pat thought, is the weather. A perfect seventy-five, just right if you had to be on the street.

He wandered into the captain's office to chat with George Reilly. Captain Reilly, a veteran of the tough precincts and, as Tom Henry had written in an article, one of the gentlest gentlemen he had ever met on the force, was reading reports. He looked up when Kenney walked in and smiled genially.

"Hey, Pat. We're about 10 per cent behind the eight-three in collars last month."

"Shit, George, I can make collars all day. But goddamn it, all the paper work, then half the night in court and the motherfucker is back on the street shooting up before I've finished his case."

"Even when the judge lets him go, we at least get credit for the collar."

"Tell you what, George, I'll give you ten collars today and take tomorrow off. I promised Tom I'd help him promote his book."

"I'll settle for five, Pat." George smiled fondly at his prize detective. To have such a famous character assigned to his precinct had shocked him. He would have figured they'd have had Kenney doing community relations work for the department. But then every star narcotics man in the Bureau had been given an undesirable transfer. It was the talk of the department, that is, the officers talked about it nervously, among themselves, never in front of a superior or a friend of long standing. The shooflies, department informers, were everywhere. Just a wrong statement could get a cop with twenty years of good service time behind him in trouble.

Pat Kenney was certainly a bit of a braggart, but in an amusing way, Captain Reilly thought. Never did Kenney show anything but absolute respect for his superior, if tinged with familiarity few other first grade detectives would display. But Pat Kenney was different.

And he was a tough, uncompromising, honest cop. Reilly boasted to his fellow precinct commanders of having the officer who had made the world's largest heroin arrest and followed through with the conviction as his new top detective.

Carlos poked his head in the door. Reilly invited him in. "OK, Rivera, I expect a big day out of you and Kenney."

"We'll do our best, sir."

"I'm sending a Mr. Carrera with you. He's a postal inspector. We suspect that there's a group of mailmen selling welfare checks."

"Shall we pick up Modalino again?" Kenney asked wearily.

"If you catch him in the act of cashing a check, bring him in. At least we can keep harassing the bastards."

"Yeah, that's about all," Kenney growled. "OK, Carlos, let's get cranked up." Pat's partner left the room and Kenney sidled around the captain's desk so that he could see the sheets of paper in front of the commander. It was the first day of the month and Reilly would be making his evaluations of last month's performances of the uniformed and plainclothesmen in the eight-one. Reilly left the papers face up as Kenney checked the names. Naturally, Kenney's name was first on the list in number of arrests made. He looked down the list to see which officers were significantly below the quota of arrests for the past month and noted six names.

"OK, George, we'll get those collars for you. And I'll give those guys at the bottom one collar each, before the day is over."

Kenney walked out to the detectives' room and found two of the men from the bottom of the list.

"OK, Shaughnessy, Fuentes. In one hour, you be at the corner of Atlantic and Seventh. I'll give you each a collar and you can spend the rest of the day doing the paper work. You guys didn't do so well last month."

The two looked sheepish and thanked Kenney; his

ability to make unlimited arrests of addicts, pushers and dealers with the evidence on them was legend. Pat walked down the hall from the detectives' room to the squad room where the uniformed patrolmen were getting ready to go out. He found the other four men who were delinquent in arrests the previous month and told them where to be two hours hence to receive at least two collars, courtesy of Pat Kenney. Then he and Carlos and the postal inspector Carrera went out and took off in a squad car to tour the precinct. Carlos drove, Kenney lounged beside him, and Carrera sat in the back seat alertly watching the postmen they passed.

After a few minutes, Kenney turned slightly to Carrera. "These people come up from the poor southern states for just one reason, to get on welfare. Every month we get a few thousand more, right out of the cotton fields or wherever they come from. You can hardly understand them. That's the difference between here and Harlem. Up there the people go back three and four generations. They have roots and usually some sort of an education."

"That's an interesting sociological note," the postal inspector remarked.

"The entire industry here," Kenney continued, "the only industry is welfare. You got any idea how much money comes in here in checks every Mother's Day?" Carrera shook his head. "Me and George Reilly tried to figure it out one day when we didn't have much to do. We figured that just into Bed-Stuy, with the average check running around a hundred and thirty bucks, and the population about fifty thousand that's three quarters of a million dollars your postmen are delivering today."

"I never thought of it that way," Carrera said.

Kenney stared at the sidewalks, crowded with Negro women clustered around the postboxes in the entranceways to the tenements. "Slow down," Carrera suddenly hissed. Carlos applied his brakes gently. "Look at that," the inspector said.

A mailman was handing the welfare check envelopes

to a group of women, their children milling about among their mothers' legs. "That's against all regulations."

"Well, if he sticks the checks into the mailboxes, even with the women right there, they can get stolen."

"How does he know he's handing the envelopes to the right people?" Carrera asked, making notations in his book.

Kenney shrugged. "It happens in every block." He was staring ahead down the street. He had spotted a black youth furtively dart into a tenement doorway. "Keep going, Carlos," Kenney ordered. The unmarked dark green patrol car moved ahead. "Stop here!"

Kenney threw open the door of the car, dashed into the tenement entrance, strangely empty of women, and threw open the door into the hallway. The slender dark youth had started up the stairs but Kenney was after him, grabbing him, and roughly throwing him down the stairs and with a hammerlock led him to the tenement entrance. "OK, what are you doing here?"

"I live here." The young Negro rolled the whites of his eyes in fear.

"What apartment?" There was a pause. "Let's see some identification."

"I left it home so I don't lose it."

"Yeah? You take me up to your apartment." Kenney gave a twist of the arm which elicited a cry of pain. "Now."

The youth started up the steps again uncertainly, Kenney behind him. On the second-floor landing he turned toward the rear and stopped before a door uncertainly.

"This it?" Kenney asked.

"I think so."

"You think?" he roared. "Don't you know where you live?"

"Right here."

Kenny knocked on the door. There was no answer. "You got a key?" he asked.

"My mother got the only key."

Kenney banged on the door again and finally a

scurrying sound came from within. The door was opened slowly. At first Kenney couldn't see anyone opening the door. He flattened himself against the wall. Then, looking down he saw a small black boy, huge white eyes turned up to him. "Where's your mama?" Kenney asked.

"Doan know," came the faint reply.

Kenney sat on his haunches, his face now on a level with the boy's. "Tell me, boy," Kenney's tones were kindly, "where's your mammy? I just want to talk nice to her."

"Mammy go to get her check. Then she go to do the shopping. Then she go to see the landlord," he recited, "and pay the rent. Then she go to the police to say the check stolen. Then she come home."

In spite of the underlying squalor and sordidness of the whole situation, Kenney laughed aloud. At the police station, there would soon be a line-up of welfare recipients reporting their checks stolen. They would take down the particulars and notify the welfare board, which would issue another check the following day. Welfare cases were allowed to report three stolen checks a year and receive new ones with no investigation whatsoever. After that there was a minimum investigation made, but unless a recipient seemed chronically unable to keep her checks from being stolen, new ones were liberally reissued.

Kenney stood up and grabbed the youth beside him by the back of the neck and jerked him into sight of the child. "You know him, son?" Kenney asked. "You ever see him in this house?"

"Naw, sir. I doan never see him."

Kenney turned to the black. "This where you live?"

"I guess I went to the wrong door by accident."

Without another word, Kenney dragged his charge back to the stairs and down them to the entrance.

"You little check-stealing motherfucker. You was waiting for the mailman, is what you were doing."

"I never took nuttin' in ma life."

"All right, out in the street." Kenney gave him a

heave against the door, which flew open and the crying youth hurtled out across the sidewalk and into the
street. When he scrambled out of the path of oncom-
ing traffic, he saw the large bulk and flaming red hair
of the detective above him. "I catch you so much as
breathing in my precinct again, I'm going to run you
in and you'll never get out of jail. You hear me?"

"Yessuh." The youngster scrambled away down the
street.

Back in the car, Kenney shook his head. "I don't
know why I bother. Nothing stops these jungle animals. He'll steal a couple of checks before the day's
over." He looked at his watch. "OK, let's make a
couple of collars, Carlos."

Just as Carlos was about to put the car in gear and
move ahead, a taxicab passed them. The driver was
white and three Negroes were in the back seat.

"They're dirty," Kenney rasped. "Pull 'em over."

Carlos took off after the cab and turned on the siren.
The cab pulled over and Carlos stopped behind it.
Again, Kenney was out of the car and pulling at the
cab door, shouting at the three in the back to get out.
Carlos came up on the other side of the cab just in
time to see one of the Negroes stuff something behind
the seat, between it and the back rest.

"Get out. Put your hands on your head," Kenney
commanded. "All right, start jumping. Jump, motherfuckers." The three blacks began jumping up and
down. "Give the car a toss, Carlos." To the driver,
"Where did you pick them up?"

"Bushwick and Flushing," the driver answered impassively.

"Got something here," Carlos called, his hand reaching behind the seat. He pulled out two glassine envelopes. And then two more. "Sure looks like H." Kenney meantime began a search of the three passengers,
allowing them to stop jumping up and down. Finding
nothing incriminating on them, he ordered them back
in the cab. "OK, driver. We'll follow you. Drive over
to Atlantic and Seventh. Your cab was dirty, like I
figured."

"Now look, officer," the driver began to protest. "I can't help what my job's got on 'em."

"It was in your cab, not on 'em," Carlos said. "Do what we say and you'll be all right. I saw one of them stash the stuff."

"All right, junkies, get into that cab," Kenney thundered.

Cowed, the trio scrambled into the cab. "We'll be right behind you," Kenney went on menacingly. "I promise I'll break your nigger skulls if you try anything."

The cab proceeded at a slow pace for the several blocks to where a marked police patrol car was parked. The two uniformed officers in the front seat grinned broadly as they saw Kenney shepherding the cab toward them. Kenney motioned to the cab driver to halt behind the patrol car.

"OK, Shaughnessy, you and Fuentes got three collars between you," Kenney said magnanimously. He handed one of the officers the glassine packs of heroin. "We didn't give the cab a thorough toss," he went on. "I think there may be a stash in it. These motherfuckers didn't come over to Bed-Stuy on Mother's Day for the air. They were cruising around waiting for the checks to be cashed and the addicts out trying to score —which is every nigger in the precinct."

"Thanks, Kenney," Fuentes said. "We sure appreciate the collars."

Pat Kenney and Carlos Rivera started out again. From the back seat Carrera asked, "How did you know they were dirty?"

"I don't know," Kenney answered thoughtfully. "Everybody asks me that. I just get, like a revelation. Of course, three niggers in a cab out here isn't exactly usual, especially with a white man driving."

Carlos drove the patrol car back into the precinct, Kenney watching the throngs on the sidewalk making for the banks. Each bank they passed was jammed with welfare recipients cashing their checks. Farther down the street, Kenney called for a halt in front of a real estate office. As they watched it, black men and women meandered in and out.

"That's Modalino's place," Kenney pointed out. "He cashes the stolen checks at fifty cents on the dollar. I've wasted more time collaring him. If I hit him now, he'll be back on the street cashing stolen checks while I'm still on the paper work."

"Ever see a postman go near him?" Carrera asked.

Kenney laughed. "Any of your boys stealing checks would be smart enough not to be seen with him."

They drove down a one-way street. Ahead on the right was parked a large trailer truck. Beyond the truck, turning up the street from the next block against the traffic, they saw two blacks strolling along. "Look at the way that motherfucker is walking," Kenney said hoarsely. "He just scored. Keep driving. I'll slide out of the car this side of the truck. You drive on past them. About the time they see you, I'll be hitting."

Carlos drove slowly along as Kenney opened the door on his side of the car. Crouching below the windshield he rolled out of the car onto the street. Stealthily he crept up behind the truck and remained concealed from the sidewalk. Rivera continued to drive down the street, past the truck and then facing and suddenly abreast of the two Negroes Kenney had spotted. One of them turned, saw the car and started running as Rivera called at them to halt. The one running reached in his pocket, pulled out something and stuffed it in his mouth just as Kenney stepped from around the back of the parked truck.

"Stop," Kenney cried. The black did not slacken his pace and made as though to run around him. Nimbly, Kenney cut off the fugitive, and cocking his right arm, slammed a hamlike right fist into the side of the Negro's jaw. He went down, sprawling on the sidewalk. Kenney grabbed for him, pulled him to his feet and hit him in the jaw again. This time his mouth opened and Kenney retrieved four glassine envelopes slimy with saliva. Suddenly, the Negro dodged, threw himself to the sidewalk, rolling under the parked truck and emerged on the street side of the truck just as Carlos completed a U-turn and drove up beside him. Jumping out of the car, Carlos grappled with his quarry, threw him over his leg onto the street and ordered him to get into the car.

The Negro refused to get into the car and swore at the detective. Just then, Kenney came from around the truck and walked up to the man he had just knocked to the pavement. He held out the envelopes for the Negro to see. "OK, we've got you with the shit. You should be glad I didn't let you swallow the stuff. You know what I would have done? I'd have taken you in and you'd be in the cage until you shit everything out of you and the chemist analyzed it. You'd get five years' minimum for possession and another five for attempting to destroy the evidence."

Now Kenney walked the man away from Carlos and the car, talking to him confidentially. They reached the end of the block and turned left. He was suddenly a friendly cop, concerned for the people of his precinct.

"Ah doan wanna go back to jail, I swear I doan, Mr. Kenney."

"Yeah. Be a shame. I wish I could help you."

"Couldn't you let me go this time?"

Kenney pondered the question, frowning, shaking his head. "I don't know. What could you do for me?"

"I don't know nuttin' or I'd help you."

"You just scored somewhere," Kenny pointed out.

Carlos had driven around the block and come up across the street from the sidewalk where Kenney and his addict were standing. "Take a ride with us," Kenney said.

"Please, suh, just this time. I swear on my mother I won't do it again."

"What are you shooting now?" Kenney asked sympathetically.

"Bout four a day."

"You'll do it again."

"Not in your precinct, Mr. Kenney."

Kenney opened the back door of the car and pushed the addict in beside the postal inspector. "Let's go, Carlos."

"Maybe I could help you if you let me go."

"Know where I can find a stash?"

"Lemme go. I'll find one."

Kenney nodded. "Pull over, Carlos." The car slid up beside the curb and stopped. "OK, call me at the station when you got something."

"Yessah," the addict cried happily, wasting no time opening the door and getting onto the sidewalk. He paused, looking at Kenney, something resembling an imploring look in his eyes. He seemed about to say something, then turned away. "You goan hear from me real soon, sir."

Carlos started up the car. "The mother was going to ask me for his shit back," Kenney growled. "When I let 'em go, half the time they do that. He gives me something good, I'll give him ten bucks so he can score and shoot up before he goes crazy."

As they patrolled the streets, Kenney looked back at the postal inspector. "Christ, it's a lousy jungle out here."

"Are you doing anything to really get the junk off the streets?" Carrera asked.

"What can you do? Those collars I gave Shaughnessy and his partner, they'll be out. We didn't have a search warrant so the stuff we found isn't admissible as evidence. What do you do, tell a guy to wait until you get a search warrant and you'll be back and make the collar? Junk is the most profitable business in the city because it's the safest now. Every time that old fool on the Supreme Court opens his senile mouth, the junk business gets safer. I'd like to have one of those decision makers spend a Mother's Day with me. By the end of the week, between junk and policy, the mob ends up with more than half of all the welfare money the city lays out. And we can't touch 'em. Well, ten months and I can retire on three-quarters pension. I wouldn't stay the whole twenty years for a full pension for anything."

"What do you want to do, Pat?" his partner asked.

"I promised those rookies a collar. Then we'll go in for a while." As they drove along, Kenney spotted two black youths in tightly cut peg pants and broad-shouldered sport jackets.

"They're dirty," he growled. Carlos pulled up beside them and Kenny jumped out. "OK, hands on the head, don't move."

The Negroes stood quietly as Kenney searched them. He found nothing incriminating on the first one and turned to the second. On his belt the black had clipped a sunglasses case. Kenney whipped it off the belt, took a look inside and threw it in the car window. "Works." Then, "Come on, both of you, get in."

"I didn't do nothin'," the first one said.

"You were in company with a man carrying works. That makes you guilty too. Get in."

As they entered the car, Carrera was examining the contents of the glasses case. The needle, eye dropper, small pan, all the paraphernalia to cook the heroin with water and then inject it in a vein. Five minutes later, Kenney delivered the two collars to the rookies who thanked him profusely and they drove back to the station house.

"What a lousy way to finish out my time, helping the precinct make its quota of collars every month. I should be out after the big guys, the ones that keep the shit flowing into the city and this country."

"Whatever happened, Pat?" Carrera asked.

"Who knows? If the mob could reach one of the mayor's commissioners like they did, no reason why they couldn't get to others. All we know is that the Bureau was getting too good, we were costing the mob millions a year in the big heroin hits we were making. Even though most of their guys were acquitted, at least we were getting the shit off the street. Then a couple of our guys were framed, the commissioner didn't back 'em up and the next thing we know—no more Narcotics Bureau. Every one of us is doing something like this."

In the station house, Kenney went upstairs. It was almost noontime. He found Reilly. "George, me and Carlos are going over to Bailey's for a sandwich."

"Yeah? And a couple of rye and gingers, I bet."

"Every other motherfucker in this precinct is high on something. Makes me understand them better if I get a small buzz too."

A uniformed policeman came into the captain's office. "Detective Kenney, a call for you. Sounds like one of your stools."

"Excuse me, George." Kenney left the captain's office and went to his own desk. He picked up the phone. "Kenney."

"Yes, Mr. Kenney, this Albert. I promise I get to you. There's two guys playing chess on Bushwick and Maple. They got the stash maybe five feet away from them, under a wire fence where a section next to the ground is torn away."

"Thanks, Albert. We get it and you get twenty dollars, get you through the rest of the day just fine." Kenney hung up. "Let's go, Carlos."

Together Pat and Carlos left the station house, climbed into the patrol car, and Carlos slid the car through the traffic at maximum speed to the corner of Bushwick and Maple. Sure enough, two older-looking Negroes were playing chess and beyond them was a wire fence between an empty lot and the sidewalk. There were several younger blacks watching the game and others wandered by, pausing and moving on. Kenney and Carlos left the car and strode over to the game. Then, leaving Carlos standing over the players, Kenney walked down the fence line.

Elaborately, the players ignored the police officers. Kenney located the hole in the fence, reached in and sifted through the litter. His fingers clamped onto a brown paper bag, which he pulled out and opened.

"Well what in the world do we have here?" he cried out gleefully. "Little glassine bags." He bent down and his fingers searched through the rubble further. This time, he pulled out a red and white bread-loaf package and found it to contain even more small envelopes. He stood there, counting the bags, as the chess players continued.

"Hey," Carlos cried at one of the players. "You

stupid or something? He'll take your queen. I don't think you are concentrating."

"Thirty bags," Kenney called to his partner. He walked over to the patrol car and dropped them into the front seat and then returned to the chess game.

"Stand up," he commanded. One of the players obeyed and Kenney began searching him, starting with the porkpie hat. When he got to the wallet, he began counting five-dollar bills. "You sold twenty five-dollar pops so far this morning, I see." Then at the other player he growled, "Get on your feet, motherfucker."

By now the rest of the Negroes had faded from the corner.

"OK, get in the car."

"We haven't done anything to warrant arrest," the older Negro argued.

"Warrant fuckin' arrest," Kenney cried as though wounded. "Get in that car before I slap your pointed heads flat."

"We don't have to listen to this abuse," the leader of the two said. "We have violated no law."

"No law? What do you call selling heroin to these addicts, coming in with money from their wives' or mothers' or girl friends' checks?"

"We were just playing a game of chess in the open air."

"Get in that car," Kenney growled ominously. He grabbed the verbal chess player by the arm and with one hand opening the back seat of the car, he hurled the black in with such force that he crumpled onto the floor. Kenney turned to the other. "Are you going to be lippy, too?" Before he could answer, Kenney clamped an arm around his elbow. The man yelped in pain and then stepped into the back seat. Carlos drove back to the station house, Kenney turned in his seat watching his two captives.

"The sons of bitches are loaded with five-dollar bills. Too bad that isn't evidence in a court of law."

Captain Reilly was waiting for Kenney and his partner as they arrived with their prisoners, now silent and docile. The Negroes walked into the station house and up the stairs to the booking room. The police officer and detectives were about evenly divided between black and white in this totally black precinct.

"Book 'em," Kenney said. A Negro booking sergeant began going through the procedure of taking their names and examining identification. Kenney walked into Reilly's office adjoining.

"Those mothers have been selling all morning from their stash."

"Either one have anything on them?"

Kenney shrugged. "I didn't toss 'em too carefully. I figured that could be done better here when they book 'em."

"How we going to tie them to the stash? It was five feet away from them, you say."

"Hell, even if we could, I didn't have a search warrant. With the number of bags they had, they've got to be high enough so a mob lawyer will be down and spring them."

There was a call for Kenney from the other room. Followed by Captain Reilly, he walked over to the booking sergeant.

"Hey, Kenney, did you toss these guys before you brought them in?"

Kenney shook his head. "No. I looked into that mother's hat band and then checked his wallet. Loaded with fives. I didn't even bother to toss the other one. After all, sergeant," Kenney smiled sanctimoniously, "I didn't have a search warrant, so anything I found wouldn't have been admissible as evidence." Kenney never really trusted the black sergeant. Somewhere in the back of his mind, he suspected the sergeant was really more on the side of the black prisoners than the police.

"Well, I sure found 'em dirty," the sergeant said. "Each of them had a couple of pops on 'em."

"Well, that's interesting," Kenney said.

"That detective framed us," the voluble prisoner accused. "He planted those bags on us."

"That," Kenney said definitively, "is what every prisoner who has ever been caught with a bag on him says. Right, Sarge?"

The sergeant nodded.

"This is outrageous. A deliberate frame-up," the captive cried, for the first time frightened, his former aplomb gone completely. "He planted that stuff when he brutalized us and threw us in the patrol car. I want to call my lawyer."

"In time," the sergeant barked. "Lock 'em both up. Mark the bags as evidence."

"Better get a chemist to see if the bags in their pocket were from the same batch of stuff as the stash," Kenney advised. He turned to Captain Reilly. "Well, it's time to go over to Bailey's. I'm buying."

Reilly looked at his star detective suspiciously. "It's not often you bring a guy in with junk still on him."

"I guess I'm getting careless," Kenney said. "Come on, let's take the postman to the only place in Bed-Stuy where a cop dares eat and drink."

Kenney, Carrera and Rivera walked over to Bailey's, Reilly promising to follow. They passed several bars catering exclusively to black patrons. "That one, there," Kenney remarked. "You see that big buck at the bar? Now if we watched him all day, we'd see three women come up to him and give him half their welfare checks. He's got a wife and three kids, a girl friend with two of his little bastards, and another girl friend with one. Not only that, but he makes his mother contribute too. First thing they do after the bank is come here and give him his share. And of course he has a policy racket going out the back door of the place."

They sauntered on through the gay throngs on the street, shopping, drinking, gambling, scoring off heroin pushers, a gala festival atmosphere everywhere. It was Mother's Day after all, checks for everyone.

With a sigh of relief, Kenney and his companions settled in at the end of the air-conditioned bar and ordered drinks. Kenney downed his first one promptly and ordered another. "They don't know how lucky they are out there. Mr. Kenney is going to be detained all afternoon in court with his collars."

"When did you do it, Pat?" Carlos asked admiringly. "I knew what you were going to do, but I never saw you."

"The lippy one had it right. When I shoved them into the car. They never knew it at the time." Kenney laughed. "Those two we'll send up. They'll have two to five years each to think about how not to get caught again. What a lousy way to live." He worked his second drink to the bottom of the glass and ordered one more. "Tomorrow the weekend starts and we get two more days of this shit. Fuck it!"

CHAPTER TWELVE

At 9 A.M. Saturday morning, Brad was just waking up from a sound sleep when the phone rang in the living room of his suite. He cursed the operators sleepily for not ringing the phone beside his bed. He told himself he would give Knute hell about the operators. He swung his legs out of bed, stood up, and holding his pajama pants from falling off him, he made for the parlor phone.

Just as he reached the phone, it stopped ringing. He picked it up and heard only a dial tone. Then the phone began to ring in the bedroom and he shambled back in, fell on the bed and reached out for the instrument.

"Kendall here."

"Did I wake you, Brad?" Ciano's voice seemed to reflect amusement. "Sorry. I wanted to remind you this is a good day to come out to the country. We'll talk at leisure."

"I'll be out there before 1 P.M., C.L.," Brad said as cheerfully as possible. After hanging up he dialed the hotel garage, requested his car and Williams and then called Luciana. She sounded as though she had been up for some time.

"I'll pick you up at eleven-thirty."

"I'll be waiting."

Goddamn, he thought. At my age, I'm falling for

that girl. I love her. I'm jealous. Is Ciano making some kind of a play for her? He put the thought out of his mind. Now he had to call Andrea. At least it was too early for Gwen to answer. And Ed never answered. Too many creditors always calling him.

Andrea did answer, happy to hear from him. "I'll have to ask Mama when she gets up," was her reply to the invitation to drive out to the country.

"Ask Mama to go out for an afternoon drive?" he exploded. "At almost nineteen? Oh, for Jesus Christ's sweet sake—"

"OK, OK," she cut in. "I know I'll be able to go. I just like to ask her."

"I'll be in front of your building at eleven-fifteen. Will you try to be ready, dear?"

He dressed hurriedly and took the elevator down to the health club. After a steam bath and a rub-down, he felt fit to face the world, even Ciano. He picked up an attaché case with his sport clothes in it. Williams was waiting in front of the hotel.

Andrea was actually standing outside the apartment house as he drove up, chatting with the doorman. She was certainly an attention getter, he thought. Her figure was lovely, her legs long, though he was proud that she did not bow to the current fashion of ultra-short skirts. He opened the door and she walked to the car and slid in beside him. "What a beautiful car. Is it yours?"

"No. Belongs to the company."

"Same thing," she said as Williams drove off for Luciana's hotel.

"Not really. I could go anytime, but the car stays."

Brad was delighted to see how well Andrea and Luciana got along. Andrea was studying Italian in anticipation of her trip next summer and Luciana, on the drive out to the Westchester County home of Ciano, conversed with her in that language, helping her with words and phrases.

They drove up before a large Tudor house and another of Ciano's hard-looking men in houseman's black suit and tie opened the door to the car. Brad identified himself and with Luciana and Andrea on either side was led through an ornate reception hall to a flagstone terrace.

C. L. Ciano, wearing a blue blazer and white slacks, an ascot tie about his neck, walked over and greeted them effusively. Accompanying him was a truly beautiful girl who in a vague way resembled Luciana. Her features were near perfect and there was an easy, outgoing air about her. Ciano said she was twenty-two, Brad recalled, although she seemed to have a maturity beyond that age. Her brown eyes were warm with compassion and understanding. The young, generous earthmother type, he thought.

Ciano introduced them to Elda Ciano, his daughter. Elda's eyes met Brad's squarely as she shook hands. "I've heard about you from Pop. I'm so happy to meet you at last. Someday I'd like to get into the hotel business myself."

Charmed, Brad took her hand, wondering how much she really knew about Whitehall. Both Andrea and Luciana established immediate rapport with Elda, who took charge of the two women as though on cue.

Ciano put his arm through Brad's and led him away from the people about the pool terrace. Brad looked after the girls a moment and then turned his attention to his employer.

"What a beautiful daughter you have," Brad couldn't help remarking.

"Your girl is a beauty too, Brad," Ciano replied.

"If only I could talk to her," Brad said wistfully. "How do you and Elda communicate?"

"Perfectly. She's a wonderful girl. We've been very close all her life. We still are. She tells her pop everything. We have long talks about what she wants to do with her future."

"I envy you, C.L. I guess the fact that I never lived with Andrea is why we don't really talk."

"Too bad. Maybe if Elda and Andrea get to know each other, Elda could help you."

"That's a nice thought, C.L."

"We'll have a drink later, Brad," Ciano said, getting

down to business. "Shall we take a stroll around the place?"

"You're the leader, C.L."

Ciano led Brad across a sweeping green lawn, under spreading trees toward a stable house out of an old English lithograph. "First, Brad, I want to put a ten-million-dollar expansion program into effect immediately. I anticipate going a hundred to two hundred million in the next two years, but within three weeks, a month at the most, you have ten million in cash to put down. Can you do it?"

"No problem spending it, C.L. The sensitive decisions will be made in putting it to best advantage."

"You'll buy the Tropic Plaza out of that money."

"If I can crack Unger. He's a tough bastard."

"Unger will sell. Plan to fly down there in a week. No sooner, not much later."

"You sure are sure of things."

Ciano grinned. "By the way, Luciana should be working for Ascot Hotels. She could be a valuable asset to us. As a hostess, a symbol of what is attractive and chic in international living." He gave Brad a side-wise glance. "If you took her around the country in the company jet on this acquisition trip—"

"What acquisition trip, C.L.?"

"The one you're going to take when the jet is delivered. I want deals in every major city. By the way, why didn't Ascot ever put together a deal in Las Vegas?"

"I tried to, as a matter of fact. That was before old Rafe Leighton exiled me because I didn't like his girl friend or the risks she was talking him into taking." Brad laughed self-consciously. "Of course, if he hadn't you wouldn't have gotten your hands on Ascot and I wouldn't be going out to spend one hundred million for starters. Maybe Lilli Darlene was a piece of luck in disguise."

"I don't believe in luck," Ciano declared. "There is no such thing as luck. Any so-called luck I have ever encountered, I made or bought myself."

Brad felt a chill run down his spine. He remembered Rafe Leighton's speculations on the origin of Lilli coming into his life. Then Ciano laughed softly. "Well, maybe I should amend that statement. You did have a piece of luck finding yourself sitting next to Luciana on that plane trip to New York, didn't you?"

"C.L., I agree with you," Brad declared cheerfully. "Luck is something a man goes to some lengths to create."

Ciano nodded approvingly. "You put it perfectly. I think I'll have those words immortalized on a plaque and give it out to all my employees."

They walked a few moments in silence. Brad couldn't remember having seen an estate of such magnificence. A beautiful chestnut horse, a mare, was being led out of the stable by a groom as they approached.

"She's my sweetheart." Ciano's facial lines, even his eyes softened as he looked at the chestnut.

"She's fifteen hands. Cara Mia, my heart, that's her name. Elda has won a wall full of blue ribbons with her. In the conformation hunter class. That's the big one. Does your daughter ride?"

Brad tried to remember the last batch of bills he had paid. There were some from a riding stable on the west side of New York. "I guess she does some riding. She never had a chance, her mother always keeping her in the city, to do any serious riding."

"She should come out and ride with Elda."

Ciano paused, his mind slipping back to business affairs. "I meant to ask you, Brad. Has your membership come through in Copper Rock?"

"I was notified yesterday," Brad replied. "I don't know how it happened so fast. I've played several member-guest tournaments there and I know a number of members. And Bryant Beddington helped, of course, though I thought he might have opposed me. He was another of the gang that got old Rafe to rusticate me when I opposed the Ascot Towers deal."

"Beddington is a great admirer of yours, Brad."

"Even Bryant must have had a problem. Old Ferdinand DePaul Lowell, the chairman of the Board of Governors is famous for opposing anybody for membership without an extensive investigation."

Ciano chuckled mirthlessly. "Quite. I couldn't qualify. Wrong ethnic background. But Whitehall pulled Lowell's investment house out of the worst jam they ever got in. Remember the vegetable oil scandal? The old bastard has been of great use to me ever since. And will continue to be," he added, his facial expression hardening again. They walked past the stables.

"Now, Brad, there are a lot of things I want to get done and get done fast. This week. I don't believe in memos. I remember what I tell my people, and," he paused and looked directly at Brad, "they never forget either. I know it is customary in big business for the guy at the top to make," his voice took on an ironic edge, "suggestions. Well, I don't make suggestions. You understand?"

"It isn't difficult to understand what you mean, C.L. I can take orders as well as I can give them. Go ahead."

"Good. Now on Monday I am sending over a special engineer and construction team. Their orders are to rebuild two luxury suites on the top floor of the Ascot Towers."

"We have pretty good hotel engineers at the main office, C.L."

Ciano ignored the remark. "I will introduce you to the man I want in as manager of the Towers."

"You couldn't ask for a better man than Knute Bjorgund. He's one of the most respected men in the business and he's made every dime of profit that could be wrung out of the property. I can assure you—"

"The new manager Maurice D'Estang will take command, under your jurisdiction of course, on Tuesday. He'll pick a new resident and assistant manager."

"But C.L.—" Brad began.

"Within a month all the executive positions in the hotel will be filled with experienced Whitehall people. Remember, we are not new to the hotel field. We operate fifteen hotels right now. None of them as prestigious as Ascot, of course. But we know how to make a profit out of the hotel business."

Brad felt the old lump in his stomach as Ciano went on. "I'm not for a minute taking the operating authority and responsibility out of your hands, Brad. But for many reasons, particularly in our flagship hotel, I want Whitehall people in the important posts. I think you will find that an amalgam of our methods and your experience and contacts will make for one of the biggest international business ventures in the world. What I'm particularly anxious for you to do is acquire more properties. Put your private jet to work. Hire another good international man, of your own choosing, to assist you in buying hotel sites around the world and working out financing deals as you always have. You're the man up front. You're the president of Ascot Hotels, the boss. Think of me as a commissioner, a guide, the person who provides the money and with the money the final word on how we move ahead. You understand?"

Well, it was out in the open. He could quit now or do things Ciano's way. Brad thought about the jet. He thought about traveling with Luciana. And he thought about the money he would make and be able to save. All his salary after taxes, everything, could be invested in blue-chip securities, gilt-edge bonds. He'd lived well all his life but he never really had accumulated wealth for himself.

"Now about that business we're starting with you on the side," Ciano went on persuasively. "An associate in Chicago has located a small meat packer who is about bankrupt. He packages a good-enough product but he has never had a good sales force. You go out to Chicago this week, look the situation over, and if you like it we'll buy it. You'll own 51 per cent of the action, a Whitehall subsidiary will own the other 49."

"Meat packing is a little out of my line, C.L." Brad's uncertainty registered in his voice, he knew. The entire Ciano method was way out of his line, for that matter. Still, he could learn as well as the next man.

Yes, if that was what he wanted to learn, the nagging voice way down there proclaimed.

"Nothing to it. All sales. The line is good. We keep the operations people and put in our own sales force. Mid-America Meat Company will sell all the Ascot Hotels to begin with. And in the South, Whitehall, through an associate, owns three large chains of supermarkets and controls several more. There isn't a big military installation south of Washington, D.C., that we don't have ringed with retail outlets. Everyone will push the Mid-America line. And, Brad, don't think for a minute that the big northern chains, Safeway, A & P, the others, will ignore our product."

Brad had to struggle to retain his sense of reality. Ciano could throw so much out, so fast, that it was a fight to think logically. Actually, he realized, Ciano, until now, was making him think with a totally foreign sense of logic, to say nothing of ethics. He realized Ciano had stopped walking. He had automatically halted too. Now this human dynamo of unconventional financial activity was staring at him, searching him for reactions.

"Well, what do you think, Brad? If you don't like it we'll look for something else where we can force big sales. Personally, I can't think of anything better."

"Sounds outstanding to me." Inwardly Brad sighed. One step deeper in his commitment to what Ciano called "the fifth estate."

"Good, I thought you'd feel that way." Ciano began walking and Brad moved along beside him.

"You certainly gave an interesting party last night, C.L.," Brad said after a few moments' silence.

"Yes. A number of people were there who are or will be important to us."

"I didn't know you were interested in the military," Brad prompted.

"The military is the basis, the implied threat of a national leader's power. With the exception of the United States every major nation on earth has at one time or another been taken over and ruled by a military dictatorship. How much longer do you think this exception will last?"

It was getting so that Brad didn't dare ask Ciano a question for fear of the answer he would receive. "The point is that in our country the military has been subservient to the civilian political structure so completely and for so long that there is still time to establish a civilian-oriented self-perpetuating oligarchy with the help of the military. General MacFarland sees it that way."

"And you see a military-supported dictatorship taking over this country?"

"Certainly. Some President of the United States, perhaps sooner than we think, will decide to suspend the electoral process and stay in office indefinitely with the aid of the military. I want this man to be mine."

"You think Ev Jamison from Texas, or Bill Adams could be that man?"

"They or a dozen others I've been watching."

"I've always wondered how Adams got so powerful on the Crime Committee so fast," Brad asked more than stated.

"That is something you will know as you get more involved in our operations."

After a few moments' silence Ciano started in again. "There's a fellow out there at the swimming pool now I want you to meet. His name is Larry Wolfmann. He's been very successful in running wholesale supply houses."

Now what? Brad thought.

A complete circuit of the grounds ended with Ciano satisfied that he and Brad Kendall understood what measures were to be taken over the following two weeks to develop Ascot Hotels. They reached the group of guests at the swimming pool. Andrea was in earnest conversation with the cleric who was introduced as Monsignor Mallory. Jorge Ramirez and several other United Nations delegates, two of them blacks from neighboring emergent African nations, were talking animatedly in a group surrounding Luciana and several other attractive ladies. Somewhat withdrawn from the group stood Larry Wolfmann, the associate with whom Ciano wanted Brad to discuss business. After a brief talk Brad dutifully made an appointment with him for the next day and joined Ciano and the United Nations group.

Ciano waved to a tall, thin, European-looking man with long, thick gray hair who walked across the flagstone patio to them. From his mouth, at a raffish angle, dangled a cigarette. As he approached them Brad, a non-smoker, was aware of the strong, acrid smoke charactristic of certain French cigarettes that wafted from the cigarette. "Brad, meet Maurice D'Estang. He has been with us since the company was founded ten years ago." Brad held out a hand which D'Estang took firmly and bowed his head slightly as he shook hands.

"C.L. tells me we're going to be working together rather closely," Brad said pleasantly.

"Yes. I'm quite looking forward to the association," D'Estang replied.

"By the way, Maurice, Jorge Ramirez," Ciano brought the Latin-American UN diplomat into the conversation, "wants to give a little party for some of his special friends among the delegates. I told him the Ascot Towers was the place for it."

"Of course." D'Estang smiled at Ramirez. "It will be my pleasure to personally supervise the arrangements."

"That's what I told Jorge," Ciano nodded cheerfully. "I think one of those luxury suites we're redecorating would be what he wants."

"Will they be ready in time?" Brad asked.

"Surely it won't take more than a week to do them over," Ciano remarked.

Brad noticed that Andrea and Elda were now talking to a young man, handsome in a swarthy Mediterranean way, whose white teeth flashed as he smiled.

Ciano followed Brad's glance and frowned slightly. "That's Tony Falcon. He met Elda at a party and has been chasing her ever since."

"I'd better warn Andrea that she's poaching." Brad laughed.

"Oh, no. She's welcome to him," Ciano said, perhaps a little too hastily. He looked over at Luciana. "Excuse me a minute, I haven't had a chance to really welcome Mrs. Blore."

"Just remember, I saw her first." Brad smiled but he felt a pang of jealousy.

"Of course, Brad," Ciano said soothingly. "Sometime today I just want to convince her to join the organization—through Ascot Hotels of course."

"Good luck, then," Brad said.

D'Estang walked over to the Latin-American diplomat, presumably to discuss the party.

Seeing that Brad was alone Elda Ciano strolled over to him. "I'm so enjoying talking to your daughter, Mr. Kendall. She is really a very interesting girl."

"She is?" Brad asked, surprised.

"Of course. Don't you talk to her?"

"Unfortunately, I've been away a great deal and haven't had the opportunity to see as much of her as I would have liked."

"That's too bad." Elda seemed sad about it.

"I think so. Now it is almost too late. I never quite know how to draw her out."

Elda smiled shyly. "You need some practice, that's all. You could try your conversation out on me and then perhaps you'll be ready for Andrea."

Brad chuckled. "That's a good idea. Well, where to start?" He thought a moment. "I think this move to legalize pot has a lot of merit."

"Do you, Mr. Kendall?" Elda asked seriously.

Already Brad was flustered. "I don't mean to say I smoke it myself. But I can't see that it does all that harm."

"I personally am against smoking grass, particularly for girls. It can make you do things you might not otherwise do."

"Same is true of liquor, isn't it?"

Elda laughed. "You'll be all right. You're arguing the way the boys do." Brad noticed Elda looking about, spotting Tony Falcon talking to Andrea, and turning back to him.

"Is he someone special in your life?" Brad asked, following her glance.

"No. But he could be I suppose. He seems to like Andrea." She said it matter-of-factly, without a trace of resentment.

"Andrea has too much else to do to get interested in young men."

Elda laughed. "Now you're talking like a father, my father as a matter of fact. But he and I communicate right on key."

"I suppose if I saw more of Andrea we would be able to understand each other better."

"Of course. Next time I'm in the city why don't you take both of us to lunch at the Ascot Towers?"

"Would you like that?" Brad asked eagerly. "Andrea doesn't really seem to like my hotels, your father's hotels, I should say," Brad amended.

"I'm coming in next week so let's make a date today."

"You're on, Elda." Brad was impressed and enchanted with the girl. "Shall we see if we can get her away from Tony Falcon long enough to nail down a time and day?"

"Sure." Brad and Elda walked across the terrace toward Andrea.

"Mr. Ciano," Luciana said as he walked over to her, "I have been looking forward to hearing you play the piano. You promised last week, you know."

"You really want to hear me play?" he asked, pleased.

"That's how you persuaded me to come out here today."

"Very well." Taking Luciana's arm he led her to the Steinway inside the large sitting room overlooking the pool. Several guests followed. Ciano sat down on the piano bench and patted the place beside him. Luciana sat next to him and Ciano began to play. Brad who had followed them in expected to hear a sort of note-missing, playing-by-ear rendition. Instead he was surprised at the near professionalism of Ciano's music. He started playing some of the popular songs and show tunes and then worked into a medley of operatic arias.

Ciano paused in his playing as his daughter Elda walked in. He nodded to her, they exchanged smiles, and then he went back to the introduction of a musical comedy number. In a clear voice, obviously well trained, Elda began to sing to her father's accompaniment.

The applause at the end of her first number encouraged the father-daughter team to give their guests another and finally a third. Then Elda and Andrea left the guests to go outside again and talk together.

"But you are marvelous, Mr. Ciano," Luciana enthused. "How did you ever become so truly accomplished when you were building such a business empire?"

"My mother believed in music before all else," Ciano replied. "I took piano lessons until I left home at eighteen. After that I never stopped playing for fun and in college I found it a useful way to earn extra money."

Brad fought back the smile of bitter irony that threatened to twist his lips. Here was one of the country's most powerful figures in big business making use of money generated by organized crime. And to see him at home on a Saturday afternoon, playing the piano, his daughter singing, guests milling about the house, one would think he was just another successful middle-class American far removed from the mighty power he had become in business.

This Maurice D'Estang was undoubtedly one of Ciano's chief hatchetmen, Brad thought as he shot a glance at the suave, though strangely menacing-looking European. For a moment he again began to have doubts about his involvement in the new Ascot Hotel organization, but he quickly forced them from his mind.

"It really was a lovely afternoon," Luciana said as they drove back into town. "Andrea, are you going to join your father and me for dinner?"

Andrea shook her head, a dreamy look in her eyes. "No, I promised Mama I'd go to a party with her. I know it's going to be boring, but I promised."

"I noticed you were having quite a conversation with that young man, Falcon." Brad dropped the statement tactfully.

"Oh, yes. He's so interesting. He's been to Italy."

"Sicily mostly," Luciana said. "I talked to him. His father was born in Sicily."

"I think Italians are so romantic," Andrea sighed.

"They beat their women, the brave things," Luciana said cuttingly.

"Tony isn't that kind of Italian. He doesn't even have an Italian name." She looked out the window of the car. "Thanks for taking me out today. I had a wonderful time. And, Dad, I'm really looking forward to our lunch with Elda on Wednesday."

"She wasn't worried about all that time you and Falcon had your heads together?"

"She didn't seem to be. As a matter of fact, he told her that he was afraid he wouldn't be seeing much of her any more. He's starting a new job with a lot of travel."

Brad felt a sense of relief which proved short-lived. Andrea giggled and went on. "Just between us, Tony isn't going anywhere. He just was being polite. He thought that Elda could get too intense about him and she really isn't his type, he says. He prefers auburn-haired girls like me."

Brad thought about Andrea's last statement and the fact that Ciano didn't like the young man. "Now look, dear, you have a lot of time ahead of you," he faltered. "Why don't you just forget that bird." The attempted humor fell flat.

"Don't you like Italians?" Andrea asked accusingly, looking directly at Luciana.

"You heard what Luciana said about Italian men. She should know."

The limousine rolled up in front of the apartment building. Williams came around and opened the door and Andrea stepped out. "Thanks again, Brad. I hope I'll see you soon again, Luciana."

"I'll call you tomorrow, dear," Brad promised. He watched her walk to the door and the doorman open it for her.

"She is a beautiful girl, Brad. You must be proud of her."

Brad's hand found Luciana's. "Yes, I guess I am. It's just so sad that her mother, on every conceivable pretext, kept her from visiting me. I think I'd feel a lot more strongly about her, her life, her school, whether or not she sees that rather sinister young man, if I had ever been allowed to know her. Now I'm going to be too damned busy to fight her mother on such things as—well keeping Andrea in New York instead of sending her away to college next fall."

Luciana put her hand on top of Brad's. "Don't worry. She seems a very sensible girl. Well, what did you have planned for tonight?"

"Beyond being with you I hadn't thought much about it. When are you moving into the Ascot Towers?"

"Is tomorrow all right?"

Brad's heart leaped. "You mean it?" He sat up straight.

"Why not. If I'm going to work for the company I might as well live free at the hotel until I can find an apartment." She clapped a hand over her mouth and looked at him wide-eyed. "Oh, I was supposed to wait until you made the job offer."

"That's C. L. Ciano." Brad grinned and shook his head.

"He told me you were the boss but that if you didn't ask me again to come work for Ascot he was going to hire me away to work in some other division of Whitehall."

Brad laughed and shook his head some more. "Did he talk salary?"

"He told me that if I had any trouble with you, he'd act as my agent. He did say you were the boss, but he'd do his best to get a living wage for me out of you." She leaned over and kissed his lips. "I said I thought I could handle the negotiations myself."

"We'll negotiate tonight. Do you want to go back to the hotel before we go out?"

"What did you have in mind?"

"Actually what could be nicer than going back to my place." He grinned and squeezed her hand. "We could negotiate a bit, and have dinner sent up. After this day of so-called relaxation at Ciano's place in the country I could use a quiet evening."

"Let's do just that then." She squeezed his hand again and he leaned across to kiss her and found himself looking out the window of the limousine directly at the doorman of the Ascot Towers. They were here. It was uncanny how she took his mind off things. There was, of course, the command performance golf game tomorrow morning. His heart sank as he thought of it and what he had done to arrange it. Still, that was tomorrow and now he was with Luciana, a whole night before them.

CHAPTER THIRTEEN

Brad had rented a car to drive out to Copper Rock, leaving the limousine for Luciana so she could go out and visit her aunt and uncle for lunch and move into the Ascot Towers late that afternoon before he returned. He knew he'd play a miserable game of golf. There was too much on his mind. Yet he couldn't help marvel at how Ciano manipulated things.

Yesterday Ciano had told him to drive over to Copper Rock and hand Ferdinand Lowell the check for his initiation fee. Ciano had alerted the old boy at his home by phone to be at the club. Brad introduced himself at the pro shop and caddy house, had his handicap posted, and picked out a locker. Things just didn't happen this way at an exclusive club like Copper Rock, even to as eligible a man socially and businesswise as Bradford Kendall. Yet, surprisingly, it had.

Then Ciano had taken Brad into his study and told him to telephone Mike Brashears, executive vice president of Allied Electric. Naturally Brad knew Mike, had golfed with him and been to his home. After all, Ascot Hotels had long been a prized customer of Allied. Mike quickly agreed to playing golf with Brad at Copper Rock the next day at eleven. Mike was effusive in his congratulations on Brad's ascendancy to president of the Ascot Hotel chain. When Brad suggested that

Mike bring along Don Tynan, vice president of sales, Mike sounded even more enthusiastic on the other end of the phone. This was tantamount to saying that in a relaxed way Brad wanted to discuss a big order, perhaps even a complete electrical engineering job for some of the hotels about to go under construction. Brad did not mention who would make up the foursome.

As he drove into Rye in the rented Ford, Brad's heart was heavy. The thought of that unctuous, offensively perceptive Larry Wolfmann playing in the first foursome he would host at his club robbed him of most of the joy in his new membership. And having to put Wolfmann together with gentlemen like Mike Brashears and Don Tynan chagrined him to the point of near physical illness. Well, in another week or ten days he'd be off in the executive jet, making new deals, the part of the business he enjoyed most.

Brad arrived at the pro shop half an hour early. His clubs were brought in and a member's tag placed on his golf bag. He placed a set of golf clothes in the locker along with toilet articles and began to feel a sense of permanence here. It was the sort of club he had always wished he could join. Ray Sanders the club pro and his assistant welcomed Brad profusely. Ray said he looked forward to playing with him if he could get away from the office during the week and Brad said he'd make a point of it.

Followed by a caddy, Brad walked out to the practice tee and began knocking out shots. He hadn't played for a month, the international property acquisition game didn't lend itself to frequent golfing. He plowed about seven or eight drives two hundred and fifty yards straight out when he heard Wolfmann's voice behind him.

"By George, Brad, you sock 'em out there."

"Take a few," Brad invited. "I'll look around for Mike Brashears and Don Tynan." Somehow he would have to appear enthused about Wolfmann's deal in front of the two men from Allied Electric.

Approaching the caddy house he saw Mike and Don

coming from the direction of the clubhouse carrying their golf bags. Brad strode toward them and shook hands. Two top-notch, straight guys, he thought. He led them to the locker room where they changed into golf togs.

"You guys want to hit a few off the practice tee?" Brad asked.

Both shook their heads. "Any good shots I might have I don't want to waste on the practice range," Don said. "Let's start right out."

Larry Wolfmann sidled up to Brad and stood smiling at the other two. "Don, Mike, meet Larry Wolfmann." They all shook hands and compared handicaps. As host it was Brad's prerogative to set teams. Ciano had wanted Larry to get close to Mike Brashears, so Brad said he and Don Tynan would play Mike and Larry. After fixing bets they started out.

To Brad's surprise, Wolfmann drove his ball damned near three hundred yards down the middle of the first fairway, by far the longest ball of the foursome. Mike nodded in satisfaction at his partner's performance. Brad, trying to hide the consternation he felt, dubbed his second shot and overdrove the four-par hole on his third shot. Wolfmann was on the green fifteen feet from the pin on his second shot. Both Don and Mike were on in three. Brad now knew he must play golf and forget his annoyance at having exposed Don and Mike to this Wolfmann. There was nothing he could do now. He might as well try to enjoy the game. Settling down he took his wedge and pitched his ball up a few feet closer to the cup than Wolfmann's ball. He lay four.

"Well, Brad," Mike needled. "You play a little different after a couple of years living in Latin America and Europe."

"Just want to give everybody a chance," Brad retorted.

Both Don and Mike two putted for one over par fives. Wolfmann sank his putt for a birdie three, and somehow Brad managed to sink his long putt avoiding a double bogey.

By the fifth hole it was obvious that Ciano had known what he was doing setting up this golf game. Mike Brashears was delighted with his partner's game. In five holes Wolfmann had two birdies and three pars. At the ninth hole, Wolfmann and the executive vice president of Allied Electric were four strokes ahead of Brad and Don. Brad suggested a refreshment on the ninth-hole stand and over Cokes Mike asked Wolfmann what his business was.

"Wholesale electric appliances," Wolfmann answered.

On cue Brad added, "He's pretty much proved to us that we should buy all of our appliances through his outfit. Looks like we'll be signing a contract with him next week. Reason I called you both was that I wanted to be sure we kept using Allied appliances and I figured if you and Larry could get together next week maybe you could work something out."

Don Tynan, who had been waiting to hear the reason for this hastily called golf game, immediately became interested. He asked Wolfmann a few questions and then they started out to play the back nine. Brad had performed. He had done just as much as he had agreed to do. From now on it was up to Wolfmann.

Mike and Don seemed to be enjoying the game tremendously. Brad noticed that Mike and Larry Wolfmann were doing a lot of talking together, Mike nodding his head frequently. Somehow, he didn't know precisely, but in some manner he was going to be responsible for Allied Electric getting screwed. He wondered if the jet, the limousine, the club, the co-op apartment, the expense account, having Luciana working for him, the meat business, and the rest of the action were worth what he suspected he was becoming. A member of the fifth estate, Ciano called it. Brad missed another shot. He sweated and swore through the back nine and never had he been happier to get to the bar.

"Well, Brad," Mike said heartily as Brad and Don paid off to the winners, "great game. But what I like is you're going to be with us for a while. You ought to find a place up this way, near the club. Get back your game. Christ, last time we played you tore us all up about the way Larry here did."

"Yeah, it's hell when you have to go to work for a living."

Wolfmann let the gibe go by. Don Tynan took up the standard. "Well, I guess Mike and I and Larry are going to have to talk some business. You sure are making changes fast in the Old Ascot structure. You've been president a week now?"

"That's right. Just wait till you see what we're doing. I expect that we will have ten new hotels under construction in the United States before the end of a year, and at least that number, if not more, abroad."

"Well, you're going to need Allied." Mike captured the attention of a waiter. They all gave their drink orders.

"That's for sure. Our guests really like those bedside consoles you designed for us."

"That's right," Don said. "You can press a button for anything from radio and television to air conditioning to room service—anything."

"But a broad." Mike laughed.

"The way we're going we'll probably be able to provide that too." Brad chuckled. "Mr. Ciano believes in the utmost in service."

In spite of his feelings, Brad couldn't help but approve the soft-sell method Wolfmann used on the two top executives as they drank their highballs and munched crackers and cheese. Wolfmann and his organization would be ready anytime to consult with Allied.

The two appliance executives left to go home finally, and Brad was impatient to get showered, dressed and back to the city to help Luciana move.

"C.L.'s going to be real happy about this little get-together, Brad," Wolfmann said. "I think we work real good together. Allied is only the beginning. We'll get 'em all in line."

"We had a pretty good purchasing system at Ascot up to this morning," Brad answered.

"Oh, come on, Brad," Wolfmann pleaded. "You know what's going on."

Brad smiled, with an effort. "Sure, Larry. Well, I've got to get back to the city. See you next week."

CHAPTER FOURTEEN

At four-thirty Brad arrived back at the Ascot Towers Hotel. Turning over the rented car to the doorman he asked that it be returned to the rental car agency in the hotel garage. In the lobby he summoned the assistant manager.

"Has a room been assigned to Mrs. Blore?" he asked.

"We're expecting her but she hasn't come in yet."

"Let me have a key to the suite assigned to her. I want to take a look and make sure it's in order."

The assistant manager went behind the desk and consulted the room reservations. "Twenty-five fifty," he said, handing Brad the key. Brad walked over to the elevator bank, and was whisked up express to twenty-five. He walked down the hall and opened the door. The living room was large, furnished in what he called institutional French Provincial. The view was beautiful, looking south toward the UN buildings and east over the river. He walked into the bedroom, took one look and strode to the phone.

"Give me the assistant manager." He waited a moment and the man was on the other end of the line. "Look, Mrs. Blore requested a double bed, not twins. Have you got a suite with this same exposure and a double bed?" He waited while the assistant manager consulted his room cards. "Yes, fine, send a boy up to twenty-six fifty. I'll meet him at the door."

Twenty-six fifty was perfect for Luciana he decided after inspecting it. Also it was on the same floor as his suite although he hadn't made a point of arranging this. From the suite he telephoned room service and ordered a bottle of champagne and a small jar of beluga caviar sent up. He called the florist and asked for a dozen roses to be sent up, a vase of red roses for the parlor and a vase of yellow roses for the bedroom. Then he telephoned the St. Regis. It was just five, the time she had planned to move. He was informed that Mrs. Blore had just checked out. His heart beat faster as he went back to the lobby where he waited for the limousine to drive up in front of the hotel.

He looked in on the florist who was just sending the roses up and then arranged with the bell captain to have Mrs. Blore's suitcases sent directly to her suite when she arrived. He paused in front of the newsstand. Since he had last been a New York resident three newspapers had been struck out of business and he missed the variety of papers he used to enjoy. He mused on the difficult job hotel publicists had justifying their fees nowadays. He had intended to have Luciana start in the public relations division of the company. Instinctively he turned from the stack of New York *Times* and saw Luciana entering the lobby. He was at her side in a moment, reaching for her hand, briefly pressing it to his lips.

"Hello, Brad. My suitcases are following me."

Both Williams and the doorman came in carrying her luggage. Brad motioned to the bell captain and then took Luciana's arm, leading her toward the elevators.

"What about my bags?"

"They'll be brought up."

"Don't I have to register?"

"There's a card in your room. We'll send it down by the bellboy."

"I must say this is the most convenient way to check into a hotel I've ever seen."

Brad opened the door to the suite for Luciana and

she gasped in delight. "Oh, Brad, it's beautiful." She turned to him, pressing close, and kissed him on the lips. He held her a moment, kissing back, and then just as they were about to hold each other tightly, their kisses becoming more demanding, there was a knock at the door. Grinning at each other they pulled apart and Brad went to the door and opened it for the bellman who wheeled a truck into the room piled with Luciana's luggage. Luciana walked into the bedroom, saw the double bed, turned and smiled at Brad who followed her.

"The closets are behind the mirrored french doors," he advised.

While Luciana with the help of the bellman hooked up her hanging clothesbags, Brad wandered back to the parlor and took the champagne bottle out of the ice bucket. He wrapped it in a white napkin and slowly worked the cork. Finally with a pop it sailed across the room and he poured two glasses full of the pale bubbling wine. The bellman came out of the bedroom, Brad handed him two dollars and held the door open for him in a silent gesture signifying that it would be unnecessary for the man to go through any further items on the check list for rooming guests.

Brad carried the two glasses into the bedroom and silently handed one to Luciana. He held his glass up to her. "To a bright future in the hotel business. Welcome to Ascot."

She clinked his glass with hers and they sipped their champagne. She walked back into the parlor and sat down on the sofa looking out the picture window at the view. "You know, I was thinking when I left to come over here that I might like to work at the United Nations."

"I think you'll enjoy working for us more."

Luciana took a long, thoughtful swallow. "I told my uncle about perhaps working for Ascot. He asked me if I knew the company had been taken over by Whitehall Development. I said yes and that I'd even met Mr. Ciano." Luciana turned abruptly to Brad. "What do you know about C.L.? My uncle says he is a very mysterious, shadowy figure in the financial world."

Brad chuckled deprecatingly. "Oh, there are as many rumors about him as you want to hear. Because of his Italian background you'll hear that he is somehow mixed up with the Mafia or the Cosa Nostra, if there really is such a thing."

"There certainly really is such a thing." Luciana looked at him seriously. "My uncle is Italian, I think I told you. He's head of a small investment banking house here which does a lot of business with Italian firms. It was once part of my father's house in Milan. He knows some of the Cosa Nostra leaders. They have asked him to handle investments for them."

"Has he done it?"

"He didn't say. But he said I certainly should be cautious about getting involved with Whitehall."

"I don't think that working for Ascot Hotels is going to tarnish your reputation." Brad laughed.

"Of course not. I was just telling you what my uncle said. He is close to the financial scene, especially where Italian interests are concerned." She finished her glass of champagne. Brad stood up and poured them another glass each and brought the caviar and squares of crisp toast to the coffee table in front of the sofa.

"You aren't worried about working for us because of Ciano, are you? He's making it possible for me to build Ascot into something that its founder, old Rafe Leighton, wouldn't have dared dream he could accomplish."

"I'm not worried. I'm looking forward to getting into something exciting, something international and important, even something with intrigue. I want to put my experience, my use of languages to work." She accepted a piece of toast heaped with caviar and popped it into her mouth. "Umm. That's so great. Champagne and caviar. Just what I felt like but I wouldn't have known if it hadn't been here." She was silent for a few moments. "I want to be with you, Brad. So tell me. What is the real background of what we'll be doing? I don't care really if something is a little shady. My

God, the whole world seems to be that way. My husband used to say that behind every great fortune lies a great crime."

Brad washed down some caviar with champagne. "I don't know too much about C.L.'s background myself. Well educated, his father was in some kind of financial business. What I do know is that in ten years he has risen from obscurity to become one of the biggest real estate operators in the nation. He has almost unlimited cash assets, or at least unlimited access to cash. Ciano, I believe, is probably the world's most successful laundry man."

"Laundry man?" Luciana laughed aloud.

"Yes. He launders money. People come to him with money which they can't spend without attracting the attention of the Internal Revenue Service—that's our tax department. If this is their problem they probably came into this money in some illicit manner. Ciano, through a network of connections and business enterprises, takes the money and is able to get it into circulation and gives back to his investors legitimate dividends in legitimate businesses."

"So that means that Ascot Hotels will grow by leaps and bounds on stolen money," Luciana summed up.

"Not exactly stolen. Probably money made in questionable enterprises like gambling. It seems to be the biggest source of money to racketeers."

"Don't you feel funny about that?"

"Why? The reason money is made on gambling is because people want to gamble. They'd be miserable if they couldn't gamble. Somewhere down Ciano's line of power men are providing this vital service. If a great hotel chain serving the travelers of the world can benefit by what's going to happen anyway, why should it bother me? Does it bother you?"

Luciana thought about it. "No, why should it?"

Reflectively they sipped champagne and munched on caviar and toast. After a few minutes of silence, a comfortable intimate silence, Brad continued to talk. "I had to work this philosophy out for myself last week when I made the decision to go with Ciano."

Almost as much for himself as for Luciana he went on.

"C. L. Ciano is the ultimate leader of what he calls the fifth estate. You know, the estates of a nation are business, government, the clergy, they call the press the fourth estate. You follow?"

"Yes. And the fifth?"

"To put it crudely, far more menacingly than it should be expressed, the fifth estate is organized crime."

"Then Whitehall is a clever criminal organization?"

"Who's to define crime nowadays. Half the United States Senate and House of Representatives indulge in practices that could be defined as anything from conflict of interest to extortion. The point is that Ciano seems to have locked many important members of the other four estates into his operations. Clergymen, legislators, businessmen and press lords benefit from Ciano's immense power. How can Whitehall be termed criminal any more than the congressman who owns large shares in radio and television stations as a result of his power with the federal government and garners huge funds which he spends on personal living by influencing legislation not in the public interest?"

"I guess it can't," Luciana replied.

"Ciano, I happen to know, is a big contributor to the Catholic Church and handles real estate transactions for them financed by money that filters up through the system. And who are the clients of the labor racketeers? Legitimate businessmen."

"Oh, wow!" Luciana shook her head and drank some more champagne. "No matter how you rationalize it, I'm going to work for a division of the world's criminal element."

Brad chuckled. "I guess I didn't get through to you. On the level of Whitehall Development, Ltd., there is no such thing as organized crime. It's another way of doing business."

Luciana finished her champagne. "Sounds fascinating." Brad filled her glass again.

"Hey, you're going to get me tipsy." She lifted the glass to her lips and took a long swallow. "Well, I

didn't tell you this, Brad, but I guess you've made it
your business now. I became so disgusted with my ex-
husband after the first three years of marriage that I
thought I'd lose my mind every time he forced himself
on me physically. At the end of five years I thought
my life was done. I spent months every year in sani-
tariums just to get away from him for a while.

"Finally, I met a psychiatrist who changed my life.
He told me to get a divorce from Blore. I explained
that Barkley didn't want a divorce, I was his show-
piece when I was not hiding in some kind of a rehabilitation place for mental cases."

Brad listened, almost unbelieving.

"Andre Thireault saved me. I fell madly in love with
him, as do most female patients with their psychiatrists,
I understand. And it was Andre who told me to get
my divorce and ask nothing from Blore. I needed to
be free so badly I went to Barkley and put it that way.
Fortunately, Andre was interested enough in my mental
well-being and future to have provided me with names,
dates, places and signed affidavits from witnesses concerning Barkley's affairs."

Luciana laughed. "You know he's a randy old bug-
ger. He liked two and sometimes three girls at a time
and even an occasional homosexual thrown in. So when
I got my divorce I was on my own. I had freedom but
no money."

She stood up and went closer to the window. "No
amount of money in the world is as important to me as
this wonderful, magnificent freedom." Luciana raised
her arms as though to embrace the whole world outside
the window. She stood thus a few moments. Brad stood
up and walked up behind her and clasped his hands
around her waist. She turned to him, leaning back
slightly, from her waist on down to her knees she was
in close contact with him.

"I'll make a good employee, Brad. I have no desire
to get married, I want an exciting career, I need my
paycheck, and the hours will mean nothing to me. I
want to live and work and be part of something big.

Your fifth estate will suit me just fine. I suppose we have the machinery to bump off a Barkley Blore type if he gets in our way."

"It's Ciano's fifth estate, not mine. And the need for bumping off people who get in the way is as obsolete as a muzzle-loading musket. On this level we mousetrap them financially. But you'll do fine." Now Luciana arched her upper back toward him, her breasts pressing to him. The kiss was the most passionate they had shared. For several days he had been concerned that despite her beauty she might be frigid. The kiss, her fluttering tongue between his lips, her arms pulling him tightly to her, and the pelvic undulations made him shudder with desire for her. He thanked himself for never having in any way tried to force this moment. If it was to come it would come naturally, when she was confident and ready. Now! Still holding her closely to him they turned and she walking backward, he leading, they did a tantalizingly slow dance step to the bedroom, to the bed, and one more step backward. She tumbled on to the bed, laughing, as Brad fell on the bed beside her. Once more the intimate embrace.

"Oh, darling," she whispered. "My new Bergdorf dress."

"Let me help."

"No. Wait right here a minute. I'll be back." She rolled off the bed and stood up heading for the bathroom, then turned, an impish smile on her face. "And what about those beautifully pressed slacks and the blazer?" She walked into the bathroom and closed the door behind her.

His heart pounding, his face flushed with excitement and anticipation, his knees rubbery, Brad stood up and undressed, neatly hanging his clothes over a chair. When he was down to his undershorts he remembered to go to the front door, hang a "do not disturb" sign on the outside knob, double-lock the door and then he went back to the bedroom. Luciana was still in the bathroom. He turned down the double bed and then went into the living room for the champagne. They had almost finished the first bottle. He wrapped a napkin around the second one and brought it to the bedroom with the two glasses, which he put on the bedside table.

He sat on the side of the bed in his shorts and hands shaking, tore off the foil and unwound the wire guard from the top of the bottle. He began working the cork up. Suddenly it popped, and the cork hit the bathroom door just as he had aimed it. A merry peal of laughter came from inside. Brad filled both glasses, put the bottle on the floor beside the bed, stripped off his drawers and got into the bed, pulling the covers up to his waist. He took one of the glasses and holding it in both quaking hands took a long swallow.

Luciana opened the bathroom door. He quivered at the sight of her beauty. Her long black tresses hung down just covering the nipples of jutting, firm breasts. She stood nude, smiling at him, and walked slowly to the bed. Reaching down she took the glass he had been clutching in both hands, sipped deeply from it, put it on the bedside table, and then lifting the bedclothes she slid into the bed beside him. She moved her body until it was over him and put her lips to his. He opened his mouth and felt a cold stream passing from hers to his. He swallowed the champagne so exquisitely passed to him and then reached to encircle her form with his arms. Luciana pressed closely to him, murmuring, "My darling, at last, at last we are the way we should be together."

Desperately he fought the desire to crush himself to her, enter her and make them one. He had forgotten how beautiful love-making could be, so long had it been since he had made love and loved at the same time. This he must make last, this their first time. But Luciana felt his need and passion, hard and demanding.

"No, don't wait, darling," she whispered. "Now."

"My beautiful girl. I love you so desperately. I'm so afraid. It's been so long for me."

"Go ahead, my darling. I understand. Later you'll be able to wait for me."

Joyously, ecstatically, he felt her move to make the

penetration come more easily. And then they were joined tightly, and in his life Brad had never known anything as exquisite. Pressing his open mouth to hers he let himself go, she moved under him, holding him tightly in her driving him toward the uncontrollable release he knew was seconds away.

The telephone shattered the room with its ring, startling Brad sharply at the moment of what would have been the most momentous ejaculation of his life. As it was he poured inside her, crying, "Luciana, I love you," and then, "Goddamn that phone." Why hadn't he, a hotelman, remembered to put a "no ring" on the line? Luciana purred in his ear, patting his back, telling him how marvelous he had been.

"Shall we let the damned thing ring?" Brad asked.

"I'd better answer it. It could even be Mother calling from London."

"At midnight her time?"

The phone pealed again. "She knew I was going to be with Uncle Alberto all afternoon. It could even be Uncle Alberto. I told him I was moving over here. He was a little worried about everything. You must arrange to meet him as soon as you can."

The phone rang again. Luciana rolled away from Brad to pick up the instrument. "Hello?"

"Mrs. Blore?"

"Yes." She looked at Brad and shrugged, pulling the phone from her ear so that Brad could hear what might be said.

"This is Knute Bjorgund, the manager of the Ascot Towers."

Luciana flashed her impish grin at Brad. "Oh, hello Mr. Bjorgund."

"I am calling to make sure everything is all right. Have you got everything you want?"

She stuck her tongue out at a suddenly enraged Brad. "I think so, thank you."

"We want you to be comfortable and enjoy your stay with us. If there is anything at all I can do for you, just call me. Anything."

"Would you tell the operators not to put any calls

through to my room until I notify them. Just ask them to take the message. I'll call back."

"Of course, Mrs. Blore. I hope I didn't disturb you."

"It's all right. Good evening, Mr. Bjorgund. I appreciate your concern." She hung up and rolled back to Brad who eagerly reached for her.

"That miserable, stupid sonofabitch," he muttered. "Now I won't feel so bad about firing him tomorrow."

"Oh, Brad, he was just trying to be nice."

"I know. Of course. We did get to it rather early."

Luciana kissed him and ran her hands over his stomach and loins. "We've got each other. Now that we're going to be together it doesn't really matter so much. He sounds like a nice man."

"Ciano says he has to go. He is going to put Maurice D'Estang in as manager."

Luciana sighed. "I guess this fifth estate won't always be pleasant. Anyway, my darling." She kissed him, snuggling close. "Here we are."

"I love you, Luciana."

"I love you too, Brad. I'm so happy with you. Oh, come to me, my darling. Many, many times."

CHAPTER FIFTEEN

Maurice D'Estang was not a regular visitor in C. L. Ciano's office. Their communications were usually effected by telephone or in some out-of-the-way place or perhaps at Ciano's very private country house. But now, it appeared, faithful and sometimes distasteful service was being rewarded. D'Estang was being apparently elevated in the hierarchy of Whitehall associates. He would be a more visible member of the corporate empire henceforth.

"It really makes little difference that you have no experience in the actual operations of a hotel," Ciano was saying soothingly. "Brad Kendall will supply a competent, incurious, self-effacing hotelman to actually manage the Ascot Towers. But as vice president and general manager it will be easy for you to do at the highest levels what you are doing on a somewhat lower echelon now."

"You think Kendall will stand still for that?" D'Estang asked, the ever-present French cigarette twitching in his mouth.

Ciano sat back in his chair, swiveled it slightly, and looked out of the sixtieth floor of the Spire Building at the city. "Yes," he said slowly. "Brad is becoming one of us. Every man has his price. Kendall is no exception. Only with him the price is paid in a more elegant manner. He is a man of class and always will be no matter how successfully we corrupt him."

"If you think so, C.L.," D'Estang replied doubtfully.

"Don't waste any time starting in on the top-floor suites," Ciano went on. "We'll be needing them very soon."

"When I walk into the manager's office and take over, Julius the Genius will be right behind me, C.L.," D'Estang said with assurance. "Shouldn't take him more than two days and nights to do the job."

Ciano swiveled back from the window and faced D'Estang across his desk. "Now we have what may be a hard one for you. But it's important, imperative," he emphasized, "that we fix this one. Remember Sam DeCalvo?"

"Sam the Stick? Sure, C.L. He's still serving federal time."

"Right. He'll have done three years this month and be eligible for parole."

"Then he faces a state sentence, seven to fifteen, I think."

"Right. I want him to get his parole on the federal time and fix a suspended sentence on the state rap, or else get the corrections commissioner to count his federal time as concurrent with state and parole him immediately."

D'Estang's chin jutted forward and a frown rippled across his forehead. "With Sam it's going to be tough. Remember how even the governor hated him. I don't know why Sam had to pick on the governor's brother's bank that time he got caught."

"Sam was very helpful to us when we needed major financing. We used over twenty million in treasury bills, municipal bonds, and street name securities which he," Ciano paused and cleared his throat, "provided for us when we bought the Spire Building six years ago."

"Sam did OK out of that. He took his chances and when he does get out he's set for life."

"We have been asked to get him out, Maurice."

Ciano pronounced the name in the French way as opposed to the Anglo-Saxon "Morris."

"That's going to take a lot of juice," D'Estang replied thoughtfully.

"We've got it," Ciano stated. "I think this is one that Francis X. Flannerty will have to personally look into."

"We've got to put a few layers between you, C.L., and any effort to spring Sam the Stick. This could get another investigation of Whitehall going again."

"Of course, Maurice." There was irritability in Ciano's tone. "It goes without saying."

"Yes," he mused. "You can't call," an ironic smile tinged the corners of D'Estang's mouth, "the 'sneaker of the house' on this one like you did for Adams."

"Correct. I expect we should contact our friend Casper Orellian in this case."

"The old con man shakedown artist," D'Estang growled.

"He wouldn't shake us down, would he?" Ciano asked mildly, though his eyes glinted sharply.

D'Estang chuckled. "Casper knows much better than that. We're not some straight Lionel family he can take for a hundred grand. That poor bastard Fred Lionel is still doing time."

"See Orellian today. Work through him on Flannerty," Ciano commanded.

"He's working on fixing draft cases now, but I'll find him. I'll try Flannerty's office in Washington. Casper has a desk and telephone right in the old mick's office."

"He's getting too confident," Ciano observed. "One of these days that U. S. Attorney is going to catch up with him and Flannerty and Flannerty's administrative assistant, what's his name?"

"Jack Klung."

"Yes. And when that investigation gets into high gear they won't be letting the FBI in on it like they did last time. Between Fred Black and his friends on the Appropriations Committee they can cut off the funds to the Bureau if it gets out of line."

"I'm grooming a couple of good younger men to take over Orellian's functions, C.L. He's pretty old-fashioned but still effective."

"Not for much longer, I'm afraid. We want all our machinery right up-to-date, Maurice. The next four years are going to be the most important in the history of the fifth estate."

D'Estang suppressed a smile at the way the super boss referred in such a grandiose phrase to the structure of which Whitehall associates was such an integral part. But better than almost anyone else in the organization he understood the power Ciano wielded and the frightening acumen with which he administered it.

"My section will be operating the way you want, C.L.," D'Estang declared. "The hotel setup will be a big help."

"Just let Bradford Kendall at least think he's the boss," Ciano cautioned.

"Of course, of course," D'Estang said assuringly.

Ciano stood up and leaving his desk walked across the large office and looked at the map of the world above the mantel, savoring the sight of the multicolored pins protruding from locations throughout, each indicating a different Whitehall project or going enterprise.

"How is our United Nations program working out?" he asked.

A huge grin split D'Estang's rugged countenance. "We are doing very well in that quarter and when the suites at the hotel have been completely finished by Julius we should do even better. Señor Ramirez has been particularly," he paused as though searching for the word, "pliable. He and the girl I found for him leave tomorrow. We have five other couriers going out this week, all as well insured as I was able to make them."

"Excellent, Maurice." Ciano was pleased. "It's a disagreeable trade we're in, but I see no alternative. If we do not exercise ultimate control others will. Since the U.S. Government renders itself helpless to stop the importation of heroin, the traffic will continue."

Ciano walked up to the Mercator projection and

tapped the pin stuck in Beirut. "We must go ahead with the hotel here. As long as Lebanon is the center of the opium trade route to Marseilles and the U.S. we need control in this area. Someday," he turned from the world chart, "when our plans have materialized politically, we will destroy the entire narcotics trade. But if until that time we do not control it at its source, Lebanon and Marseilles, and of course more and more Saigon, Hong Kong, and San Francisco," he paused, then continued, "if we do not control the narcotics traffic, then when the time comes we will not be able to obliterate it from American life."

"In the meantime," D'Estang remarked, "we grow steadily stronger on the heavy profits it turns over."

"Yes, but the very power those tax-free gains afford us is what will one day end the H problem forever."

Ciano walked over to his desk and standing behind it he pressed a button. A section of wall slid silently aside revealing a large room bright from the light that streamed through the windows. An organ stood back to back with a spinet piano. Ciano sat down at the organ and slowly placed his hands on the keys as though trying to decide what he would play. Then the powerful and melodious chords poured from the small organ as Ciano played the Duke's aria from *Rigoletto*.

D'Estang realized the meeting was over and walked to the door.

CHAPTER SIXTEEN

Jorge Ramirez stepped out of his sedan, immune by virtue of its United Nations-bestowed diplomatic license plates to molestation by the New York City police. Under the no-standing sign in front of Tiffany's on Fifth Avenue, Jorge bade his driver wait. He walked into America's most famous jewelry store and over to the counter at the rear that dispensed the relatively less-expensive jeweled pins. A distinguished-looking, white-haired gentleman, tightly rolled umbrella hanging on an arm, wearing the striped pants and morning coat of a diplomat or luxury hotel manager, was examining a pin. He looked up as Jorge peered at the brightly shining articles in the glass case. Then he continued to examine a pin, placed for his inspection on a black velvet tray.

A clerk materialized behind the counter, smiling. "Is there anything special you are looking for, sir?"

"It is my niece's birthday. I wanted to bring her something. She is in Geneva."

"How old is she?" the clerk asked.

"She is fifteen." Jorge smiled apologetically. "I am not looking for something expensive. By the way, I leave on Pan American flight 657 tomorrow at 5 P.M. Is it possible to have the article put directly on the flight and avoid the New York City sales tax?"

"Excuse me," the diplomatic type broke in, talking

in a middle-European accent. "Will you be so good, please, as to take a check on my bank? The Queensfield Bank on Grand Central Parkway?"

"You have identification, sir, of course; I am sure we can accommodate you."

"Yes. And I will be in the bank manager's office tomorrow afternoon precisely at three o'clock. You can confirm me then."

"That won't be necessary, sir, if your identification is in order. Just let me finish with this customer." He turned to Ramirez. "I'll go back and check the matter for you."

"No," Ramirez said. "On second thought I'll just buy this small ruby chip pin for fifty dollars. I think it will be easier to pay the tax and take it with me."

"As you like, sir."

Back in the car Ramirez directed the driver to take him back to his apartment in the luxury Place d'Etoile apartments. Jorge came from a fine old family in Santo Morango and from early youth had been accustomed to gracious living. At thirty-five he had been appointed to the United Nations sinecure and had really been able to taste luxury in all its refinements. Not that the diplomatic post paid so munificently, but after three years' experience he had become exposed to certain individuals on the periphery of the UN who recognized a man of influence and persuasion among his colleagues. They were willing to pay well for the benefit of his good offices. Such a one had been Maurice D'Estang and ultimately his wealthy associate, C. L. Ciano.

Dismissing his driver until nine in the morning he went up to his six-room apartment and private office on one of the top floors of the building and let himself in. This was truly his pride. The hacienda in Santo Morango was spacious and grand, befitting his family background and political ties with the palace, but he had become a truly international man in these years since his arrival on the New York scene and here was where he loved to be and from whence he adored to operate. Eugenia, his wife, conveniently spent at least six months a year in Santo Morango, where all her friends from childhood resided, and where they both wanted their children to be brought up. As an international diplomat it was well understood why he could not be home with his family as much as he would like. His wife could boast to her friends and relatives about her husband's importance. This, in addition to the five children, were her only real interest in life.

Jorge Ramirez walked through the living room, decorated in modern American style, as he called anything which departed from the traditional heavy mahogany furniture and rich hangings of the Spanish influence inflicted for centuries on Latin-American aristocratic homes. The living room divided his apartment into two sections. There were the two bedrooms he and his wife occupied on her infrequent visits and a third bedroom for guests or one of their older children on vacation in New York. On the other side of the living room, beyond the dining room and kitchen, with its own hall entranceway, was Jorge's office den and adjoining it a small parlor and bedroom suite. He walked through the kitchen and into his office, closing the door behind him.

"Christa?" he called.

"Ya, Jorge," came the Scandinavian accent of the beautiful, blond-haired girl who was his private secretary and mistress.

English was their only language in common and there were those uncharitable enough in the Latin section of the UN to question the value of a non-Spanish-speaking secretary. However, the surprisingly small salary paid to Christa Bergman was considered a bargain. Only Jorge knew where the real money paid her came from.

"Are we packed for tomorrow?"

"Almost, Jorge. Come in."

Jorge walked through his den into the parlor and then the bedroom. Christa, absolutely nude, her long hair falling all around her, was placing last-minute articles of clothing into her suitcases. Jorge caught his breath. He marveled at her exquisite blond beauty, so different from all the black-haired women of his part of the world. He threw off his suit coat, loosened his tie, fell to his knees in front of her and grasping her buttocks pulled her to his face, the soft platinum tuft below her hard, muscular belly against his mouth. Greedily he began kissing her here, his tongue penetrating the hairs to the lips he sought.

"Jorge, Jorge." She laughed. "Let me finish everything first. Please, darling."

He released her, running his tongue inside her thighs a moment, then standing himself. "We must, unfortunately, go to dinner with Umulu. I thought maybe before we went out we could . . ."

"Oh. Those nigras. Always they are so, as the Americans say, uptight. They make the air so heavy around them. So intense."

"I know. But Umulu is having several other members of the African delegations. You know how they like blondes. And I am trying to do some business with the right Africans."

"I am almost finished packing."

"We'll travel light. We're going to come back heavy. You might even have to leave something in Switzerland."

"I know, darling. But it takes much longer for a girl to pack light, you know."

"You have until two tomorrow afternoon. Are all your documents in order? Your passport?"

"Of course."

Christa was a marvel to him. His wife complained for days before making a trip and was never ready when it really came time to go. More than once he had missed important flights because of her and now at least she understood why he had forbidden her to ever travel on business with him. He hoped she would never leave Santo Morango again.

Jorge couldn't take his eyes off Christa's perfectly formed, athletic body. It was almost two months since Maurice D'Estang had introduced them and his lust for her was as great as the first time he had seen her, maybe stronger, since he never failed to discover some new, erotic detail in the art of love-making each time they embraced. She laughed at the naked desire mirrored in his face and eyes.

"OK, Jorge. We make love now. We need strength to eat with those uptight blacks."

The Santo Morango delegation automobile drove up in front of the Place d'Etoile apartments at exactly 2:20 P.M. Ramirez and Christa Bergman were waiting, each with only a single light suitcase. Ramirez carried a neat, thin, black attaché case with no initials, just a combination lock. The driver took their suitcases and put them in the trunk of the car as Christa, followed by Jorge, climbed in. Jorge placed the case on his lap. "Go out to Kennedy, Rafael. Stop at the Queensfield Bank. It's just off Grand Central Parkway after you pass La Guardia."

Jorge and Christa sat silently beside each other. Both were rested. They had slept until mid-morning after the strenuous late night with the African members of various UN delegations. Ramirez couldn't help but feel self-satisfied at the job he had done over the past six months. D'Estang's money and personal services had gone a long way toward forging the organization which would make Jorge a millionaire several times over. He was especially pleased with himself for getting Christa a Santo Morango diplomatic passport.

The car turned off the parkway and soon came to a stop. The Queensfield National Bank was beside them. It was exactly two minutes before three, Jorge noticed, looking down at his watch. "Wait here, I'll be out in a few minutes." Carrying the case he stepped out of the car.

He was the last customer to enter the small, unprepossessing-looking bank. He had never heard of this bank, much less ever been in it before. A bank guard came up to him as he walked to the rail behind which sat three executives at desks facing the tellers. Jorge asked to see the manager. No questions asked, he was led to an office behind the row of desks. He walked in. A very conservative banker type, blue pin stripe and vest, cropped gray hair, watched unblinking as he crossed the room. The door behind him closed. The banker said nothing.

"I am pilot on Project Immune," he said. The banker glanced at his watch, stood up, went to a wall safe, turned the combination and opened it, and took out a slender, black attaché case. The twin to the one Ramirez was carrying. The banker placed the case on his desk. Wordlessly Ramirez placed his case beside it and picked up the one which had come out of the wall safe. The banker nodded and Jorge left the inner office and walked past the bank officers. The guard opened the door for him and he was back in the delegation car within two minutes of the time he had left it.

"That was quick," Christa remarked approvingly.

"Sí," he said in good spirits. "Well, darling, off to Europe for a few days' working holiday. Are you happy?"

"Yah, Jorge. We have good times together. And we do important things for the world too. I love to travel."

They arrived at Kennedy Airport an hour and a half before the Scandinavian Airlines flight was due to leave for Zurich. Checking in occupied only a few moments since they were ticketed and on diplomatic passports.

"You know, Jorge, we could have stayed home almost another hour."

He shook his head. "I had to be at the bank at exactly three."

"Why?"

He realized he had needlessly disclosed information and pursed his lips. He was distracted, perhaps apprehensive about the mission, but that was no excuse for carelessness. As D'Estang had said, the way this operation was set up, if a man was careless or changed his mind, he and he alone would suffer. Very badly, D'Estang had added.

"No, reason, really," Jorge answered the girl's question with a smile. "I just wanted to be at a bank before it closed." He pressed her hand.

After checking in and receiving diplomatic status on the flight they went up to the SAS first-class passenger lounge and had a coffee and brandy. Christa chatted happily in Swedish with the blond hostess. Jorge, conscious of an overwhelming burden, clutched the attaché case. He looked down at it, saw his knuckles were turning white, and said to himself, Relax, Jorge. In only eight hours the mission will be half accomplished. He reassured himself with the knowledge he was dealing at the very top. On a level above the president of his native Santo Morango or almost any other president in Latin America. He was dealing with a world power, comparable to the United States official government in Washington. He was proud to be a part of this power from which he would, and already had, realized so much.

The flight was called on time and Jorge, still gripping the case, it had not left his hand since he picked it up at the bank, led Christa on board. They sat to the rear of the first-class section, Jorge taking the window seat, his left arm around the attaché case wedged between his buttock and the arm of the seat. For twenty minutes he waited uneasily until the door closed and the plane taxied out on the ramp.

Once airborne, Jorge sighed with relief, pushed his chair back, reached for Christa's hand and closed his eyes. He did not intend to sleep but merely to doze, always conscious of the attaché case pressing against him. In spite of himself he did fall asleep and it wasn't until the stewardess came around to serve cocktails that he woke up with a start. His fingers clawed, found the case, and he relaxed. Christa and the stewardess were chatting in some foreign language he didn't understand.

Jorge and Christa enjoyed cocktails, talking of the places they would visit after the UN committee meetings were completed in Geneva. He placed the attaché case under his seat.

They hurtled through the darkening sky from west to east, losing hour after hour. Jorge had planned the flight carefully. They would arrive in Zurich just as the banks opened and he would make an immediate delivery of the attaché case.

An hour after the cocktail service, dinner was brought to them and they finished eating at eight-thirty New York time, three-thirty in the morning at their destination. Now a screen was lowered at the end of the first-class cabin and a movie began. It was an insipid love story which bored both of them after five minutes. Jorge knew he was nervous about this mission and was finding it difficult to disguise his unease. Christa noticed his nervousness and squeezed his hand.

"What's the matter, darling?"

"Nothing, really. I have too much on my mind, that's all."

"Just put your head on my shoulder." She brushed his lips with hers. "Let me caress your face. Soon you go to sleep."

Jorge laid his head beside the softly scented long blond hair and Christa began to stroke his forehead and eyes. He started to breathe deeply and soon, forgetting his fears, he fell asleep.

The jetliner made its first stop at Paris just on time. It was five in the morning. Jorge and Christa dozed aboard for the hour lay-over and then they were airborne.

The sun was rising over the mountains as they landed in Zurich. On their diplomatic passports they cleared customs and immigration with no inspection and walked out into the waiting room. Hardly had they appeared, before a man in a chauffeur's uniform walked up to them.

"Señor Ramirez?" he asked. Jorge nodded. "I am the driver you contracted for."

Ramirez knew he had made no plans for a driver to meet him but he expected to be met. "Thank you. Please take these two bags." The driver took his and Christa's suitcases and led them out into the glistening air. They both breathed deeply.

"That is the good air from the mountains," Christa said appreciatively. "I miss it in New York."

The driver ushered them to the black Mercedes he was driving, put the suitcases in front and drove off. It was seven-thirty in the morning. Ramirez gave no instructions to the driver. Forty-five minutes later the black car pulled up in front of a bank, ancient-looking grillwork protecting the doors and windows. As they came to a stop the iron lattice swung open from within. A bank guard stood before the opened door. Asking Christa to stay in the car Jorge walked up to and through the doorway and into the bank. A bald-headed, smiling man wearing a black coat and striped pants that seemed to be a uniform of upper-level management in Swiss banks inclined his head slightly and led Ramirez into an inner office. On the heavy, dark-wood refectory table in the cubiclelike room with a black attaché case like the one Jorge had brought in. He laid his case down and picked up the other one.

"Would you care to open it?" the banker asked. "The combination is set for zero zero zero." Noticing the lock was set to open, Ramirez nodded and pressed the two spring catches. They sprung and he lifted the top. Inside was a plain manila envelope. He opened it. Inside he found a sheaf of hundred-dollar bills. He counted them. Five thousand dollars. Five thousand tax-free, unaccountable dollars. He restrained the pleasure he felt, nodded to the banker, placed the envelope back in the case, closed it and walked from the bank, carrying the case with the money.

"Where next, sir?" the driver asked.

"Hotel Splendide." He turned to Christa. "We'll rest until afternoon, then fly to Geneva for the committee meetings. Reception tonight, meetings the next two days. Then on to Paris. We'll stay a couple of days and then go home."

"Good. I do some shopping."

"I think, darling, we must travel light. We do our shopping back in New York. All you want."

CHAPTER SEVENTEEN

Casper Orellian strode jauntily down Fifth Avenue. It was fall and the air was crisp. People stopped and openly stared at the dapper elderly boulevardier, complete with a carnation in the buttonhole of his morning coat. The Continental gentleman arrived at the main entrance to Saks and walked through the doors. As he sauntered down the aisles of merchandise, salespeople and customers alike eyed him.

This was the first step in accomplishing a rather delicate mission which only his close friend Congressman Francis X. Flannerty, often referred to as the "sneaker of the house," could help him effect. Two speakers of the House of Representatives had vociferously objected to Flannerty's sobriquet on the basis that the sneaker and his *modus operandi* might become confused with them. But the sneaker, over the past thirty-six years, had become even more entrenched in Congress than the men who had succeeded to the office that put them third in line for the nation's presidency. As Orellian approached the women's cosmetic counters he grinned to himself, thinking of the old "sneaker's" fatal weakness. He stopped before the appropriate counter.

"Give me half a dozen jars of Erno Laszlo special face cream," he requested.

The woman behind the counter looked at him in surprise. "A year's supply for your wife?" she asked.

"I know several ladies who can't live without the product," Orellian replied, his eyes twinkling, his smile indulgent. The saleslady smiled back at him and disappeared down behind the counter, straightening up with a six-jar case of the cream.

"That will be ninety-six dollars with tax," she said.

Orellian peeled a hundred-dollar bill from the roll of bills he had produced from his pocket and handed it to her. He waited while she put the case of the cream into a bag and handed it to him with his change. Thanking her, Orellian briskly walked out of Saks and at the Fifth Avenue entrance he caught a cab. "La Guardia Airport," he told the driver. "Eastern shuttle."

Two and a half hours later, the shopping bag containing the skin cream held in his left hand, Casper Orellian entered the Van Buren Hotel in Washington, D.C. His eyes traveled about the lobby and he walked toward the figure of Francis X. Flannerty sitting on a sofa at the end of the room. The sneaker of the house stood up, his tall, rangy form, the sharp features topped with the thatch of white hair, the black, tight suit and black tie presenting an imposing appearance. He stood almost a head taller than Orellian who walked up to him and placed the shopping bag on the floor. Flannerty glanced down at it and then called a bellboy over. "Jenkins, will you take this up to my suite?" he asked deferentially.

"Yes, sir," the elderly-looking colored bellman replied eagerly. "Yes, sir, Congressman Flannerty."

Flannerty gestured toward the sofa and he and Orellian sat down. "How is everything, Casper?" the senior legislator asked pleasantly.

"Good, Frank. Except that I was just given a delicate case to handle. By no less a person than C. L. Ciano."

Flannerty nodded. "I hope he is quite happy with the job we did for Bill Adams at his request. Very unusual to place a second-term congressman in the number-two spot on any committee, especially the Organized Crime Committee."

"C.L. is very pleased, Frank. So much so that

through his man D'Estang he has asked us for another beauty."

"Don't keep me wondering, Casper."

Orellian nodded. "He wants to get Sam DeCalvo, popularly known as Sam the Stick, out of federal prison and also have him pardoned on the state time ahead of him."

"C.L. always has a tough one for us," Flannerty said after a few moments of thought. "Very well, we'll see what can be done. We must always remember that Ciano is most generous with remunerations, both in cash and kind. He was certainly able to stop all FBI co-operation with the U. S. Attorney in New York when they tried to investigate certain of our activities last year. Ciano owns Fred Black, of course."

"What is the best way to go from here?" Orellian asked. "Contact Corrections Commissioner Harvey in New York?"

Flannerty stood up. "I think we want to go over to the office. We'll have Jack Klung do a little investigating for us."

It was a short walk from the hotel to Capitol Hill and the new House Office Building where Flannerty had a suite of offices befitting his seniority and influence in the House. "Give me a few minutes to look over my messages and then we'll go in and talk to Jack," Flannerty said. Orellian nodded and walked into the office which Flannerty had made available to him. He sat down behind the desk and took out a list of the long-distance phone calls he needed to make, putting one through to London first at the taxpayers' expense. The fixer had just completed his second call when the intercom buzzed and Flannerty asked him to come in.

In the "sneaker's" office Orellian found the stout, bull-necked figure of Flannerty's administrative aide, Jack Klung. "I've just been talking to Jack about our problem," the congressman began. "He has some ideas that I think could be productive."

Orellian turned his gaze to Klung, sometimes referred to as Dr. Klung although nobody knew what he was a doctor of, certainly not medicine.

"The easiest way to go about it is the way we did it last time, ask the President to grant him a pardon," Klung suggested.

Orellian shook his head. "It's one thing to pardon a powerful labor leader who happens to be a racketeer, but a pardon for a man like DeCalvo just can't come from the level of the White House."

"I realize that, Casper," Klung said. "I was just going through the alternatives. Where we have to place our wedge is with the federal Parole Board which sits on DeCalvo's case next week. It happens that the chairman of this board might be susceptible to some slight political pressures that this office can bring. Of course he can easily be outvoted by the other members of the board and he can only use just so much influence on them without making them suspicious, but this is one road we can take. If it doesn't work—"

"Sam stays in another year before being considered," Orellian finished for Klung. "That's unacceptable."

"I will of course have a conversation with the federal corrections commissioner," Flannerty interjected. "He has found it convenient to come to this office for help from time to time. His word has a lot of weight with the Parole Board. The real problem is that there are people who do not want DeCalvo paroled a single day before he serves out his sentence."

"If the Parole Board turns Sam down," Orellian replied gloomily, "only presidential influence can spring him."

Leaning back, the palms of his hands together, the sneaker of the house smiled knowingly. "I suspect we can work out the problem with the federal Parole Board. It's at the state level where we may be in trouble. Ordinarily I could call Richie Harvey and he'd take care of an immediate parole for DeCalvo but in this case the governor will have a strong interest. We'll have to attack this matter through the governor's office as well as through Richie."

"How are you going to do that, Frank?"

"I wouldn't even try except that we are doing it for C. L. Ciano. You can appreciate, Casper, the repercussions that could be caused if some journalist brought out that I had personally interceded for a mob type like Sam the Stick."

"Of course, Frank," Orellian replied. "C.L. will, of course, be most grateful to you. As a matter of fact, Maurice D'Estang was talking about switching all the Ascot Hotel division's travel business to your nephew's travel agency."

"I'm sure that Eddy would appreciate it. But that isn't why I am going to try to do this thing for C.L. There are other reasons." He paused and then turned to Klung. "Jack, let's hear you perform."

Miming the act of picking up a telephone and holding the instrument to his mouth, Klung began talking in the nasal twanging Yankee accent that characterized Representative Francis X. Flannerty.

"Richie boy?" he began. "Frank here. Been a long time since we got together. Remember back home when you were running the state prisons and I made the governor let you spend five million dollars fixing up your old jailhouses? Yass, my boy. Ha ha ha."

Casper Orellian was openly astounded at the ability with which Klung could imitate the senior congressman's voice. Flannerty chuckled at Orellian's surprise. "Jack should of been an actor."

"He could fool me anytime." Orellian gave the aide a wary look. "He could be dangerous."

Klung laughed and shook his head. "I only do it at Frank's request."

Orellian shrugged slightly. "I've been around this office for quite a few years now but I never heard Jack do that before."

The sneaker stood up and put a hand on Orellian's shoulder. "I'm going over to the floor to listen to the debate on the welfare reform bill and be recorded as present. While I'm there Jack will put through a few key calls. Then if anything does come out later I can say I never made such calls as are being talked about on behalf of a mafioso named Sam DeCalvo. And when Richie and the governor mention the date and time of these calls I can prove I was on the House floor at that very moment."

Orellian shook his head, admiration in his expression and tone. "Frank, you think of everything."

"They don't call me the sneaker of the house for nothing." Flannerty laughed to himself.

"Can we have a drink this evening when you come off the floor?" Orellian asked.

A shy, slightly sheepish smile spread over Flannerty's face. "I expect I'll be busy this evening, Casper. I want to check out what help we can expect from the Justice Department."

Orellian smiled back understandingly. The existence of the sneaker's close male friend in the Justice Department was a fairly open secret on Capitol Hill. The affair had been going on for fifteen years or more and Flannerty had discovered that Erno Laszlo's cream rendered his part of their consummations of the affair the most efficacious and stimulating of any lubricant he had yet discovered.

"Good, Frank," the stylish fixer replied. "I'll be down from New York again this week and check on progress with you and Jack."

"I'll try to have something for you at that time, Casper." The sneaker of the house nodded and left his office.

CHAPTER EIGHTEEN

It happened seldom that C. L. Ciano took an incoming phone call when he had a visitor. This Friday, as Brad sat in the office, enthralled as always by the view of New York from the top of the Spire Building, Ciano was talking in guarded sentences to his partner, Hyman Steinert. Late Friday afternoon was a sort of round-up day for Ciano, Brad gathered. It had been one hell of a week. Yet never had a week started with so delightful a Monday morning.

He had wakened to find himself beside Luciana in her bed. After that first, uncontrollably premature ejaculation of suppressed desire for her punctuated by the strident ring of the telephone, he had been able to pace himself perfectly to her uprising curve of passion and hold himself in until she writhed and called out to him in ecstasy to join her. Several times they had awakened during the long, beautiful night and each time the passion was equally intense though taking different forms, once wildly active, another time slow and extensive. They had gone to sleep joined and come awake to gentle motions that had started in their sleep. And finally, with the sun flooding in the bedroom at eight o'clock he was refreshed and passionate. He almost feared their morning love-making might be heard out in the hall. By now he had forgiven Knute for his ill-timed phone call the previous evening.

Brad was so happy with his life, prospects and Luciana that it was difficult to adopt the somber mien he deemed appropriate to telling Knute that he was no longer the manager of the hotel. In fact, had not Maurice D'Estang arrived at the hotel at ten o'clock looking for him, Brad would have telephoned Ciano and asked him to reconsider. D'Estang's first words when he met Brad in the lobby were "Is he out yet?"

Brad shook his head. "I'm on my way up to see him now." D'Estang had nodded impatiently.

Brad Kendall arrived in Knute Bjorgund's office and found the hotel manager his usual exuberant self.

"I hope everything is well with Mrs. Blore." There was a pleasant, cheerful lilt in Knute's Scandinavian accent.

"Yes, she's very happy with the hotel." He paused, wondering how to proceed. Then he decided that in the ensuing period of serious bloodletting he could only come right to the point on each occasion.

"Knute, I am sorry to have to be the bearer of bad news but Mr. Ciano has decided to put in a new general manager, a new resident manager, and God knows where it will stop. Until he puts in a new president it's my job to carry out his orders."

The manager swallowed, a sick look coming over his face. "It is something I hoped wouldn't happen, but of course knew might. I'll never get a finer house than this one for the rest of my career."

"Don't you believe it, Knute. Now you are entitled to many benefits, as you know, and Ciano wants to be very generous in severance pay. You'll receive a check today for your salary for the next six months. The new manager will be in this morning."

"They move fast," Knute observed dourly.

"Very."

"OK, Brad." Knute stood up. "I clear out my desk now. You can have the office in half an hour."

Brad badly wanted to tell Knute to take his time but he knew D'Estang expected to take over immediately. "Thanks, Knute. Thanks for understanding."

"Oh, I understand plenty. I been in this city the

last three years while you were in exile—yes, that's the word."

Brad nodded. "Productive exile, however."

"I think I know much more about this Whitehall than you do."

"You can't believe a lot of rumors. They've been investigated thoroughly, by banks, the FBI, the financial sections of newspapers. Every time they came up smelling like a rose."

"Yeah, sure. You know how many times I make what is almost a scandal in this hotel smell like a rose? About one time a week." Knute busily cleared out drawers, piling the contents on top of his desk. "Maybe I'm the lucky one."

"Well, you sure won't have any trouble getting another good job. And by the way, if you see anything for your top staff members let them know. You know I'll do everything I can to help."

"I know that, Brad. It's not your fault. You can come to me if you have to someday and I will help."

"Thanks, that's good to know."

Brad was jolted back to the present as Ciano put down the phone. "Hy Steinert just asked how the move is coming to get everybody into this building?" He gave Brad a questioning glance.

"We're already trying to sublet our space on Sixth Avenue. Before I made any definite personnel moves I thought I'd better see where the bloodletting stops."

"You don't like this substitution of personnel, do you, Brad?"

"We're letting a lot of highly experienced people go who will have to be replaced."

"We'll find replacements right from our own organization. We always move fast. You'll get the habit."

"Well, secretaries and clerical help have already been assigned space in this building and many of them moved this week. I never thought we could move so fast. Usually the moving-van services have to be notified a month or two in advance."

"We control the leading transport companies. There's no sense paying rent to a building Whitehall doesn't own. And don't worry about subletting. We have a special office that makes and breaks leases."

C. L. Ciano turned in his seat and looked northeast out the picture window. The Place d'Etoile, indeed star shaped, towered above the surrounding apartment buildings near the East River. "How's your apartment coming? Have you decided on one yet?"

"Thanks, I have. A beauty. I'm all set to close the purchase."

"Good. We'll make you a loan to buy the apartment. You'll be able to pay it out of your salary in a year, tax free. We like all our employees living in company-owned apartment buildings and working in company-owned office buildings. No point their paying rent outside. And we have buildings in every location at every price to suit every income."

"That's cozy, C.L.," Brad remarked. "I sure can't complain."

"Good. We don't like complaints on either side," he added significantly. "As long as everyone does his job we're all taken care of. Security for every man and woman on the Whitehall team."

"How about the Miami deal, C.L.?" Brad asked. "I'd like to get that one nailed down before making the big push into Latin America."

"Timing is everything, Brad. I moved very fast on stage one of that acquisition. I would say give it another week or two and we'll be ready to go into stage two. That's where you come in."

"I read they've been on strike since Monday, the whole place had to close down."

"I heard about it. Those labor unions can sure make some impossible demands."

"Morrie Unger is a damned tough guy," Brad observed. "That's why his partners would like to sell out, just to get away from him, but a strike isn't going to make Morrie sell out. He's got too many rackets going for him in that hotel. He either owns or has a piece of every supplier that takes a dime's worth of stuff into the Tropic Plaza."

"We'll look the situation over in another week. Unger

is a vulnerable man." Ciano smiled deprecatingly and spread his hands out on his desk. "He works with a very loose group down there. He tries to keep so much for himself there are a lot of people would like to see things different. The way things work in the world nowadays you have to have a tight organization, everybody does his job the way he's told, nobody gets out of line, not even a little. That way lies success."

C. L. Ciano stood up and paced to the window and back. "If our organization were as loose, say, as the United States Government, we'd be dead. You know that even the law-enforcement agencies and departments of this country so mistrust each other they don't share information. Well, let's hope things stay that way."

"Look, I'm a team man, C.L.," Brad suddenly burst out as though he had been struggling to contain himself. "But does that mean Luciana Blore—and I'd like to do something about changing that last name—has to go out at night with hotel guests Maurice D'Estang thinks are important?"

Ciano smiled in friendly fashion and walked back from the window. He gripped the back of his desk chair and leaned across toward Brad.

"First, congratulations on your taste and intentions. Second, Luciana is on the Ascot Towers Hotel payroll, as hostess and promotion officer, for a generous amount, I might observe. She will prove to be worth it, I know. It is my information that Maurice asked her to have dinner and spend the evening with Representative Everett Jamison of Texas who is coming back into New York next Tuesday."

"I would have thought he might have asked me first," Brad said petulantly.

"She is directly on the Ascot Towers payroll." Ciano's voice clearly reflected impatience. "She was asked to handle a special and important assignment. She accepted with enthusiasm, I'm told."

"She couldn't very well say no." Brad regretted the statement as soon as he'd made it, but he hadn't counted on falling in love with Luciana.

Ciano's eyes turned dangerously glinty. He stood up straight, looking down across the desk at Brad. "Look, you are way up in this organization. There are a lot of men who have been with us since we started that have the talent to be president of Ascot Hotels. I tried to make you understand what being part of us means. It means staying in line, doing your job, giving orders and taking them. It means we don't have time for pettiness. My God, Brad. If you don't know who we are and what we are doing, I've badly misjudged. There's still time for you to leave us, but you'd better make up your mind."

Brad realized that he might well give a subordinate an even more severe reading out for complaining about company policy. "I'll have to be more objective about Luciana."

Ciano nodded, satisfied with the response. "The reason I want you with us is twofold. You have a fine reputation in the industry. Hotelmen as a whole, I've learned, realized you were right when you opposed Leighton, and they appreciated your loyalty when you stayed on with him even though it meant leaving your center of power in Ascot Hotels." Brad waited for the second reason. Certainly there was far more involved than Leighton's glib expression "Wops need WASPs."

"I am aware of your activities in national politics," Ciano pronounced.

Brad shrugged. "Only in that political conventions mean big business to hotels. Both national and state conventions."

"I know about some of the favors, many of an intimate nature, you have done for some of the big city and state party leaders."

Brad smiled. "We try to take care of good customers discreetly, when they have special needs or problems."

"I know of few politicians who have been as intimately associated as you have with the bargaining and dealing that goes on at the last minute before candidates are nominated by their parties."

"I've always been fascinated by politics," Brad admitted. "As a matter of fact, I was figuring on trying to land a campaign job and boot home a winner this election year if I was through with Ascot."

"That's what I wanted to hear you say, Brad. Stay with us, play it our way, and you'll have the best of both worlds, your hotel chain and influencing elections, using the power of Whitehall's political section."

As usual Brad was both elated and disturbed at the way Ciano could manipulate him. Take him to the top of the mountain, so to speak, and show him the world that could be his. "I figured you'd have me doing something for William Fortune Adams. Too bad he's not a little less pompous."

"Bill Adams is one of a dozen possible candidates I could promote for the presidency within the next two elections. Another strong possibility is Ev Jamison. Our organization in Texas has been quietly behind him for four years. We want to run him for the Senate this year. He's an ideal candidate. Native-born Texan married to a Texan girl. Five good-looking kids. People like him. Nothing wrong with him for senator which four or five million dollars can't cure."

"That would certainly get the ball rolling nicely in Texas." Brad whistled softly.

"We're going to do more than run Jamison in Texas for the Senate." Ciano gave Brad an owlish look. "He's going to enter the New Hampshire primaries."

"Directly challenge the leader of his own party?"

"He's been a voluble critic of the Administration's war policy, as you know. No other Republican has so openly criticized the President since Charlie Goodell tried it and failed to get re-elected to the Senate in 1970. If he can make a good showing in New Hampshire he should be a prime Republican candidate in 1976. That's the year we're shooting for."

"Are we going to help him in New Hampshire?" Brad asked. "I have some good connections there."

"I'll know better after I talk to him next week. And it may be that Luciana will pick up some interesting information from him which will help us decide."

"You're convinced that the Vice President won't run in '76, C.L.?"

"I'm not convinced of anything."

"It appears to me that your political section is going to be spending one hell of a lot of money," Brad observed.

"We're prepared to spend a minimum of fifty million dollars over the next five years to elect our man President."

"In my opinion you will do it," Brad said thoughtfully. "So how come this paragon of public acceptance from Texas is getting fixed up with a date in New York?"

"Other highly qualified presidential candidates have been swingers," Ciano remarked. "That's one reason we're behind Ev Jamison. We want some protection on our investment in him."

"I see what you mean." Brad couldn't keep the sarcastic edge from his voice.

"I don't think you do," Ciano replied sharply. "Ev has very good taste. He could only enjoy spending an evening with a woman as beautiful and cultured as Luciana. She could give a man who's lonely and away from home some pretty heady ideas. She doesn't have to go up to his suite and get in bed with him; all she has to do is give him a good time, make him feel relaxed, and without trying she'll make him want a woman. Maurice will see he gets what he wants after Luciana goes home."

"You're not going to," Brad's tone was ironic, "take out insurance on William Fortune Adams that way."

"No," Ciano agreed. "But his ambitions are far beyond his means. In our many campaign contributions, and in defraying his expenses, there will be considerable evidence which only we would be in a position to discover and release as to misuse of funds and questionable origin of certain funds. Once someone is with us," he gave Brad a sharp look, "he stays with us."

Ciano walked around his desk toward the table in front of the leather sofa across the room. He ran the fingers of his right hand down the fuselage of the model jet. "We'll use the jets, Ascot Hotels, money, girls, muscle, whatever we need. But I expect to see Bill Adams nominated as the Democratic candidate for the Senate at the state convention."

Ciano looked up from the model jet. "It's almost six o'clock. Can I fix you a drink?"

"You having one, C.L.?"

Ciano shook his head. "Never use it but don't let that stop you. I've got a theory, never trust a man that doesn't drink." He laughed easily. "Of course I can afford that theory. Everyone I work with *has* to trust me."

"What do you do for pure pleasure?" Brad asked, sincerely curious.

Ciano gave him a broad grin and then pressed a button under his desk. The wall slid back, revealing the organ and piano back to back.

Ciano left his desk and walked over to the organ. "I'll play you a song I wrote. I've been thinking of starting a company to publish music and make records."

Brad was surprised and pleased at the sweetness of the theme Ciano had composed. A man who played and wrote music as well as he did couldn't be an evil person, he thought.

As Brad listened to Ciano playing his composition his thoughts went to the luncheon he had given for Elda Ciano and Andrea. It was a good thing he and Luciana were so strongly tied together, he thought, or he might have had ideas about Elda even though she was only a few years older than his own daughter. Elda was truly the most considerate, warm, and yes—sensuous—young woman, despite her wholly demure mien, he had ever met.

With Elda's help he and Andrea had enjoyed one of the most satisfying conversations they had ever carried on together. When the luncheon was over they made another date for the following week. Brad wondered whether Elda had mentioned the luncheon date to her father. He decided not to bring it up himself. Despite his overwhelming attraction to Luciana, Brad couldn't help but have the slightest of guilt twinges about his frank admiration for Elda.

After playing his composition Ciano stood up. "How about that drink?" he asked.

"Scotch and soda. I'd sure hate for you not to trust me."

"Help yourself." Ciano walked over to a blank stretch of paneled wall behind the sofa. He pressed a catch and a fully equipped bar, complete with a small refrigerator, revolved out.

As Brad made himself a highball Ciano said, "By the way, you did a fine job setting Larry Wolfmann up with the Allied Electric people. They let him order as big as he wanted, filled his warehouse with merchandise, thirty-day terms, and made him a fair price on everything."

"Why does he want to warehouse so much stuff? He could have all Allied appliances sent direct from factory to consumer and take a commission without the extra expense of warehousing."

"Larry's a conscientious boy. He wants to assure all his customers of immediate delivery. Only way he can do that is to have the goods on hand. You understand?"

"I hope not," Brad replied. "But I probably do."

"Just take your time, Brad. You can't do everything all at once. Bit by bit you will become one of us. One of our best. Someday when things aren't going the way you think they should be in the world, you'll be able to pick up the phone, call the White House and straighten things out."

Brad met the gleaming black points of light that were the pupils of Ciano's eyes. He held his glass up, Ciano nodded back, and Brad took a long drink.

"Do you trust me?"

Ciano nodded.

Brad took another swallow. "Good. Now there is a lot that is none of my business going on and I'll never ask about it unless you want me to. But if I'm carrying the title of president of the Ascot Hotel chain, just within my own command I've got to know what's happening or I can't function efficiently."

"What's the beef?"

"For the last few days D'Estang hasn't let me onto the floor where all this mysterious so-called decorating is going on. He works for me, on the organization chart anyway, and yet when I try to get on either the passenger or service elevator that goes to that floor, a new elevator man hired by D'Estang won't let me on. I wanted to fire him and D'Estang said I'd better check with you first."

"I'll tell Maurice to give you the tour. The job's got to be done by Monday night." Then, abruptly changing the subject, "Who are you golfing with this weekend?"

"I set up a date with Bob Fullerton, executive veep of General Brands Food Company. Maurice is playing with us and your new appointee to vice president of food and liquor purchasing, Dom Corbi. I figured Fullerton has the right to put up an argument before Corbi does whatever it is you want him to do."

Ciano grinned. "Good thinking, Brad. We want to stay close to General Brands. Corbi knows that. You know what we're going to do? In two years we're going to sell that meat company you own 51 per cent of to General Brands. We're going to make it worth up high in seven figures. And even after you've paid a legitimate capital gains tax you'll put a solid million or better in the bank. Then we'll go with another company. We should be able to turn a nice solid supply or service company over every eighteen months to two years. Got any ideas about the next one?"

Brad nodded. "Sure. Carpeting."

"Hey, I like that. Besides the hotels, we control maybe two hundred restaurants around the country. They all have to recarpet every year or two."

"You ever figure government contracts on carpeting? And then there's always paint."

"We're big in paint. Anyway, Brad, you're more with us every day. I can see it. Why don't you drop over and see us tomorrow after you finish golf? As a matter of fact, you could drive out, leave your daughter, Andrea, with us, she and Elda get along great together, and then come over for a late lunch."

"Good idea, C.L." He put his glass down. "If there's nothing else, I'll move along."

"See you tomorrow, Brad."

By the time Brad was down on the street his spirits were soaring once again. Luciana was waiting for him and for the first time that week since Monday night, they would be able to have a quiet dinner alone together. The evenings had been a series of farewells to home office executives, explanations and several talks with the hotel trade press writers trying to smooth over the all-too-evident corporate executions at Ascot.

CHAPTER NINETEEN

Tony Falcon had never been more polite and charming as he conversed with Gwen and Ed Connor. Andrea Kendall watched the scene approvingly. Tony played golf and talked a good game with Ed.

Tony had covered his initial shock very suavely, he thought. He had seen Andrea leave the Ciano home with her father in a limousine and he instinctively felt that somehow Andrea's companion, Luciana Blore, represented great wealth. So what was Andrea doing living in this dump? It was a good address but what a run-down pad for grown-ups with two kids. There could only be one answer, her father had the money. But surely this bitch broad, Andrea's mother, would have shaken down her first husband pretty good. He wondered now if Andrea really did have a lot of rich girl friends. If she was around Elda Ciano she must know some important people. The thought of Elda made him shudder. Not since he was fourteen years old had the old man lit into him the way he had the other night about not seeing her any more. His father had been so scared he could hardly talk. He kept running off in Italian.

At this point Tony wasn't much concerned whether Andrea's parents let her go out with him or not. If she came out of this kind of a rat trap there couldn't be much value. Probably her rich old man had told all of them to screw. That's what he would have done. Maybe he could get out of the whole thing right here. He wanted to get laid anyway. He shot his french cuff and glanced at his watch. It was seven o'clock.

"Say, Mrs. Connor, I was hoping Andrea could have dinner with me. I have to meet some friends of my parents at seven-thirty. I told them I might have a date."

Gwen looked at her husband questioningly. Andrea stood up. "I'm ready, Tony," she said.

"You haven't asked your father yet," Gwen said sharply.

Who the hell was her father? Tony wondered. He hoped the old Irishman would say no, and to prod him, Tony stood up. Connor looked from Andrea to her mother helplessly. Hesitantly he began, "If Andrea wants to go out . . ."

"You won't keep her out late, Tony?" Gwen asked worriedly.

"Oh! Mother!" Andrea cried in exasperation.

"Certainly not, Mrs. Connor."

"Where did you plan to go for dinner?" Ed Connor asked halfheartedly.

"We'll be going to the Salerno Restaurant on East Forty-sixth Street. It's listed in the book."

Andrea was blushing with embarrassment. She prayed her real father would win out and make her mother let her go to college as far away from New York as possible.

"Well, you both go on and have a nice dinner together," Gwen decided. Then unsuccessfully trying to sound offhand she said, "Andrea, you call me when you've finished dinner."

Out on the street Andrea was so happy to be away that she reached impulsively for Tony's hand. "Let's walk a couple of blocks before we get a cab."

"We'll have to walk one block to my car," Tony answered. To himself he thought, hey, maybe there is something here. She sure as hell looks, acts and talks cherry but who knows what could happen.

"Ha, Tony!" The headwaiter at the Salerno greeted

him. "Lady," he bowed acknowledgment to Andrea. "Come, I have a nice table in the back for you two." He seated them in a secluded booth.

"How about a drink, Andrea?"

"A sherry maybe."

"Aw, try a real drink. It won't hurt you."

"Well, what do you suggest?"

"Martini?"

She shrugged. "That's what Brad would probably suggest."

"Brad?"

"My father. My real father. You met him at the Cianos'."

"Sure. I guess I got a little confused." He ordered two martinis and looked across the table at Andrea. She really was a pretty-looking chick now that she was away from her drag parents. In fact, she was beautiful. He was still confused about her circumstances.

"Is your father a friend of Mr. Ciano?" Tony asked.

"I suppose so. My father is the president of the Ascot Hotel chain."

Suddenly Tony was impressed. This was big money. Very important. He had been so shaken up that day that he could hardly remember who he had met. All he remembered was making the most polite and final bye-bye of his life to Elda Ciano, telling her he was soon leaving the country, which his father had decided he would do the night before. Then a little of his cool returned, and he had talked to this lovely chick who had to be rich. He had found out how to call her at home before he left the Ciano residence forever.

"I should think you'd have a lot more fun living with him than where you are," Tony probed.

"We have a very happy home. You didn't meet my brother." She was silent a moment. "It's true, though. The few times Mama has let me visit Brad we had great times. And then when I'd come home and tell her she would be furious. I learned that I had to tell her I had a dull time, that Brad was too busy to do anything with me if I wanted to see him again."

"Sounds pretty confusing," Tony prompted. "Don't

you feel sometimes that you want to get like away from it all?"

"Yes. Yes, I do. But I can't control my life. Sometimes I just wish I could fly away from everything." She looked across the table at the darkly handsome young man. His deep brown eyes seemed to her pools of sympathy. He made her want to confide in him, yet she hardly knew him.

"Maybe you need some fly-away pills?"

"What are you talking about?" She laughed.

"I could give you some pills that every time everything was going wrong and you wanted to get all the way away, you just take one, and you're away, even if you're just sitting in your bedroom."

"Drugs?" she asked uneasily.

"Look, didn't you ever wish you could stay awake and study a couple more hours, and enjoy your studying, get like high on work?"

Andrea nodded. "Sure. A girl in our class has a brother who gets her amphetamine pills at exam time. She gave me one. It was just like you say. My work suddenly became a gas." She frowned. "And then I was back, studying in my room, my brother asleep in the next bed. It's terrible not to have your own room."

The cocktails arrived and Andrea sipped hers very slowly. Tony's interest was aroused anew. Maybe somehow he could get close to some action around the Ascot Hotel chain if he worked things right. Anyway, this girl might have friends who could afford what he had to offer.

"Shall I order for both of us?" Tony asked.

"Please. I don't know much about Italian food."

Tony ordered and then repeated his suggestion made at the Cianos' that they might meet in Italy next summer. She really is a warm chick, he thought. Real class. Maybe more than Elda had. But then Tony didn't really like Italian girls.

Andrea enjoyed her Italian dinner tremendously, and although she only drank half her cocktail, the Chianti wine disappeared as fast as it was poured into her glass.

When the dinner plates had been cleared, Tony said, "I see you don't smoke. Did you ever try grass?"

"Not really," Andrea replied after a pause. "Some of the girls at school tried it this year. The girl I told you about got some from her brother and we all had a few drags. It didn't do anything for me except make my mouth taste funny."

"Probably you didn't take it right."

"Maybe so."

"Did the other girls like it?"

"They said they did."

"Would you like to try some?"

"What? Right here?"

Tony laughed. "Of course not. But some friends are having a party downtown. They've got some real good grass, Acapulco gold, just in from Mexico."

"Do you smoke marijuana?" Andrea asked curiously.

"Sometimes. I can take it or leave it. But if the company is good, it's kind of nice. Makes you really dig music, and paintings and each other."

"I guess I've led too sheltered an existence. I never had any LSD, or speed, or pot, or, or anything. I know girls of seventeen, even sixteen and fifteen who take some of these things."

"You should give it a go, grass, that is. Acid is good but you have to have lots of time, like you don't have to be anywhere for a whole night."

"No way." Andrea laughed.

"Do you want to go down to this party? They're all nice people. You can try a joint if you want to or just groove. They have great music. Everybody just sits on the floor."

"I'd have to call Mama. What would I tell her?"

"Tell her those older friends of my family want us to go to a movie with them."

"I forgot all about those friends." Andrea giggled.

Tony waved to the waiter for the check as Andrea stood up and went to the telephone.

In Tony's sports car convertible, driving downtown, Andrea leaned against him. His right hand strayed from the wheel and rested on the top of her thigh. Andrea put her hand over his and his fingers massaged her, walking upward. She was very attracted to Tony and wanted to see more of him. She enjoyed a delicious sense of freedom in the open car and the pressure of his fingers excited her. She knew it was wrong. She also knew that she was practically a retarded child. Girls her age were having affairs, traveling free of their parents, and she always had to be right where her mother could find her. Especially since Brad was in town. Andrea laughed aloud.

Tony shot a questioning look at her. "Let me in on the joke."

"I was just thinking that in the two or three weeks my father has been back, Mama is stricter with me than ever. She's always afraid I'm going to see him or be with him without her knowing it." She laughed again. "You and I could be in bed together, and if Brad were someplace where she could actually see him, she wouldn't worry about me at all."

"Let's work out a deal with your old man." Tony leered at her.

"He's not so old. And you took what I said the wrong way."

Go slow, Tony, he warned himself. This one is worth time. And you were ready to blow it, you dumb ginzo.

Tony pulled up in front of a brick apartment building on West Tenth Street. "Here we are," he announced. "If you decide you don't like the scene, we'll split. But give it a shake. OK?"

"OK, Tony. Are you going to leave your car under that 'No Parking' sign?"

"Sure. No cop's going to waste his time writing out a ticket. Even if he does—hell, I've got twenty, thirty of them. When it gets too bad, we have a guy in my father's company who goes and fixes them."

They walked into the dark entranceway of the apartment house, and Tony pressed a button without even looking at the name cards.

"You've been here before," Andrea said.

"Of course. This is where it's at weekends. Old buddy of mine lives here. He's going to college down-

town. His old man stakes him to the pad to keep him
from bothering them at home."

"That sounds kind of desperate."

"Wait'll you see the crowd."

The buzzer squawked and Tony pushed the door
open. Holding her hand they walked up three flights
of stairs. A door opened a crack and then was thrown
open. "Tony!" a young man's voice cried. "Come in.
You brought a bird. A beautiful one."

Andrea was suddenly in an apartment dimly lit with
red and yellow and green and blue light bulbs. As her
eyes became used to the multihued gloom she saw well-
dressed girls and boys, who looked to be about her
age, sitting or sprawled on the floor, the one sofa and
the few chairs. She was surprised not to see even one
hippie type. They all looked like college kids to her.
There was no mistaking the musky odor of the hand-
rolled cigarettes they were passing around, first one,
then another taking a deep draw.

"Hi, honey," a droopy-eyed, long-haired blond girl
said and offered Andrea the remnants of a cigarette.
"It's only a roach but there's one more good pull left."

"No, thanks," Andrea said. "Maybe later."

The blond girl wandered off. Tony led Andrea
around the room and introduced her to several young
men and women she thought quite attractive. To her it
seemed an orderly party. Everyone was quietly listening
to the persistent beat of the rock music or staring off at
a wall. Several couples were embracing, kissing and intimately stroking each other. "Shall we try a joint together?" he suggested. Andrea shrugged. It seemed to
be the thing to do. Tony led her from the living room
to a smaller adjoining room. The reek of musty smoke
was heavy. A couple, half dressed, were actually doing
what Andrea instinctively knew must be absolute sexual intercourse. They moved together languidly. She
watched as the girl passed a sloppy-looking cigarette
butt to the boy on top of her and he took a long drag
and then held it to her lips. She drew in, lazily un-
dulating her hips under the boy whose belt was well
below bare buttocks.

"Oh, Tony, let's split."

"Come on, baby. One joint won't hurt either of us. There's another room."

"Well, if we're going to smoke let's go in where everyone else is," Andrea said insistently.

"Sure. Why not." They went back to the weird lighting of the living room and sat on the floor, their backs against the wall. Everybody was talking to them now and when they heard that Andrea wasn't a pot smoker, joints were produced from all corners of the room.

Tony grinned in satisfaction. "Nothing like bringing a beautiful girl who's never smoked grass to get a free joint."

"I'm glad I could be of some use." Andrea giggled. A bunchy-looking hand-rolled cigarette was placed in her hand. Tony took it, lit it and taking a deep pull on it, holding the smoke deep down in his lungs, handed it to Andrea. She held it in front of her looking at it.

Letting the smoke trickle out of his mouth, Tony said hoarsely, "Just breathe in deeply, right through the joint, baby."

Everyone was watching, laughing and encouraging her. But it was Tony she wanted to impress. If he thought she was a square he wouldn't want to see her again. She looked at him, his eyes upon her, smiling. "Come on, nothing to it." She couldn't let his friends think that Tony was with some child. Andrea lifted the cigarette to her lips and sucked in the smoke, and then drew it down into her lungs.

"That's my girl. Now hold it as long as you can down there." To emphasize his instructions, Tony placed a hand over her mouth so she couldn't exhale the smoke. The smoke was hot and she began to panic. She pulled Tony's hand from her mouth and expelled the smoke. Neither the taste in her mouth nor the tickling sensation in her throat was pleasant. She handed the butt back to Tony. "Takes a while to get the hang of it," he said understandingly.

Already the smoke that had reached her lungs and what she was breathing in the heavy air of the room made her dizzy and her head swirl. "Oh, Tony, I feel so funny." She wanted to ask him to take her home but that would have marked her forever in his eyes as a spoilsport.

He handed her back the joint after taking a long pull from it. "Take another drag, Andrea," he urged.

"Yeah, Andrea. Come on. A couple more and you'll be up there," the others in the room chorused.

Andrea tried to smile and then put the butt to her lips and inhaled deeply, directly through the cigarette. "Hold it down there as long as you can, baby," Tony said, taking the nearly burned-out cigarette from her and puffing the last of the weed himself. Now Andrea felt as though her head was a balloon lifting her off the floor. And she suddenly wasn't concerned about her mother waiting for her. Actually, she realized for the first time that she was always worried about her mother waiting at home and what her mother would say to her when she returned. Now she didn't care. Tony, watching her closely, said approvingly, "Hey, there you go." He looked around the room. "Who's got another joint?"

"When are you getting some more of that Jamaican grass in, Tony?" someone called. Andrea stared at Tony. Was he some sort of a pusher? she wondered absently. Another lighted joint was in Tony's fingers. He took a drag and handed it to her. She took it and inhaled and then closed her eyes, leaning back against the wall. "Come on, baby, let's go back and do this privately." He took the butt from her.

She allowed herself to be pulled to a standing position and led from the room. So this was what a high meant. She giggled. "Tony, I think someone's using the bedroom."

"There's another one."

"What are you going to do?" she asked.

"Nothing. I just thought we'd be alone a few minutes."

In the dark back room, which seemed to be empty, they sat down on the bed and Tony held out to her the smoldering joint. She shook her head. "I'm floating as it is." He took a drag and handed it to her insistently. He watched the red tip burn down close to her fingers as she drew the smoke in and handed it back to him. "Hey, you're great, baby. I'd never believe it was the first time."

Her giggles became uncontrollable now. "First time, not counting the time Alicia and her brother and I tried it, but I didn't inhale."

"You like the high?"

"Yes. No problems. I couldn't care about anything."

Tony took a last drag and stubbed the finished butt out. Then, reaching for Andrea with both hands, he fell back on the bed pulling her with him. He put one hand on the inside of her thigh, the other was under her back and she felt his fingers at the side of her breast.

"Can't we just relax and do nothing, Tony?" she asked. "Let's just relax and not worry."

His hand went further up the inside of her thigh. "Hey, Tony," she sang. "No more. I'm not ready for that. Can't we just have fun?"

Tony's hand continued up and his fingers crept under her panties and then stopped, making contact with the sanitary napkin. "I told you, Tony." She laughed mockingly.

Disappointed and frustrated, Tony took his hand away and lay beside her a moment and then sat up. "We'll have other chances, baby."

"Not until we're married," she heard herself say. The words shocked her as much as they did him and she sat up too. The effects of the marijuana began to recede. She realized how closely she had come to letting the one thing she had vowed would never happen to her occur. "Hey, I'd better get home pretty soon or Mama won't let me go out again with you. Or with anyone else."

"OK, baby." They stood up and as they reached the doorway to the hall another couple slipped by them.

"We thought you'd never get through." The girl giggled.

Out in the main room there were disappointed protests when Tony announced he had to get Cinderella home. "Come back, Tony," a girl called out as they left the apartment.

Out in the cool night air Andrea breathed deeply. Tony helped her into the car, closed her door and then went around to the driver's seat. Saying nothing he drove off in the car and was cruising up Eighth Avenue when Andrea turned in her seat.

"Tony? I'll bet you are going back to that party."

"Maybe."

"And you'll start with one of those girls where we left off."

Tony grinned. "No. For something as special as you I'll wait."

She wanted to see him again and again. Something hard and masculine, yes and mean, about him fascinated her. She had never met any man like him, but where would she? She was determined that the first time she went to bed with a man it would be after they were married, but she knew it would be corny to tell this to Tony. She wondered if he would keep taking her out after he realized she would not go all the way.

Tony reached into a pocket and brought out a stick of gum. "Chew on this. It'll take the smoke smell off your breath."

Ten minutes later, in front of her apartment building, he saw her inside. He watched as she entered the elevator and waved and smiled. Then he turned back to his car and started downtown again. This girl had really gotten his juices flowing. He had to have something tonight, even if he paid for it. The pot party was his best bet. Besides, they were all good customers and potentials for when he moved into the hard stuff where the money really was.

CHAPTER TWENTY

Christa leaned on Jorge's shoulder as he sped along the winding highway, the azure blue Mediterranean to their left, the mountains on their right. The wind blew the blond hair casually out behind her. "What a beautiful three days, darling. I wish we could have stayed longer."

"My duties call," Jorge replied. "Besides, my darling, the Riviera, the beaches, the restaurants, the sun, our little inns, they all seemed to arouse your passions and make you so consistently and deliciously demanding that I don't think my body could have supported life many more days."

Christa laughed happily. "Jorge, you are fantastic. I never get enough of you."

They passed a sign saying Marseilles 50 KM. "Well, we'll soon be there," Jorge said.

Half an hour later Jorge was maneuvering the little sports car through the winding streets of Marseilles. "How do you ever find your way around this horrible city?" Christa asked.

"I've been here once or twice. And I studied the city map carefully. You know most people drive right into a city and hope to find their way around without even bothering to study a street map for fifteen minutes first. Now, the garage should be ahead."

He rounded a curve and drove into a modern-looking

garage and gasoline station. "All right, my sweetheart, here is where we change cars."

"I like this one." Christa pouted.

"But they want us to drive a Paris car from here to Orly Airport. Remember? We promised when we took out the MG."

"I hope it's a good car."

"It will be."

It was twelve noon when Jorge and Christa transferred their two light suitcases from the MG convertible to the heavy Mercedes sedan. They put them in the back seat. A garage attendant opened the trunk for Jorge's inspection. He reached inside and pulled at two sturdy leather suitcases. On each suitcase was sprinkled a generous amount of travel and hotel stickers. The Latin diplomat nodded and the trunk was closed.

"We will have one more night in France. We find a nice inn about two thirds of the way to Paris and then tomorrow we have plenty of time to make our twelve noon plane to New York."

Jorge was pleased with himself and the world as he tooled along the highway toward Paris. Christa's hand lay languidly on his thigh and every so often she affectionately leaned against him and kissed his neck or cheek.

What good was life if you could not enjoy it completely, Jorge thought. Of course this took money but that was a plentiful commodity if you knew where to look for it. If, as he had been told to assume, he had been under surveillance every moment from the time he and Christa left his apartment in New York to this moment, he had made not one suspicious move. The trip had a point to it, the committee meetings in Geneva. There was no reason why he should not have visited the bank in Zurich where he kept a special account. And after the Geneva and Paris meetings there was certainly no reason why he would not take his beautiful secretary for a three-day tour of the Riviera. Perhaps eyebrows would be raised, mostly in jealousy, but certainly not the hint of any wrongdoing could have been raised. Who could suspect anything because he and Christa flew to Marseilles to rent a car for the Riviera visit? And, of course, it is cheaper to drive a Paris car back, rather than keep a Marseilles car and pay the intercity exchange rate. And why wouldn't he want to drive back through the vineyard country of France to the airport?

Twice they stopped at vineyards, were graciously received, tasted samples of the wines and drove on. They stopped for the night in Dijon, staying at the inn those two famous American authors Scott Fitzgerald and Ernest Hemingway had made famous as the scene of a prolonged revel.

The following morning Jorge and Christa combined all their essentials into the smallest of their two suitcases. The larger suitcase contained the clothes they would replace back in New York. It was an easy drive from Dijon to Orly Airport. At the car-rental service an attendant identified Jorge, took the two big suitcases from the trunk and the light one they had repacked, and carried them to the Air France counter. Three suitcases for the two of them, two big ones and the small one, could hardly be ostentatious. They simply left the big suitcase with most of their clothes in the car. All would be taken care of.

Ramirez was given full diplomatic courtesy at Air France. His suitcases weighed a total of sixty kilos, the precise amount allotted to two first-class passengers traveling together. They were checked onto the plane scheduled to leave at 1 P.M., and Jorge and Christa were ushered to the VIP lounge for a drink before departure time.

It was three in the afternoon when the Air France flight from Paris pulled up to the ramp at Kennedy Airport. Jorge and Christa were among the first to disembark. An Air France officer was waiting for them inside the terminal and they were escorted to the baggage ramp. Their three suitcases were the first off the plane and their Air France escort put them on a cart and pushed them through the diplomatic office where Jorge and Christa showed their diplomatic passports and were politely waved through. Outside, on the street, a limousine with diplomatic plates pulled up to the curb where they were standing. The driver got out of the car and put the two heavy suitcases in the trunk. Jorge carried the light suitcase they had packed that morning in Dijon and slipped it in the back seat of the limo with Christa and himself.

Forty-five minutes later, just after 4 P.M., the limousine drove down into the garage of the Place d'Etoile apartments and stopped beside the elevator. Both Jorge and the driver looked back at the entranceway. No car had followed, no pedestrian was in sight. Jorge, carrying their one suitcase, and Christa entered the elevator. Jorge pushed the button for the sixteenth floor. The door closed and Jorge leaned against the side of the elevator.

"Tomorrow, my darling, you will go out and shop for whatever you want. Maurice D'Estang will be over for a cocktail at six."

CHAPTER TWENTY-ONE

Pat Kenney walked into Captain Reilly's office and threw the envelope on his desk. Reilly looked down and saw in the upper left-hand corner the name Representative Fred Black.

"What's he want, Pat?" the captain asked.

"He says he wants to see me at his office this afternoon. Think I should go?"

"I guess you should. Wonder what it's all about."

"Ah, some nigger probably complained about police brutality. I guess I'm the first cop out here won't take any shit from these animals."

"I'm behind you all the way, Pat. We don't have to take any abuse from some congressman looking for votes in an election year either."

"Thanks, Captain. I'll drop by Bailey's and then see what the hell Fred Black wants."

"I'll wait here until you call me after you've seen him."

Pat Kenney dropped by Bailey's and after fortifying himself with a hot pastrami sandwich and three rye and gingers he went out to his car and drove over to the other end of Bedford-Stuyvesant where Representative Black's office was located. He arrived in a combative mood. The first thing that slowed him down was the congressman's sloe-eyed, bosomy receptionist. An

Italian girl. Looked like she'd make a nice evening. Maybe Black would keep him waiting.

Kenney identified himself and the girl buzzed the office and announced the visitor. "You can go right in, Mr. Kenney," she said with a smile.

"Yeah? Then I'll see you when I come out. You live around here?"

"Not in your precinct, thank God, Detective Kenney." She gave him a hostile look.

"You should get to know me when I'm not working. I'm really adorable, they say."

"Representative Black is waiting for you."

Kenney pushed open the door into Black's private office.

"Come in, Detective Kenney," Black said affably, standing up and coming around his desk. "By God, you look just like your pictures. A pleasure to meet you." Black strode toward the burly redheaded detective, hand out. He shook the beefy paw, reached up and clapped a hand on the big man's shoulder and led him toward a chair.

"Glad to meet you, sir," Kenney said, taken aback. He became aware of another man seated.

"Detective Pat Kenney, meet Commissioner Colten." Colten stood up and the two men shook hands. "Dave Colten," Black explained, "is the mayor's commissioner of special projects. Let's all sit down and we'll tell you, Pat, if I may call you by your first name . . ."

"Sure. Everyone does," Kenney said, bewildered at the friendly course the meeting was taking. He sat down next to the commissioner.

"Pat, I've been working for a long time on one of the biggest problems, not only in my district out here, but all over the country. And you are one of the top experts on this problem. Narcotics."

"I just read that book about you," Commissioner Colten added. "A great story. That was some case."

"What we wanted to talk to you about, Pat, is this. I have started a congressional committee to investigate drug abuse, particularly as it concerns the big cities. We want to go all out and get to the bottom of the problem. Where the stuff comes from, how it gets into the hands of the wholesalers and then the retailers, how people become addicts, and who, what individuals are responsible for this national menace and disgrace."

"That's very interesting, sir," Kenney replied noncommittally. "I hope you get better results than the other committees always being started around the country."

"We think we can do a definitive job for one reason." Black paused, letting Kenney's suspense build. Then, "If Detective Pat Kenney served as the committee's special investigator our chances of success would be tremendous."

Pat Kenney sat back in his seat and blinked. Now he really was surprised. What the hell did this mean? "I'm a New York City cop," he said, as if this was some sort of an explanation.

"Of course, Pat. But the city is willing to assign you to our committee. Right, Dave?"

Dave Colten nodded. "Right. I checked it out with the mayor and he and I and the police commissioner had a meeting. You still stay on the city payroll, building up time against retirement and pension. What do you say, Pat?"

Realization sunk in. Instead of spending his last year out with the animals before he could retire on 75 per cent pension, Pat could serve on this committee. Anything was better than the streets of Bed-Stuy and maybe he could even do some real good. Get the death pushers of heroin at the top, the machine that brought the stuff in. Maybe even catch the smugglers right out at Kennedy International Airport. "This is kind of sudden," he managed to say.

"We've got to work fast on this problem, Pat," Black said. "You won't be out catching in slum precincts any more. You'll be investigating. You have the run of the city, go anywhere in the country, if you want to search out the source of the narcotics coming into America and particularly New York City. You can even hire a staff."

"My old partner for seven years in the Narcotics Bureau is working up in Harlem, doing the same thing I am here. How about him?"

"Hire him," Black agreed. "Get him off the streets of Harlem and into investigation work with you. Just remember, you report to only one man, me. It's my committee. Got it?"

"Yes, sir," Kenney said happily. "When do I say bye-bye to the eight-one precinct?"

"When you leave here. You're cleared to start with us tomorrow. Captain Reilly will be notified by the time you get back."

Kenney could hardly restrain his exuberance. "What about any clerical or secretarial help?"

"You can use this office. You met Rose on the way in?" Kenney nodded, restraining the grin spreading across his face. "She'll help you until we get you organized. Your paycheck will be sent to you at this office. Expenses will be reimbursed weekly. Any large amounts of cash you have to spend for narcotics buys, air tickets, special entertaining, temporary help or the like will be advanced to you here."

Black stood up and thrust out his hand. "It's your ball game, Pat. The committee will be counting on you."

"Yes, sir!" Kenney took the small hand and shook it gently. "See you tomorrow."

"I will probably be in Washington for some special hearings. You just carry on as you see fit. So long, Pat."

Black walked to the door with the detective and ushered him into the outer office. "Mr. Kenney will be with us, now, Rose," he said to his startled secretary-receptionist. "Help him in every way you can."

Back in his office Black turned on a transistor radio medium high as he and Dave Colten burst out laughing for several moments.

"Goddamn, that C.L. is a genius." Colten chuckled.

Black nodded. "He gets Kenney off the streets and Kenney's partner too. And if anything at all is slipping up in the system, the great Detective Kenney will come across it and we'll be the first to know. Anything else to tell me, Dave?"

The commissioner shook his head. "C.L. says to be super careful no matter how secure we think we are," Black said as he turned off the transistor radio.

CHAPTER TWENTY-TWO

The crisp, clear late November weather added to the excitement, although Brad Kendall was playing the scene as a routine event in a corporation president's schedule. Nevertheless, the imminent acceptance of the Gulfstream executive jet was as keen a thrill as he had ever experienced in his business career.

Even the imperturbable Maurice D'Estang showed signs of excitement as the Ascot limousine turned in to the Lincoln Tunnel heading for Newark Airport. Luciana, seated between Brad and Maurice, didn't even try to hide the excitement she felt at the prospect of making the maiden flight on the company jet. The only truly unmoved occupant of the car besides Williams, the driver, was Harry Hirsch, the new traffic manager for Ascot Hotels. Harry would probably never fly in a company jet, or be driven about New York City in a company car or fly to another city and find a company-leased car waiting for him. Yet it was Harry's job to assign transportation to Ascot and Whitehall executives all over the world.

Harry Hirsch took a notebook from his pocket as they approached the New Jersey end of the bridge. He had been in this job just a few weeks and wanted to make no mistakes. It was the best-paying traffic position he had ever held in a long career as both a corporate and a government executive travel dispatcher.

"In Miami," he said, consulting his notes, "the plane will take Perez, Calderone and Thompson to the Dominican Republic, Puerto Rico and St. Croix in the Virgin Islands, respectively, after your meetings with them, Mr. Kendall."

"That's right, Harry. I'll brief them on Ascot's willingness to invest with their governments in hotel development and we'll send them home in style."

"By the time the jet returns to Miami the next day you will be ready to go on to New Orleans and then back to New York."

"I hope so, Harry." Brad frowned to himself. "Of course, the opposition in Miami may not be as pliant as Mr. Ciano thinks."

"Mr. Ciano said that he will need the jet next Tuesday for Congressman Jamison."

"Correct, Harry," Brad said crisply. "I will be accompanying Jamison for a few days of meeting the New Hampshire primary voters."

Twenty-five minutes after the limousine entered the tunnel it reached Newark Airport and cruised down the row of hangars until Hirsch, keeping watch, announced that the next hangar was theirs. Williams turned left and drove them along beside the hangar out onto the ramp. Luciana cried out in pleasure as they saw the sleek Gulfstream twin jet executive aircraft with the Ascot Hotels logotype smartly painted on the fuselage. With no stockholders to account to for corporate expenses, C. L. Ciano had ordered the Ascot identification to be boldly displayed. Few executive planes bore the name of the owner corporation.

The pilot and co-pilot, in crisp powder-blue uniforms and gold-braided bill caps, stood erectly in front of the steps leading up to the passenger door. The limousine stopped and the pilots came forward. Williams opened the rear door and the Ascot executives stepped out on the ramp.

As they started toward the plane a short, round, softlooking man with the barest fringe of light hair around his dome-shaped head stepped down from the front entrance to the jet. He peered out at them through glasses thick as the bottom of a Coke bottle and protectively clutched the black satchel he was carrying.

The meeting was obviously not intended to occur, Brad surmised, as Maurice stared at the man a moment in surprise and then walked up to meet him.

"Everything in good working condition?" he asked.

The pudgy man nodded, saying nothing. Maurice turned to the others. "This is Julius. He does a lot of special instrument work." With that he hustled Julius away from the others and into the limousine. Luciana looked after Julius questioningly and D'Estang came back to her, a businesslike smile on his face.

"Julius checked some of the instruments out for us. Mr. Ciano trusts him more than any other electronics expert and wanted him to have a look at our new plane's instrumentation. Now, let's go aboard her."

Brad and Luciana looked at each other, smiled, shrugged and followed D'Estang to the plane.

Harry Hirsch, who had hired the pilots, made the introductions and while the co-pilot and Williams loaded the suitcases, Maurice led the inspection of the plane. "Now that is probably the sleekest-looking sight I've ever seen in my life," he exclaimed as he stepped into the cabin. The interior was fitted with a long sofa which, the pilot explained, could pull out to double its width and make a bed. There were large swivel seats arranged around a table on which was a telephone and a console which showed the readings of the plane's principal instruments.

Altogether the plane seated eleven passengers. "There's a head to the rear," the pilot pointed out. "A toilet," he added, seeing Luciana's puzzled expression. "You can telephone anyplace in the world, most of the time," the pilot went on "There's also a teletype you can hook into the wire services or contact with the Whitehall communications center. There's even television, though at the speed we travel you can't keep any one station too long."

"Beautiful, she's got to be the sweetest bird in the

world," D'Estang murmured. "Wait'll our campaigning political friends have a week in this job."

"There'll be another just like it delivered in two months," Harry Hirsch said without any particular enthusiasm in his tone. Then, a note of pride in his voice, "This one was supposed to be delivered to another corporation but, due to some connections I had, I was able to intercept it."

"It is the most beautiful airplane, the most beautiful anything that moves that I have ever seen," Luciana echoed.

"Is everything cleared for Miami, Chuck?" Harry Hirsch asked the pilot.

"Yes, Mr. Hirsch. She'll go anyplace in the world you want to send her."

"Miami and the Greater Antilles will do for this trip. You have the schedule."

The pilot nodded. Maurice D'Estang stepped out of the plane almost reluctantly. "I envy you, Brad. Have a good trip. And come back with the Tropic Plaza Hotel."

"I'll try, Maurice." Brad was learning, out of necessity, to get along with D'Estang and found it wasn't too difficult as long as he bowed to the fact that Maurice was the true link, so far, between Ascot and Whitehall. D'Estang walked over to the limousine and from the back seat took a neat, thin black attaché case with three heavy locks on it and went back to the plane.

"Here, Brad. Give it to Calderone, our banker in Puerto Rico." Brad took the case, shook hands with D'Estang and Hirsch, waved good-by to Williams and stepped inside. Luciana was sitting on one of the chairs. The pilot pulled up the steps and closed the door into which the steps nestled. He turned the long handle that bolted the door securely shut and turned to Brad, who took the swivel seat beside Luciana, both facing front. "One thing I forgot to point out, Mr. Kendall. That cabinet is a well-equipped bar in case you want anything. We estimate two and a half hours' flying time to Miami." He looked at his watch. "We're right on schedule. A car will meet you at our private ramp at

Miami Airport." He walked up to join the co-pilot in the forward cabin, turning in the doorway to the flight deck. "You can lock this door from the inside. If anything comes up you should know I'll tell you over the intercom and if you want to make any calls, pick up the phone and the co-pilot will switch into the right frequency for you. Have a nice flight."

"Thanks, Chuck."

The bulkhead door closed and they were alone. They looked out the window and saw the limousine drive away from the ramp. Brad sat back, smiling across the table at Luciana.

The jet engines started up and soon the plane was rolling along toward the runway. Studying the console a few moments, Brad turned on the VHF receiver and they listened to their pilot talking to the air controller, getting takeoff instructions and instrument clearances.

"Buckle seat belts, please," the pilot's voice came over the intercom. "Ready for takeoff." Impulsively Luciana reached out and Brad took her hand in his as the jet started down the runway, gathering speed, suddenly leaping into the air and assuming a high angle of attack.

Ten minutes later, just as though they were on a commercial flight, they heard the captain say they could unbuckle seat belts, he would advise of any turbulence ahead. They continued to sit back comfortably, still marveling at the luxury and convenience of having a private jet plane to take them around the country, the world.

Finally Brad broke the contented silence. "Well, at last, for the first time in five days we have a chance to be alone together and talk. They've certainly been keeping you busy."

"You haven't exactly been sitting still, darling," Luciana retorted.

"No. It's been frantic. I wonder if it will always be this way."

"It's fun, exciting." Luciana's eyes sparkled.

"I'd be a lot more excited if I had more time with you." Brad looked in her eyes and then kissed her.

Her lips moved provocatively against his. "Damnit, I've missed you this week," he said after the kiss.

"But, darling, we've been in bed together every night."

"Sure, after you came home from entertaining D'Estang's VIPs. And I've had to be up every morning too early to wake you up and find out what's going on."

"The price we pay for success. But what we have had has been awfully good. At least I thought so."

"So did I, darling. I just—I love you."

"I love you too, Brad."

"What happened with the Texas congressman that C.L. is setting up?"

"He's really awfully nice. I enjoyed being with him. He was so sweet, and he wanted me so badly to stay with him Tuesday. When I finally made him leave me at my room, I felt so guilty going out again, straight to your bed and body."

"According to Maurice the rest of that night didn't go so badly for him. He had a beautiful brunette standing by for Jamison that looked almost like you. That bastard really is one of the world's slickest corrupters. You provide the class, the intellectual excitement and the sexual stimulant. Then another girl takes care of the sex."

"You make me feel like a Judas goat." Luciana pouted.

"You should feel proud of yourself. The guy has very high standards. He wouldn't have let himself get involved with the average girl. It took you to get him so stimulated that it impaired his judgment."

"Oh, Brad. Do we have to talk about it?"

"Do you think he has what it takes to be a serious contender for the presidency?" Brad's face became serious. "He's on the young side."

"He's the same age JFK was when he was running. And he is so handsome and virile-looking," Luciana added.

"Your type, eh?"

"You're my type and you know it, Brad. Seriously, if I was an American woman I think I'd vote for him."

"Well, it will be interesting to see how he does in the New Hampshire primaries. If he makes any kind of a showing against his own President he has a good chance of winning the Senate race next fall and, knowing C. L. Ciano's thinking, your friend Jamison won't be out of the public eye for long during the next four years."

"I think he can go all the way," Luciana declared.

"You should know," Brad remarked. "You have been his confidante, the beautiful companion who, he said at one of those parties, was his intellectual and cultural superior. You must have learned a great deal about him."

"He's gay, urbane, well traveled, extremely bright about foreign affairs; he knew more about Communist Party activities in Italy than I did, and he has a beautiful speaking voice. Women will love him and vote for him." Luciana gave Brad a mock fierce glare. "I'd have gone to bed with him and loved it if it hadn't been for you, you bastard. I was jealous of that other girl."

"That's why you were so active with me." Brad laughed. "Well, anyway, C.L. was delighted with the whole thing. And just think, when we go to Texas you can meet his wife and five kids, have dinner with them and have not the slightest feelings of guilt."

"I wouldn't anyway."

"Well, he would." They sat quietly for some time, looking out the window. Then he glanced at his watch. "Hey, the sun's over the yardarm. How about a drink?"

"I wonder if we have the makings of a screwdriver?" She laughed softly. "Remember? On our first flight together?"

Brad stood up. "OK, I'll be the steward, ma'am. One orange juice and vodka, and the steward will have a Bourbon and soda." The bar proved to be as well stocked as the pilot had said and Brad returned and put their drinks on the table in front of them.

"May this flight prove as fruitful as our last one together," he said picking up his glass and holding it to hers.

"I was so lucky to have you as a seatmate." She took a sip of her drink. "You were lucky too."

"I've got news. Now it can be told. I planned it that way. I watched you in the airport, I was right behind you in line so I could pick the seat next to you."

"Is that true?" Luciana was genuinely surprised.

"It sure is."

Luciana chuckled, pleased. They sipped their drinks silently a few minutes and then Luciana asked, "We've all been so busy I haven't had a chance to ask you about your daughter."

Brad shook his head. "I have only seen her once in the past week. She seems to be enjoying her last year at high school. Being a year older than the other girls she seems to want to be doing what college freshmen do. Of course her mother won't give her much freedom."

"That's probably just as well. I hope she isn't seeing that young Sicilian hood, what was his name?"

"Tony Falcon. I hope not, but far be it from me to interfere in her private life. You only make them more determined when you try to stop them."

"Is she any happier about living at home?"

"I doubt it. But Gwen gets to her in the most excruciating way. She makes Andrea feel guilty. Guilty about all she and that guy she's married to have done for her. By Gwen I'm a deserter who left them all in the lurch. Andrea never hears about how well I've taken care of her mother, stepfather and half brother."

Luciana leaned to him and put her hand on his thigh. "Don't worry about it, Brad. Don't let it upset you. I think Andrea knows how much you've done for them. Give her another year or two and see how she blossoms out. Once she gets away she'll be a new girl."

"If Gwen will let her go," Brad replied gloomily. "I've got to see more of her and I'll try to find out if she's getting together with Tony Falcon. It's just that there's so damn much to do. The hotels, my two dark horses to manage, Jamison and Adams, and now C.L. wants me to look into some new educational project he's interested in."

"That doesn't sound like Ciano's line," Luciana murmured.

"No. I thought the same thing. What this company does is distribute audio-visual training aids to colleges around the country. I think it specializes in community colleges which don't have any campus life. It brings in new audio-visual tapes each week and takes the old ones on to the next college."

"Very, very un-Whitehall-like."

"Well, ours not to reason why." He held up his glass to Luciana. "Ours just to do or die. Something like that." He finished his drink in a last gulp and put the glass in a holder attached to the armrest.

"Luciana?" The seriousness in his tone startled her. She turned to him, a worried look about her eyes. "I don't think I was right suggesting you come to work for Ascot. I didn't think you would have to play hostess for Maurice D'Estang. I had no idea that Ciano would so suddenly and drastically change the face of Ascot. You shouldn't have to be subjected to demands on your private life."

"But I don't mind, Brad. I rather enjoy it, the excitement. I'm happy with my job. This last week I lunched with three television producers and visited the woman's editor at the New York *Times* as a start toward publicizing the new look at the Ascot Hotel chain."

"That part is fine. It's the nighttime engagements that worry me."

"All part of the job. I love it."

"And I love you."

She reached for his hand. "I know you do, darling. And I love you."

"Let's get married, Luciana. You can still work at Ascot, but your entertaining would be done with your husband."

Luciana stared at him, her eyes wide in surprise. "Get married?"

"Yes, I mean it."

"Oh, Brad. That's the dearest, sweetest thing you could have said. But you don't want to get tied down now, just when your career is blasting off, so to speak."

"I'd be better if we were married, and I wouldn't be quite so worried about you when I was away."

"I think it's a lovely idea. When the pace slows a bit let's give it some thought."

"I've given it a lot of thought, especially this past week. Why should we wait? We're both free. We love each other. We want to be together. Why not soon? We could get married in Miami?"

"Oh, lovey, we can't just like that. I'd have to notify the whole family. Mother should at least have a chance to meet you before we announce anything."

"Don't you want to marry me, Luciana?"

"Of course, darling. But it's so complicated just now. Here I'm only just divorced and now we're talking about me getting married already. Let me catch my breath. Give me time to get the feel of life as an unmarried woman. Believe me, I'll appreciate marriage again much more if I've had a year on my own first."

Luciana looked at the woebegone expression on Brad's face. She threw her arms around his neck and kissed him. "I do love you, Brad. It's just—" she paused helplessly—"just give me time, my sweet. Try to understand." Still he remained silent. She put her hands on his face, one on each cheek and made him look at her. "OK?"

He smiled at her sadly. "OK, dearest. It's just I want you to be protected."

"I will be." A mischievous expression flitted across her face. She glanced at the other side of the cabin of the plane. "Do you suppose that really makes a bed?"

Brad's smile widened to a grin. "I don't know. Shall we find out?" They stood up and examined the brown leather sofa. Brad noticed a handle in the middle of the front of the sofa, close to the floor. He took hold of it and pulled.

"You did it, Brad!" Luciana clapped her hands as the seat pulled out into the aisle and what had been the back rest swung down to double the width. Luciana sat on the side of the sofa bed and bounced up and down a couple of times. Brad walked forward to the door between the flight deck and the cabin and slid the bolt. He took his suit coat off and threw it over the chair, taking off his tie and loosening his shirt. Luciana had discovered two pillows and put them at the forward end of the bed.

"So, darling, we christen the new plane properly." She laughed throatily. "I'm glad we are doing it, not some special person Maurice is working on." On his knees in front of her, Brad reached up under Luciana's skirt and catching the waistband of her pantyhose began to pull it downward.

"Let me, darling. I don't want anything to happen to them. I can't get at my suitcase." Smoothly she slid them down her legs and off and tossed them onto the chair. Then she unzipped and slithered out of her skirt, placing it on the table. She watched as Brad heeled off his loafers and stepped out of his trousers and underpants. He sat down beside her, his bare bottom on the cold leather. He hardly noticed it though as he tried to open her blouse. Laughing, Luciana pushed his hands away and undid her blouse herself and then reached behind to unhook the bra. "Now, darling," she whispered. "I never thought I would do this in an airplane, at least not in such comfort and luxury."

Brad lay down beside her and they kissed long and hard and then she guided him over her and they were together. They became conscious of the outside world again when the pilot's voice came over the speaker.

"We will encounter turbulence ahead. Please fasten your seat belts."

"What shall we do?" Luciana's eyes were wide.

"We sure as hell aren't going to stop now." Brad laughed. "We'll just hold onto each other and let the turbulence do the work."

"What a beautiful way," she agreed.

They were tightly joined when the plane hit the air currents and began to jolt them up and down. Luciana laughed as they jounced up and down together, kissing and holding each other tightly.

"I love this turbulence, darling. I love it," she cried.

After another ten minutes the pilot's voice came over once again. "We're out of the turbulence. It should be smooth going all the way into Miami. We'll land in one hour."

Half an hour later Brad and Luciana pulled apart for the third time. "Oh, Brad, that was delicious. What a sensation! We are better together every time."

"I love you, Luciana." His lips were against her ear. "I don't see how I can stand not being married to you much longer."

"You promised, darling. Give me time. Besides, we have each other anyway. Like crazy."

Brad rolled over, looked at the clock and the airspeed indicator, made some rapid calculations and asked, "Have you ever made love steadily for seven hundred miles?"

"No," she replied seriously. "But it was beautiful. Next time let's go for a thousand."

"You're on." Brad laughed.

"If I'm on, I want some turbulence to help, like you had."

"You are a hoyden." He stood up. "We have twenty minutes to get back to looking like two serious-minded executives."

"A lovely interlude. As soon as we get to Miami I will have to start working on the dinner tonight for our Latin friends."

"And I've got the Tropic Plaza problem to solve. But we shall prevail. You have made me an *hombre muy fuerte.*"

CHAPTER TWENTY-THREE

A Lincoln Continental convertible was waiting at the private aircraft terminal when they arrived on schedule at 3 P.M. Brad reminded the pilots that they were off until tomorrow morning at ten. Although it was all on the itinerary Harry Hirsch had given the pilots, Brad gave them the phone number of the Coco Bay Club where he would be staying, and after the suitcases had been put in the trunk of the car he drove off with Luciana, reveling in driving the powerful convertible himself.

It took about half an hour to reach the club out on the Seventy-ninth Street causeway between Miami and Miami Beach. The Coco Bay was the newest of a series of small luxury private clubs, far more intimate than the hotels on the beach. It was here that Luciana would be hostess to a party for the Latin-American bankers, businessmen and government officials with whom Ascot was negotiating to jointly finance hotels that Ascot would manage. After they had checked into their adjoining rooms Brad left her to visit Bob Heller, vice president and general manager of the Tropic Plaza Hotel.

It was a twenty-five-minute drive to downtown Miami and across the Brickle Avenue bridge to the hotel. He drove up the broad entranceway to the front door, before which a few pickets listlessly wandered, carrying signs proclaiming the Hotel Workers Union was on strike against unfair practices by the management of the hotel. Parking the car he walked into the deserted lobby. It was palatial in its dimensions, huge two-story-high plate-glass windows affording a view of Biscayne Bay. The elevators were shut down so he found the staircase and walked up the flight of stairs to the second-floor offices of the manager and his staff. There was not even a secretary in the area and he wandered between desks to the back office of Bob Heller. Heller was on the phone but he hung up when Brad entered. He neither stood nor offered to shake hands when Brad entered. He merely gestured at a seat across from his desk.

"Looks rough," Brad commented uneasily.

"Remind you of anything?" Heller asked curtly. "Like when Leighton had to sell out Ascot to your friends, the Whitehall mob?"

Brad ignored the statement. "I've been through strikes before," he replied.

"Not even supervisory personnel dare come in. Ever see, actually see, your top assistant get his leg broken by some hood swinging a baseball bat?"

Brad shook his head. "Did that happen?"

"Did that happen?" Heller mimicked. "Even my secretary isn't coming in. Of course, I'm sure you'll settle this strike ten minutes after Ascot takes over the place."

"I don't appreciate the implications you're making," Brad said dryly. "I came here to make a deal."

"I was always in favor of selling this hotel to Ascot and getting my own money out at a profit. Now we have to sell and I hate to see you get it. I'm sure you'll be able to settle the lawsuits arising over the food-poisoning incident three weeks ago when our chef was drugged. I'm sure you'll be able to negotiate with Wisenmann who is suddenly foreclosing on the mortgages he had assured us from the beginning would be renewed. I'm sure you'll be able to fix all the little nuisances that suddenly hit us after I told you I'd like to see us sell out, but Morrie Unger didn't want to let go."

"Morrie Unger had promised to sell out to Ascot two years ago when Leighton, already overextended, bought out the bondholders who were giving you a hard time. And then Morrie welshed." Brad stared across the desk at his one-time friend. "Unger helped get Ascot into the problems that ended with Leighton having to sell."

Heller held up a hand. "Brad, I'm ready to sell out our equity this minute. And I think Unger is ready too. Why don't you go up and see him? Don't expect him to be friendly. You guys play pretty rough. But I think he knows he's licked." There was a moment of silence. Then, "Hey, how come you"—he paused— "what's the expression? Got mobbed up so fast? This isn't the way a former American Hotel Association president does business?"

Brad stood up and leaned forward over Heller's desk. "Look, Bob, I've let your innuendoes go by up to now but I don't need to hear any more of this shit. Just because I work for a powerful-enough company to force Morrie Unger into keeping his word doesn't mean we're mob connected. If there was anyone who operated in that area it was your partner, Unger."

Heller jumped to his feet, facing Brad. "Either you're a great actor or you really don't think you are Brad Kendall, pride and front man of the syndicate. If you don't know who's using you, if you don't know what Whitehall is, I can tell you you're the only innkeeper in America who doesn't know."

"You don't know what you're talking about," Brad protested.

"No? You spent the last three years outside the United States and joined Whitehall two days after you got back. So maybe you don't know what it's all about."

Brad started to interrupt but Heller held up his hand. "No, wait. Hear me out. For your own good. Drop in on the Association sometime. Watch how they treat you. Respect? Sure. But respect born of fear. They figure they cross you or Whitehall and it's concrete kimonos for them. You are big-time organized crime and every man in the hotel game knows it. So why don't you wise up? Stop trying to kid us. Like I said, if it's yourself you're kidding I feel pretty damned sorry for you."

In a quiet voice Brad replied, "Why don't you just call Unger and tell him I'm here in Miami. If he's ready to make the deal let's do it."

"Go on over to the beach and see him. You know where his office is. He's there and waiting to see you." Heller smiled grimly. "For old times' sake, Brad, one word of advice. Miami is an open city. Whatever protection you have personally in New York doesn't go here. Just remember Morrie Unger doesn't take a licking lying down."

"A licking? We're paying him 20 per cent more for his equity than it's worth."

"Equity," Heller repeated in disgust. "He doesn't care about the money you're paying him half as much as he cared for the house. It was the big prestige point in all his little deals and rackets. Personally, it's a blessing to me. I don't like being that closely associated with a mob guy. I guess you think differently."

"Cut that stuff, Bob." The menace in Brad's tone even surprised himself. "Do we close tomorrow? Or the next day?"

"Depends upon how much more punishment Unger wants to take. I'm ready."

Brad Kendall drove across to lower Miami Beach in a thoughtful mood. The traffic was light and he pulled over to the side of the road after he had left the causeway. He suddenly realized, he finally admitted to himself, that yes, he was part of what was colloquially referred to as the mob. It was a shock to him. He wanted to have all the luxuries and advantages of what Ciano called the fifth estate yet still preserve his self-image as an honest, talented businessman. Shit. One way or the other he was connected with that penumbral organization which the newspapers called La Cosa Nostra or the Mafia. That meant he was liable to gangland-type extermination as the next hood. For a few minutes he sat literally trembling at the enormity of this final realization. It had taken Bob Heller to bring him face to face with himself. He looked at his watch. There wasn't much time if he was to meet Unger and be back at the Coco Bay Club to meet the Latins. Maybe he could put off the Unger meeting.

Hey, he said to himself, you're part of it all. If you're going to take the risks you'd better make use of whatever protection goes with the organization. Lie to anybody, everybody if you have to, but never, never lie to yourself. You're a fucking mobster, one way or the other. He reached for the mobile telephone and put through a call to the number D'Estang had made him memorize just in case he needed help fast locally. The mobile operator put the call through and he heard a voice say, "Mendes Market."

Brad pushed the transmit button with his middle finger.

"This is Kendall. I may need some help on the delivery to 75 Lincoln Place, Unger." He released the button.

"We sent a delivery truck out there a couple of hours ago. We also had one at the Tropic Plaza Hotel. We have one at the Coco Bay Club. Look around and you'll see one behind you now." There was a raucous laugh on the other end. "You must be a new driver." Brad looked in the rear-view window, saw the black sedan and slowly depressed the button.

"Yes."

He hung up the phone, started the car again and in ten minutes was parked on the curb near the entrance to Unger's office. Furtively looking around he was aware of the sedan he had seen just off the causeway slowly driving past him. Two men were in it. One was looking at him. He felt a sense of relief as he walked into the office building. He took an elevator to the third floor and walked down the hall to the offices of Unger Enterprises. There was no receptionist inside but a young man appeared.

"I think Mr. Unger is expecting me. I'm Bradford Kendall."

The stocky-looking young man nodded and motioned him to follow. He was led to a solid door. His escort opened it and pointed inside. Brad entered. He had met Morrie Unger a few years before when Rafe Leighton had first started negotiations on the purchase of the Tropic Plaza Hotel. Today, Unger's projecting underlip, heavy jowls and hooded eyes gave him an even more surly expression than he remembered. Unger didn't even bid him sit down.

"All right, Kendall." He stabbed the air with a forefinger, "I know why you're here. Yeah. We'll close tomorrow on the deal. Just remember one thing. You're way over your head in this game. Your boys know where my family lives. I know where your daughter lives. You want to play rough? OK. You're not some ordinary businessman any more. Don't forget it. Because I play rough, too."

"I came here to discuss business, not audition for a B movie," Brad replied. "Shall we review the deal so we both understand it before our lawyers finish it?"

Unger's growl might have been a laugh. "OK, play it your way. We don't have much to talk about. Yeah, we gotta deal. You take over the mortgages, a million three for the equity. The place is yours."

"Congratulations, Mr. Unger, you have sold a very thin equity for a very substantial price."

"Yeah? Well, you son of a bitch, get your substantial ass out of my office. I could of done this on the phone with Bob, but I wanted to see you again. And just remember, Miami is open territory. Win one, lose one. I got you down personal."

"We'll let the lawyers close in a less emotional atmosphere." Brad turned and walked out of the office. He found his way to the front door and into the corridor. At the elevator he rang, his eyes ranging the hallway for any sign of trouble. He noticed the exit sign over the door at the end of the hall. He heard no answering sound of grinding machinery to his signal and decided to walk down the stairs. As he approached the exit he heard a door open and close behind him and saw the stocky youngster accompanied by a much larger-looking hulk of a man wearing a sport shirt and slacks coming down the hall after him. He pushed through the door and began to descend the stairs. He heard running feet behind him and the two men burst through the door and began pursuing him.

Brad, gripping the rail, ran down the steps. He was almost at the first landing when another enforcer type pushed through the first-floor doorway to the stairs and started up them toward Brad. Looking behind him he saw that his pursuers were half a flight behind him. There was only one answer, get through the hood coming up at him. At least he had the advantage of gravity and height. He continued down the stairs, holding the rail with his left hand, his right hand, fingers outstretched and held together stiffly, was ready to inflict what damage he could. He rounded a landing and was almost on top of the grim-looking thug coming up to meet him. There was no possibility this was a casual visitor to the building eschewing the elevator to walk upstairs. The hood stopped, bracing himself against the rail, both hands held poised. With all his power Brad pushed off from the steps and sent himself hurtling by the stolid form in front of him. Two enormous hands on the ends of two thick, muscular arms grabbed at him, fingers digging into his biceps. Taking careful aim Brad shot his stiffened fingers at the big man's throat. But the lantern jaw was suddenly a solid connection with the barrel chest arresting the jab. Brad turned the plane of his hand upward and spread his fingers, as they stabbed toward the assailant's eyes. The tough jerked his head back to avoid taking the fingers and his grip loosened. Brad's momentum was such that he tore out of the strong grasp as he hurtled downward. He caromed off the wall and continued down the last flight of stairs, all three goons now after him. He reached the door to the lobby and burst through it. Outside through the glass door the sidewalk and street seemed deserted. Before he could reach the door he felt two hands grab him by the shoulders and spin him around. Instinctively, he ducked his head and threw himself at the floor as a pistonlike fist lashed out at him, driving through the air just above his face.

Brad heard, rather than saw, the street door slam open. Heavy footsteps pounded toward him. All he wondered now was how bad a beating Unger had decreed for him. Covering his face and leaning over to protect his stomach he heard a hard splat and then another above his head. He felt himself pushed roughly out of the way and when he looked up he saw four new men had appeared in the lobby, one of them already reducing the face of his antagonist to a bleeding unrecognizable mess.

"There are two more on the stairway," Brad cried out.

Immediately two of the four rushed through the door just in time to run headlong into the heavy-set, mustached youth and the other enforcer who had chased after him from Unger's office. Brad's rescuers savagely began beating the two. Brad saw a spiked brass-knuckled blow swing into the kneecap of the younger man who let out a shrill long scream as he collapsed to the floor. He continued to shriek in pain as the one who had wounded him shifted his attention to helping his companion batter the giant-sized enforcer. The punishment sickened Brad. There would surely be one less goon on Unger's staff. He went down, one leg bent at an impossible angle, blood poured from his mouth, and the bridge of his nose was crushed.

"Isn't that enough?" Brad cried.

The two turned to him wonderingly. "You shudda seen what yudda looked like, mister. Lucky we was here," one scarred and grizzled gladiator panted. "We got orders whadda do they tried something."

The other two brutes dragged the blubbering remains of the third Unger goon out of the main entrance to the office building and through the door into the stairway vestibule.

"I'm sure glad you guys showed up," Brad said gratefully.

"You was lucky," one of the stalwarts rasped. Then

to his men, "OK, let's finish the job and get oudda here."

"You're going to kill them?"

"Naw, that's too good for them, now." He turned to his men. "Let's go."

Two of them grabbed the feet of the giant-sized thug and started up the stairs, dragging him, his back and head bumping each step as they ascended. Unconscious, he moaned and blubbered. He had at least a broken leg, a broken arm, a crushed face and surely other injuries. The other two each grabbed the feet of their vanquished rival hoods and started up the stairs with them. The heavy youth with the broken kneecap regained consciousness. His screams of pain reverberated through the cement stairwell. Methodically, the goon hauling him upstairs dropped the feet, walked down five steps to the head of the shrieking wretch, and with one sharp kick of his pointed, metal-capped shoe to the temple silenced the victim. He plodded back up the stairs, took the feet and continued to drag the limp body after him.

"You go on wherever you want, mister. We'll take care of this. Our orders are to deliver Unger's boys back to him personal."

Brad needed no urging. "Thanks again, fellows," he said weakly. In a moment he was back on the street. He took the keys out of his pocket, climbed into the car and drove up Miami Beach to the Seventy-ninth Street causeway, turning westward toward Miami and the Coco Bay Club.

He was still too shocked at the brutality he had witnessed, at the punishment intended for himself, there was no telling how badly Unger had instructed his goons to injure him, and the fact that this sort of thing was now an integral part of his business affairs. So shaken was he that he drove by the entranceway to the Coco Bay Club and had to drive all the way over to Miami and turn around and head back out the causeway again toward the beach. This time he made the turn, drove up to the parking space outside his room, and still in a slight state of disconnection let himself into the room. The door between his and Luciana's room was closed. He was glad, he wasn't ready to talk to her just yet.

CHAPTER TWENTY-FOUR

Brad Kendall waited somberly in his office at the Spire Building for the call from C. L. Ciano. The convenience and luxury of having two executive offices, one at the Ascot Towers, the other right in the heart of the Whitehall associates complex, had considerably paled since his return from Miami.

He was still shaken by his experience there even though he had carried out his mission in Miami and in New Orleans. Until the scene with Unger and the hoods he had never squarely faced the fact of his involvement with organized crime.

It was one thing to be intellectually aware of what he had become and where the money he was using to expand Ascot originated, but it was something else to witness the brutal facts of life that obtained when one became "mobbed up." He was now a mobster, an Ivy League, WASP, Social Register gangster. This realization when it finally hit him with its full implications had so shocked him that he had been unable to come into the office his first day back from the southern trip.

How could he get out? Could he, in fact, get out? Did he really want to get out? Was Andrea safe from rival mob vengeance? This must be a circumstance that all of Ciano's high-level people faced twenty-four hours a day. Even C.L. must surely give thought to the safety of his daughter and wife.

Brad ran through a little speech he had prepared asking Ciano to allow him to resign peacefully. But did he know too much now? And then Luciana. She had taken the whole matter so calmly. After all, he had his hoods, didn't he, she pointed out. And the hoods Ciano provided were better than the others or he would have been badly beaten himself. All part of the game Luciana had argued lightheartedly and proceeded to thoroughly enjoy her own mission of entertaining and gleaning information from the Latin diplomats, businessmen and government people who had come to Miami to discuss hotel expansion in their respective countries with Brad.

Brad winced when the phone on his desk rang. He picked it up and heard his secretary tell him that Mr. Ciano was ready to see him. Almost in a trance he stood up, walked across his office and out the door to the hallway. He passed people but did not hear their greetings as he made his way to the bank of elevators. He pressed a button and waited for the car which would carry him up several stories to C. L. Ciano's floor.

On Ciano's floor, even though Brad was well known, the security guard escorted him through the two sets of sliding doors. Outside the door to Ciano's office Brad shook his head and, pulling himself together, entered into the presence not knowing what he would say or do.

Ciano was smiling genially when Brad walked into his office. "Congratulations on several jobs well performed," he said, walking toward Brad, holding out his hand. Brad shook it warily and followed the maximum boss to the conference area, sitting on the sofa. Ciano sat on a chair opposite him.

"Sorry about the unpleasantness with Unger," he said.

"The unpleasantness was all Unger's as it turned out," Brad replied, trying vainly to muster a smile. "Anyway, we closed the deal the next day."

Ciano chuckled. "I don't suppose the sight of his goon squad delivered back to his office in such damaged condition encouraged him or his lawyers to quibble."

The relish with which Ciano made the remark reminded Brad that despite all his polish and veneer of culture Ciano was still basically a mobster, albeit the top mobster in the country, if not the world.

"Luciana did a fine job with our Latin friends," Brad observed. "We'll have hotels going up all over the hemisphere."

"Yes. I think she should accept some of the invitations extended to her to visit in those countries we are particularly interested in. And for many reasons I would put St. Croix high on our priority list."

From the point of view of pure hotel operations and profits Brad didn't agree with Ciano, but he had learned that there were many important if obscure reasons for everything he did and the way things were going it was not his place to question the boss.

"We'll have the money to go ahead with the new hotel in New Orleans when the plans are completed," Ciano was saying as Brad tried to concentrate on the words. "You came up with a fine piece of land for it. Expensive, but that's why we were able to get it after all the other hotel companies decided they couldn't afford it."

Ciano laughed. He was in a good mood that day and appeared not to notice Brad's despondency. "Tell me, Brad, how did you like the way our banker in Puerto Rico came through with the million-dollar loan in one hour when you had to put up the money for that land?"

"It was quite impressive." Brad's tone was reserved. "I suppose that black attaché case I handed him at Miami Airport just before our jet returned him to Puerto Rico had something to do with his making the loan."

"You are learning fast, Brad." Ciano chuckled and then stopped, becoming aware of Brad's generally dour mood.

"Anything wrong, Brad?" he asked.

"No," he replied uncertainly. "Everything seems to be all right."

Ciano regarded the president of his hotel chain speculatively. He shifted in his seat and then stood up. He walked over to the mantelpiece above the interior decorator's fireplace and leaned on it, glancing up at the map of the world over the mantel.

"Brad, I sense you feel uncomfortable with us today."

Brad started to reply but Ciano held up a hand and then continued. "My concept here is not one that would be evolved by the traditional American businessman brought up in the American middle-class mold. I am a third generation Italian-American. Because of this and the point of view I inherited from my father before he died I went out into the world after receiving an excellent education thinking differently from most people.

"Many Italian boys dreamed of joining the Society of Honor, the Mafia if you will, and rising through the ranks up to *capo,* or boss. It was my dream when young to become President of the United States. Why not? I used to ask when they told me an Italian could never be elected President. Napoleon wasn't even French, I would argue, he was Corsican. Of course he used the army to become the emperor. As a boy I studied the life of Napoleon and read every book I could find on the subject. At the same time, as I grew older I became acquainted with the Honorable Society, many of its leaders and soldiers, or button men, as we used to call them. My father was *consigliere* to the *capo* of one of New York's five families. It was his desire that I go to college and then law school and not enter the Society but rather go into business. Even then, when I was going through Columbia Law School, just after World War II, my father foresaw the decline and fall of his Society. He knew that eventually law-enforcement agencies would not be so easily bought off and they would cripple the families through advanced methods of harassment.

"A legitimate business empire, built on the foundation of the money the families took in but would find more and more difficult to invest, was the way of the future, my father used to tell me.

"In the meantime, my political ambitions never abated. Today, I use the enormous sums of untaxable money generated by organized crime to achieve the power Napoleon derived from his army and WASP Presidents of the United States gain from compromising with politicians." Ciano fixed Brad with a near fanatical gleam in his eyes. "Whitehall is more powerful than any other business or political organization in the free world.

"And even though as an Italian I can never be elected President, as a powerful-enough businessman, with all the connections of the family enterprises and labor unions at my command, I could eventually own a President of the United States."

Ciano paused in his monologue and stared at Brad to see how he was reacting. As always the hypnotic quality of this boss of the boss of bosses, for that Brad realized is what Ciano was, held him in thrall, changed his reasoning process and made him forget the severe trepidations that disturbed him.

"Such a thing is impossible," Brad replied.

"It might seem that way to you, as a traditional upper middle-class businessman, but to me, a minority group member, so to speak, it is obvious that such a thing can and will happen. There has been a revolution, culminating in a dictatorship in every country the world has known. Do you think our country is going to be different?"

"I don't know," Brad replied.

"The reason I'm telling you all this, Brad, is that you have not really made up your mind, committed yourself to our power structure. When I have finished talking to you it will still be possible for you to walk out my door and go back to your old limited life style. But if you stay, as I hope you will, it will not be possible for you to change your mind at some future date. Do you understand me?"

Brad nodded. "Perfectly." He wanted to add, "Do

you mind if I leave now?" But he couldn't bring himself to say the words to the compelling man standing above him.

"Good. You see, Brad, you have an enormous opportunity to make your will and opinion felt in the four other estates of American life. If you stay with us you will find little by little what a pinnacle of power we are here in the Spire Building. We can tie up America with strikes if we so choose and at the same time we can settle them if it is advantageous to us. In five minutes I could stop the longshoremen's strike that has been tying up the docks of the West Coast for months. But why? It doesn't suit us to display power prematurely.

"When we control the United States we will solve most of its problems, but not through endless and usually fruitless debate by self-interested legislators. No. But in the manner of Alexander the Great. We cut the Gordian knot with a sword. This country, the big cities in particular, have become ungovernable by the old system. In almost two hundred years the basics of the Constitution have become obsolete. We have grown faster in two hundred years than any other country in the world has grown in its entire history."

Ciano paused, prowled about the office a few moments and then once again fixed Brad with his gleaming black eyes. "Can't you see that we are the forerunner of the new way of doing business and governing a great nation? In four years from the time we take over there will be no such thing as crime on the street. There will be no narcotics problem. There will be no need for welfare, which paralyzes the cities financially and feeds the petty criminals. We will not permit foreign entanglements which lead to sending men to war. Every citizen left in America," the phrase chilled yet strangely thrilled Brad, "will be a producing human being.

"And, Brad, the interesting thing about our methods of accomplishing these objectives is that the hard-working and achieving members of our society will hardly be aware that a revolution is going on. They will only realize that gradually our worst problems are withering away."

Ciano stopped talking as though to invite some response from Brad who was too overwhelmed to speak for several moments.

"It all sounds like Utopia, C.L.," he managed. "How are you going to do it?"

"The way it's always been done, with the backing of the military. Our man in the White House roots out all or most of the causes of dissent among the officers who make the military operate. He demands that the nation respect its military men from the top down to the recruit. We gain the loyalty and respect of men like General Alton MacFarland, the general you met at my home two months ago. With him firmly behind us in the position of chairman of the Joint Chiefs of Staff we rule America without regard to the shackling political problems which impede progress. In six months there will be no more narcotics problem in America. I know the source, routes and handlers of 90 per cent of all the narcotics that come into America. The government of the United States will never be able to stop this traffic as long as it has to go by the laws that hinder law enforcement. But we will pick up and execute every known narcotics trafficker from the importers down to the level of the pushers." Ciano smiled grimly. "Present company excepted, of course. This would all take me no more than two weeks.

"Do you know how mainland China cured its narcotics problem?" Ciano continued. "China had more addicts than all the rest of the world put together up to the nineteen thirties."

"I'm familiar with the China solution. The estimate is that Mao had over three million people shot out of hand."

"Numbers mean little. Do you think three million less dissidents, criminals, unemployables would hurt the United States? Not only that but it is not our plan to execute them. We will move them by the thousands to the great deserts and let them either make their new land bloom into something they can be proud of, thus rehabilitating them, or they can die."

Brad tried to fight the emotional appeal of Ciano's rhetoric which he knew was far more than mere rhetoric. Ciano would quickly and efficiently carry out his plan if given the chance. But Brad couldn't help becoming excited at the sheer grandiosity of this very plausible revolution, as Ciano saw it, to save America.

"What we get back to," Ciano went on, "is the American society of the eighteen hundreds where every man, woman and child had to achieve to survive. My methods will insure that a society based on class by achievement will endure in our country. Non-achievers and anti-achievers will be eliminated and a highly productive society will emerge. The concept of the labor unions to make their members work as little as possible for constantly increasing wages will also be eliminated. Crime itself will disappear.

"It's ironic, Brad. Using the power of crime to eventually destroy crime. But there is a precedent in this hemisphere for such an unlikely occurrence." Ciano walked back to the fireplace and pointed out a spot on the map of North America. "Captain Henry Morgan became such a powerful pirate that he was knighted by Charles II of England and elevated to the rank of Royal Governor of Jamaica. His first act was to hang all his former associates and he eliminated piracy from the British West Indies."

"But in the meantime Whitehall continues to aid and abet organized crime," Brad stated flatly.

"That is true, although on our level we don't consider ourselves criminals. We are a new type of businessman. Someday, if you elect to stay with us, I will go into the specifics of the programs we expect to put into being when we take over in 1976. A fitting year, the bicentennial of our nation, don't you think?"

"Yes, very fitting, C.L."

"Well, our work is cut out for us, Brad. The ideal situation is to do so well in the primaries in 1976 that our men are running against each other for the nomination at both conventions and in the election we own both the Republican and Democratic candidate."

"I think we can do it, C.L.," Brad enthused suddenly. "We should be able to build Jamison and Adams into top contenders. I assume that you have other likely candidates I don't even know about backed by other people on your staff I haven't met."

Ciano nodded and smiled. He walked over to where Brad was sitting and put a hand on his shoulder. "You've got the two best prospects, Brad. But yes, I have others including two who might even be elected in '72. That is if the President can be beaten. You watch the '72 primaries, you'll see who I mean."

"I hope you have the kind of insurance on our men that's still good four years from now," Brad remarked dryly.

"We do." Ciano paused and glanced quizzically at Brad. "I take if you aren't going out that door today."

Brad stood up and put his hand out. "You take it correctly, C.L. And you don't have to remind me what that means."

The two men shook hands firmly.

"Very well, Brad. We don't go in for oaths and mixing one another's blood. But at a certain time, and this is it, the end result is the same. You're with us now."

"Right," Brad replied—and knew with frightening certainty that he was committing himself for life.

"By the way, Brad, I've been thinking about our last conference," Ciano said thoughtfully. "You are perfectly right about wanting to know everything that's going on within your command. Everybody, including Maurice D'Estang, will report to you on all matters involving Ascot in any way."

"I appreciate that, C.L."

"But you must remember that Maurice and others have additional responsibilities beyond hotels, as you yourself will have when we start launching the political campaigns for our horses in the big race."

Brad nodded. He felt he couldn't take any more of

Ciano's plans just at the moment. He changed the subject. "By the way, C.L., you ought to take a trip in the new jet one of these days. She's a honey."

Ciano nodded. "That little bird and her sister ships are going to do a big job for us in the next few years."

The interoffice phone buzzed and a secretary's voice said, "Mr. Ciano, Mr. Steinert asked if you could come down to his office as soon as possible."

"Tell him I'll be right there," Ciano said in the direction of his desk. "OK, Brad. See you later. Give my best to Luciana. Maybe next Sunday we'll get together again. You have a good golf date scheduled?"

"I'm working through the list you sent me."

Brad left the office feeling relieved. For better or worse he had committed himself. How was it that Ciano manipulated his people, making them happy to do things his way?

CHAPTER TWENTY-FIVE

It was six o'clock when Brad Kendall finally left his office in the Spire Building and headed for the Ascot Towers Hotel where he had a seven o'clock engagement with Maurice D'Estang. Luciana was spending the night with her uncle out on Long Island so he would be alone. Had it not been for the altercation with Unger's thugs the southern trip would have been a dream. He and Luciana had even had a whole day together to lounge around the pool, make two trips back to the bedroom for love-making, and a whole evening to themselves. Then came the hectic, successful days in New Orleans. It surprised and worried him how much Luciana was on his mind. He had sent her out to Sands Point in the limousine and so was obliged to try to find a taxicab.

It was a raw, windy evening and no cabs were to be found so he started walking the fifteen blocks to the hotel. When he had only another five blocks to go he spotted the first empty cab. By now, cold and annoyed at all cabs, he decided to walk the rest of the way. You had to take a walk like this now and then to appreciate the luxury of a company limousine, he thought to himself.

Brad arrived at the hotel with just enough time to spare to shower and change. At 7 P.M. on the dot he was in the lobby cocktail lounge waiting for Maurice.

All the Whitehall people, Brad noticed, were ridiculously cautious about where and when they would talk frankly to each other. D'Estang wouldn't even converse, except on the most routine of matters, in his own office. He appeared in the doorway of the cocktail lounge, the ever-present cigarette dangling from his lips, looked around, saw Brad and came over to him, pulling out the chair opposite and sitting down. Instantly the headwaiter was at his elbow and they both ordered extra dry martinis with a lemon twist.

"Everything went well, I hear," D'Estang opened.

"C.L. is happy."

"Yeah. I just talked to him. I was glad to hear about the New Orleans deal. A big new luxury hotel there will help us a lot with our other action down that way."

They talked for a few minutes and then the martinis arrived. "Well, here's to you, Brad." Maurice lifted his glass. Brad did the same. They both took long, appreciative sips. Then Maurice put his glass down.

"C.L. told me that you should know everything that happens in the Ascot picture."

"I am supposed to be running the company. However, I would never ask you to elaborate on that, quote, other action, unquote, in New Orleans. But I have to know everything, no matter how trivial it might seem, about the hotel itself."

"C.L. wants me to show you what we did up on the twenty-eighth floor."

"I think I damn well should know if I'm responsible for this and all the hotels in the Ascot chain."

"Sure, Brad. I agree." He gave Brad a familiar smile. "C.L. says we can all talk frankly now." He took another long sip of his martini. "You know what my basic job with C.L. is, I guess."

"I figured it out. On a lower level, with the families, you'd be the corrupter."

D'Estang nodded slowly. "I get the important people working with us on the outside. People like state and federal judges, the commissioners we need, the Washington-elected crowd, all those. Right now, C.L. has me working on the United Nations people. As manager of this hotel I can do them all a lot of favors, that's why C.L. put me here. And when it comes to buying these guys to do special jobs for us, it's my job to see they stick with us."

"You take out your own brand of insurance." Brad grinned suggestively.

D'Estang smiled back broadly. "Yeah. That's the word. Now what we did on twenty-eight was to figure out another way to insure that our people stay with us. Finish your drink and I'll show you. I set up a party for Jorge Ramirez in one of the suites on twenty-eight. He's giving a party for his special friends and associates with diplomatic status at the United Nations. We are very interested in keeping Jorge and his associates in line. They're up there now."

Brad finished his martini. "All right, Maurice. Let's go see what you've put together up on twenty-eight."

D'Estang led Brad to the elevator bank. Eight automatic elevators serviced the guests with vertical transport. They stepped into a car and rode up. But instead of going to twenty-eight, Maurice pushed twenty-nine, a utility floor between the last story of bedrooms and the roof dining room and cocktail lounge.

"I thought we were going to look in on twenty-eight," Brad remarked.

"That's what we're going to do. You'll see."

Brad followed Maurice out of the elevator on the twenty-ninth floor. A large section of the floor comprised the kitchen for the Star Club above and the rest was used for storage and air-conditioning machinery for the top-floor luxury dining room and cocktail lounge. Brad did not often visit this floor, trusting the maintenance men to do their job without his supervision. The back-up manager Brad had hired for the hotel had complained to him, he remembered now, that the few times he had come up here he had been kept from visiting one section of the floor by special employees of Maurice D'Estang.

Arriving at a sliding door Maurice inserted a key in the lock and turned it, sliding the door back. Brad was stunned at what he saw inside. It looked as though he had wandered into the master control room of a television station. Silhouetted in the bluish lights that glowed from a bank of monitors he saw the bald, dome-shaped head of a man hunched over a control console. Suddenly he became aware of what he was seeing on the monitor tubes. Men and young women were clustered around in hotel rooms, the rooms of the suites on the twenty-eighth floor.

The man who was operating this array of electronic gear turned around as the door slid closed and in the flickering light of the television tubes Brad saw a vaguely familiar face. Where had he seen this gnomelike individual with the fringe of weak hair about his head, the thick petulant lips and the heavy glasses?

Maurice chuckled at Brad's puzzlement at the scene before him. "First, Brad, meet Julius the Genius. And, believe me, when it comes to electronic surveillance, Julius is a genius."

Now it came back to Brad. This was the man he had seen coming off the company jet the morning he and Luciana had flown to Florida. He felt a sinking feeling at the realization that the Genius had been working on the jet.

Maurice watched as Brad stared from Julius to the monitors and back to the pudgy technician. "You want to look into the twenty-eighth floor." He laughed. "That's what you're doing. Sometimes we call him," Maurice pointed at the man standing in front of the monitors, "Julius the Genius. From here we can see and hear everything that happens in the four suites on the twenty-eighth floor. That's the job that's been going on up here for the last two weeks. Nifty?"

Brad shook his head speechless. "I can't believe what I'm seeing," he finally said. "You know there are some fairly stringent laws against this sort of thing."

Now it was Maurice's turn to look surprised at Brad. "Law?" he bleated. "C.L. said you were with us now."

Suddenly the grim humor of the situation hit Brad. One of these days he had better realize what he had become. He began to laugh, bitterly at first and then with mirth. Maurice, staring at him, broke into laughter too. Julius stared at them and they ceased laughing as abruptly as they had started.

"Julius has hidden television cameras in the ceilings and walls of every room on this floor," Maurice explained. "We can even see into the bathrooms if we want to. Furthermore, he has two video tape machines to record what the cameras pick up." Until now the room had been silent but at a gesture from D'Estang Julius pressed a switch and they heard sound. The party in the living room of the main suite was getting under way.

"It seems to me, Maurice, that I've seen something like this before in the movies."

"An old-and-tried insurance firm is the best."

"It didn't faze James Bond, as I recall. And then there was the guy who ordered a dozen copies of each picture to send out to his friends."

"Perhaps. But this is one of the methods we have found most effective," D'Estang reiterated dryly. "You'll see some of the variations these girls employ."

"I've never really regarded sex as a spectator sport, Maurice."

"Nor I, my friend. This is purely an exigency."

"By the way," Brad interjected. "As I recall, you put that pride of Texas virility and virtue in Congress, Representative Ev Jamison, on the twenty-eighth floor."

D'Estang laughed. "Oh, yes. He christened this system."

"Where are people safe from surveillance?" Brad asked rhetorically.

"Practically nowhere." He grinned insolently, looking significantly at Julius. "Not even in private jet aircraft."

Brad flinched. He wondered whether or not he would tell Luciana. It might make her realize how completely depraved the character of the company he had just pledged his allegiance to really was.

"There is virtually nowhere you are safe from surveillance without taking the most thoroughgoing precautions." He gestured at Julius who had taken his seat again before the console. "Our own electronic experts

are better than those employed by the government as
you will see, but the FBI uses the best they can get.
That's why so many of our friends are in such trouble
now. When Whitehall was first founded Mr. Ciano provided for security against every type of surveillance
known or anticipated. That's why we're clean. And
why we'll stay clean." He put a hand on Brad's arm,
leering. "Hey now, watch this." He leaned toward Julius. "Give us a little volume."

In the living room which was on the monitor, Doreen, the lowcut flimsy dress falling wide at the breasts,
was standing close to a tall, distinguished, graying Negro. Doreen, a statuesque blonde, her hair hanging loose
behind her, was saying, "Gentlemen, shall I do my ballet exercises?"

There were shouts of "Go ahead, Doreen," and
"Show us how!" as the males voiced their enthusiasm.
The other girls, about seven of them Brad estimated,
in the group of twelve men, hugged themselves close
to the United Nations envoys, stroking them, kissing
them and moving tantalizingly against them.

With a quick movement Doreen shed her dress and
pirouetted nude before the mirror that covered one
wall of the room.

"If there was a hall of fame for what she does,"
D'Estang muttered hoarsely, "she'd be on a pedestal."

Doreen began to press herself against the Negro diplomat as two of the girls passed a tray of cham-
pagne-filled glasses.

"These UN people really live it up," Brad remarked.

"They are the easiest to insure," D'Estang agreed.
"I'm sure they're not all like these pals of Jorge. It
just happens that he moves with a swinging group.
That's the type we need for our special courier jobs."

"To carry the black attaché cases to bankers the way
I did?" Brad stated, more than asked.

"That's part of it," Maurice replied noncommittally. "A lot of these smaller Latin and African countries
send their well-connected bums to the UN to get them
out of their own country without embarrassing their
powerful families. The UN is also a fine way to give

an unwanted popular politician a very posh exile without offending his followers at home. Those are the types we're after." He looked at the monitor in disgust. "You don't think any of the serious diplomats from important countries would be getting involved in one of Jorge's parties? Hell, no! But we have ways of getting to them too. There isn't anyone we can't reach one way or another if it's important to us."

Doreen, rubbing herself against the big Negro, was saying, "Oh, I'll bet you could make a girl feel good." She darted her tongue into the black ear below the wiry, tight curls that covered his scalp.

"Go on, Clive, give the girl what she wants," Ramirez encouraged. The African diplomat needed no urging. He followed Doreen into one of the bedrooms, the others cheering. A stunning, raven-haired girl pulled at a tall, blond man and he followed her to another bedroom. One of the remaining girls stripped and did ballet exercises before the mirror.

In the control room Julius punched up a picture on the main monitor of Doreen and the handsome black in the bedroom. She undressed him with no resistance. Soon he was lying flat on his back on the bed, the camera in the ceiling recording the entire scene. Doreen knelt over his loins and both hands on the epic erection she had caused, she bent over and slowly lowered her mouth over it, onto it, taking it deeply between her lips. The estatic groans of the diplomat came clearly into the control room.

To Brad's amazement and disgust another picture came up on the monitor showing Doreen and the black diplomat from a different angle and then proceeded to go in for a close-up on Doreen's act of fellatio.

"A zoomar lens. I'll be goddamned," Brad exclaimed.

"I told you he's a genius," D'Estang muttered.

"He seems to enjoy his work," Brad observed. "I've heard of voyeurism, but this is ridiculous."

Julius switched from one room to another as the party rapidly developed into an orgy. "Hold it there, Julius," D'Estang growled. "Now this looks promising."

Apparently two homosexuals had discovered each other and were tolerant enough to permit a girl to join their exercise.

"Now," D'Estang commented in satisfaction, "we have the real hammerlock. The business with the girls is usually enough to keep our friends in line when we play back the video tape for them. But there are those who, as you suggested, request wholesale prices to buy the pictures in quantity. However, the world still despises a queer."

They watched as the girl tried vainly to derive some kind of physical gratification. One man, in classical style behind the other, consummated a most vigorous orgasm, his excitement heightened by the girl who was screaming imprecations at the two as she tried to somehow insert herself between them.

Brad turned from the monitor to D'Estang. "I get the picture," he said, smiling faintly.

D'Estang nodded. "I've had enough. Before the party is over every son of a bitch in the place will have compromised himself. Doreen picks up a nice check and we have our insurance."

"And Julius the Genius has spent his favorite kind of an evening getting paid at the same time." Brad started for the sliding door.

"Hold it a minute, Brad. I want to talk to Julius a couple of minutes and we'll be out of here."

This was all part of his business, Brad realized. He had made his choice. What right did he have to be disgusted now. He turned and watched the monitor as D'Estang and Julius conversed in low tones. Ramirez was lustily pushing into one girl from the rear and she in turn fluttered her tongue in the groin of the second girl who was lying on her back shrieking with delight.

"The lousy little bastard," D'Estang snorted. "I got him one of the most beautiful little broads in the city for his own and he's using the girls for himself that should be compromising these other guys for us."

"No honor among thieves, Maurice," Brad replied wearily. "Didn't you know?"

D'Estang looked at him uncomprehendingly. "Sure, I guess we can go now. I'll buy you a drink downstairs."

"I think I could use one."

As they waited for an elevator to take them down Brad said, "I suppose it's none of my business, but what do you do with these fellows later?"

"They are all very useful to us. Nobody has discovered a better way of bringing certain products into this country than using the immunity of foreign diplomats."

The elevator dropped them down to the lobby where they went into the pub for a drink. Brad shuddered at the thought of what he didn't know about Whitehall Development. Still he had made his decision and would stick to it. His life would certainly be one of excitement, wealth and wielding great power. Already he was learning to regard the unsavory activities of Whitehall not as crime but merely as another more efficient way of doing business.

CHAPTER TWENTY-SIX

Daddy Ed, as her mother still liked to have Andrea call her stepfather, was on his second martini. Ordinarily Andrea would have been quaking inwardly with fear. It didn't take much more than two drinks for the Irish temper to break loose at the slightest provocation. All evening her mother had been saying the usual nasty things about Brad, Ed Connor agreeing and adding his own evaluation of the bum. But the pills, the blessed pills that Tony Falcon had given her, made everything seem dim and a little funny. Everything was just fine.

Then, with a sudden whoop, Little Eddie, at thirteen almost as tall as Andrea, burst into the living room carrying a leather folder which Andrea instantly recognized. Three days ago after she had been out smoking pot early in the evening with Tony Falcon he had given her the photograph of himself she had requested. In the blue morocco folder were two pictures of him. One a portrait, the other a blown-up snapshot taken of him at the beach in a male bikini, hardly more than a jock strap.

Despite the euphoric effect of the pill a twinge of anxiety attacked Andrea as Little Eddie brandished his prize. Neither her mother nor Ed quite approved of Tony though they couldn't say why. They did not forbid her to see him for an early evening on a Friday or Saturday night but there was always an edge of disapproval in their tone of voice when they said good night to her and told her to come back before midnight.

Little Eddie must have gone through her dresser drawer in the room they shared, she realized, and found the pictures. In the two days she had not yet had the chance to use the pictures as she had planned. Her idea had been to get home early from school, before Eddie was back from afternoon sports, her stepfather was still working, and her mother was out shopping or seeing friends. It was all planned in her mind. She would take a downer pill, prop the picture up on the bedside table where she could see it, and fantasize Tony making love to her. At a certain point the downer pills made her feel very sexy and she would masturbate, staring fixedly at Tony's face and strong body.

But for the last two days her mother had been home, complaining about some new illness and nagging at Andrea about her father, who, she insisted, had never taken care of his obligations to her and Ed, what with rising prices and the expenses of properly clothing an eighteen-year-old girl, almost nineteen.

Little Eddie whistled boisterously. "Hey, Andrea, some picture of your boy friend. What is he? The muscle man from muscle beach?"

Ed Connor gulped down his martini and strode across the room to his son, snatching the picture from his hand and staring at it. "Look, Gwen, look at this!" he cried. "Look what Andrea keeps in her room."

Gwen inspected the picture. "What a disgusting thing to give to a girl."

"I never liked that smart-ass guinea," Ed ranted.

"It's just a picture of him," Andrea protested mildly. "And Eddie shouldn't be going through my drawers. It's time I had my own room anyway or else I should leave here."

"Leave the home we've made for you at such sacrifice?" Ed Connor cried out. "God knows that bum of a father doesn't do anything for you."

Gwen clutched at her heart and fell back on the sofa. "I'm feeling bad enough and now my daughter wants to leave me when I need her. After all I've done for her. If it wasn't for me you wouldn't be on earth. Your father wanted me to have an abortion but I made him marry me so you could be born and have a name. Even *his* name was better than none."

The effects of the pill were wearing off and her mother's words assaulted her ears. The same old story. So maybe it was true. She did owe her mother everything she had in life. But she had tried to repay her mother and Daddy Ed as best she could. They hadn't had a maid in over a year, since Andrea had been able to do the household chores before and after school.

"I'm sorry, Mama, of course I wouldn't leave you. But it isn't fair for Eddie to go through my things."

Ed Connor had poured gin over a couple of ice cubes and gulped it down, still holding the offensive leather picture folder.

"How dare you bring this obscene thing into my house. You go to confession tomorrow and make your peace with God."

"God and I are on good terms," Andrea said thoughtfully.

"Blasphemy!" Ed screamed. He hurled the leather folder at Andrea, catching her in the face and the corner of the eye. Andrea clapped a hand over her eye and rushed to the bathroom where she turned on the cold water, groped for a washcloth, and began bathing the eye which was giving her pain.

After a while it stopped hurting her. She put down the washcloth and reached under the sink. Finally her fingers found the bottle she had taped into the crevice under the molded sink and took it out. She took a downer and then retaped the bottle back where it had been. Since she cleaned both the bathroom Eddie and she shared as well as her mother's this was a secure place to hide the precious pills Tony Falcon had given her.

When she went back to the living room, after the pill had begun to have some effect, her mother had calmed down and Ed Connor was sullenly drinking, sitting at the dining-room table in the alcove.

She looked around for the leather folder but it was nowhere in sight. "Never mind," her mother said primly. "Ed has already taken care of that nasty thing. We have decided that we don't want you seeing any more of this Tony Falcon. Trust your father to seek out and find the most disreputable possible characters for you to associate with."

"What's wrong with Elda Ciano?" Andrea asked.

"Nothing. She is a fine young woman. It's the men your father introduces you to that Ed and I object to."

"Brad didn't introduce me to Tony Falcon. He just came up and introduced himself." Despite the pill Andrea realized she had made a tactical error. She had met Tony at Elda's house. She hoped her mother would not belabor this point.

Fortunately, Ed Connor interjected himself into the conversation. "I don't want to hear of him again, you understand? Goddamned wop, probably a mafioso. I don't want you to see him ever again!"

Although she wanted to defend Tony she was afraid to upset her mother and Ed any further. It had all been worked out with them that tomorrow, Saturday, she would spend the night with Elda Ciano at her place in the country and go to Elda's church with her on Sunday. She did not want anything to interfere with this plan. How she longed to leave this apartment forever and just come back to visit her mother and Little Eddie, even though he was a brat.

Now the pill was lulling her and everything once again seemed pleasant. "All right, Daddy Ed, if you say so," she agreed.

"Goddamned right I say so," he grumbled.

Andrea sat on a chair in the corner of the room with a history book on her lap, which she pretended to be studying. Soon she had drifted into her own private world and was far away from the depressing scene in which her body was seated. Tomorrow night was the most important thing on her mind. Elda was such a wonderful friend. And what great fun they had at their weekly luncheons with Brad.

Because she was a senior, the oldest girl in her class,

in fact, Andrea could take Wednesday off after the last morning class and meet her father and Elda at the Ascot Towers Hotel at 1 P.M. And much as Andrea liked Luciana it had thrilled her when Elda confided that she thought Brad was the most attractive man she had ever met.

As a result of this confession, Elda had even said she hoped Brad would take some notice of her in a romantic way. Andrea had told Elda about her own romance with Tony Falcon. Tomorrow, Andrea would tell Elda the truth of what her plans were for the night. Tony was becoming understandably irritated that they could only have an hour or two together when she could find an excuse not to be home. The evenings were short and though Tony became so amorous it was difficult to resist him, she had done so up until now.

But tomorrow night she had promised to go to the Saturday-night pot party at his friend's apartment in Greenwich Village and then spend the entire night with him. She knew he was an experienced man, but she hoped he was looking forward to having her for the first time as anxiously as she was. It would be her first time with a man and she had planned it carefully, reading up on the Catholic system of rhythmic birth control. Elda would cover up for her.

"Now, what's so exciting in that history book you get that look on your face?" Ed Connor suddenly called out from the dining-room table where he was hunched over his glass.

Andrea was shocked out of her reverie. "Nothing," she replied.

"Nothing? Let me see what you got there." He pushed his chair back and walked over to Andrea. Jerking the book out of her lap he turned it around so he could read it. After a few moments of study, his eyes squinting at the page, he shoved it back at her.

"I don't see anything to make you look the way you did. What are you? Daydreaming. You thinking about that wop?"

"No, Daddy Ed," she replied demurely. "I guess I'm just tired." She gave her mother a pleading look.

"Oh, Ed, leave her alone," Gwen said.

Ed turned on his wife. "I know what she's doing. She's thinking about that wop. I've got friends on the police force. I think I ought to have him picked up and questioned."

"Ed, let's talk about it tomorrow," Gwen replied wearily. "You know I'm not well. I think I'll go to bed."

"I think we ought to get it straight right now. Andrea might even be seeing him tomorrow night?"

"I'm going out to the country with Elda," Andrea replied in sudden alarm. "You can call me there if you want to check on me." She hoped they wouldn't but she would give Elda the number at Tony's apartment so she could call them back if need be.

"Andrea, you aren't going to see Tony Falcon again, are you?" Gwen asked.

"I promise I won't, Mama." You made me the liar I am, Mama, she said to herself. You taught me how to lie to Brad, how to get money out of him for you and Ed.

"She better not," Ed said ominously.

Gwen stood up. "Come and kiss Mama good night, Eddie," she called. Little Eddie appeared in the hall to his and Andrea's bedroom and obediently walked to his mother, kissed her and returned to his room. Andrea kissed her mother good night and then said she was also ready to go to bed.

"Don't you want to stay up a little and talk to Daddy Ed?" Ed asked huskily.

"I'd like to but I'm so tired. And tomorrow I want to get up and study for a couple of hours before I make breakfast for Mama."

Ed growled something and returned to the dining alcove. Andrea wanted to ask if she could at least have the handsome leather folder back without the pictures but decided not to make things any worse. The downer she had taken in the bathroom was soothing her and she wanted to lie in bed and let what thoughts she enjoyed come into her head.

In the bathroom she quickly changed into her night-gown, brushed her teeth, combed out her hair and went into the bedroom. Her bed was nearest the bathroom. Little Eddie had wanted his bed next to the window and Mama had given it to him.

She slipped into her bed and almost immediately fell into a comfortable doze. The downer she had taken began to make her feel warm and sexually desirous. Tomorrow night she would be with Tony. It was funny how her whole attitude toward virginity and sex had changed. Partly it was because she didn't want Tony to lose interest in her that she had decided to let him have her, take her virginity. But more than that she wanted to be a woman, have her own life and get away from this apartment. Then she thought of Mama and her illnesses and all Mama had done for her and she knew she could never leave her while she was needed. Brad didn't really need her or she might have gone to him to get away.

CHAPTER TWENTY-SEVEN

Brad Kendall stared out at the lights twinkling all over the city. While it is traditional for a hotel executive to have his office close to the action on the lobby floor, Brad had chosen the top floor beside the Star Club for the executive suite of the Ascot Hotel company. It was Saturday, early evening, and Luciana had been given an entertaining assignment for the night leaving Brad alone.

In the outer office he heard his phone ring. The secretary had left for the day at noon so he punched the lighted button on the instrument in front of him and answered.

"Brad?"

He recognized the contralto voice of Elda Ciano and was pleasantly surprised. She had done more to get Andrea and himself back together again as friends as well as father and daughter than anyone or anything had since Andrea was old enough to communicate.

"Yes, Elda. Good to hear your voice."

"I'm sorry if I'm bothering you, Brad."

"In no way is it ever a bother to hear from you."

"I think we ought to talk. If I come into town can I see you?"

"Of course. What's the problem."

"If it wasn't important I wouldn't disturb you. You've probably got an important evening lined up."

"Nothing could be more important than talking to you if there's something on your mind."

"It's about Andrea. She needs help and doesn't know it."

"Where do you want to meet?"

"How about your apartment? I can park in the building's garage."

For a moment Brad hesitated. Having Elda and Andrea together in his apartment was one thing. What would C.L. say if he knew that Brad was meeting Elda alone in the apartment?

As though sensing Brad's quandary Elda laughed over the phone. "I don't think anybody is going to think there is anything improper about my meeting you at your place alone, even my father." Then her voice took on a note of urgency. "Andrea is in trouble."

"When do you want to come in?"

"I'll leave now, Brad. I should be there in an hour."

"I'll be waiting."

Brad hung up the phone, gathered some memos and papers that had to be read by Monday, turned out the lights and left his office.

Elda arrived at Brad's apartment just as he had finished showering and changing clothes and put out some hors d'oeuvres. "I hope you don't think this too forward of me, Brad, but it is important for us to talk about Andrea."

"Even if it wasn't important to talk about Andrea I would be charmed and delighted that you came to see me." He gestured at the sofa and Elda sat down. "Can I make you a drink?"

"Just some sherry, thank you."

Brad poured a glass of sherry for Elda and a highball for himself and sat down opposite her. "Now, tell me about Andrea."

Elda sipped her sherry and then put the glass down. "First, I hope you realize I have no personal interest in Tony Falcon or he in me." Brad nodded.

"Andrea had made plans to visit me today and spend the night."

"How nice. I didn't know."

"It came up after our luncheon last Wednesday. Anyway, Andrea called me this afternoon to say her plans had changed. She swore me to secrecy and admitted she was going to see Tony and in fact be out all night with him. She was so happy and excited I didn't know what to do. I couldn't refuse to cover for her if her mother called and I certainly wasn't about to call her mother and snitch on her. I didn't know what to do, Brad. But one thing I do know, Tony Falcon is not good for her. She hasn't the experience to cope with one of those Italian lotharios. I finally decided to call you."

Agitated, Brad sipped on his drink and then put it down. "You mean her mother thinks she's out in the country with you right now?"

"That's what Andrea told me."

"And she's planning to spend all night with that bird?"

Elda smiled fleetingly. "So she says."

"Why?" Brad asked. "She's still young, there's plenty of time."

"It's not so much what she's doing, it's who she's doing it with," Elda replied. "At nineteen most girls have had their first experience with a man, and probably enjoyed it."

"What can we do, Elda?"

"I think we'd better find them before it's too late. If Andrea has made up her mind she's going to lose it, let's at least try and let it be with someone who won't hurt her." She looked up at Brad, smiling. "Do I shock you? We haven't gotten up to this point yet in teaching you to talk to nineteen-year-old girls who happen to be your daughter."

Brad shook his head. "I'm aware of today's trends." He took another long swallow. "How do we find them?"

"I have been out with Tony and I think I can predict the routine, particularly since Andrea described to me some of her dates with Tony when she was home before midnight."

"I'm listening," Brad said after Elda had paused in her discourse.

"It's only eight o'clock now. Tony will take her to some Italian restaurant and then they'll go down to Greenwich Village to a certain apartment I know where there's a permanent pot party every weekend. That's where he is most apt to—in his vernacular—score."

Brad couldn't repress a slight shudder. "Are you suggesting that I go down and bust her out of this place?"

"Unless you want Tony to be successful."

Brad shook his head. "Let's go get her now."

"Wait until a little later. You take me to dinner and then I'll take you to Andrea."

"Anyplace you have in mind?"

"Anyplace that has no connection with Whitehall."

"That shouldn't be so difficult. We'll finish these and go."

Were it not for his anxiety for Andrea Brad would have enjoyed dinner with Elda. He never would have thought of asking her to spend an evening with him but now that it was happening he found her more delightful than ever. Were it not for Luciana with whom he was, he knew, obsessed, Elda would have been the ideal girl for him to escort to the various parties and functions about town. But no, C.L. would not approve. C.L., despite his modern approach to business, was very old world in his family life style.

"I really enjoyed dinner, Brad." Elda's warm tones and sparkling eyes delighted him. "I'm just afraid you're going to think this thing with Andrea was an excuse to get a date with you."

"You don't ever need an excuse to see me. The next time I'll ask you, and there'll be no other reason except I want to see you."

"True, Brad?"

"Wait and see." He paid the check. "It's almost ten o'clock. Do you think we ought to find Andrea? Before—"

"Before it's too late?" Elda filled in. "Yes. I'll show you where they almost surely are."

Outside the restaurant in a cab Elda gave the driver an address in the Village and then sat back beside Brad who now wore a grim, set look on his face.

"It's not going to be all that bad," she said.

Fifteen minutes later the taxi pulled up before a shabby-looking apartment building across the street from an active, saloon-type bar. Brad helped Elda out and, paying the driver, he followed her into the building.

"Just remember, I'm your chick taking you to a pot party. Pretend you're out for kicks. If Tony and Andrea aren't here they soon will be."

Elda checked the names and pressed a button. Almost immediately there was an answering buzz and she pushed the door open. They walked up three flights of steps and Elda rapped on a door, which opened a crack.

"Baby!" a young man's voice rang out. "Where you been? We've missed you. Looking for Tony?" The door opened and Elda and Brad walked in. The door closed behind them. "You brought your own date? No sweat. Tony's got a gorgeous little chick in here somewhere." He chuckled gutturally. "I think they went through three joints and now they're out back." He turned to Brad. "Got your own grass or do you need some of ours?"

Brad looked helplessly at Elda. "Give him five bucks, sweetheart," she said. "His stuff won't quit."

Obediently Brad handed their host five dollars and received three tightly rolled homemade cigarettes. Elda took one from him. "Light me up, Brad?" She gave him a sly wink and drew herself closer to him. "If we aren't smoking we'll be conspicuous. You don't have to inhale."

Brad lighted the marijuana cigarette. Elda and he passed it back and forth a few times. Then Elda took his hand and led him among the young men and women sitting on the floor smoking and petting and talking. In the dim red and blue light, flashing and changing in psychedelic patterns, Brad tried to find Andrea. As his eyes became accustomed to the peculiar lighting he could make out faces. Elda led him to the rear of the room and then into a hallway. There was a bedroom at each end of the hall. Elda pulled him into one of the rooms where two couples were lying half dressed, smoking and all seemed entwined with each other.

Elda shook her head. "Must be the other room." They walked down the short hall to the other room. This time the door was closed. Elda took hold of the doorknob and pulled it partly open.

"Hey!" It was unmistakably Tony Falcon's voice. "We got this room reserved. Close that fuckin' door, you mother."

Elda turned to Brad and nodded. She pushed it all the way open and stepped in, Brad right behind her. He heard Andrea's giggle as Tony cried out angrily, "No shit, goddamnit!"

Looking down, Brad saw that both Tony and Andrea were lying together almost nude. Andrea was down to her bra and panties and Tony was wearing only a pair of black socks, one hand on Andrea's panties as though getting ready to pull them down, the other hand holding the joint.

"Somebody's going to get the shit beat—" Tony stopped in mid-epithet as he recognized Elda. "What the hell are *you* doing here?" Now there was fear in his voice as he remembered what his father said would happen to him and their family if Tony ever saw Elda Ciano again.

"Andrea," Brad said in hurt tones.

"Brad!" she screamed, trying to cover herself with her hands. "How? Why?" Surprise and mortification tied her tongue.

"Get dressed, Andrea," he said gently. "I'm taking you home."

"No. I don't want to go home," she protested. "I love Tony. We're going to be married." Then looking from her father to Elda she cried, "Elda, you're in love with Tony, that's why you brought my father here."

Tony was struggling to cover his nakedness and pulled on his underpants backward, groping for his pants. "You better go with your old man now," he said. Then he whispered something into her ear.

"No, I don't want to leave you. We were just going to have a beautiful night and now Elda and my father spoiled it all. I hate both of you."

"She's still high, Brad," Elda said quietly. "She'll come down and be glad we showed up."

"Bullshit I will!" Andrea shouted. "You can all go fuck yourselves."

Shocked, Brad reached down, cupped his left hand behind Andrea's neck, pulled her upright and slapped her across the face, first with his palm, then the back of his hand.

"Get dressed. Now! We're getting out of here."

"Tony, don't let them take me away."

Elda stared down at the frightened, chagrined, half-dressed Tony and grinned insolently at him. "If you know what's good for you, Tony, you get out of here like now. Andrea's father will take care of her."

Picking up the rest of his clothing in one hand Tony Falcon fled the room. Andrea, alone, gave Elda an appealing look. "I'm sorry," she said.

"I'll help her get dressed, Brad. Wait outside for us in the hall. She'll come down fast."

Brad retreated to the hall and waited for Elda and Andrea to come out of the room. The disturbance seemed to have had no effect on the party or the two couples in the other bedroom who were performing a number of different acts upon each other while still managing to keep the glowing ends of their joints alive. Tony had chosen that bedroom to dress in but the orgiasts paid him no attention.

Andrea and Elda came into the hall. "She's all right now, Brad. We'll all slink out of this den together." The three of them wandered through the pulsating room to the front door and Brad opened it, let the girls out and followed them outside.

He breathed several deep lungfuls of air as they walked down the stairs. "Thank God you called me, Elda."

"Did you and Tony have a nice dinner together?" Elda asked, as though nothing had happened.

"Yes. We had only been at the party ten minutes when you arrived."

"You see Brad? I know Tony's timing."

Back at Brad's apartment Andrea finished pulling herself together. She was properly contrite now.

"What would you like to do, Andrea?" Brad asked. "You can stay here in the guest room with me or you can go back to your mother."

"I don't want to go home," she replied softly.

"Why don't you drive out to the country with me, Andrea?" Elda offered. "You'll get a good night's sleep and we can go to church together in the morning and spend the day in the country." Elda looked at Brad. "Your father, I'm sure, would come out for lunch and drive you back to your mother's."

"Of course, Andrea."

"Is that all right, Elda?" Andrea smiled gratefully at her friend.

"Of course."

"After those terrible things I said?"

"I've said as bad when someone disturbed me when I was way up there. I'll have a sherry and we'll start out."

"Elda?" Brad took her hand. "I don't know how to thank you."

"We did our best. We'll just have to see if it takes."

Brad went down to the garage with his daughter and Elda and put them into Elda's car. He and Elda exchanged a long meaningful look. "See you tomorrow, about one," he said. Elda started up her Aston-Martin and gunned out of the garage.

For the first time, when Brad returned to his apartment, his heart wasn't threatening to fill his mouth while he waited and wondered whether Luciana would be calling him when her evening assignment was completed. Sometimes she did, sometimes she didn't.

CHAPTER TWENTY-EIGHT

Despite the discomfort he felt telling Ciano of his personal problems, Brad Kendall continued his carefully pruned narrative of Tony Falcon's corruption of Andrea. Brad wasn't yet ready to apprise C.L. of Elda's recent participation in his life.

C. L. Ciano, his lips compressed, his palms held together, listened intently. Finally he said, "I'm sorry, Brad. I feel responsible."

"No reason for you to feel that way, C.L.," Brad replied. "The only reason I bring it up is that I thought you might know some way to persuade this Falcon character to leave Andrea alone."

"I'll give the matter some thought, Brad. And again, I'm sorry."

"These things are nobody's fault. What do you say to a nineteen-year-old girl when you don't like her boy friend? There's nothing you can say that won't make her more determined to see him."

"I'll speak to an associate who knows Falcon's father," Ciano promised.

The telephone on his desk buzzed softly and Ciano picked it up. He listened a moment and put it down. "Fred Black is outside. I'll have to see him. Is everything else going all right? How's Luciana? I haven't seen her lately."

"She's very busy. Maurice seems to find a lot of entertaining for her to do," he added dryly.

"There are busy days for all of us, Brad. This year of 1972 is the crucial one in plotting our future strategy."

Brad stood up. "So I realize, C.L. I'm planning Jamison's campaign in the New Hampshire primaries already. Is there anything I can do for Adams? He is a singularly colorless candidate for anything. We'll have to do something dramatic to get him elected to the Senate next fall."

"I have some ideas along that line. I'll talk them over with you when they have achieved definite direction."

Brad walked across the large office high above the city and opened the door. Outside, Representative Fred Black was waiting to see Ciano. Brad shook hands with the swarthy, diminutive congressman and then strode down the hallway to the elevators.

"Come on in, Fred," Ciano greeted him, walking across the space separating them. Ciano gestured at the chairs and sofa under the huge map of the world, dotted with multicolored pins. Ciano sat down opposite Black and leaned forward. "Now, what's so urgent?"

"My sleuth. Kenney. The guy we took off the streets of Bed-Stuy as a favor to someone."

"What about him, Fred?"

"I don't know just how he did it but this morning he laid out for me the entire series of routes from Marseilles to St. Croix and into Florida, the southern states and New York. He even had names and dates. Right on through to Sal's wholesalers and the big niggers in Harlem and Bedford-Stuyvesant."

"He's some cop," Ciano said unperturbed. "Good thing we got him away from the Narcotics Bureau. I wonder how he got his information?"

"I asked him," Black replied. "He was noncommittal. Said something about informers. I know he's been giving a lot of money out lately."

"There are a number of courses we could take. We could tell him to work with the FBI or the federal

Bureau of Narcotics and Dangerous Drugs. They'd so frustrate him he'd give up on the whole thing. We could send him to the state Crime Commission and let him get into a controversy with the district attorney for not letting him make the case. They'd all get into such internecine fighting that they'd forget about Kenney's information."

"I thought we might set Kenney up for a police commissioner's investigation," Black said. "There's so much jealousy of him in the department since that book came out about him they'd love to disgrace him out of the force." The little congressman's eyes glittered as he made the suggestion.

Ciano stood up without replying and walked over to the large plate-glass wall that looked out over the city. He contemplated the view for a few moments and then turned and reached for the telephone on his desk.

"Ask Mr. D'Estang to come in," he said crisply. Then he returned to the window, staring out meditatively. After a few minutes of silent contemplation he went back to his desk and sat down. "Maurice will probably take a while to get here if he's at the hotel."

Ciano was silent a moment and then gestured at the chair across the desk from him. Black stood up and crossed over to the desk and sat down again.

"As you know, Fred, we are anxious to elect Bill Adams to the Senate this fall. He'll have rough going no matter how much we spend on the campaign unless we do something very dramatic on his behalf."

Black nodded. "You can say that a few more times, C.L."

"His big chance is to get elected on a strong law-and-order campaign, we all know that."

"It's his only chance," Black echoed. "I had to do a hell of a lot of compromising with the sneaker of the house to get Adams made a member of the House Committee on Organized Crime. Flannerty had promised the only opening to another man."

"I understand, Fred. And now, as I sit here, I begin to see how we can make the dramatic impact for Adams we've been looking for."

"I'm listening," Black replied dubiously.

"We put Kenney and his findings into Adams' lap and let William Fortune Adams, junior member of the House Committee on Crime, break up the East Coast narcotics syndicate and its wholesalers and retailers in this country and France."

Ciano fixed Black with an almost fanatic stare. "What could be more dramatic than that. We'll plan this event for late spring or early summer so that Adams will be at the height of his popularity just as the state convention opens. I'd say there's every reason to believe that he'll receive the party's nomination to run for senator. Then we'll take him down to the Democratic National Convention in Miami and see what happens to him there. If we ride this thing right there's no reason why Adams shouldn't be a strong candidate in '76."

Black was still reeling under the impact of Ciano's highly unorthodox thinking when the subdued whirring indicated Ciano's secretary wanted him on the phone. Ciano lifted the instrument to his ear, listened a moment and said, "Send him in."

The door opened and the large figure of Maurice D'Estang, the ever-present cigarette dangling from his lips, pushed into the office. Fred Black was dwarfed by D'Estang as he stood up to shake hands.

"Fred," Ciano said, "go back and tell Kenney he's done a great piece of investigative work. He's done his work so well, in fact, that you're going to have him join forces with the House Crime Committee which will act on his information."

"If that's what you want, C.L.," Black agreed dubiously. "You're going to make a lot of problems for the organization."

"Everything will be thought out and controlled. I'll be in touch with you."

Black turned a rueful smile on D'Estang. "Wait till you hear this one, Maurice!" The representative shook his head and left.

Rapidly Ciano explained his thinking to Maurice D'Estang. "We'll have to sacrifice a number of middle-level wholesalers from Miami to Boston and of course we'll have to set up one of our French connections for a bust."

D'Estang pursed his lips around the cigarette, a troubled look coming across his face, but he remained quiet as Ciano expounded his idea. "We'll give away one UN courier in New York and this might also be the opportunity to get rid of the big black man in Harlem who's becoming so troublesome. I expect that we'll have to blow three hundred pounds of heroin but what a story for the newspapers and television news. They can honestly say Bill Adams and his courageous committee were responsible for the apprehension of a hundred million dollars' worth of narcotics at street value."

"And we might have to come up with as much as half a million dollars in Marseilles," D'Estang replied.

"Right. And well worth it, Maurice. Just one thing I want to be sure of. Do we have Bill Adams fully insured?"

"Not as much as I'd like. He isn't interested in sex, he's never made a big loan, he lives fairly quietly. I haven't found the wedge yet."

"But he is very ambitious politically." Ciano stood up and began pacing in front of the picture window. "As campaign expenses mount we'll find ways of insuring him. It won't be hard to tie him to taking money from criminal sources. Give it some thought, Maurice."

"Sure. By the way, when this all happens there's going to be one hell of a panic in the streets. The addicts will be going insane."

Ciano smiled. "I've thought about that. By the time Adams busts this case we'll have the routes set up and working from the Orient through Mexico and California and into New York. That reminds me, I must tell Brad to scratch the hotel deal we were about to make in St. Croix."

"He'll be disappointed," D'Estang said cheerfully. "He's put a lot of work into that one including two trips."

"Then there's the matter of the half a million dol-

lars. We can't use any of the family money for this.
It will have to be generated out of our activities here."

"Larry Wolfmann's operation is getting ripe,"
Maurice replied helpfully.

"Yes. Just what I was thinking. Now, the next step
is to set up a meeting with Sal. Take care of that for
me as soon as possible."

"Check. And .C.L.," he paused hesitantly, then,
"when you're in the mood I'd like to discuss what
we're doing in the termination section, as you call it."

Ciano frowned a moment. "Not now, Maurice. That
is a necessity in our business that I regret, as you know,
and now isn't the time to discuss it."

Ciano sighed deeply, walked over to his desk and
pressed a button. A section of the wall slid back revealing the organ. He turned to Maurice and said,
"I assume recruiting in that department is coming
along."

"Doctor Wormsinger has two or three more prospects
under observation. Real nutcakes."

"That's what it takes. Come campaigning time next
spring and we'll do what we have to do."

Ciano moved across the office into the music room
and sat down behind the organ. Slowly he raised his
hands above the keys and brought them down. A chord
reverberated through the room. Maurice D'Estang re-
ceded from the office.

CHAPTER TWENTY-NINE

Salvatore Di Siccerone stepped out of his limousine on Madison Avenue in the sixties under the watchful eye of one of his most trusted soldiers who had jumped to the pavement from the front seat first. He looked with satisfaction at the façade of the newly renovated building. This was one of the properties owned by Whitehall on his behalf. It produced handsome rentals. He walked through the glass doors and directly to the elevator bank of the seventeen-story building.

A car was waiting and he stepped in and pushed the button for the tenth floor. Immediately the doors closed and he was lifted to his floor. Leaving the elevator he walked down the hallway and opened an office door. A bell tinkled as he stepped into the reception room. A door opened.

"Mr. Di Siccerone," a cadaverous young man said in pleased tones. "We are so happy to have you come back to us."

"My wife loved that little trinket you made for her, Georgio. For five grand she should," he added.

"What can we do for you today?"

"My daughter's got a birthday coming up. She's gonna be eighteen. I want you to design something special for her, some kind of a trinket a girl her age would like."

"A pin perhaps? A butterfly of rubies nesting in diamond chips?"

"Yeah, something like that. Two grand. I don't want to spoil the kid or anything like that." He looked at the watch on his wrist. "Show me some of what you got, maybe I'll get an idea."

For five minutes Sal the Hand examined pieces of jewelry that Georgio had designed, checking the minute hand on his watch every so often. "OK. Georgio, fix the kid up one of them nesting butterflies. You can even go twenty-five hundred if you want. I'll have someone pick it up when it's ready." He reached into his pocket and pulled out a thick fold of hundred-dollar bills. He counted out ten, which he handed to the jeweler.

"There's a grand on account. I'll pay the rest on delivery."

"Yes, sir. Is there anything more you'd like to see?" But Sal was already leaving the jewelry designer's shop and heading for the outer door.

"We'll look forward to your next visit, Mr. Di Siccerone."

"You bet, Georgio," Sal said as he walked out into the hall. He stood in front of the last elevator door on his left and consulted his watch again. He nodded to himself and waited, not touching the signal button.

Moments later the door opened and Sal walked in as the door slid shut behind him.

"Good morning, Sal." C. L. Ciano was standing in the elevator cab.

"Hi ya, Charlie," Sal responded. "Good to see you again."

The cab started downward and then, halfway to the ground floor, it stopped. The doors remained shut. "We'll be between floors for five minutes," Ciano said. "I'll try to make this quick."

"I'm with you, Charlie. And by the way, there isn't any way I can thank you like I want to. When Sam the Stick was paroled the whole organization knew that I did it. Anything you ever want is yours."

"That's good to hear, Sal, because I have a plan so radical it will scare you—at first."

"Anything, Charlie. The commission knows I work with someone up there, but they don't know who. My word is double law now. So go ahead."

"I'll talk fast, Sam. First, the planning for 1976 is coming along great. I need a top man in New York State as a candidate, maybe I need several, but right now I have a chance to make William Fortune Adams the powerful senator I'll need. Using Flannerty, Orellian and Fred Black I got Bill Adams on the House Crime Committee. Now I need to make him a hero, get me?"

"Sure, all the headlines and that. Like I said, anything I can do."

"You can do it all, Sal. Now listen carefully." Ciano's voice was low and intense. "Remember you asked me to get that cop Kenney off the street, he was bothering your black wholesalers?" Sal nodded impatiently, straining to hear and comprehend Ciano's plan. "What I did was get Kenney assigned by the police commissioner's office to Representative Black's special narcotics investigation in his district. We all figured this would bury Kenney but what happens? Kenney somehow made all our routes from Marseilles through St. Croix and into the East Coast. He has some locations and the dates where entries were made. He may be onto some of our UN couriers. In other words, his information compromises your narcotics operations."

Sal the Hand cursed quietly but vigorously. "How the hell did he do it?"

"Informers. But that isn't the point, Sal. I want to make a hero out of Adams. The way I'm going to do it is have Adams make a big narcotics haul, the biggest in history. We give Kenney to Adams and from behind the scenes steer them onto the big bust. They get a lot of middle-echelon people who look important but don't mean too much to us. We've got to give them a couple of the Frenchmen, and you've been wanting to get rid of that big black dealer in Harlem anyway. Maybe you've got a few men in your own organization you'd like to drop."

Sal the Hand shook his head. "I'll find stand-up guys I can trust. Guys willing to do time for the whole organization, guys who we can make look bigger than they are."

"I guess you're right," Ciano agreed. "We'll get them the best lawyers, of course, and see they are well compensated. If we work it out in advance with lawyers we might set things up so they don't get convicted in the end. The main thing is the big splash up front. The American public doesn't know or care what happens in court six months or a year later."

"When does this big bust happen, Charlie?"

"In April. That gives us four months to set it up. There's going to be a hell of a lot of work to do on this and I'll have Maurice D'Estang assign one of his top men to co-ordinate between your organization and the Crime Committee."

Sal the Hand suddenly burst out laughing and Ciano regarded him in puzzlement. Sal looked at Ciano's serious expression and guffawed anew. "Don't it seem funny to you, Charlie? Here you own the House Crime Committee and we are talking about coordinating my operations with the committee?"

"It's the only way, Sal," Ciano replied earnestly. "This is going to be a very delicate operation."

"Of course it is, Charlie. And I'm with you all the way."

"Good. Now, one other thing. I want Tony Falcon picked up in this bust. And him I want sent up for a good long time."

"Why, Charlie? Didn't he say bye-bye like I promised?"

"Sure. And he went after another young girl from a nice family and he's trying to get her hooked. I want you to tell his old man that Tony shouldn't keep seeing this girl he's getting onto pot and probably into hard stuff. She's a nice girl."

"I'll see what I can do, Charlie. I hate to go back to

Augie again. He's a man of honor who gave and got respect. I hate to set his son up."

"Why does he have to go after nice girls?" Ciano's anger made his tone tremble. "Let him leave them alone."

"He's just trying to increase his business, Charlie."

"Let him stick to blacks and Puerto Ricans."

"You know where the big business is in his line."

Ciano held up his hand. "I don't want to hear about it, Sal. Just make sure Tony gets hit in the bust. And for him no lawyers paid for by me."

"Hey, Charlie," Sal protested, "don't get all excited. I'll take care of everything. You'll have your hero, this Adams. But between you and me I don't think the kids voting in '76 will go for him. They don't like law and order. We're the heroes these days and the cops and feds are the bad, brutal guys. You gotta keep abreast of the times." Sal chuckled.

"We'll make him attractive in '76, just let me get him into the Senate as a hero in '72," Ciano countered. "We'll set up another meet in a couple of weeks."

"I'll be around."

Ciano pressed the down button and the elevator began to descend. It stopped on the second floor and Ciano stepped out, turning to smile and give a small wave to Sal as the doors closed.

On the first floor Sal the Hand briskly strode out to the sidewalk and into his waiting limousine.

CHAPTER THIRTY

Brad Kendall stood on the snow-packed slope stamping his feet for warmth and watching as Ev Jamison and Ron Jarrett, the famous star of rugged movies about cops, bandits and cowboys, greeted the skiers as they waited in line to get on the tow. This was not the first New Hampshire primary in which Brad had been involved, politics had always been in his blood, and the state was just as cold as always after the Washington's Birthday holiday in February.

State Representative Jack Bath, hand picked by Ciano as coordinator of Jamison's efforts to make a good showing in the New Hampshire primary, was standing beside the actor who seemed to be able to ignore the cold and wear his typical leather clothing without an overcoat. Although half the skiers were from out of state, Jamison's efforts would not be wasted. Here he was, a Republican defying his own party and President. He couldn't help but emerge as a highly attractive candidate in 1976 and every friend he made among the country's young people now would count.

A flash bulb popped and then another. "They really like him here," Brad said, leaning to Luciana who was holding his arm.

"Yes, he has great presence."

"Any idea where the photographers are from?"

"One of them is from *Life*. The other from the Boston *Herald,*" Luciana answered. "I had a talk at breakfast with the man from *Newsweek* who wants to do an interview."

"Good. The more the better. You're really keeping busy on this campaign." And with a touch of sarcasm he added, "Night and day."

"Now, Brad, don't start that again. I'm doing my job and trying to do it well."

"I'm sure Jamison is happy. You haven't been out of his sight for a week."

"Except when I'm sleeping," Luciana snapped.

"And then you're not with me either," he countered.

"You know what the deal was. We're not supposed to look like lovers while I'm working on Ev's campaign."

"We can preserve appearances and still be together after the children are put to bed," he replied petulantly. "Damnit, Luciana, I love you. I can't help it."

Luciana's tone softened. "I know, Brad. And I love you too—in my own way." She paused, staring across the snow at the group around Ev Jamison. "This campaign will be over soon and we'll be back in New York again."

"And Maurice will have you out entertaining all night."

"Maybe in recognition of a good job done here, C.L. will give me a week off and I'll give it all to you." She smiled up at him and teasingly made a kiss with her lips.

A young campaign aide hurried across the snow to Brad. "Mr. Kendall, an important telephone call for you. You can take it in the lodge."

"Probably Smith at the paper. I've been trying to get an interview with him for two days." Brad followed the aide into the lodge, thankful to have an excuse to get out of the cold for a few minutes. A telephone was off the hook, lying on the cashier's desk.

"Just pick it up, sir," the college youth said.

Brad picked up the telephone and identified himself. "Hello, Brad," he heard a voice say. "I'm really sorry to bother you out there. Mike Brashears here."

Why, Brad wondered, would the vice president of Allied Electric be calling him. He felt an odd sinking sensation in his stomach, remembering the golf game he had set up last fall between Mike Brashears, Don Tynan, sales manager of Allied, and Larry Wolfmann, Ciano's associate.

"Yes, Mike," Brad replied. "You must have had a hell of a time reaching me."

"I did. If it weren't urgent I never would have bothered you. I had forgotten that you get worked up over politics every four years. How's the campaign coming?"

"We're doing better than I expected. What's the trouble, Mike?"

"The trouble is that a couple of days ago Larry Wolfmann discovered his warehouse had been robbed over the long weekend. Everything at General Hotel Supply was stolen. Over a million and a half dollars of our merchandise is missing."

"Surely Wolfmann had insurance," Brad said into the phone. "Has he paid you for the stuff?"

"No," was the cryptic reply. "And no insurance. Wolfmann's auditor called us this morning. They already have filed bankruptcy proceedings. What can you do to help us? We're out well over a million dollars."

The enormity of the situation began to hit Brad. For a week or two he would forget what he really was part of, what he really was himself, and then something like this would happen to remind him.

"Mike," Brad said, "I don't know what I can do but I'll come back and personally look into the situation. This part of New Hampshire is as remote as the North Pole, but I'll do my best."

"I would appreciate that, Brad. I'm in real trouble over this thing."

"I'll call you when I get in." Brad hung up the phone and walked slowly from the lodge out to the ski slope.

Luciana gave him a questioning look, noticing the set, serious expression on his face. His only words were "I keep forgetting what we are."

"What happened, Brad?"

"I'm responsible for Allied Electric suffering a loss of over a million dollars. God knows what other companies are out that much too."

"It's nothing you can legally be held for, is it?"

Brad shook his head. "No. No, of course not. None of us at Whitehall expose ourselves that way." He sighed. "I guess I just wasn't cut out to be a criminal. I worry about other people too much."

"I don't know why you can't accept things as they are," Luciana replied coldly. "You certainly made it clear to me what I was getting into. If you couldn't understand your own words that's too bad. I certainly did."

Brad glanced at her. The determined look on the beautiful face chilled him for a moment. "I'm afraid I'd better get back. Maybe I can keep the problems down to a minimum."

"What actually happened?"

"A variation on the old bankruptcy racket. Thanks to me and the Copper Rock Club it worked out very successfully."

"Then why the long face? C.L. will be happy."

"Will you be all right for a few days if I go back?" he asked, ignoring the question.

"Of course. In fact, things are so well under control I don't know why you bother to come back. You did your job, made the contacts, talked to the Republican leaders and the delegates. Between Jack Bath and myself we can take good care of Ev."

"I'll be back in a few days and I'll keep in touch by phone," Brad replied. "Explain to Ev for me." He leaned to her and kissed her. Her response was disappointingly casual. "I'll take one car to the hotel and send it back to you." He paused. "I'll miss you, Luciana." She made no reply and he walked away toward the parking lot.

It was early evening when Brad reached his office at the Ascot Hotel. The company jet had been waiting for him at the Lebanon Airport, a two-hour drive from where he had been campaigning, and whisked him to Newark Airport. As he had requested, C. L. Ciano had waited for him.

"How is our man doing up there, Brad?" Ciano asked exuberantly. He seemed unusually genial this evening, Brad thought.

"Jamison should do even better than we thought, C.L." Brad took the seat in the informal conference corner of the office opposite Ciano. "If we can do some dramatic things for him these next four years and keep the voters reminded of the fact he opposed his party leaders on some key issues I think you have a leading Republican for America's two-hundredth-anniversary-election year."

"Good. Now what brings you into New York so unexpectedly?"

"What happened with Larry Wolfmann?" Brad countered.

Ciano nodded. "Now I understand. The Allied people called you."

"Mike Brashears called. After all, I set them up."

"There really wasn't any reason for you to come back because of that," Ciano said.

"Will you explain the whole caper to me, C.L.? I'd like to know the details. And I'd also like to figure some way to protect Allied."

"A loss of a million and a half doesn't mean anything to them," Ciano answered expansively. "Uncle Sam pays for it."

"It might be useful for us to stay friends with Allied," Brad pointed out.

Ciano sat back smiling. "All right, Brad. You're one of us—irrevocably." The word had a cutting edge not lost on Brad. "You might as well know the whole story. After all, we're only beginning."

Don Tynan, sales vice president of Allied Electric, was put in charge of the General Hotel Supply deal. Two weeks after the golf game sponsored by Brad Kendall, Tynan and Larry Wolfmann toasted the beginning of a new relationship in the offices of General. The toast was sipped in scotch and Wolfmann handed Tynan a check for $100,000, the wholesale cost of the merchandise delivered over the past three days to the warehouse.

Although General Hotel Supply was the only company that either Brashears or Tynan had ever sold that kept so much merchandise warehoused at any given time, the explanation seemed logical to them. Brad Kendall, in a crash program to redecorate and refurbish the Ascot Hotel company's older hotels, insisted that immediate delivery be available on all appliances and furniture needed by the decorating department.

Only by having the needed equipment on hand could the hotels meet the exacting redecorating schedule demanded by the company.

Larry Wolfmann, meanwhile, was setting up a series of smaller warehouses throughout the southern states of America. Each warehouse was located to serve the maximum number of department stores in the White-hall-owned Super-Save chain. Super-Save stores were strategically located near the large military posts and the budget-conscious military market was the store chain's chief source of business.

Each month Wolfmann ordered and paid promptly for a minimum of $50,000 of television sets, radios and many different consumer and commercial products. General Hotel Supply was a cherished Allied customer. In December, January and February, Wolfmann asked for, and was promptly granted, sixty days' credit for the merchandise with which he filled his warehouse and the orders became enormous. Several other large manufacturers of items used extensively by hotels began to follow the example of Allied Electric in reaching the Ascot Hotel chain.

By the long Washington's Birthday weekend, General Hotel Supply's warehouse in Queens County was bursting with merchandise purchased on sixty-day credit. On Saturday morning, a fleet of trucks drove up to the warehouse and spent the entire day loading up. This was not a remarkable occurrence in itself, only the magnitude of the move might have been surprising.

Every week trucks disgorged cargo and other trucks picked up. Even over weekends occasionally transfers of merchandise were made from the warehouse to another destination.

By Sunday morning, the warehouse was bare and the fleet of trucks had fanned out in myriad directions bearing their loads to the web of warehouses Wolfmann had set up from Virginia to Florida, from Georgia to Arizona.

Forty-eight hours later, on Tuesday morning after the holiday, shocked employees of General Hotel Supply discovered to their horror that the company had been looted of everything. Security guards hired by the company were found locked in an office with an adequate supply of food and drink. Although none the worse for their long weekend ordeal they were thoroughly chagrined by their capture and inability to stop the record-breaking theft.

By the time police authorities were called in it was too late to send out effective alarms. The trucks would have already reached their destinations, unloaded and dispersed. Over the next few months the merchandise would go into the Super-Save stores and be quickly snapped up by pleased, bargain-conscious customers, amazed at their good fortune to buy a second color TV set at half price or under. Even the military PX system was unable to offer military personnel such bargains. General Hotel Supply immediately declared bankruptcy, sorrowfully telling its several million dollars' worth of creditors that there were no assets left in the company.

"So you see, Brad," Ciano continued, "Super-Save buys from the warehouses Larry set up down there and that little operation will generate a million to a million five in cash over the next three months."

Brad absorbed the entire process as Ciano talked. At first stunned, he then began to understand that in reality there was no limit, no depths, to which the man sitting opposite him would not go to achieve money.

"Isn't this whole thing a little risky for one lousy million dollars, C.L.?" Brad asked sincerely. "It seems to me that Whitehall must generate, more or less honestly, that much every day."

Ciano nodded. "But that money is strictly clean. Every penny of it must be accounted for—where it came from, where it is spent. For a while we suffered through an investigation a year. First the New York *Times,* then the *Wall Street Journal,* then the U. S. Attorney gave us a lot of attention and even the FBI made some sort of check on us but we always came out, as the *Times* had to admit, 'smelling like a rose.' "

"And this money you can use any way you want." Brad nodded. "I see. Would it be presumptuous of me to ask how you plan to use it?"

"No. When the time is propitious you will be told."

"And there's no way Whitehall can be implicated?" Brad asked incredulously.

"Even if Ascot might be suspect, and that's not likely to happen, there's no way we can be tied to Larry Wolfmann's operation. He keeps whatever he can make for himself over one million dollars. The deal should have been worth three hundred thousand to him."

Ciano smiled owlishly at Brad. "All that money, by the way, is going into Project '76. You'll be directly involved. This time as an adviser to Bill Adams."

"Fine, C.L. In the meantime, I want to at least commiserate with my friends at Allied."

"Yes, a good plan. I should have thought of it myself. If nothing else you can keep track of what sort of investigation is being made into the matter. It shouldn't take Larry Wolfmann more than two months to liquidate his stock. As a matter of fact, he should be able to do it in a few weeks. The general manager of Super-Save has been building up to a giant sale for a month now in anticipation of the merchandise that has just become available. But if there is a chance of investigators getting a line on Larry's final phase it would be well to be able to warn him."

"I'll stay on top of it, C.L."

Four days later, after numerous inconclusive meetings with Allied Electric and the other companies who had lost large quantities of their merchandise in the robbery, Brad returned to New Hampshire. There were only a few days left to the primary election and the campaigning pace had stepped up.

"Goddamn, Ev," Brad said at the nightly strategy meeting, "I'm sorry I had to pull out at just this time. I might have persuaded the Manchester paper to support you."

"I'm sorry too," Ev replied, though Brad could see that here was plainly a more radiant candidate than the Ev Jamison he had left four days ago. Brad couldn't help but intercept the looks passing between Ev and Luciana as the meeting progressed.

"The polls give Ev a hell of a good showing, everything considered," Jack Bath was saying. Brad lost the train of the conversation. Instinctively he knew what had happened in the four days he had been away. But no use crying about it, he told himself vainly. It was the way of the fifth estate.

After the meeting Brad managed to catch Luciana alone in the bar as Ev talked earnestly to his staff over nightcaps.

"I take it," Brad said, smiling bravely, "that while I was away Ev Jamison was insured."

Luciana smiled saucily and nodded. *"Pro bono Ciano."*

"Shit," Brad said. He gulped the last of his drink and left the bar.

CHAPTER THIRTY-ONE

"Beautiful countryside, this Laos, Jeff," Brad commented, looking out the round window of the descending Gulfstream executive jet. "Too bad they have to keep a war going to spoil it."

Colonel Geoffrey Woodholt smiled ruefully. "The war doesn't affect the capital Vientiane. The people live as they always have."

The voice of the pilot came over the speaker. "We'll be on the ground in five minutes, Mr. Kendall. Buckle seat belts." The three men, sitting in swivel chairs, buckled their belts. Etienne D'Estang seemed, as always, imperturbable. He bore a close resemblance to his older brother, Maurice, and spoke English with a hard French-Corsican accent.

"Both the Minister of Finance and the Minister of the Interior will be at the ramp to meet us," Woodholt was saying. "You will have a short audience with the premier, Souvanna Phouma. The government, such as it is, is very impressed with your arrival in your own jet and the importance of the Ascot Hotel chain has been magnified in their eyes. This all gives much face to Etienne who will be staying here."

Etienne did not smile, indeed, he appeared not to hear. "You'll have your pick of the best girls in the city," Woodholt continued. "My boys will help you to choose an important woman as your mistress." This last statement brought some vestige of a smile to the Corsican's face.

The plane set down smoothly and rolled to the small terminal building. When the engines stopped the co-pilot came back and opened the door. The aluminum steps unfolded. Brad and his group were ready to disembark.

The colonel was the first to leave the plane, followed by D'Estang and then Brad. They walked across the ramp and into the air-conditioned terminal. Here a group of Laotian officials dressed in Western garb, white suits, were introduced to them. Several Americans were also in the party and Colonel Woodholt introduced them to Brad and D'Estang. "You'll meet with my people after the ceremonial luncheon," Woodholt said.

The government ministers and their aides left the airport with Brad, D'Estang, and Woodholt and climbed into waiting limousines which sped them to the decrepit Hotel de Paris, the city's best. Inside the hotel they were led to a private room where an elaborate bar was set up for refreshments. All of the party accepted drinks and then sat down around a table for the formal meeting, conducted in French.

While both Brad and Woodholt spoke a rusty brand of French, Etienne D'Estang was in his element and seemed to quickly establish a rapport with the ministers. Brad noticed that Etienne wasted little time in letting the ministers know that they would be embraced in any deals he made, hotel or otherwise, he was careful to say. In fact, he understood that both of the ministers had studied law in France and he wished to retain them both, on behalf of Ascot Hotels, beginning now.

Obviously, Etienne had been the perfect choice for this mission, Brad realized, as the two ministers glowed their satisfaction and promised to be helpful in every way possible. They were impressed, of course, with the fact that Etienne's brother was the manager of the world's most prestigious hotel, adjoining the United Nations in New York. But the promise of immediate remuneration clinched the co-operation between Ascot Hotel negotiators and the royal Laotian Government. For an hour the men talked of the great day when the Ascot Hotel would be finished in Vientiane and important persons from all over the world could be properly accommodated. A whole new tourist boom would lift the economy of tiny Laos and make the country a must stop on all tourist itineraries.

After luncheon had been served the ministers and their aides left for their homes, promising Etienne they would be available to him anytime at home or office. When Woodholt, Brad and D'Estang were left alone the colonel said, "OK, now that the bullshit is over let's go over to the house we rented for Etienne where we can talk. One of my boys will be around once a week to make sure that there are no bugs installed in the place."

The house Etienne would occupy was large and comfortable. One room, a study, was air conditioned and to that room they repaired. In the room two Americans wearing sport shirts and slacks were waiting.

"This is Bob and Eddy," Woodholt introduced the two. "Everything under control?" he asked.

"As much as it's ever been in the last ten years," Bob, a tall, lanky young man with sandy hair, replied. "It's coming up crop time again and we better find a market or we're gonna lose our guerrilla army. When I left camp yesterday half my native troopers were out harvesting poppy."

"That's why Mr. D'Estang is here," Woodholt said crisply. "Now, here's the drill. General MacFarland arranged through highest level contacts for a big outfit to buy all the opium our Montagnard tribesmen can harvest."

The colonel turned to Brad. "It isn't by choice that we are in opium. But our job here for the past ten years and I guess for the next ten or twenty years is to keep the tribesmen out in the mountains along the North and South Vietnam border armed and fighting against the communists who bring supplies down the Ho Chi

Minh trail. So far they've been loyal to us because we make sure they are supplied with everything they need. But they only have one way of making money, that's growing opium poppies. We'd give them the money but they're a proud people. They want to earn what they get. Maybe that's what makes them good people to work and fight with."

Woodholt stood up and walked over to the bar and made himself a gin and tonic. "So in order to keep our indigenous army fighting we gotta peddle their poppy juice."

"How much can you supply?" D'Estang asked sharply.

Woodholt turned to Bob and Eddy questioningly. "From all the tribes where we have control, all over the country?" Bob asked. "I suppose in the next three months they'll bring out maybe ten tons of raw opium. That includes what the Meos in Burma bring out too."

"We'll handle it," D'Estang snapped.

"Good," Woodholt replied. He paused. "I don't have to tell you how sensitive this is. My agency of the United States Government could never be associated with opium trafficking but the orders from the top say that we have to do everything in our power to harass the enemy supply lines to the south with indigenous troops and prevent the communists from coming through the mountains to western Laos and Vientiane. The only way we can do this is with happy, prosperous Montagnard guerrilla fighters. And the only way we get them is to make sure their opium is purchased at a good price."

"Anytime we can be of service to the government, it's our pleasure," D'Estang answered. "I'll have the machine ready to pay for and move ten tons of crop. You got no worry."

"You know," Brad said dreamily, "a fine new hotel in Vientiane isn't such a bad idea."

"Sure," Woodholt agreed. "And at the speed they negotiate in this country you just might get one financed and built in twenty years."

"I'll start working out pickup points tomorrow," D'Estang said to Bob and Eddy. "I wouldn't know how to find you but I expect you to find me."

"You got any bush clothes?" Eddy asked.

"I thought I could buy what I need."

"We'll take you over to our place. We have everything you'll need."

Brad looked at his watch. "Well, if I'm going to make it back to Bangkok before six we'd better get going. You seem well set here, Etienne."

"Yeah. I'll be all right. Tell Gaglia to get his equipment and be ready to come out here next week. Ten tons he's going to have to boil down to morphine base."

"Right, Etienne. And don't lose track of the fact you're supposed to be negotiating the financing of a new Ascot Hotel."

"Don't worry about it, Brad. Everything is going to be just fine."

Leaving D'Estang with Bob and Eddy, Colonel Woodholt and Brad stepped into the chauffeured car waiting for them and started out for the airport. Woodholt noticed that Brad seemed reflective if not downcast as they drove along. "What's the matter, Brad? Don't you like what you're doing?"

"In a corporate empire the size of the one I work for you learn not to become emotionally involved in its activities. But it is hard to avoid reflecting on the results of operations in which you become involved."

"You sound like some of the more intellectual people in my agency talking," Woodholt replied. "The by-products of the means we employ to achieve America's national objectives are none of my business."

After a long pause Brad said, "We really will have a damned fine hotel in Bangkok next year and also in Hong Kong. It's been a successful trip."

"I'm sorry it took so long to set up the Vientiane deal. But something like today, simple though it looked, took a hell of a lot of planning and investigation. It was fortunate that you had General MacFarland's influence behind you."

"I wouldn't have been sent otherwise." Brad looked out the window. "Here's the airport. Bangkok next stop. I hope you and Kitty are planning to have dinner with Luciana and me tonight."

"We sure are. That is some woman."

At the end of the long drive into Bangkok from the airport Brad found a message waiting for him at the Intercontinental Hotel where he and Luciana were staying. François Gaglia wanted to see him right away. Even before calling Luciana's room Brad rang Gaglia. "Come right up," the Corsican rasped.

"Come down. We can talk in the bar." Brad intensely disliked the Corsican chemist Etienne D'Estang had brought on the trip. He couldn't explain what it was about the short little man, a partial hunchback, which so repulsed him but Luciana had felt the same way. "It will be safer talking in the bar," Brad added, playing on the chemist's paranoiac obsession that he was always being watched.

"Yes, yes, I come down," Gaglia hissed.

Brad strode into the air-conditioned bar and ordered a double gin and tonic and was well into it, experiencing a pleasurable lift, when Gaglia appeared. Brad had chosen a corner table with his back to the wall and no one was sitting near him. Gaglia saw him, rolled his eyes around the room, and then came over to the table and sat down hesitantly.

"We can talk, François," Brad said. "I have a message for you from Etienne. But first, what's the big emergency?"

"I 'ave foun' ze laboratory I need," he announced dramatically. "I mus' pay today."

"Is it secure?"

"The best, I assure you. I have good friends here. It need only to pay certain man in the government and we are," he grinned, "how you say, cooking."

"How much do you need?"

"Only one thousand dollar the month. And pay one thousand dollar to police chief office. There are other laboratory here, many I think. What does Etienne find?"

"Ten tons raw opium in next three months."

Gaglia hissed. "Oh, that is good, very good."

"He wants you to come to Vientiane. He will send for you. The jet will take you."

"Yes, we will make the morphine base in Laos, then in Bangkok we refine to heroin. We have big, very big operation."

"The biggest there is out here," Brad agreed unenthusiastically.

"We can be bigger than Marseilles, and much safer," Gaglia went on happily. "We make almost full ton of heroin."

Brad stood up. "Order a drink for yourself, François. I'll leave two thousand dollars in cash in an envelope in your box."

"Yes? Thank you. I see you later."

Not if I see you first, Brad wanted to say, but he nodded and left the bar. He went directly up to Luciana's room and knocked on the door. "It's me, Brad," he called.

Luciana opened the door. She was wearing a tropical-weight cocktail dress and she looked beautiful and tanned. He wanted to reach out and scoop her up and hold her and kiss her.

"You'd better hurry and get ready, Brad. We'll be late for cocktails with Commissioner Thannit."

"How about a kiss first?" He put his arms around her gently and she turned her face up to his.

"I'm still mad you didn't take me to Vientiane today."

"It was men only and very strictly business. I'm sorry, Luciana."

"I know. I was only teasing you. So did you get your dope trade off the ground?" Luciana laughed at the pained look that came over his face.

"I think an Ascot Hotel in Vientiane would be profitable," he replied.

"Oh, Brad darling, come off it. Now get ready. You

know how important Commissioner Thannit is going to be to the success of your—" her tone became heavily tinged with irony—"hotel venture in Thailand. After all, you do want complete co-operation with customs so guests of the new Ascot Hotel won't have to have their suitcases searched when they enter the country."

"I'll be ready in fifteen minutes. I just have to leave some cash for François."

"That crippled little creep? I'm going to scold C.L. for making us take him with us. I'm going to tell him —he rides in the john all the way back across the Pacific to San Francisco."

"That won't be necessary. He's staying in the Far East for a while."

"Good. Gee, Brad, I guess I will be happy to get home. We've been out here a month now."

"A very successful month," Brad added. "OK, see you in fifteen minutes. After the Thannits' we're having dinner with Jeff and Kitty Woodholt."

"I like Jeff." Luciana's eyes sparkled. "I don't know why but I always seem to be attracted to spies and secret agents."

Several days later Brad accompanied François Gaglia and a young Frenchman named Duroux who had mysteriously appeared on the scene to Vientiane in the jet. They were met by Bob and Eddy accompanied by Etienne D'Estang who had by now acquired a large-size Land Rover. With no interference by Laotian officialdom Gaglia and Duroux transferred the cartons of chemicals and equipment they had brought with them to the Land Rover and they drove across the runway to an area where several unmarked small and medium-size airplanes were parked in front of a freshly painted white house.

"Would you like to come with us and see how our operation actually begins?" D'Estang asked Brad.

"I would indeed," Brad replied. "I'll be expected to give a comprehensive report on the whole situation when I get back."

"I've just leased this STOL aircraft—that means short takeoff and landing—from a fellow Corsican pilot in Vientiane. Climb in."

"Is there room for all of us?" Brad asked.

"We'll let Duroux fly with Eddy and Bob in their plane." D'Estang, Duroux and Gaglia loaded the heavy chemicals and equipment into the high-winged, single-engine plane and then the three of them climbed in. Etienne started the engine and let it warm up.

"I didn't know you were a pilot." Brad said, surprised.

"I can tell you, my friend, there is very much that you don't know about me and it's just as well. All you have to know is that in one month I will be the biggest operator out here. I am the source of the entire trade routes you and Maurice and the ultimate boss who I do not know are setting up."

D'Estang watched the plane Eddy and Bob were flying taxi out of the area and he released the brakes and followed. "Do not be alarmed if I seem to fly crazy," Etienne called above the noise of the engine. "The communists down there shoot at everything that flies. But I know where they are."

In moments Etienne had gunned the plane and it was taking off. Airborne he headed northeast toward the mountains. "We will fly over the Plaine des Jarres and land at a camp on top of a mountain where over three thousand of the Meo tribesmen have their home. They have been harvesting their opium for a month now and have a big supply."

After almost an hour in the air Brad saw the mountains towering beyond the odd-looking plains full of stones that indeed looked like crockery jars. Etienne kept the other plane always in sight and soon it seemed to be swallowed up by the mountains.

"We're almost there," Etienne said. Suddenly, without having changed altitude, the ground or the tops of the hills were only a few hundred feet below them. The plane circled and Etienne brought it in for a landing although Brad could not actually see a strip. Then they were bumping along the rough ground and the plane came to a halt after a landing roll of less than one hundred feet.

Brad opened his door when the engine was cut and stepped out onto the ground followed by Etienne. A strange sight greeted them. They were standing on a flat dirt clearing surrounded by jungle with mountains towering above them to the east, north and south. To the west from where they had come the terrain was flat. Now, coming out of the trees, was a crowd of short, squat, broad-faced men wearing U.S. Army fatigues, jungle hats and combat boots. They carried carbine rifles, and as they approached they seemed friendly and happy to see the airplanes.

"Now, François," Etienne said, "I will ask the chief to assign some men to help you and Duroux set up your field laboratory. I have already brought up here four steel oil barrels which have been set up over fires for you and filled with water. You can reduce their opium to morphine base right here where we purchase it." He turned to Brad. "It takes ten pounds of opium to make one pound of morphine base. Not only is this the safest place to reduce the opium to its essence, but it saves us carrying a lot of extra weight out of here. At this one station alone we will buy almost a ton of raw opium and carry out two hundred pounds of morph."

"What is your plan? To drop in on these camps all over Laos and make the morphine base on the spot?" Brad asked.

"That is exactly what we will do. For twenty years I have been in narcotics, all over the world. I was last here in 1962 and I have always dreamed of an operation like this one but I could never get the backing to do it." His eyes glistened with zeal. "Now, at last I can show how to really exploit this trade. When we fly out of here with the morph it will be the highest quality produced at less cost to us, the originators of the shipment, than ever before in the modern history of heroin. You just watch our operation today."

Eddy and Bob followed by Duroux came over to Etienne. "Are you ready to start buying?" Eddy asked.

"Ready. Did they set up a table for me over by the steel drums?"

"Everything is just the way you want it. Naturally, we're anxious for you to make the buy as quick as possible so we can get these little monkeys back to killing communists."

Etienne, carrying an attaché case, strode across the dirt airstrip and into the trees. There the oil drums were carefully suspended over crackling fires, boiling the water which filled each drum. Already Gaglia and Duroux were setting out the chemicals and glass testing equipment. Etienne was followed by a tribesman carrying a scale. The Corsican set up the scale on the table, sat down behind it, placed his briefcase on the table in front of him and snapped it open. It was full of Laotian dollars, and a cry went up from the tribesmen as they saw the money.

"Tell them to start putting their poppy on the scale," Etienne called to the two Americans. In the Meo dialect the word was passed, and one by one the Montagnards began piling their bricks of the musky-smelling, sticky-brown opium on the scale.

Each of the tribesmen weighed his opium and was paid at the rate of twenty-five U.S. dollars a pound. "It is impossible for you to know what a shocking good price we are paying, including the cost of the plane, even the cost of flying the jet all the way over here," Etienne said as he weighed the opium and paid the tribesmen. As the opium bricks came off the scale Gaglia and Duroux took them and dropped them into the steel drums full of water, into which they had meticulously measured the chemicals necessary to start the processing.

The Corsican chemist seemed swept up in the spirit of the operation, humming to himself as he filled first one drum, then the next with the brown bricks. "I suppose this is very primitive to you, François," Brad commented.

"Yes," Gaglia agreed. "But it is often this way. In Lebanon I made the base outdoors as the opium from the fields in Turkey was brought in to me. I shouldn't be wasting my time on this process. After today young Duroux here, my apprentice, will do this job. Where the skill, the experience is needed is in refining the morph to heroin."

"What is the ratio of base to heroin?" Brad asked.

"One for one. But it is a very delicate process and a dangerous one. I know chemists who became careless and died miserably, poisoned by the fumes." He scraped a brick with his knife, dropping the sliver into a glass retort of chemical. "Very fine quality," he observed. "When I refine the base, the results should be far purer than anything that's been seen in New York before. The cutters must be warned of the purity of the product," he said with pride. "A new addict particularly could easily take a fatal overdose."

As Brad watched, the buying process went on for almost two hours during which time Etienne had purchased just under two thousand pounds of raw opium. "Well, you've bought out the whole crop harvested by the villages in this part of the mountains," Bob said happily. "I always knew there must have been an easier way of doing it."

"How did you do it before?" Brad asked.

"We had to let two companies, about three hundred men, make the trip back to the nearest city. They were always afraid of being attacked and their poppy stolen. It took over a week and there was always a lot of fighting over the money when they came back."

"Then I'm glad we're able to do a real service for the agency and the government out here," Brad said.

"*Out here,*" Bob emphasized the two words, "you sure are doing the U.S. of A. a service." Brad sensed an expression of the American agent's true feelings about the operation. One ton of heroin would keep every addict in the United States supplied for a month. Five years ago such an amount would have hopelessly flooded the market. Now, Brad read, it had been estimated that two thousand new addicts were being created every month in 1972.

Brad turned to D'Estang. "Now that you have made the buy you must be ready to go back to Vientiane."

D'Estang shook his head. "I will stay with François. He and Duroux will be working all afternoon and night and most of tomorrow. Then, while they rest I will go with Eddy and Bob to set up the next complex of villages for the operation you are seeing here."

"There must be other people in the business out here," Brad suggested.

"Oh, certainly. But thanks to Colonel Woodholt and whoever in Washington set him up with you we have the makings of the slickest machine in the Orient. And, of course, the real trick here is to get the heroin directly back to the United States. Most of my old companions here have been specializing in smuggling their heroin or raw opium into Saigon to hit the military market there. But that market is drying up fast."

"The routes from the laboratories in Bangkok and Hong Kong to big cities at home are being set up," Brad said. "All you have to worry about is getting the base to Gaglia's labs."

Brad looked around the clearing, taking in the entire operation. It seemed a long way from Ciano's office in the Spire Building in New York, and yet it was Ciano who was responsible for setting up this strange source of narcotics in the battle-ripped Laotian jungles. The four steel drums of chemically treated water and opium were boiling merrily away. Duroux hovered over them anxiously, skimming the surface with a long-handled spoon and examining the sludge, Gaglia giving him instructions. This was just the beginning of an enormous operation, and it gave Brad goose bumps to think that he was here at the beginning of an entire new trend in world-wide narcotics trafficking. The old routes from Turkey to Lebanon to Marseilles and thence to the lucrative markets of the new world would soon be destroyed, by the very people who were exploiting them and this would be the source of heroin in the 1970s.

"Just one question, Etienne. How do I get out of here now? I have an important dinner engagement back in Bangkok tonight."

"I'll take you back, sir," Bob volunteered. "Eddy had better stay out here until your people finish their job. These Meo know him and do anything he says."

"Thanks, Bob. I'm ready to go back now if that's OK with you."

"We're on our way." Brad said good-by to the three Corsicans, Duroux was also one he had learned. They were a fraternity in this trade apparently. He followed Bob out to the dirt landing area and climbed into the agent's plane.

It was a slow trip back to Vientiane, Bob having to dodge around areas known to be communist infiltrated. Talking was difficult over the noise of the small plane's engine so Brad was alone with his thoughts, something he tried to guard against these days.

As always he thought about Luciana. It had been difficult for him to accept the fact of her short affair with Jamison in New Hampshire. It had been even more bitter for him to realize that she had done it not merely because Jamison was an attractive and vital man but as a deliberate act of business. The business of binding Jamison to the fifth estate. She had soon gone back to Brad as though nothing had happened, and he was as sick in love with her as ever. Maybe not in love, but certainly wildly desirous of her, sensually and intellectually. This trip had been for the most part one of the most enjoyable and interesting experiences they had shared since joining Ciano's establishment.

The marring aspects of the Far East adventure to him had been Luciana's growing delight with her participation in an overwhelming criminal conspiracy and her exasperation with Brad when he made allusion to the lamentable state to which his character had sunk.

"We are part of a fifth estate in life," she would remind him. "The leaders of our estate are on an equal, if not superior, level with the leaders of the other estates. We develop business and industry when and where others cannot. We are the logical entity to administer the government of the United States and become the greatest influence on world affairs."

Brad's answer was always the same. "You are memorizing verbatim what Ciano tells you."

"And who else should I memorize?" she would retort. More and more, Brad understood, Luciana was having an intellectual love affair with C. L. Ciano. He sometimes wondered if it went any further but the thought of Ciano being seriously interested in anything but power was impossible to accept.

Finally the small plane landed at Vientiane and Bob drove Brad across the runway to his jet. The agent looked it over covetously. "That's sure the way to travel around this part of the world," he said admiringly.

"As long as you can get the landing clearances," Brad amended.

"You haven't had much trouble."

Brad nodded. "True. But my old man has more connections than most traveling businessmen, even those whose companies can afford a private jet."

"Yes, sir. You can say that again."

Brad felt a deep sense of relief and satisfaction as he sat in the command swivel chair of the Gulfstream, a gin and tonic in his hand, looking down at the scenery of Thailand forty thousand feet below. Another week and he and Luciana would be flying back to the United States. Meantime, it was his responsibility to get the routes to the United States set up. As a hotel executive, transportation facilities were second nature to him and it was expected of him to make a thorough investigation of all types of carriers, public and private, serving any area in which Ascot Hotels might decide to build.

CHAPTER THIRTY-TWO

Ascot One landed in San Francisco after five weeks in the Far East with several important personages aboard. Brad and Luciana had been host on the trans-Pacific flight to one of the top advisers to Prince Souvanna Phouma, the Deputy Minister of the Interior of Thailand, and one of Hong Kong's most powerful Chinese lawyers, Joseph Peng. All had brought their wives, were guests of Ascot Hotels, and would be flown back to their homes after a three-week junket around America. All were vital links in C. L. Ciano's affairs in the Orient.

They passed quickly through customs, and limousines sped them to San Francisco's new Ascot Hotel where they would start their junket. It was April now, a beautiful time all over America. Not too hot, not too cold. The visitors would be in Washington for the Cherry Blossom Festival. Luciana would be their hostess for most of the trip since Brad was needed back in New York.

In Luciana's room, after the three visiting couples had been settled, Brad opened an envelope which had been personally delivered to him by an emissary of Ciano. He read it carefully and put it down, puzzled.

"Now why on earth would Ciano want this company?" he asked.

"What one?" Luciana asked.

"It's called Educational Aids, Inc." Brad studied the communication again. "The company distributes audio-visual films and devices to community colleges throughout the western part of the United States."

"What's a community college?" Luciana asked.

"That's a college for local students. There are no dormitories. Usually just a small cluster of classrooms and other facilities. Why would C.L. want to get into something like this?"

"Have you ever seen him do anything without a good reason?"

"Never."

"Then you'd better give the company a phone call and make an appointment." She looked at her watch. "It's only two o'clock in San Francisco. You can probably arrange a meeting this afternoon."

"After thirty hours off and on in the air over twelve different time zones?" He smiled suggestively at her. "I thought maybe we'd take a nap. It's been a long time since we've had a chance to lie down together."

"We don't take our little group to dinner until eight-thirty tonight. You'll get back in time for a nap, baby."

The warmth in her tone delighted him. She had a way of turning it on and off. "Well, if you put it that way." He sat down on one of the twin beds in the room and picked up the phone.

"Besides," Luciana went on, "I'm curious to know what it's all about. Let's see if you and I can figure out what the genius is up to before he tells us."

"Get me Dawson Peterson at Educational Aids, Inc.," he instructed the operator, giving her the phone number on his instruction sheet from Ciano.

One hour later Brad Kendall was standing in front of a large map of the United States in the office of the president and owner of EAI, as the company was called. Peterson, who had left one of the largest advertising agencies on the West Coast, was explaining the workings of his company to Brad.

"I was surprised and delighted when the Ascot people first contacted me about buying control of this company," Peterson said frankly. "It's a great concept, but I had no idea how much capital it would take to make the thing work. With your resources you can make a gold mine out of it. As I told Mr. D'Estang when he called from New York in answer to my advertisement in the *Wall Street Journal,* I would like to stay on and manage the company for you in a minority stockholder position; of course you would want control."

"Yes, that would be necessary," Brad answered, still completely confused as to how EAI fitted into the Whitehall picture.

"In the East where there are as many as twenty-five community colleges in a state like North Carolina alone, one man, two at the most, can cover them all in his car. But out here," he laid a pointer on the map, "the distances are greater. Being an enthusiastic amateur pilot I thought I could combine my hobby and my business and fly to the colleges with my visual-aids devices."

"Is there a market for such things at the colleges?" Brad asked.

"An inexhaustible one. I showed you my hardware, a cassette player that projects one-hour illustrated lectures by our country's noted educators and lecturers. Then there are the sound slide projectors and various other devices to bring the latest educational programs right to these out-of-the-way campuses which have no facilities to provide truly exciting teaching methods."

"You're in business now?"

"Certainly. I cover almost a hundred community colleges west of the Rocky Mountains with two planes and regional salesmen driving their cars. My people visit every campus at least once a week to bring in new cassettes and sound slide films and take back those that have been used. Our EAI men, and in some cases women, are the best-known people on campus."

"Then why do you want to sell control?"

"We have one problem. Software." He noticed Brad's puzzled look. "That's the programming for these devices. I need about three hundred thousand dollars to go into producing the educational programs that we take around. And I haven't got it. With the money this company could be the biggest force in education today."

With a pointer he tapped various networks of lines east of the Rocky Mountains. "There are about five other companies doing the same thing I am. They all have the same problem, financing the software. I could sell twenty hours of educational programming a week, thirty if such programming was being made. And we could produce it all, for all systems, out here in California. The small colleges and even the large ones are crying for it. Look."

Peterson turned from the map and picked up a cassette cartridge about six inches square and an inch thick. He inserted it into a device about the size of a portable television set and immediately a famous author was discussing aspects of the creative process.

"Every English department in the country wants this one. Fortunately, I know this particular writer personally and he did it for me free as a test. Don't you see what this can mean?"

"I begin to, Mr. Peterson, I certainly begin to." He smiled inwardly. No, C. L. Ciano never did anything without far-reaching reasons. "Now you feel that it would be possible to acquire all the companies in the United States presently engaged in this field. In other words, with the proper financing EAI could cover every community college in America."

"That's right, sir."

"And the local EAI man or woman sort of becomes a campus fixture, visiting every week with new programming, or software, as you call it."

"Yes, sir."

"And with an infusion of three hundred thousand dollars you could get the programming going onto these campuses."

"Without doubt."

"What do you think it would take to bring the other regional companies under one central control?"

"It's hard to say, but I feel it could be done with a

minimum amount. I'm not the only person in this business in trouble. You see, we all got excited and jumped in to be the first to get our hardware around to the colleges so we'd have a kind of exclusive. And then we found out that we just couldn't get enough software to make our operations profitable."

"The whole concept sounds most interesting. I'll be in San Francisco for several days and we'll see if a deal can be worked out. I've been in the Orient for over five weeks so I'll have to call home office, talk to my people and see what we can do."

"That will be fine, Mr. Kendall. Just don't wait too long. To be truthful, I do have a couple of other outfits looking over the system and, frankly, the way I am now I'd just have to take the first definite offer that came along."

"You'll hear from me tomorrow morning. I can see several applications of your community college network to our own aims."

"And bear in mind that I produced television shows for fifteen years at my advertising agency. I can put together the software division for you within days of the time we're funded."

"Yes. I'm sure that we would want to take over all aspects of sales and distribution with our own people."

"I have some fine salespeople out in the field," Peterson protested.

"I'm sure you do. But we're getting ahead of ourselves. By the way, did it ever occur to you that this system would be an excellent way of a political candidate getting himself across to students just coming up to voting age?"

Peterson frowned. "As a matter of fact, I really hadn't. My thinking was always in the field of pure education and training."

"Well, as an old ad man yourself you can see that this would be a powerful medium for politicians to make a long-term, slow sell to the students."

"Yes, I can see that. Perhaps we can get into commercial messages, frankly labeled as such, of course."

"Of course," Brad repeated.

"Now, what was it all about, Brad?" Luciana asked.

Brad smiled mysteriously and put the chain lock on the door to the room. "Tell you later. Right now I need a shower and a nap, euphemistically speaking, with my beautiful girl."

"Oh, Brad." Luciana laughed. "All right, it has been a long time since we've had the chance to be together." As Brad took off his jacket and tie and unbuttoned his shirt, heeling off his loafers, Luciana opened one of the beds. By the time Brad returned from taking a shower, Luciana was waiting for him, undressed, in the bed.

"Come to me, darling."

Brad needed no encouragement and he quickly slipped into bed beside her. It was three days since they'd last made love, he figured. And all the time her presence, her lithe movements, the way she looked at him had tantalized him. How much he wanted her. Just as he was about to totally become part of her, one practical thought went through his head. He rolled over, picked up the telephone and told the operator not to ring the room until further notice.

"Do you think you should do that, baby?" Luciana asked. "C.L. might be trying to get through to us."

"I'll call him—later," he replied huskily. And he pulled her to him, feeling her strong, well-toned body and firm breasts against him again. For a fleeting moment a picture flashed through his mind of Ev Jamison having her but so great was his desire now that the image had little effect.

"I love you, Luciana, I can't help myself, I love you," he moaned.

Luciana patted his head. "Come to me, darling. I want you now. Right now."

CHAPTER THIRTY-THREE

Brad Kendall's first desire upon reaching New York's JFK Airport via commercial airliner was to try and reach his daughter. He would have tried to reach Elda Ciano to make contact except that a limousine was waiting to take him immediately to C. L. Ciano's office. And to underscore the urgency, Maurice D'Estang had come out to meet him.

"This is an unexpected gesture, Maurice." Brad's tone was neutral. Professionally he had to work with Maurice but he was not anxious to see more of the tall, heavy-set Corsican than necessary.

"I wanted to hear what happened. How's my brother?"

"Last seen your brother was in his element putting together his poppy route. He'll do very well over there."

"How does he like that place?"

"He seemed happy. He told me this was a deal he'd been wanting to set up for a long time. I'm sure he'll be the biggest operator in his field very shortly."

Maurice nodded in satisfaction. "That's good. He's always been the problem kid in the family. Never could settle down to any one thing."

"He'll do a good job for the company." Brad turned sidewise facing D'Estang. "What's so urgent that I have to get right over to C.L. this evening?"

"He'll tell you. I think you're going back to politics for a while."

"Fine with me. We gave our all for Jamison. By the way, how in hell did C.L. get interested in this educational caper?"

"You told us on the phone it looked like a good deal."

"I think it can become a profitable enterprise with the proper seed money. I see what Ciano is getting at, of course. He figures he can use the system for propagandizing for his candidates with the college students. But it seems to me that he could do the same thing with less effort in other ways. Why get into building up a company?"

Maurice stared back at Brad a moment, an incredulous look on his face. "Propagandizing the students?" He began to laugh. "Is that why you think he wants EAI?"

"Well, he certainly didn't want me to acquire it for the average profits involved and I don't think he feels some sudden benevolent urge to improve the educational standards of community colleges."

Maurice chuckled. His chuckles turned to guffaws and then derisive laughter. "No, no, you are quite right. But influencing students politically isn't what interests him in the company. At least not primarily."

"Then what is his interest?"

"What has been your primary purpose in the Orient?" D'Estang asked. "And don't tell me setting up hotel deals."

"I thought that's what it was," Brad replied innocently.

"All right, have it your way." D'Estang chuckled. "But all that stuff my brother is getting out of Indochina is going to be coming back to this country. And out of Latin America through Mexico are coming new shipments of cocaine. And what is the primary market for this stuff?"

"The ghettos."

"Used to be. But the emphasis is shifting. The kids outside of the cities want their share, the kids in colleges around the country, and those half-assed community colleges are no exception. Since you've been back from the Orient, what outfit have you seen with the most acceptance on college campuses? Who can go every week to the small colleges without ever being suspected of anything wrong?"

D'Estang saw Brad's expression change to one of horror and pain. "That's right," Maurice went on, "your friendly educational-aids distributor. Get it?"

"We're going to get the kids on campuses around the country hooked?" Brad asked hollowly.

"No. That they already are. EAI is just the most convenient and safest way of getting to them what they're going to buy anyway."

It shouldn't have shocked him, Brad thought. It was a logical extension of what was happening, what he had helped cause to happen, in the international narcotics routes. He sat back silently and said little for the rest of the trip, answering D'Estang's questions perfunctorily.

The limousine stopped in front of the Spire Building and Brad and Maurice went in. "C.L. will be glad to see you," D'Estang said. "He considers you a top man now that you're really one of us."

Brad nodded but didn't answer. The special elevator that only stopped at C. L. Ciano's floor swiftly lifted them the sixty-six floors. The security guard passed them through to Ciano's office and once again Brad found himself in the huge, though somehow comfortable, office with the man who had efficiently and progressively made a criminal, albeit a high-level malfeasant, out of him.

"Brad," Ciano greeted him, "forgive this precipitous summons but I couldn't wait to hear a complete report of everything that happened on the trip. In our case such reports can never be committed to writing or discussed over the telephone."

Ciano led Brad and D'Estang over to his conference alcove around the fireplace with the big Mercator projection of the world above it, and they all sat down. "First, would you like a drink, Brad?" Ciano offered.

Brad felt in the mood for a stiff highball and said so. Ciano pressed a button beside his chair and almost immediately his office butler materialized. Maurice D'Estang joined Brad, and Ciano got down to business. "I want to hear everything," he demanded. "From the moment you took off from New York almost six weeks ago."

Almost an hour later, Ciano had been listening intently, Brad brought him up to the incidents surrounding the Meo tribesmen and Etienne D'Estang's methods of bringing morphine base into Vientiane.

"And how about the routes from there?" Ciano asked eagerly. "We have no time to lose bringing product in. In a week from now the routes from Europe will be closed down, but I'll get to that later."

"We'll be in action. I took the liberty of loaning Ascot Two to the Ministry of the Interior for a month. His aide and the lady of his choice are touring America as our guests in Ascot One right now."

"Good, good, Brad. How are they going to use it?"

"I made several trips to Vientiane and persuaded the government that if a major hotel were to be built in Vientiane it was necessary to have better transportation between Vientiane and Bangkok and Saigon and Hong Kong. Then, playing on national pride, I suggested that they form their own international airline to take passengers and cargo between those cities." Brad winked. "Naturally, I offered to assist in financing such a venture and loaned them a jet to get started."

"So we have our own Air Opium," D'Estang exclaimed. "Just like Air Vietnam."

"Exactly, Maurice. We can get whatever quantities of material necessary safely delivered throughout the Orient. Now we come to the problem of shipments between the Orient and here." Brad paused, glancing idly at his empty glass.

"You've been doing a lot of talking, Brad. Make yourself another drink," Ciano urged.

"Thanks, C.L., I will." Brad walked to the bar behind the sliding wall and poured another highball. "Joe Peng, another guest of Ascot Hotels in this country, is the leading Chinese lawyer in Hong Kong. He represents a Chinese syndicate that is purchasing two VC-10 jets from Britain and starting a world-wide jet charter service available to groups all over the Orient who wish to visit the Western Hemisphere. Needless to say, any extra payload they can carry will be welcome. We can count on two flights a month between Hong Kong and Acapulco. I assume that our contacts in Mexico are sufficient to—"

"No problem," D'Estang broke in. "In Mexico we're golden."

"Then," Brad smiled and spread his hands, "I have done my job. And by the way, C.L., it really wouldn't be a bad idea to put a lovely small hotel in Vientiane. I made up a pro forma statement. We could see a respectable profit out of it."

"Go ahead with it, Brad," Ciano decreed. "After what you've done, I'll give you a hotel in Peking if you want it."

"Things are still a little draggy there, boss." Brad grinned.

"Whatever you say, Brad. Now, let's discuss the EAI deal. I take it Maurice has enlightened you on its value to us. At this point the most important project we are mounting as far as you are concerned is building up Bill Adams into a national figure. The planning has been extensive, as you will realize when Maurice gives you a complete briefing. Your job is to squeeze every drop of political juice out of the tremendous victory Bill Adams is going to score over organized crime this week."

"He is?" Brad asked.

"How many people in America know that there is a House Crime Committee?" Ciano asked. "And if they know there is such a thing I'll bet they couldn't even name the chairman, much less any of the members. Well, Bill Adams is going to put that committee on the map and make himself famous. The chairman won't like a junior committee member taking all the credit, but we'll have Adams out of the House and into the Senate this fall."

"Politics are my favorite bag, C.L. Lead me to the fray," Brad toasted, holding up his glass and then drinking.

"Maurice, when Brad's finished with his drink take him down and show him the congressman's New York office." He turned to Brad. "As you know, there are all sorts of restrictions on how much a candidate can spend these days, but for every restriction there are two ways to get around it. Now when you see Adams' office you might well ask yourself, how does a congressman afford such opulence? And we have the answer. With all the new office buildings going up in New York the Spire Building needs to build its prestige. What better way than by having our congressman who may become our senator in the building? So it is worth it to the building to give him the space for a nominal rental and decorate it so that we can show it to prospective tenants of the building."

"You have whetted my appetite, C.L." He put down his drink. "Let's have a look."

After taking their leave of Ciano, Maurice and Brad rode the regular elevator down to the sixtieth floor. They stepped out of the car into the reception room for the entire floor. "Adams has the whole floor?" Brad asked.

"His law firm has part of the floor and pays full price for its footage." A security officer in uniform sat at the reception desk. He recognized D'Estang, who pulled out a special laminated card and held it up.

"Go right on back," the officer said. "Mr. Adams is at his desk."

"He works late," Brad observed.

"He hasn't been out of here for almost a week." Maurice pushed the door to the congressman's section of the floor open. "He even has a small apartment up here."

"What's the big excitement?"

"You'll see." D'Estang led Brad down a corridor with closed doors on both sides of it. "Here's where the permanent New York staff works." At the end of the corridor stood impressive wood-paneled double doors. Above them on a wooden plaque was printed in block letters "Communications Room."

"This is something. Julius the Genius put everything he had into it. Too bad Whitehall doesn't have press conferences, this is where they'd be held." D'Estang reached into his pocket and drew out a key which he fitted into the lock on one of the double doors and turned. He pushed the door open and switched on the lights.

Brad followed D'Estang into the room and then stood still, silently admiring it. To his right, the back of the rectangular room, was the viewing area. There were three stepped platforms for the members of the press to stand, sit, set up cameras and take notes.

"There's toilet facilities and changing rooms behind the press section," D'Estang pointed out. "Mr. Ciano had the top public relations firm in New York design this room."

"Let's hope Adams makes it to senator," Brad breathed. "This is, to use C.L.'s own word, a bit opulent for a congressman."

"Senator? He ought to make it all the way in '76."

Brad studied the elaborate communications layout to his left. A chart of the world dominated the back wall, with round clocks above each time zone indicating the time all over the world. Furthermore, the part of the world in darkness was in shadow on the large chart. At a glance one could see the approximate time of day anywhere in the world.

"C.L. has a thing about maps of the world," Brad remarked.

"That map is something else," D'Estang replied. "It's all what you call rear projection. The technical guy at the console over there," he pointed at the console of the side of the room, radiant with dials, lights, switches, buttons and a row of television monitors, "can turn off the world and throw anything he wants up on that screen. He can even throw two or three pictures beside each other up there or run a movie or TV show. You gotta see it to believe it."

"I believe it, Maurice," Brad said wearily. "By now

I believe anything. But why does a congressman need all this?"

"The whole thing was put together for one big show, coming up next week. C.L. wanted you in on it all the way. All you have to do is get Adams elected senator."

"I'm glad he isn't asking me to do something difficult," Brad retorted sarcastically.

"Wait until you see what you got to work with." D'Estang looked around as though making sure nobody else was in the large room. He lowered his voice. "Right above here is a control room where everything that happens down here is duplicated. Up there you can even hear what the news people are saying to each other as they watch the show."

"What show?"

"I'll give you the complete morning line after we see Adams. I'll show you to his office." Maurice turned off the lights, locked the doors after him, and led Brad back down the corridor of staff offices and around to another double door above which was the legend "Representative William Fortune Adams." He pushed open one of the double doors, and they found themselves in another reception room, one in which a working secretary presided by day, Brad thought, judging by the size of the desk and the piles of papers and green-covered transcripts of congressional investigating committee hearings. Hardly had they entered when Congressman Adams pushed open the door from his office and greeted them. He looked as fresh as morning, ready to go out and give a political speech.

Maurice chuckled. "You'd never know to look at him he's been working twelve straight hours."

Brad shook hands with the representative. "Hi, Bill, I've been looking around the place. Too bad an important congressman like you can't afford something with a little more class."

A worried expression came over Adams' face. "You think the place is too sumptuous? Maybe I'll be suspect?"

Brad shook his head. "We can explain it away. As soon as someone tells me about the big show I'll work out what to tell the press when they get their first look at the place."

"He just got back to New York a few hours ago, Bill," Maurice explained. "I'll give him a thorough briefing tonight."

"It's so big it even scares me," Adams said. "But if we pull it off—Lord have mercy—" he searched for a word, "it will be apocalyptic."

Brad looked at D'Estang. "Maurice?" there was mock plea in his tone.

"Bill, we'll see you tomorrow," D'Estang said. "Brad hasn't eaten, hasn't slept and doesn't know what we're talking about."

Back on the street in front of the Spire Building the limousine was waiting for them. "Thanks for sparing me a long session with Adams," Brad said as the limousine headed for the Ascot Hotel.

"We'll have a quick supper and I'll hit the highlights for you. Tomorrow we'll get into details."

Inside the hotel Maurice headed for the elevators. Brad held back. "I don't feel like all the bowing and scraping that goes on at the Star Club tonight. Let's just grab a bite downstairs where the tourists eat," Brad suggested.

Maurice shrugged. "As you wish." He followed Brad through the lobby to the River Room.

"Ah, Herr D'Estang," Brad heard someone with a Germanic accent say behind him. "I tried to call you earlier." Brad turned and saw a gray-haired man in a black suit with pearl-gray vest, peering through thick glasses, standing up from the table he shared with a young man who looked to be in his early twenties. Brad always felt an immediate antipathy toward people who wore sunglasses indoors, and the youth had on shades that included two wide strips of translucent black plastic that ran from the glasses back to his ears. He stared at the young man who wore his blond hair close cropped. He had a strange, fixed preoccupied smile on his face but otherwise seemed of conservative dress and manner.

"Doctor, I'll call you in your room later," D'Estang said briefly. "I'm quite busy now."

"Yes, yes," the doctor murmured. "Please not to forget." He sat down and Brad continued on to a corner booth followed by D'Estang.

"Who was that?" Brad asked when they had seated themselves and ordered a drink.

"That is Doctor Ulric Wormsinger, a psychologist originally from Vienna. He now does some work for us in the field of psychological testing."

"That young guy wearing the shades looks like he could do with some psychological help."

"Yes," D'Estang answered vaguely. "Someday we'll get into Wormsinger's function but right now, let's talk a little about Adams."

CHAPTER THIRTY-FOUR

Detective Patrick Kenney surveyed the scene with professional suspicion. Even at the federal Bureau they didn't have this kind of a setup for following an investigation in progress. And with the addition of a press gallery full of people ready to report the culmination of six months of intense effort on his part, Kenney could feel his nerves twitch and his stomach pulsate. As always, since Representative Black had turned him over to Representative Adams, the unprecedented speed and smoothness with which his operations moved ahead alarmed him almost as much as they satisfied him. Things just didn't go this well if everything was kosher, he thought.

Kenney was under no misapprehension that Congressman William Fortune Adams was spending so much of his time, effort and somebody's money because he believed wholeheartedly that it was his mission in life to curb organized crime. If such was the case this elaborate setup would be unnecessary. Adams wouldn't be playing to the press so openly, possibly, even likely, jeopardizing the entire operation.

Of course, Kenney had known the score for the past two months. Adams was looking to get elected to the Senate in the fall and who could tell what was his final goal. Kenney recognized stark political ambition when he saw it. The New York Police Department was the favorite football of city and state politicos.

So why, he asked himself, was Pat Kenney playing along? Was it really because he had one all-consuming passion to seriously cripple the narcotics syndicate he knew existed but had never, until now, been able to isolate and attack? He wasn't getting anything else out of working for Adams. Long hours and no days off featured his existence. Yes, he was making a very fair bonus on top of his salary as a first grade detective and the frustrations of having been transferred out of the Narcotics Bureau and into a ghetto precinct were notably absent. In fact, he had far better resources and more money to work with under Adams than he ever had in his best days with the city Narcotics Bureau.

He thought about the jet that had been available to fly him at a moment's notice to any part of the world his investigation covered. He had unlimited funds to pay informers. He had even bought a top police officer in the Virgin Islands by paying him more money than the narcotics smugglers had paid him.

Why was it then that he couldn't get rid of the nagging feeling that somehow he himself had been bought and paid for? He was doing the most effective job of his lifetime, so if anyone was paying him off to do what he believed in and wanted to do was there anything wrong? The problem, almost one of theological proportions it seemed, was too much to wrestle with now as he sat behind the console at one side of Adams' elaborate communications room. Beside him was the technician who made all the electronic apparatus function.

Kenney could look to his left and see the big world map which showed where it was dark and where light in the world. In front of him was a row of television monitors. The technician could throw the pictures that appeared on them onto a large screen which appeared when needed in the middle of the Pacific Ocean on the big map that covered the back wall of the communications room. Another screen in the South Atlantic could be flicked on with a switch. Directly in front of him, sitting at a desk, was Representative Adams, facing the members of the press who had been invited to personally witness what was hoped to be the largest international narcotics roundup ever achieved. If successful the entire Middle East-European-American narcotics syndicate would be destroyed.

Kenney focused his attention on Adams as he stood up and addressed the battery of newsmen, photographers and TV cameramen gathered before him.

"Ladies and gentlemen of the fourth estate," Adams was saying to the press, "I'm sorry that it was necessary to impose certain restrictions on you but this is the only way we can let you witness the pay-off. The operation we launched against the highly organized narcotics syndicate would be blown if a word leaked out prematurely."

He gestured toward the table behind them that contained a silver coffee urn and plates of sandwiches. "There are more than adequate facilities to make you comfortable while you watch the operation unfold from our control room here."

Adams looked at his wrist watch. "It's ten o'clock. Hopefully by tomorrow morning everybody will be free to leave, but if our operation has not been completed successfully we will have to ask you to stay. So—" he smiled at the press group "—is it understood? If anyone feels he can't stay with us until the end he's free to leave now." Adams gave the newsmen a questioning look but nobody moved.

"Very well." He turned to the console and his eyes met Kenney's. "You have all heard of Detective Patrick Kenney. Probably most of you have read the book about his exploits while he was a member of the New York Police Department's Narcotics Bureau. Detective Kenney has been working with me for many months in an effort to break the power and effectiveness of the international narcotics syndicate that is bringing in the quantities of dope to our country that is weakening our national structure and creating increasing numbers of addicts every month."

As was planned, Pat stood up facing the press a moment and then sat down. Adams continued. "When this operation has been wrapped up Detective Kenney will give you a summary of what you have seen unfold here."

Then Adams turned to a severe-looking, middle-aged man with a crew cut, gray hair and a wiry figure sitting on the other side of the console technician from Kenney. "Now, let me introduce you to Mr. Jackson Potter of the New York office of the federal Bureau of Narcotics and Dangerous Drugs. I have co-ordinated my investigation with the Bureau through Mr. Potter and all the arrests you will witness will be effected by his agents." Potter stood up, nodded and sat down.

Kenney noticed that in the front row of the press section Brad Kendall, president of Ascot Hotels, was seated. He had met Kendall a number of times recently and had reached the conclusion that the hotelman was somehow tied in politically with Adams as an adviser and probably a campaign contributor. He expected that Adams would explain Kendall's presence, but Adams made no further announcements regarding his associates.

"My investigations turned up one little-known fact," Adams continued. "The syndicate we have had under surveillance operates in a way never before revealed. When it makes a major move in one area, it makes all of its moves here and in Europe simultaneously. The reason for this, we have learned, is that should any one of its operations become compromised, all the others will have been achieved before a full-scale investigation can be undertaken. Of course, it is impossible, the leaders of this syndicate believe, that the entire apparatus from the top down, in Europe and America, could ever be penetrated and destroyed. Yet that, for the first time, is what my investigators have done. Led by Detective Kenney on loan to my staff by the New York Police Department and Mr. Potter, we have been able to identify the leaders and chief smugglers and wholesalers involved in this syndicate. Shortly you will see the results of their efforts."

Brad glanced about the press section attempting to gauge the effect on the newsmen of Adams' speech. While he had of necessity been selective regarding the newsmen invited, he was mindful that the big push here was to make Adams a statewide hero. Therefore, he had invited representatives from all the major newspapers in New York State as well as the important local TV channels to be present. Excitement mingled with disbelief seemed the tenor of the press.

On the screen flashed a picture of a trawler with a picturesque seaport in the background. "This is target number one," Adams recited. "This is a picture taken by Bureau agents two weeks ago of a trawler owned by a Corsican narcotics trafficker named Robert Tradeux. Tradeux at this moment is sailing just off Marseilles where he will land about a thousand pounds of morphine base from Lebanon for the underworld chemists who will turn it into heroin. As you can see by the world map it is now 4 A.M. along the Riviera with sunrise expected in about one and a half hours. At that time agents from Mr. Potter's Bureau, accompanying French police agents, will intercept the trawler and search it. The bags of morphine crystals are behind bulkheads in the ship's hold."

The picture of the trawler disappeared. "Now, you will see over a hidden closed-circuit TV camera a scene from Kennedy International Airport coming to us live." On the screen was a room which looked like it might be a customs station.

"A few minutes ago an Air France jet landed at Kennedy International Airport non-stop from Paris," Adams recounted. "Aboard that plane was a man named Jorge Ramirez. He is the United Nations representative from Santo Morango, a small country in Latin America. As such he enjoys diplomatic immunity. In a few moments you will watch him walk out through the diplomatic passport exit at JFK International Airport Terminal. You will see him on the screen. Through a network of paid informers we know that he is bringing into the country well over one hundred pounds of pure heroin. When cut and retailed in so-called five-dollar pops that load is worth thirty-five million dollars.

"Also tonight, from St. Croix in the American Virgin Islands a courier is bringing into Miami Airport another hundred pounds of heroin. He will have no trouble at the airport since St. Croix is part of the United States and there is no customs inspection of passengers arriving from the American Virgin Islands. For several years St. Croix has proved to be one of the easiest and safest parts of the United States into which heroin and cocaine can be smuggled."

Adams looked up at the picture on the screen. A few men and women were coming through the room with porters carrying their baggage. They showed passports to immigration agents and were waved through, their luggage unopened. "There's Ramirez now," Adams exclaimed, excitement in his tone. He glanced up at the television cameramen trying to focus on the screen. "This scene is being preserved on video tape and will be available to all the TV representatives when the operation is over."

Ramirez, followed by a beautiful, long-haired blonde wearing a short skirt and the porter pushing the diplomat's sturdy-looking suitcases on a cart, identified himself with his diplomatic passport and walked on through the special customs office with the girl out onto the street.

"It was the girl who really led me to him," Kenney commented. "My informant said to look for a Latin UN diplomat with a sexy blond girl friend."

The picture on the screen cut to the exterior of the diplomatic exit. "Another camera will show you what happens from here," Adams went on. A limousine drove up to the United Nations representative and stopped. The driver jumped out and came around the car, opening the back door. Ramirez helped the girl into the back seat and stepped inside beside her. Then the driver motioned to the porter to push the cart closer to the limousine's trunk. He opened the trunk and then personally hoisted in first one and then the second large, heavy suitcase and slammed the trunk closed.

"Even if we wanted to, we could not arrest Ramirez here," Adams explained. "His diplomatic immunity holds within the city of New York where he is on United Nations business. Agents from the Bureau out at the airport now will maintain the surveillance on the Ramirez car." The limousine quickly drove out of the picture, which was wiped from the screen.

A red light glowed on a telephone beside Adams. He picked it up and listened. "Our agents report that the limousine is being followed. There are a number of unmarked cars along the route into the city which will take turns following Ramirez in order that he doesn't become suspicious. I'll keep you informed as the limousine nears the city.

"And now," Adams continued, "let's switch our attention up to Harlem. There has been, for the past few days, a panic brewing. Heroin has been in short supply and in all the ghetto areas of the city the addicts are restless, terrified that their sources may dry up before a new shipment comes in. Street crime and petty thefts are rising as the addicts steal enough money to get ahead on their supply. Before tonight is over, were it not for our operation, at least half of the pure stuff Ramirez brought into New York would reach the ghetto cutting shops to be adulterated for sale on the streets. It is our hope to follow this shipment from Ramirez to the American importers and from them to the major wholesalers. One big Harlem operator in particular we hope to catch with the evidence on him, named Permagon Antilles, is referred to as the Big Nig. That's not my name for him, I assure you," Adams added hastily. "I merely work with the facts and pass them on to you." He paused to let his declaration have impact.

"Now the Italian family—and again I mean no ethnic slurs—I only am trying to lay certain facts before you—the Italian group or family tied in with Ramirez and the French connections will try to get rid of the entire shipment by morning. They should realize about a million and a half dollars on the load for which they paid perhaps four hundred thousand dollars in France. They used to make the French connections deliver the heroin to them in New York where they paid considerably more. Now they have found that by handling the smuggling end of the operation themselves they are much surer of receiving the heroin. It costs them less, and they don't have to worry about the Frenchmen getting careless and compromising them.

"What we have here is a ring made up of two separate but equal groups. There's the European section and the U.S. section, each with its own maximum leader. We believe tonight that we will apprehend the two leaders in a sort of narcotics summit conference." Adams stood up and walked toward the map.

"The two top Frenchmen, I believe they are actually Corsican, left Paris," he placed a pointer on the city, "yesterday. They flew to Montreal." He traced the route with the pointer. "And now, with the co-operation of the Royal Canadian Mounted Police, we have had the two Frenchmen under surveillance since the moment they landed in Montreal. We will be notified of what flight they take to New York City anytime now."

In the control room above Congressman Adams' communications room Maurice D'Estang, Julius the Genius, wearing earphones, and Dino Larucci, Sal the Hand's counselor and most trusted aide, watched the operation unfold. "After all this what we're going through, that bum Adams better get himself elected," Dino growled. "What a square!"

"He's got the press excited," Julius reported. "They're whispering away, making bets he won't pull it off."

"If we left it to him and Kenney and the Bureau he sure wouldn't," D'Estang agreed. "I'll bet a grand they blow Ramirez and we have to set them straight." He looked at Larucci. "I'll even give you two to one odds."

"No bet," Larucci replied. "But I hope they nail

the nigger. He's been an ice pick up our ass since he got so big."

"You got it set, don't you?" D'Estang asked.

"Nothin's never set, anything can happen," Larucci replied.

"They lost the limo!" Julius suddenly cried.

"Lost it?"

"They were trying to keep such a loose tail it got away."

"That Ramirez is a smart spic," D'Estang said. "But he's been wanting more money and implying that he could give us trouble if we don't pay up."

"He's got Forno, one of the best wheelmen in the business," Larucci added. "Forno always figures he's being followed, and nobody can snake a car through the streets like him."

"You should hear Adams," Julius chuckled. "He just heard from Potter that they lost the limo and he's probably wondering what to tell the press now."

"Let the bastard suffer," Larucci advised.

Julius, the headset covering his ears, simpered, "The ladies and gentlemen of the press are getting restless."

"Five radio cars and they lose the limo," growled D'Estang. "Well, our boy with the Bureau's posse will save Adams' ass. Just goes to prove what I always say, you gotta have insurance on everything." He walked over to where Julius was sitting at the control console. "Get Dan Gason on the special frequency. Tell him to head for the Pierre Hotel and wait for Ramirez to show. The driver is changing from the Cadillac limo to a brown Mercedes 280 out in Queens. Dan will have to figure out how to explain the way he picked them up again."

In the communications room Adams stared at the press contingent helplessly. "It appears that the Bureau has still not been able to regain contact with the Ramirez car." He gave Potter, who was urgently talking into his phone, a reproachful look.

Brad, sitting in the press section, was conscious of an air of derision among the reporters. What kind of a stunt had they been asked to participate in? they seemed to be asking themselves. Brad's worst fears were being confirmed. Adams was an unexciting figure to begin with. And now, at the very start of what should be his moment of glory, he was blowing the operation. Something had to be done to recapture the interest and confidence of the press.

Brad stood up. "Mr. Adams?" he began.

Adams nodded dubiously. "Your question, Mr. Kendall?"

"I wonder if Detective Kenney of your staff could explain a little more to us about how this surveillance works, what are the pitfalls, how do you lose a tail, burn a tail, I believe, was the expression in the book about Mr. Kenney, which I suppose most of the journalists here have heard of."

Adams returned Brad's bland gaze with a hard look of his own. This was his show, not Detective Kenney's nor even Potter's. Why was Brad Kendall, whose job as Adams understood it was strictly to supply logistical support for the Adams campaign, trying to influence the conduct of this politically oriented operation?

Brad, sensing Adams' resistance to sharing the focus of attention and resolving to make Adams aware of who, in reality, was calling the shots on this campaign, appealed indirectly to the other journalists. "What I think all of us are interested in, Congressman Adams, are the views and interpretations of an experienced detective like Mr. Kenney in this case."

"Right, let's hear from Kenney while you are trying to find that car," another reporter supported.

Assenting murmurs from the group of journalists caused Adams to turn to the detective. "Mr. Kenney, would you mind giving our guests here tonight whatever further information you have which might be useful to them?"

Kenney had been listening to and watching Brad Kendall with curiosity mixed with pity and a certain feeling of guilt. He could not understand this hotelman's true function in the investigation. Certainly there seemed to be a more profound connection between

Kendall and Adams, and for that matter Black, than was apparent. Brad was more than just a political adviser and provider of accommodations, Kenney realized instinctively. He wished he knew more. It would have helped him make an important decision recently if he had known just where Kendall fitted into the big picture.

As Brad had been talking, Kenney thought about the afternoon not long ago when he had been keeping a young hood, Tony Falcon, under surveillance. Tony was selling marijuana and lately heroin to the overprivileged youths he cultivated. When a particularly beautiful girl about nineteen, a young lady with real class Kenney realized, visited Tony's apartment for the better part of two hours Kenney had become curious. When the girl finally left he had followed her to the apartment she shared with her parents, Mr. and Mrs. Edwin Connor. It had not taken much effort to find out that the girl's name was Andrea Kendall, daughter of the president of the Ascot Hotel chain.

At this point Detective Kenney found himself in an unpleasant dilemma. Tony Falcon was leading him to the higher-ups in the heroin syndicate and he didn't want Tony to suspect he was being watched. Obviously, if Kenney passed the word to Kendall that Andrea was seeing Tony at his apartment and leaving with the unmistakable look of having taken narcotics, Kendall would raise hell with his daughter—what father wouldn't?—and Tony would realize he was under surveillance.

In other words, Kenney's problem was whether or not to blow the investigation and reveal what he knew. Was Kendall more important than the investigation? Discreet inquiries provided inconclusive answers. Kenney decided to keep quiet about the girl and pursue the investigation.

Kenney ambled from the communications console to the center of the floor. Ever since he had been an instructor at the police academy he had enjoyed addressing an audience, and when the book about his exploits as a detective in the Narcotics Bureau came out he suddenly found himself in demand as a speaker until the police commissioner had told him to stop talking or get off the force. But at this moment he was free, ordered to talk by a U.S. congressman.

Kenney made an imposing figure. Big, burly, a wide Irish face topped with red hair, he commanded absolute attention. "Our problem tonight," he began, "was that we had to go with a very loose tail on the subject limousine. We know that Ramirez is very cautious and the driver who picked him and the girl up had to be a top wheelman. With this loose tail, even with several radio cars working, it's very easy to lose a car. That's what happened just now out there in Queens. The cars are all fanned out looking for the limo."

"Do you think they'll find him?" a reporter asked.

"It's hard to say. In cases like this, a driver only has to be out of surveillance for a minute or two to pass the stuff to an accomplice and then even if we get him later the evidence is gone."

"I think it's safe to say we'll pick the limo up again anytime now," Adams broke in, the confidence in his words far from reflected in his tone of voice.

"Another thing a good wheelman will do," Kenney went on, ignoring Adams' statement, "he'll pull out of sight suddenly around a corner, turn into a garage waiting for him, and he's lost. In the garage he'll change cars, come out on another street, and he's gone."

"If he's lost, is your whole case tonight destroyed?" a pretty female crime reporter from the New York *Times* asked.

"We are on several other subjects who should take us to the same place," Kenney replied. "But of course Ramirez is our best subject. I think Mr. Potter's men will pick him up again."

Kenney was practically convinced that there was no way the Bureau would find the limousine before it was too late. He had seen this sort of thing happen too many times to be optimistic. It would be some kind of a miracle if they picked the limo up with both Ramirez and the suitcase of heroin still in it.

Kenney realized that his own pessimism was conveying itself to the newsmen and to cover the gap in the proceedings he discussed the case further. "You must keep in mind that there are six different," he paused searching for a word and recalled a suitable one from the book written about him, "elements we have to think about in this case." He held up one large hand and with the other ticked the points off on thick fingers.

"First, we know about two Frenchmen coming into Montreal this morning. The Mounties are watching them." Kenney touched his second finger. "Right now Ramirez is coming into the city with over a hundred pounds of heroin. He'll be taking it to someone at the top, probably the same person the Frenchmen will be seeing, we figure. Now third, we've got this courier arriving in Miami from St. Croix sometime tonight. I'll tell you more about him later. He'll be carrying one hundred pounds or better of heroin plus maybe as much as another thirty pounds of cocaine for the Chicago market."

Kenney touched his fourth finger. "Through informers we have learned that the Big Nig's main cutting rooms in Harlem have been alerted to have their people ready for a shipment tonight. And fifth, we know that trawler with a big shipment of morph is going to unload off Marseilles anytime in the next couple of hours." Now Kenney held his hand up, fingers outstretched.

Dramatically, the detective clenched his fingers into a fist which he enclosed with his other hand. "The sixth thing is the whole syndicate we're after. Now you heard Congressman Adams say that the syndicate plans all its operations to come off simultaneous. Each of these five elements will lead us to the syndicate if we handle it all right. That's what you're here tonight to see. How we follow these five operations back to the source, the syndicate." Once again he smote his fist with his other hand.

The press was silent, staring at the expressive detective with fascination. It was Kenney who kept them interested, Brad realized, not the pompous congressman. So he would have to see that Kenney's charisma rubbed off on Adams.

"This has been a long investigation, six months that I've been on it," Kenney continued. "And despite all our work it was only in the last month that everything suddenly," he held his hands apart, fingers spread, and then moved the hands together, the fingers entwining, "came together. Good police work and development of informers finally made it for us."

Even as he said this he knew it wasn't really true. He had suddenly gotten very, very lucky or something. He couldn't even put his finger on just exactly how he had been responsible for the valuable information that flowed into the network he had set up for Adams.

"So what we're doing tonight is tracking all the five elements I was talking about and each one should lead us to the same place, the top echelon of this narcotics smuggling syndicate. We put them out of business and we're well on the way to choking off the supply of," his tone raised dramatically, "the living death that keeps coming into our country."

There was a moment of silence and then an impulsive burst of applause which abruptly ceased as Potter, the telephone held to his face, motioned to Adams who went over to him. The congressman smiled broadly at what Potter was telling him and then turned to the press. "Mr. Potter has just informed me that one of his agents has located Ramirez, his girl friend and the driver. They indeed somehow shifted to another car and at this moment are drawing up in front of the Pierre Hotel at Fifth Avenue and Sixty-first Street."

"I hope they still have the stuff with them," Kenney muttered.

"Can you tell us the name of the agent who found Ramirez again and how he managed to do it?" a reporter asked.

"I'll ask Mr. Potter to make that information available as soon as possible," Adams replied. Potter said a few more words to Adams who once again faced the press. "Ramirez has left the new car, it's a Mercedes-

Benz, and gone into the hotel. The driver, doorman and a bellman have put the suitcases on a cart and are pushing them right behind Ramirez. The agent who found Ramirez is in the hotel and will check out the room he goes to. Now the Mercedes is leaving the hotel with the girl in it and it will be tailed."

Kenney returned to the console behind which Potter and the technician were seated. As the journalists watched, Detective Kenney listened to a headset he held against an ear and then handed back to the technician. He strode from behind the console and addressed the press group.

"In about ten minutes or less the Eastern flight from St. Croix will be landing at Miami International Airport," Kenney announced. He was getting into the groove now and enjoying his share of attention. "Over the past few months I spent a lot of time down there trying to establish how heroin and cocaine was getting into the island and who was taking it from there to the United States and where in the United States. I was working undercover, of course, with the help of an old friend of mine who used to be with the Narcotics Bureau and is now one of the top cops in the Virgin Islands. With his help I was able to make the right pay-offs and meet a character named Karl Echeverrea Brandt. He's half German and half spic—Latin that is," Kenney corrected himself. "He became a U.S. citizen after spending five years in the U.S. Army where his language capability made him valuable. Today he has big social and business connections in the Virgin Islands. He is also one of the top movers of narcotics in the Caribbean. It's this Karl who's on the plane bringing in a load. We'll follow him real careful when he gets off," Kenney promised. "I have one of my own men working with the Bureau agents at the airport."

Jackson Potter looked up sharply from the console as Kenney's implication brought a chuckle from the press, but he said nothing.

Now Adams addressed the journalists. "Ramirez has taken his suitcases up to rooms 1801 and 3. We have determined that the room is registered in the name of

Joseph Sterrato and we are checking to find out everything we can on this man."

On the big screen in the Pacific region of the map a picture of the Hotel Pierre's Fifth Avenue entrance flashed on. "We have a TV surveillance truck parked outside the hotel. Needless to say it doesn't look like what it is but we want a record of who comes in and out. We also have two agents on the eighteenth floor watching Sterrato's room."

"So, now they have everything under control again." D'Estang chuckled.

"They'll fuck it up again," Larucci rasped. "That Echeverrea is slippery as a wet skin."

"I put the best man I had available into Kenney's Miami operation," D'Estang answered. "Bebbi's a Lebanese. He knows every trick in a smuggler's bag and has used them all twice. The feds alone wouldn't stand a chance."

"Hey, Genius, what's happening in Strega Joe's suite?" D'Estang suddenly asked Julius.

"Everything's going fine. They just counted the bags and put them in the two new suitcases. Joe's paying off Ramirez now."

"Right. We gotta get that shit out of the suite right away. We promised Sterrato he wouldn't get hit with possession. Where's Falcon and the nigger?"

"Right where they're supposed to be, on the corner of Sixtieth and Fifth waiting to see Ramirez leave the hotel. Then they'll go right up. Shit!" the Genius suddenly exclaimed. "Adams is getting scared."

"What do you mean?" D'Estang snapped back.

"He's asking Potter to hit Joe now. He's afraid the rest of the deal won't come off and at least he's got a big haul right in his hands now."

"That water-blooded little gutless shit heel," D'Estang swore. "After all we put into this thing?"

"Potter's shook up too. He doesn't know whether to hit now or not. He's saying they can always grab everyone else who comes to the suite and be sure of Joe and Ramirez."

"Get Kendall outside now." D'Estang strode from the surveillance office.

Brad was wondering what was going on around the console. Everything seemed to be all right now, yet what was the conference about? He could sense the curiosity on the part of the newsmen around him. Then he heard the subdued tone of the beeper in his pocket. He stood up and walked from the press section to the group around the console. Adams looked up.

"Be back in a moment." He put his mouth close to Adams' ear. "Ciano wants me."

Adams nodded and Brad went out the door behind the console into the hall. He had hardly closed the door behind him before D'Estang pushed open the emergency staircase door.

"That bastard's crazy, Brad," D'Estang whispered urgently. "He wants to hit the suite now. He's afraid if he doesn't something else will happen and he'll blow the whole thing in front of the press."

"I'll stop him."

"Fast!"

Without answering Brad ducked back into the communications room and was next to Congressman Adams just in time to hear him say, "OK, Jackson, let's order the arrest."

"No! No arrest now!" Brad's voice lashed out. Potter whirled around at the commanding tone. "Bill, come into the conference room with me a moment." Brad turned to the detective. "Kenney. Give the press some more of your personal commentary on this case. They love you."

Adams started to protest. Brad took his arm, hissing into the congressman's ear, "This is straight from the top. Let's go." The two men went through the door behind the map of the world into the well-appointed conference room.

"Now what is this, Brad?" Adams began annoyed. "It is not your position to meddle in the affairs of a congressional committee conducting its business."

"Come off it, Bill. You know who set this thing up for you. Now look, everything is under control. Don't weaken now. Let the whole show play itself out and get everybody. You hit Sterrato now and you'll miss the big international impact we brought the press here to witness."

"We were lucky we didn't kill the whole operation when the Bureau lost Ramirez," Adams returned. "Supposing it happens again. We'll have nothing, no evidence. This way at least we make a big haul and get Sterrato for sure, in possession."

"Bill, just follow the original plan. Everything will work out."

"And if it doesn't? I might not even be re-elected to the House, and even if I was lucky enough to be re-elected they'll get me off the Crime Committee." He stared at Brad with hostility. "I don't know how I got myself into this circus, the press and all that, in the first place. When Ramirez was lost I realized for the first time what a goddamn fool thing I let you talk me into."

"You wanted it so bad you could taste it!" Brad bit out the words. "Now go back in there and see it through because if you don't the press will really destroy you. Not only did you put on a big show for them to enhance your chances for the nomination to run for the Senate, they'll say, but halfway through you chickened out. And, Bill, don't forget I'll be backing another candidate if you blow this deal tonight and you can be damn sure I'll see the press has some lovely stories."

Brad saw the tortured look on Adams' face and changed his tack. He smiled. "Go back in there and really clean up—Senator," he said heartily, clapping Adams on his broad though quivering back.

"You've got a better team than you know that's with you all the way. OK?"

Adams nodded. "I guess I'm through the point of no return now anyway."

"Don't look at it that way, Bill. This is William Fortune Adams showing the state, the country why he should be senator, why he should be President! Right, Bill?"

"Right, Brad." Adams pulled himself up to his full, not inconsiderable height, set his jaw at a determined angle, and started back to the communications room, Brad behind him.

Pat Kenney was holding the press enthralled with his comments on the use of informers and undercover agents in the battle against narcotics traffickers. "In my biggest case, the one the book was about," Kenney was saying as Brad and Bill Adams returned to the communications room, "the only way we really broke the case and seized the one hundred and twenty pounds of heroin was to get Mickey Bocca to talk. You remember he was the guy we tailed through the case. When we finally grabbed him at his mother and father's place with his wife in possession of twenty pounds of heroin we really didn't have the case solved."

Kenney grinned and shook his head. "We knew there was another hundred pounds somewhere else and a lot of important Frenchmen and dons around town waiting to deliver the stuff. So what did we do? We sweated Mickey. In eight hours he forgot all about that Italian *omerta* stuff, the code of silence, you know. We made a deal. His father and mother and wife get off, Mickey gets minimum time and he gives us the big guys we want." Kenney laughed bitterly.

"You think all that surveillance and police work I told the author of the book to put in really happened?" He laughed again. "Mickey gave us the Frenchmen, his uncle, his brother in whose basement the heroin was hidden, and the members of his Mafia family connected with the case. That's how we broke up the syndicate that existed ten years ago. And it took all this time for a new one to crop up and we break it the same way, getting stools and informers."

A reporter raised his hand and was recognized by the detective. "Mr. Kenney?" the reporter asked, "this is all very interesting to us. But how come you're telling us this about Mickey Bocca now?"

Kenney nodded seriously. "Two reasons, sir. The

first one is that before the night is over you're going to be wondering how we were able to get such exact information that we dared put on a show like this for you. The answer is that I and some of my associates have made it our business to go out and buy, scare or beat what we needed to know out of the parties that came to our attention. That's how a big case is broken."

Now Kenney grinned sheepishly. "The second reason is that Mickey Bocca didn't appreciate the lengths to which I and my partner went to protect him from his own people when he turned stool for us. He has been out of jail a couple of months and is now suing me and the author of the book for a lot of money saying we invaded his privacy and held him up to ridicule and scorn."

"Is all this on the record, Mr. Kenney?" another reporter asked.

"As far as I'm concerned it is," Kenney answered.

"How did you develop the stools on this case?" the girl from the New York *Times* asked.

Before Kenney could deliver his answer Bill Adams stepped forward. "Before you all leave here Mr. Kenney has my permission to answer that question, but we have just had word that Ramirez has walked out of room 1801 and stepped into the elevator."

On the screen, which appeared in its customary position in the South Pacific, flashed the picture of the entrance of the Pierre Hotel. People were walking up and down the sidewalk under the marquee. "This is direct from our TV surveillance truck," Adams announced.

Everybody in the room stared at the screen waiting to see who would go in or out of the hotel. After a few moments Jorge Ramirez, the same man they had seen go through the diplomatic exit at JFK International Airport, walked out of the front door and stood in front of the marquee. He was carrying one of his suitcases, a bellhop was carrying another. Suddenly a limousine swooped in off the street. The driver leaped out, opened the trunk, and Jorge tossed one bag in and the bellhop placed the other one beside it. The Latin gave the bellhop a tip and then stepped through the back seat door which was held open for him by the driver and the limousine cruised off.

"What has happened, according to our informers, is that the heroin has been removed from Ramirez's suitcases in Sterrato's suite. Clothing, laundry and such were put back in them. You could see how much lighter they appeared from the way Ramirez and the bellhop handled them.

"Now," Adams looked dramatically across the room at the press, "I had two alternatives. I could have asked Mr. Potter to hit Sterrato's room, search it, arrest him with the contraband and Ramirez. My other choice was to wait it out and see who else shows up to visit with Sterrato. As you see, I decided on the latter course. We are interested in breaking up an entire syndicate, not merely hitting one wheel, albeit a very important wheel, in the machinery."

"Congressman Adams." Potter of the federal Bureau of Narcotics spoke up for the first time. "The plane from St. Croix is now landing in Miami."

"Good," Adams replied. "Let us know when your agents spot Echeverrea Brandt enter the airport." He turned back to the screen. "Now let's see who else comes in."

Maurice D'Estang nudged Larucci. "That's twice we had to save this operation, and we're just beginning."

"Yeah, and it would have been tough on Strega Joe. As long as they don't actually get him in possession he should be able to beat the rap."

"Good man, Joe," D'Estang remarked.

"Yeah. He's a stand-up guy." Larucci chuckled. "He's a real actor too. He always wanted to be a star, a big trader. Now he's got his chance to act like one. You know how much he gets for this caper?"

D'Estang shook his head. "What is Sal giving him?"

"If Joe convinces the cops and the press that he is the head of the heroin syndicate in the United States he gets twenty grand. Then on top of that he gets another twenty-five grand for every year he has to spend in jail, plus all his legal expenses, of course."

"Jesus!" D'Estang exclaimed. "For that kind of dough I'd take a fall myself."

"Oh, Joe's going to have hisself a ball playing the big man. And when this is all over he can sit around drinking strega and telling the punks how it was when he was the biggest man in horse on the East Coast." Larucci sidled over to Julius the Genius and stared at the small monitor screen before him. "Where the hell is Falconi and the big nigger's main man?"

"They'll be along," D'Estang said with assurance. "You said it was all set up."

"I don't care how good the setup, things can go wrong."

"Wait'll my colleague down below us gets a look at Falconi," D'Estang remarked. "He'll go ape."

"What's the story?" Larucci asked, curious.

"Brad's this society-type executive running Ascot Hotels for us and his daughter met Tony Falconi. Tony got her onto pot and pills and maybe hard stuff."

"So that's the story," Larucci said. "I wondered why we was walking Falconi right into this trap. If all goes right he'll do real time."

"That's the way the boss wants it," D'Estang replied. "And while we're setting people up you guys are doing the big nigger in pretty good. The real big nigger, not some stand-up guy like Strega Joe."

"The black ass son of a bitch has it coming. He's been bad to work with lately. Shit, you'd think he wasn't a nigger the way he tries to push us around. He's trying to muscle us out of cashing heisted welfare checks in Harlem. At fifty cents on the dollar that's half a million dollars a month we take in. Those fuckin' niggers can play with dope but when it comes to cashing checks they don't have the brains to read the numbers and divide by 2. This Permagon Antilles, what the hell kind of a name is that anyway, is trying to push us out of check cashing." Larucci laughed. "We'll show that spade what happens to fuckin' uppity niggers."

"Hey!" Julius the Genius called out. "There's the Big Nig's pimp mobile pulling up in front of the hotel." On the screen, duplicating the picture coming over the equipment in Adams' control room, a long Lincoln Continental, complete with round opera windows in the black canopy at the rear, slid up to the marquee.

In the communications room Detective Kenney suddenly stood up. "There they are," he exclaimed as the back door of the car on screen opened and a tall young man in expensive-looking if garish clothes stepped out. "That's Tony Falcon," Kenney narrated. "The nig-, black man," he corrected himself, "driving is one of the top boys of this Permagon Antilles."

Brad Kendall who had resumed his seat sat suddenly upright. There was Tony Falcon on the screen. He looked from the screen to Kenney, caught his eye a moment before the detective hastily shifted his glance away, and then glanced back at the screen.

Suddenly he was assailed with doubts once again. He had been working so intensely since coming back from the trip to the Orient that he hadn't had time to do more than meet Andrea for a short chat twice. He had asked her about Falcon and she had been evasive each time before looking him in the eye and telling her father that she hadn't seen Falcon since the night of her rescue from the pot party.

At least, he thought grimly, there would be no question about her seeing Falcon any more. He would be safely in jail. He felt a moment's gratitude to Ciano. He must have arranged for Tony to become exposed.

Even as the journalists were watching Tony walk into the hotel, Adams picked up a phone, listened and turned to the press. "The RCMP just called to report that the two Frenchmen they have had under surveillance for us have just boarded a plane in Montreal for New York, which will be arriving in an hour and fifteen minutes."

There was silence in the room for over a minute as the press stared at the entrance to the Pierre Hotel.

Then Kenney, holding a headset to his ear announced, "Tony Falcon has just gone into room 1801."

The screen in the Atlantic Ocean of the big map flashed on and another airport scene was punched up by the technician. Now Potter was talking. "Karl Echeverrea Brandt is just walking into Miami International Airport. What you are seeing on the screen is the baggage claim area where Echeverrea's suitcases should be arriving soon. We will actually see him claim his bags. Agents from the Bureau will keep him under surveillance."

For several minutes the press watched the baggage-claim area at Miami Airport. People from the St. Croix flight were claiming their luggage and leaving the area, but there was no sign of Echeverrea. Finally when the last bag had been claimed Adams fitfully asked Potter where the subject was. Potter was about to answer when the light flashed on his phone. He listened and then said in words that carried through the press section, "Echeverrea went directly to the English Pub where he's still sitting and drinking a gin and tonic."

"What about his bags?" Adams asked.

"No information," Potter replied tersely.

Adams stared at the screen again. "But there are no bags left to claim," he protested, a fact obvious to everyone in the room.

"We'll get back to Miami," Kenney said. "Tony just left Sterrato's room at the Pierre. He had the bellboy come up with a baggage cart to take down two suitcases." The journalists shifted their attention from the baggage area in Miami to the front of the Pierre Hotel. They were soon rewarded with the sight of Tony Falcon walking out the front door followed by the bellman pushing his cart. The black driver had already opened the trunk. It appeared to take all the bellman's strength to lift the suitcases into the trunk. Tony Falcon tipped the bellman, apparently generously from his reaction, and then got into the front seat of the big car beside the driver.

"And this car should lead us right to the Big Nig," Kenney remarked happily.

"We have four radio cars in a light tail on the limousine," Potter said. "This time we won't lose it."

"Now back to Miami," Kenney said with a grin, listening in to a headset. "My own man just called in. He was watching Echeverrea like a hawk from the time he walked out the door of the plane. My man saw him brush up against a Puerto Rican just as he entered the airport. Echeverrea kept going and the Puerto Rican stayed near the entrance as though looking for someone coming off the plane."

Kenney, a proud look on his face, continued. "This guy I just hired last month figured Echeverrea had made the pass so he kept his eye on the spic. When the last person had left the plane the Puerto Rican made a big show about his family not being on board. Then he goes down to the baggage counter and right in front of our eyes, on that screen," he pointed to it, "he claims two suitcases and walks out of the claim area. My guy tails him back to the departure deck and what does he see but the spic handing one of the suitcases to a nigger."

Kenney's excitement carried his listeners. "Now he's got two guys to tail, right? Luckily he finds a Bureau agent and puts him onto the nigger. He follows the spic and sees him check his bag on a plane for Chicago. My guy buys a ticket on the same plane and calls me. He's on the plane now." Kenney turned to Potter. "You better have a couple of your Chicago boys meet Eastern flight 21."

"Right," Potter replied tersely. "I just got a report from Miami. The Negro boarded a flight for Detroit and now Echeverrea has left the English Pub. He is carrying a large-size attaché case and is wearing a blue Pan American carrying case slung over his right shoulder. Both appear to be heavy. He's heading for the Northeast Airlines counter."

There was a minute of silence in the room as the reporters scribbled notes in their pads. Potter, listening on a headset, continued relaying Echeverrea's moves. "Subject just checked onto Flight 62 for New York.

An agent is on him and the flight will be met in New York."

Waves of high-frequency excitement bombarded the observers in the communications room and Adams instinctively knew that he must become the source of this radiating energy.

"We are following five suspects on four different domestic flights," Adams summed up. "At the moment, agents are following the car with the man who made the pickup from Sterrato in room 1801 at the Pierre Hotel. Their present location is at Lenox Avenue and 117th Street, approximately here."

A street map of the Harlem area of New York City flashed on the screen and a red dot indicated the location of the car. "The dot you see will follow the progress of the limousine, which is obviously headed for a destination in Harlem. Our present theory is that part of the load, maybe even half, fifty pounds of heroin, will be received in Harlem and the rest is intended for another destination in New York City, probably the Bedford-Stuyvesant area. This is going to be a particularly delicate operation. We will have to keep the place to which the first half of the load is delivered under observation, follow the limousine to its next delivery point and keep that under observation and then quietly pick up the limousine and its two occupants and arrest them. What we are afraid of is that Sterrato in room 1801 at the Pierre will be warned if we hit too soon and the rendezvous we expect he is keeping with the two Frenchmen and Echeverrea will not occur."

The red dot stopped moving at 126th Street and Eighth Avenue. There was an electrifying silence in the communications room as Potter listened to his telephone. "The two men have left the car and taken one of the two suitcases into a tenement house at 278 West 126th Street. One of our black undercover agents is following." There was silence in the communications room as the reporters waited for the scene in Harlem to develop.

Adams, Kenney and Potter conferred in soft tones

around the console and then Adams turned to the press. Brad was expecting his call signal to beep at any moment but it remained silent. Finally, Adams turned to the press.

"The two men who left the car with the suitcase full of heroin have entered an apartment on the third floor of the building. We don't know which apartment they have entered but whichever one it is, that's where the top Harlem man will be examining the purity of the material before making the pay-off. The white man, Tony Falcon, will make sure the money is right and it is his job to deliver it back to the syndicate, presumably through Sterrato."

Adams looked about at the attentive journalists and cameramen. "Ideally, of course, we would like to follow Tony all the way through and back to Sterrato. However, the big black man in Harlem is our most important catch. We are afraid that if we start pounding down doors on the third floor it will alarm our man and he may well escape. Therefore, we will put another black undercover agent on the third floor to help the first man and when Falcon starts to leave the apartment the two agents will slam into the door before it can be closed and arrest everyone inside. The agents outside will be ready to rush in and help the two undercovers."

Still no summons from D'Estang, Brad noted. Apparently this plan met with the approval of the planners above.

"To be completely safe," Adams continued, "one of the agents covering the Pierre Hotel will post himself in the telephone operators' room and make sure that no phone calls from Harlem get through to 1801."

Silently the journalists scratched out their notes as Potter gave orders to his men in Harlem from the console. Then Adams made another announcement. "The second undercover man is equipped with a microphone which will bring to you all the sounds made during this arrest." He motioned to the console technician. "Turn the volume full up."

Interrupted by a hum, static filled the room. Then

came the unmistakable sound of footsteps walking up a creaking staircase. "He should be just approaching the third floor," Adams reported.

Now the sound of the steps changed as the agent walked down the hall. Then came snatches of whispered conversation.

"I'll take the north end of this floor, you stand to the south," the Negro undercover agent was saying to his partner.

The seconds and minutes ticked by as the tense journalists sat in silence. Kenney and Adams hovered over the console, anxiety showing in their faces. Then could be heard a distant murmuring and the creaking grind of an ancient door being opened.

There was a sudden shattering sound as of the door being suddenly smashed in and the cry "Hold it everyone. Police. Hold it, you!"

A shot rang out and then in the background came the shouts of the other agents running up the stairs.

Above the general melee of shouts and curses came the voice of one of the black agents. "All right, you nigger motherfuckers, hands on the wall. Yeah, you, too, big boy. Hey! You want some heat across the mouth." There was a smacking sound and a groan.

Kenney listened, a wide grin across his face, rubbing his hands together. "That's where I should be, Bill," he said jubilantly to Adams.

It was difficult to distinguish between the voices now as the agents from the Bureau rounded up what sounded to be four men in the room plus Tony Falcon. Now they could hear authoritative shouts from the agents as the neighbors crowded the halls. "Get back, get back in your rooms. You want to go with them?"

"Naw, suh!" A door slammed shut.

Now the distant sound of a siren came from the bug and more confusion. Then there was silence. "Maybe we can sell it to a sound-effects man," Adams quipped. "We'll get a report on what actually happened pretty quick."

"When can we get out and report this raid?" a reporter called out.

"Just as soon as this operation is finished," Adams answered. "We're still waiting to see who shows up to meet with our friend in 1801. And," he glanced at the shadow passing across the world chronograph, "we'll soon be hearing from our agents in France about the trawler. I suspect that the reason for the visit by the Frenchmen is to discuss disposal of the heroin that will be manufactured from the morphine base being brought in to Marseilles at this moment. As you can see, it's almost daylight."

"Mr. Adams." Potter was smiling for the first time. "Perfect score. They got Permagon Antilles and two of his men with the heroin; they estimate twenty-five kilos. Falcon had a briefcase full of money they haven't counted yet, and they have the driver of the car with the other load of heroin."

"Jesus, what a panic there's going to be in Harlem when the addicts read about this haul," Kenney chortled.

"How about letting us report it now?" a journalist called.

"Gentlemen, we made a bargain," Adams replied. "The story of the arrests you actually heard made will not be released until you leave here, in time to make the afternoon papers and," he checked his watch, "it's now one in the morning, tonight's TV news. Now, right now, at JFK our crew is secretly installing two small television cameras so you can watch Echeverrea get off the plane and walk down the corridor into the main terminal. Another camera will follow him out to the taxi stand. And again, I remind the TV newsmen here, copies of all the TV coverage you have seen will be available to you as you leave. Processing and duplication is going on now so you will not have to wait." The admiring and grateful sounds from the press section indicated that Adams was making a superb public relations impact.

"It looks like we may have a lull in the activity, ladies and gentlemen. I suggest we take a coffee break," Adams suggested, "and we can all talk together informally. Detective Kenney, Mr. Potter and myself will be glad to answer your individual questions."

"Well, I'll be pulled up on the meat hook if they didn't do that one right all the way!" Larucci chortled. "We can forget the nigger for seven to fifteen years, I'd guess."

"Yeah," D'Estang agreed. "Now if they get the trawler too, and the way we set up that asshole Robert Tradeux they can't miss, Adams can claim to have pulled off the biggest international antinarcotics operation in history. He can honestly tell the press that at street value he has intercepted and confiscated half a billion dollars' worth of narcotics."

"Unless some killjoy points out that the value of nine hundred pounds of morph in Marseilles might run a couple of hundred thousand dollars," Larucci said deprecatingly. "And the poor-grade two hundred and twenty pounds of heroin you bought just to be seized ran you three hundred thousand tops direct from the labs."

"Nobody knows that." D'Estang turned to Julius. "What's the next action?"

"The flight from Miami is due in half an hour and they could hit the trawler anytime now. The sun's rising in Marseilles."

"Congressman Adams," the technician called across the room. "The flight from Miami just touched down at JFK."

The press corps needed no second bidding to put down their coffee and rolls and return to their seats. The same picture was projected on both screens, the doorway through which passengers from Northeast 62 would enter JFK terminal. It was a clear, well-defined picture.

Five minutes after the announcement by the technician the doors were opened at the Northeast ramp. A crowd of perhaps twenty people was gathered to meet the passengers as they disembarked. There was a gasp as the press members recognized the tall figure and handsomely gaunt face of Karl Echeverrea Brandt. He wore the Pan Am bag over the left shoulder and carried the large attaché case in his right hand. He plunged into the middle of the knot of passengers and the welcoming throng.

"Watch him! Watch him!" Kenney cried inadvertently as though giving the command to the agents on the scene. Moments later Echeverrea emerged from the crowd and strode down the passageway to the terminal. He had neither bag nor briefcase.

There were cries of "What happened? Did you see him pass them? How'd he do it?" from the amazed journalists. Kenney, who had been staring at the screen, called out, "Hey, there goes a spic with the blue bag!"

"I see the fellow with the attaché case now!" came from the press section.

"My agents will be right on both of them," Potter announced with assurance. As the journalists watched, the scene changed to the main terminal. Echeverrea strode purposefully toward the stairway down to baggage reclaim and taxicabs. A few moments later, with the Pan Am bag, he strolled nonchalantly across the terminal and down the stairs to the transportation level. Equally nonchalant a man followed him.

"There's one of my men," Potter proclaimed. A few moments later another man walked toward the stairway carrying the briefcase. Several people were walking behind him. "And there's the other," his voice rang out.

"I'm getting a call from Marseilles now," the technician called. Potter picked up the phone and listened.

With a few hours' sleep behind them Congressman Adams, Brad Kendall and Maurice D'Estang entered the office of a jubilant C. L. Ciano.

"Well, Bill, you did it, you did it big."

"Never could have done it without my team which you made possible, C.L.," Adams replied modestly.

The afternoon papers covered Ciano's desk. His television set was blasting out the incredible story of how New York City's Congressman Adams of the

House Crime Committee had scored his momentous victory over the heroin syndicate.

"Half a billion dollars' worth of narcotics seized by the Adams task force!"

"The top members of the narcotics syndicate from France, the United States and the Caribbean seized at summit conference in midtown luxury hotel by crime-buster Adams."

"Trawler seized off Marseilles with a thousand pounds of narcotics by international agent of the Adams team."

"Now let's capitalize on this magnificent accomplishment," C. L. Ciano said heartily. "I see Kenney got a fair share of publicity. Maybe we can use him too."

"He could be a difficult man to manage, C.L.," Brad observed.

"Manage?" Adams lifted an eyebrow.

"Well, you know what I mean, Bill," Brad went on hastily. "He'll say just what he thinks at any given time. In politics that's not always wise."

"Bill is a New York delegate to the Democratic Convention in July," Ciano went on. "We should be able to get a lot of attention for him there. We'll work on having him deliver a nominating speech and perhaps he can fight for some more anti-crime legislation in the party platform. What do you think, Brad?"

"I'll see what we can do behind the scenes," Brad said.

"Anything that old Francis X. Flannerty can do for you, don't hesitate to ask," Ciano reminded him.

"He can help all right," Brad replied. "I'll see that Miami is fixed up for Bill. I'm sure we can get him mentioned for the second spot on the ticket."

William Fortune Adams basked in the attention and high-level planning. "Maybe if I could invite a few of the right people to fly down to Miami on the jet with me it would help."

"Of course, Bill. Of course. Whoever you like."

"I'll have a few suggestions to make," Brad interjected. "We've got to ride this thing for all it's worth."

"I'd be glad to hear any suggestions you have," Adams said almost patronizingly. "I'll start putting a list together."

"Save a few places," Brad advised. "You never know what might develop at the last minute."

"I know how to put a political campaign together." Adams looked from Brad to Ciano. "C.L., if you'll excuse me, I promised my wife I'd be home early for dinner."

"Of course, Bill. Of course." Ciano stood up and started to walk to the door with Adams. "You have an experienced man in Brad Kendall to help you direct your political fortunes."

Adams made no comment but shook hands at the door with Ciano. "Thank you again, C.L. I appreciate the help you've given me in this operation."

Ciano closed the door behind the congressman and returned to his desk. "Maurice," he said after a few moments of thought, "do we have Adams well insured?"

"Pretty good, C.L. And more to come. For instance, those fancy offices he has downstairs, the decorator charged him two thousand dollars for a hundred-thousand-dollar job. The decorating company is owned by Joe Sterrato and a couple of other hoods. The press will remember that Adams deliberately refrained from having Joe arrested in possession of narcotics." D'Estang laughed. "Joe did a great job today acting the part of the kingpin but they'll have a hell of a time getting a conviction on him."

Ciano nodded his satisfaction. Then, "But I want Falconi put away good." He glanced at Brad and winked.

"I guess Falconi will get it. So far nobody has bailed him out."

"Good. And see what further insurance you can get on Adams. I think we can push him all the way. God knows he's the great American mediocrity that usually makes it."

CHAPTER THIRTY-FIVE

Impulsively Elda Ciano pushed the luncheon dishes and vase of flowers aside, reached across the table and took Brad's hands in hers.

"You can't blame yourself for what's happening to Andrea. She's just going to have to get herself out of that dreadful home atmosphere she's put up with so long."

Brad shook his head. "I should do more for her but it's still hard to get through to her, unless you are around," he added.

"You haven't been around much yourself, not that it's your fault. It seems that you are the first person Dad turns to when he needs something done." She paused, then, "In the legitimate area of his enterprises."

A bleak smile came to Brad's lips. "Is there any other area?"

Elda nodded seriously. "I know much more about my father's business than he thinks I do." She noticed the concerned look. "Oh, don't worry, I at least know enough to keep silent. Anyway, let's get back to Andrea which is why we're having lunch together at your apartment." She gave him a direct smile, her fingers exerting small, tingling pressures on his hands. "And I must say it's been a thoroughly enjoyable luncheon. I know it's wrong of me but I can't help being glad that Andrea couldn't come over until later."

Brad squeezed Elda's hands back. "Yes, so am I as long as she's doing what she has to do at school."

"I hope you can get her out of New York this summer. And it would be wicked if she has to go to college in New York City next fall and live at home the way her mother insists."

"I know," Brad agreed morosely. "When she comes over this afternoon I'll talk to her about that. It's been so long since I've really had a chance to discuss things with her. Since before my trip to the Orient in March and here it is May. She seems to avoid giving us a chance to talk."

"I think that since Tony Falcon was arrested two weeks ago she's been afraid you might give her the I-told-you-so routine."

"I never would." A flash of distress crossed Brad's countenance. "You don't suppose she continued to see him after the night we pulled her out of that opium den?"

Elda shrugged. "I don't know." Slowly she pulled her hands from his and withdrew them to her lap. "Andrea hasn't been as communicative with me as she once was. It's possible she saw Tony again. I'm sure her attraction to him was very strong even after our little scene. A girl can be a devious creature when she has been mesmerized by a man. And if you knew how a daughter can deceive her adoring father!" She laughed mirthlessly. "I should know. I hope you never have to find out."

"I don't think Andrea would deliberately lie to me," Brad replied. "There isn't any reason why she should, is there?"

"Not if she's really quit seeing Tony Falcon."

"He's in jail."

Elda shook her head. "He's out on bail."

"How do you know? He wasn't supposed to be bailed out—" Brad cut himself off, shocked at his momentary loss of presence.

"I know," Elda replied. "No help of any kind for Tony. But his father put up the bail."

Brad was reluctant, perhaps afraid, he thought ruefully, to probe the depths of Elda's awareness of the fifth estate and her father's activities. Instead he said, "Elda, I'll never be able to adequately express my appreciation for your interest in my problems with Andrea."

"And with that pompous kind of talk you'll always have a big fat communications gap with her—and her contemporaries," Elda added. Then seeing the surprised expression on his face she laughed and reached across the table and took his hand again.

"Just relax, Brad. Like talk straight, you know?" She pressed his hand and then letting go stood up. "Time for me to split. Andrea will be here anytime now."

"When will I see you again?"

"When do you want to, Brad?"

"Like, ah tonight?"

"You want to see me tonight? To analyze what happens with you and Andrea this afternoon?"

Brad pushed his seat back and, standing, was about to say how helpful it was to talk to her about Andrea. Then he shook his head, smiling wryly. "That's the right excuse—but no, I want to see you, talk about things that interest both of us, maybe put my arm around you on the dance floor, if all that doesn't add up to making me some kind of a dirty old man."

"It's a good year for dirty old men," Elda grinned. "I think older men are much more fascinating, exciting and romantic than the uptight young men just out of college."

"Good. It's a date? Here at, what time is good for you?"

"The earlier the better. I have to get out home before too late."

"I'll take you home in my car," Brad offered.

"And leave my true love, my little Aston-Martin, all by itself in some lonely garage all night? No, I can take myself where and when I want to go. I have a few appointments in town this afternoon and I'll be back at five-thirty to freshen up. Leave the key for me if you're going to be out then."

"I'll do better than that, Elda." Brad walked from the dining alcove to the living room. He stopped at the mahogany breakfront, which had been in his father's family for several generations and which he had rescued from Gwen at the time of the divorce. Pulling open a drawer he reached into it and took out two keys on an Ascot Hotel key chain.

He turned to Elda who had followed him and taking her hand pressed the key chain into it. "A souvenir of the Ascot Hotel company for you. The keys fit my door."

"Thanks, Brad. I'll give them back tonight."

"I'd be disappointed if you did. Think of here as your base of operations in town."

"What about Luciana?"

Brad was surprised to realize that he hadn't really thought about Luciana all day. "What about Luciana?" he asked.

"What would she think of you giving strange women keys to your apartment?"

"You're not strange women, you're family. Besides, what's she got to do with it?"

"I guess nothing, if you say so, Brad."

They walked to the door and Brad let her out. "I'll be looking forward to tonight, Elda."

"Should be fun." She ducked out the door and Brad watched her until the elevator came. She turned, waved and stepped into the car. Slowly Brad closed the door and walked back into his well-appointed living room with sweeping views of the city to the north and west. He was very proud of his New York apartment and enjoyed it greatly. Next he needed a place somewhere in the country. That would come soon, he promised himself.

Waiting for Andrea to arrive he meditated on what form their conversation would take. She had called him to say she wanted to see him. Usually Brad had to go through Elda to reach his daughter. He knew what sort of repercussions a direct call would bring her. He was tempted to pour himself a drink but decided against it. He still had a tough afternoon ahead of him and he certainly wanted to be fresh for his first real date with Elda tonight.

What about Luciana? she had asked. What about her? he now asked himself. He still loved her, missed her, wanted her and was desolate when he couldn't be with her. And yet from the moment he had awakened this morning, knowing he would see Elda for lunch, he had hardly thought of Luciana. And anticipating dinner with Elda he found the full ache of wanting Luciana was not with him. Obviously, there could never be anything serious between himself and Elda. Good Lord, he was well over twenty years older than she. And what would C.L. think of Brad being romantically interested in his daughter? What would he, Brad, think if a man in his forties was interested in Andrea? As a matter of fact, such a man would be infinitely better for Andrea than a Tony Falcon or some wild-haired young pot smoker.

His thoughts were interrupted by the buzzing of the doorman. He went over to the front door and pressed the answer button. "Your daughter coming up, Mr. Kendall," the doorman announced.

"Thanks, Albert," Brad replied. He opened the front door and leaving it ajar walked back to the living room to wait for Andrea. Moments later he heard the elevator come to a stop on his floor and then the door was pushed open gently and Andrea appeared. The door closed behind her and almost wraithlike she stood in the foyer, motionless.

"Come on in, Andrea," Brad invited warmly. "It's so wonderful to see you again."

Obediently Andrea approached him and Brad went toward her, putting his hands on her shoulders, which felt pathetically thin, and drawing her close to him, he kissed her just beside her lips. She made no response and allowed herself to be led to the sofa where she sat down beside her father.

Brad had not seen Andrea for several weeks, not

since a few days after his return from the Orient, and it pained him to see that she was even paler and more withdrawn than when last they had been together. "Are you all right, dear?" he asked.

"Of course, Brad," she replied listlessly. "Maybe a little tired studying for final exams."

Brad looked into her face searchingly. He sensed that it was more than final examinations troubling her but he didn't want to upset her with direct questioning.

"How's everything at home?" he asked casually.

"Pretty much the same," she replied.

"Remember, you always have a home here. I took a large apartment thinking you might want to move in with me." He thought he noticed a look of longing as she glanced around the living room. He had showed her the place before and she knew how comfortable it would be for her.

"I don't know what would happen to Mama if I left. She is practically an invalid. And when she and Daddy," she gave Brad an apologetic look, "Ed, I mean. When she and Ed fight it would be so much worse for her if I wasn't there. And Little Eddie needs me. I couldn't just desert them."

"Dearest, you have to think about what's best for you. Do you really think it's in your best interests to stay where you are?"

Andrea looked down at her hands folded in her lap. "I don't know, Brad." There was a long silence which Brad did not break, waiting for Andrea to say more.

Finally, "I don't know, Brad. I just feel I shouldn't make any change now. Maybe later."

"What about this summer? We talked about you taking a trip to Europe. Wouldn't you like to do that?"

"No," she replied with haste that jarred him. She seemed almost afraid of the prospect, he noticed. "I mean," she went on, "there's a lot I can do here. Maybe get a job and help out at home. Mama doesn't want me to go away this summer anyway. She's sick now and she's sacrificed all her life for me."

With tremendous self-control Brad managed to keep

his answer on a conversational level. "Your mother really hasn't sacrificed anything for you. Financially I have always taken care of not only you but the rest of them as well."

Andrea seemed to be suddenly contrite. "I know, Brad. You've helped all of us even though Mama will never admit it."

Mollified, Brad turned to another subject. "How about college? What are you doing to get into a good college somewhere?"

"Mama wants me to go to college in New York City."

"Oh, no, Andrea. You should see something of the world, live in other places than New York." Again he was aware of a fearful expression fleeting across her face as he made the suggestion. "You've got to get away from your mother and Ed sometime," he amplified.

"We'll see," Andrea replied enigmatically.

"We don't have much time to see. What colleges have you applied for?"

"Hunter College—"

"That's in New York," Brad interrupted. "How about Oregon or some western college? Even something in the Midwest, or for that matter in New England. But not in New York City." He couldn't contain the agitation creeping into his voice.

"I'll apply for any college you suggest, Brad."

"Just applying isn't enough, damnit. That school I pay so much to should be helping."

"I'll come over here and fill out the applications and you can send them in."

"Well, I suppose that's a step in the right direction. You've got to get away from this city, any city, when you go to college."

"You'll have to talk to Mama," Andrea said primly.

"Mama? I'm the one paying for it."

"I'm sure Mama will be reasonable, Brad." Andrea glanced speculatively at her father. "Anyway, as I said, I'll get applications for some nice colleges far away from New York and we'll fill them out and you can sign them as my parent and we'll send them off."

"Maybe the two of us should visit a few campuses together," Brad suggested.

"We'll see what Mama says and—" Andrea saw the emotional storm clouds building up in her father and deftly reversed herself—"and whatever she says we'll do it anyway."

Immediately the sun broke through, the turbulence stilled. "Good girl. You're practically nineteen. There's no way your mother can stop you. But I'll make the motions of talking to her."

"You don't have to now. Wait until she's feeling better." Andrea paused and took a deep breath. "Brad, there is something you could help me out with now. I hate to ask you but I don't know any other way."

The look of appeal on her face made him feel suddenly protective. "Always come to your father first if you have a problem."

"Well, I know how you feel about Ed and my mother and how they've been so unco-operative about letting me be with you, but there's also myself and Little Eddie at home. We really don't have any food in the house. We are about to be evicted, right out on the street. We have to pay the landlord five hundred dollars by nine o'clock in the morning or everything will be moved out of the apartment tomorrow."

"If your mother had let Ed continue as a golf pro you wouldn't be in this shape. But she insisted that Ed become a lawyer or a stockbroker. I know, he tried but he couldn't make it. I feel sorry for the poor, frustrated, broke guy but if he had any guts he'd be out at some country club teaching."

"He just got another job on Wall Street. Partly because of his golf. He'll be playing with the firm's clients."

Brad nodded. "I must say, in the days when we were all getting along, it was a pleasure to play with him. I'm a good amateur but Ed was a pro. I'll never forget the day he straightened out my wedge lob shot for me. Pity your mother had to wreck things."

"Will you help us, Brad?" Andrea pleaded.

"The sad thing is that no matter how often I help it does nothing to convince your mother that I should have something to say about what happens with you. College, for instance."

"We'll work that out between us, Brad."

"I wish you'd eat more or something. Maybe you should see a doctor, dear. You don't look your old self. I'll help out but I want something in return. I want my daughter's health back. And the way to do that is to get her out of this stinking city for the summer. You could come down to Miami with me in July. Maybe we could spend August together in Europe." Again he noticed the spasm of near terror that flicked from her eyes.

"We can talk about it, Brad."

"When?"

"Later on in the week. Maybe over the weekend."

"That's a good idea. Perhaps you could stay with Elda and I would come out and visit you both."

"I'll ask her, Brad."

He could see her impatience growing. "All right, dear. I'll write out a check to you for five—no, six hundred dollars. You might as well get some food in the house while you're at it."

"Oh thank you, thank you, Brad," she breathed.

He stood up and walked over to the heirloom mahogany breakfront. As Andrea watched anxiously, her father in careful, deliberate motions pulled out a green felt-covered writing surface and drew up a chair, seating himself at the desk. From a shelf above the writing surface Brad took his checkbook and opened it to a page of blank checks. He reached inside his suit coat pocket for a pen and then started to write the check.

"Incidentally, Andrea, I read about your friend Falcon being picked up in that narcotics raid. I hope you stopped seeing him after the night Elda and I rescued you." He looked up suddenly from the checkbook and saw the sudden flush come to her cheeks and forehead. "You can see I was right about you dropping him completely."

"I know," she said in almost inaudible tones. "Mama said the same thing."

"You didn't continue to see him, Andrea?"

"No." She hesitated. "Well, once again. I wanted to at least tell him face to face I couldn't see him any more."

"I don't think that was necessary. Why, he was trying to introduce you to dope."

"All the kids smoke pot, Brad. That isn't dope."

"It leads to it."

"Brad." There was a pleading note to her voice. "Do we have to talk about it? I'm sorry I ever met him." There was the slight edge of an accusatory tone which made Brad recall that he was really responsible for Andrea meeting Falcon.

"The important thing," Brad said brightly, "is that you never see him again. And I guess he'll soon be in prison for a good long stay so there isn't much likelihood of you seeing him. Just promise me that while he's still on bail you won't talk to him." Brad was holding his pen poised above the checkbook as he waited for Andrea to answer.

She looked down at the check, partially filled in, and back to her father. "Of course I promise, Brad. I won't see Tony Falcon again." With relief she watched him nod and then turn to the desk and finish writing the check.

"You have time to take it to my bank and get it cashed if you like," Brad said, handing the check to his daughter.

"Oh thanks, Brad. I'm so grateful."

"Too bad your mother hasn't got it in her to be grateful."

Andrea folded the check and tucked it in her handbag. "Well, I'd better get to the bank. I don't think the landlord will take a check from Ed or Mama any more."

"I'll be in touch with your mother about summer plans and colleges," Brad said.

"Oh please, Brad. Don't rub it in about the money.

I'm going to tell her it's money I've been saving from what you've given me above my allowance."

"Because she knows you've already given her all the money you officially get from me each month," Brad said dourly.

"It's just she'd be mortified if she thought I was telling you about our troubles at home. It kills her that Daddy—Ed," she quickly corrected herself, "can't make money."

"If she'd left him alone he could have made a very good living, but that's your mother."

Andrea was moving toward the front door and Brad followed. She opened the door. "Good-by, Brad. I'll see you soon."

"I hope so. Don't I get a kiss?"

Andrea bestowed a perfunctory peck on her father's cheek and then hurried down the hall to the elevators.

Baffled, concerned, a little hurt, Brad glanced at his wrist watch. It was not quite two o'clock. Andrea had plenty of time to talk with him further and still get to the bank, which was only a few blocks from the apartment house. Now he did feel like a drink and he poured himself a weak Old Fitz and soda which he drank contemplatively. Halfway through it he went to his telephone and dialed Gwen's number.

The phone rang several times and then Little Eddie's voice came over the line. "Eddie," Brad said in a friendly way, "may I speak to your mother, please?"

"She's not here," Eddie replied automatically.

"This is Brad," he said urgently.

"Just a minute," Eddie answered. They must really be avoiding bill collectors, Brad thought. What a hell of a way to live.

"Yes, Brad, what do you want?" Gwen's cold voice cut over the line.

"I think we ought to have a talk as soon as possible about Andrea's plans. This summer and next fall."

"There's nothing to talk about. Andrea is spending the summer with us here. We'll be taking a few weeks off, all of us together in the country someplace."

"What about college?"

"She'll be going to college in New York and living here. I'll inform you what college she's going to attend."

"If I'm going to pay for it I'd like to have some say where she goes." There was a long pause and then Gwen went on, "I'll ask the school to notify you which colleges Andrea has applied for." Suddenly Gwen's voice turned hard with suspicion. "Have you been talking to her, have you been seeing her without my knowing? Just remember, I have custody of Andrea."

"I am aware of that. It's just that I have to travel a lot and now would be a good time to make some decisions."

"I'll make all decisions concerning my daughter. Now, if you don't mind, I'm not at all well. I was just taking a nap when you called." With that Gwen hung up.

Brad walked to the sideboard, strengthened the drink and paced about his apartment as he finished it.

CHAPTER THIRTY-SIX

Tony Falcon paced the length of his small apartment on the West Side of New York. He wished he had some grass or a drink but he could afford neither. He had just enough heroin to give the broad a skin pop. It had taken every penny he had, and a piece of his father's savings to bail him out. He still couldn't understand why the organization's bail bondsman hadn't put him back on the street within a couple of hours after he was arrested. Instead he was in stir a week before his father had personally bailed him out. Something was very wrong with the whole setup, he knew, but what was it?

Christ, it was lousy to be broke. The organization wasn't doing a thing for him; he had to hire his own lawyer and even his own father didn't talk to him much. At least he wasn't sitting in the stinking Tombs wondering what was going on. Where the hell was the broad? She'd better get here with the bread. He wanted to go out that night, see a few people, find out what the hell was happening.

A buzzer rang and he jumped for the button to release the downstairs door. He jabbed it viciously, leaning on it, giving the broad plenty of time to get into the inner vestibule. Then he opened his door and heard her trudging up the stairs. Come on, baby, come on up with the loot, he muttered. She finally reached his landing and seeing him she smiled happily.

"I got it, Tony. Six hundred dollars."

"Let's see it, baby." He reached out for her bag.

"Can't you wait until we get inside?"

Tony almost pushed her through the door into his dimly lighted apartment and onto the sofa. "OK, doll, give."

"Not until you kiss me and tell me you love me," she replied coyly.

He felt like rapping her in the teeth, but she was the only person that had helped him since his father got him out of the can. And she could get more where this came from. "Sure I love you, baby," Falcon said gruffly. He tilted her head back and kissed her. Here she was the society girl virgin, unattainable, and now she was begging him for a kiss, and more before the afternoon was over. He kissed her hard and despite his preoccupation with the money she had brought him he felt himself getting hard.

"Feel that thing against you, baby. You want it in you?"

"Sure, Tony. A skin pop first?"

"Where's the bread? I'm going to have to get some more horse for you after today."

Andrea opened her handbag and handed him a roll of thirty bills, twenty dollars each. He took them from her and counted them and then went over to his bureau and dropped them into the top drawer.

"You're a good kid, Andrea. I'll cook up a pop for you." As Andrea watched, Tony went into the kitchen and turned on the gas stove. He tore open a glassine bag and poured the white powder inside into a tiny pan with a tablespoon of water in it. Andrea watched as though hypnotized. In a few moments the water boiled dissolving the white powder. Then Tony took out a hypodermic needle, drew the solution into it and approached Andrea.

"Ready, baby?"

"Yeah. I need it, Tony." She held up her left arm

so that the underside of the forearm was up, the back of her hand almost against her shoulder. Tony pinched her skin between his thumb and forefinger and into the fleshy wrinkle he inserted the point of the needle and pushed down on the plunger, filling a small area under her skin with the contents. Then he withdrew the needle and Andrea lay back on the couch.

"This do beat hell out of the pills, don't it, doll?" Tony asked gently.

"Oh, yes, it does. I wish there was a way I could do this at home." She closed her eyes.

"Let me make you comfortable, baby." Tony was aroused now. He unzipped her dress and pulled it off her and then pulled down her pantyhose. She was lying nude now except for her bra. Andrea moaned as he turned her halfway over to get at the hooks that held her bra together and deftly slid the undergarment off. He looked down at her and started to undress himself. He chuckled to himself as he remembered what a struggle it had been the first time he had laid this girl. Even though she had been relaxed and smoked three joints it had been tough. She really had been a virgin as the blood on his sheets attested, which excited him more than anything sexual had before. Andrea had been his first virgin. And from one of those social families too, that had made the conquest sweeter.

Andrea lay quietly as Tony mounted and entered her and frenziedly pumped away. "It's so nice this way, Tony," Andrea said lazily. "The pops really do it for sex. Just use my body, fuck me the way you like it." He grasped her buttocks holding them against his groin with both his hands, crushing his lips to hers as he expended himself deep within her. His lust temporarily slaked, Tony rolled off the nude girl.

"Nice for you, Tony?" she asked.

"Yeah, doll," he answered hoarsely.

After lying beside her a few minutes he got up, pulled on his clothes and looked into the bureau drawer at the cash Andrea had brought him. Somehow he had to keep her coming to him and bringing him money when he needed it. She had a habit now, so it shouldn't be too hard. The lawyer his father found and he had hired warned Tony not to get caught in any narcotics dealings of any sort while this case was pending. That meant that Andrea was the only safe customer he could sell until the whole thing blew over.

"Tony?" Andrea asked. "Will you miss me?"

"What do you mean, miss you? Where you going?" He tried to keep the alarm he suddenly felt out of his voice.

"Well, I graduate from school in three weeks and my father wants me to go away for the summer. He said he'd take me to Europe."

"You don't want to leave poor Tony all by himself, do you?" Falcon wheedled.

"I'd like that trip and I don't like this city and my mother and stepfather."

Tony looked down at the lovely girl lying in a semieuphoric state. He understood her perfectly. She was in the same state he was immediately after getting his rocks off. With no sex desire temporarily, he could think very rationally. But in an hour or so when the fountain of his desire had been replenished he would be thinking of the next girl he could get.

Andrea, lying there deeply relaxed from the skin pop, wasn't thinking about the next one, or where she would get the pills she had become dependent upon, or even about where she would find a few joints to smoke. But when the effects of the heroin wore off the old tensions would return and the next pill or pop or joint would never be far from the center of her thoughts.

He leaned over her. "Baby, I'll be back in a few minutes, I want to do a few errands."

"I'll just be lying here, Tony," she replied lethargically.

Falcon went back to the bureau drawer and stuffed the cash in his pocket. He left the apartment and walked down the stairs. For the moment, as he walked out onto the street with the bread in his kick, he felt like a big man again. First he dropped into the cigar store and bought a *Daily Racing Form*. Then he walked into the neighborhood saloon to discuss the racing information contained in the paper with the bookmaker who hung out there. He had two drinks, sipping them slowly, and decided upon a horse for the final race at Aqueduct, handing the bookie fifty dollars on the horse to win. A place bet or even a show would have been more conservative but putting his money on the nose made him feel like somebody again.

With the bet down he went to the liquor store and bought a bottle of cheap whiskey. Then he looked for the nigger pusher. Since Tony was basically a wholesaler and in fact supplied the pusher's contacts, this was a demeaning situation but he wanted to have enough horse on hand for Andrea. The pusher, as though sensing Tony was looking to score, emerged from a shoeshine parlor and waited for him, leaning against the glass window of the shop.

No words were exchanged. Tony handed the black pusher twenty dollars and four glassine envelopes were pressed into his hand. He kept walking. It was now almost two hours since he'd left his place. He chuckled to himself. He was feeling horney again and from experience he knew his timing was right on with Andrea's. The effects of the skin pop would have worn off and she would be tense and worried again.

Tony walked into the drugstore he patronized and winked at the pharmacist. "Gimme two boxes of amies, Al." He placed a ten on the counter. Al went back to the prescription counter and returned with two boxes of amyl nitrite. Tony slipped them in his pocket, picked up the change and, whistling, he walked out on the sidewalk.

He let himself into the apartment building and walked up the four flights of steps to his flat. He started to put the key into the lock but before he could get it all the way in and turn it Andrea pulled the door open. Her clothes looked disheveled and her makeup was streaked.

"Where have you been, Tony?" Her voice was high pitched. "I've been waiting and waiting for you."

"Just had to do some errands, baby. Relax."

"How could I relax when I didn't know where you were and I have to go home soon."

Tony set his package from the liquor store down in the kitchen and then came out to Andrea. "You gotta go home soon?"

"You know I do."

"How about this summer? You're going away with your dad, huh? I guess we won't be seeing each other. I been thinking of getting out of here myself."

Alarm and fear sparked from her eyes. "I'm not really going away this summer, Tony. I'll be right in New York. And my mother insists that I go to college here in the fall." She moved close to him and put her arms around his shoulders. "Don't you talk about going away. I need you to be near me."

"I'll be around."

"You can't go anyway as long as you're on bail," Andrea reminded him.

"Babe, I can do what I want to do, when I want to do it." He put a balled fist against her cheek. "And don't forget it."

"Will they send you to prison?" Her face eloquently reflected the worry and concern she felt.

Tony shook his head. "No. Don't worry. I'll be around to keep you supplied with what you need when you need it. All those headlines about the big narcotics roundup only mean one thing. Representative Adams is going for higher political office. He's made his point. He's got the big TV and newspaper publicity behind him now. It don't make any difference whether any of us are convicted or not. My lawyer says he'll get me off. As a matter of fact, I've got to give him three hundred tomorrow."

"I'm glad I could help, Tony."

"You're great, kid." He kissed her and she clung to him fiercely. She sure had a great figure, a fine young body. These society girls could be the best there was for a while. Desire pulsated in his groin. "Hey, gorgeous, what d'ya say? Another ball?"

"You want me, Tony?"

"Of course, don't I always?"

"Sometimes I wonder. Have you got any amies?"

"Just got a pack. I'll fix one up for you while you get those clothes off again." Tony took the tin of amyl nitrites from his pocket and a benzedrine inhaler from the top of his dresser. As Andrea slid out of her clothes he opened the inhaler and put in a fresh amyl nitrite pill. Then putting the cap back on tightly he handed the inhaler to Andrea, once again undressed and lying back on the sofa. She put the inhaler to her nostril and sniffed as Tony pulled off his own clothes and lay down beside her.

"Wow, what an amie does to you," Andrea laughed. "Have a sniff." Tony took the inhaler and drew in a deep sniff.

"Yeah, if I wasn't already so fuckin' horney I'd think this stuff was doing it." He handed the inhaler back to Andrea who applied it to her nostril again as Tony moved in between her legs.

"Oh, God!" Andrea moaned. "Make it last, Tony."

"I'll try, baby."

"Here, have another sniff." She held the inhaler to his nose. He breathed in deeply through his nose and thrust himself violently into her. Andrea screamed in wild joy as the drug heightened her sensation. She responded with complete abandon, meeting his thrusts and sniffing the amyl, and even as Tony was calling to her that he couldn't hold it back any more she felt herself gloriously ripped asunder by his phallus, her orgasm gripping her from the top of her head down to her toes. She thought she could feel him running through her body and coming through her throat, her tongue was the end of his penis and his mouth was over hers. She writhed, tried to scream and fell back into a velvety softness as slowly, deliciously, Tony's hardness withdrew from her mouth, back through her insides and finally out of her altogether. She lay in a sort of semicoma for how long she didn't know until she felt a splash of cold on her breasts and opened her eyes. Tony was standing above her, a glass in his hand. Some of the drink had spilled upon her.

She smiled wordlessly, looking up at his naked body,

his penis small and limp. It always pleased her to take his great, hard, long thing inside her and reduce it to this shriveled-up state. Slowly the responsibilities of her life flooded into her state of tranquillity. Mama would be wondering where she was. If she was late there would be a big fight and Daddy Ed would get drunk and perhaps hit her again and Little Eddie would be impossible and she would have to go through another nerve-shattering evening. She sat up and suddenly felt naked. Tony laughed as she folded her arms around her breasts and crossed her legs.

"What's the matter, kid. You getting shy again?"

"Toss me my clothes, Tony."

Tony retrieved Andrea's bra and pantyhose, handing them to her. She stood up and carried them into the bathroom with her, picking up her dress and shoes on the way. Tony finished his drink and was just pouring another one when Andrea emerged, looking neat and well-groomed despite her pale face and troubled expression.

"I'm almost out of downers, Tony," she said. "I just can't get through a night at home any more without them."

"I'll have some for you tomorrow."

"Thank you. I wish those skin pops lasted longer."

Tony went to her and put his arm around her shoulders. "Maybe you're ready for something new, something that would keep you going longer. You want to try?"

"In the vein?"

"You'll go for seven or eight hours above the world," Tony said suggestively. "Maybe more."

"Will they be able to tell?"

"Not really. You know you're there, doing what you gotta do, but nothing bothers you."

"You know, God, I'm already late. It's going to be murder when I get home. Especially if Brad called Mama about me getting away from New York for the summer and going away to college in the fall."

"Take a downer as soon as you get home," Tony advised.

"They take so long to work. Maybe I should try a real shot. It would work until I go to bed tonight, wouldn't it?"

"Sure it would."

"The only thing is I'm afraid they'll start noticing the needle marks."

"Not if you know what you're doing," Tony counseled. "I know a girl who started shooting in her thigh, then between her toes and now she puts it in under her tongue. She doesn't have a mark on her body and she's been shooting almost a year."

"Maybe I should shoot a little now," Andrea said tentatively.

"No, baby. You had a skin pop only three hours ago. Wait until tomorrow. I'll get you set up then. No point in getting too much in your system all at once." He kissed her. "Someone's got to look out for you, kid. I'll give you a downer now. In an hour it'll start to really work. Tomorrow we'll try something else."

"Whatever you say, Tony. Just don't go away someplace and I promise I won't either."

"That's my love, baby. And look, if you can figure out any way to get us some more bread we'll really be needing it."

A look of quiet desperation came over Andrea's face. "I wish you knew what I had to do to get the money I brought you today."

"I know, baby. Together we'll figure out how to get up the bread. Your father has lots of it, we just have to figure how to get it out of him."

"I'll do anything I can, Tony."

"We'll have a good afternoon together tomorrow. And if you still want it, we'll give you a real shot."

"I'll see how bad things are tonight. I'd better fade out of here fast. Every minute I'm late makes my mother wilder." She threw her arms around him, kissed him and reluctantly let go.

"You'll never know how I hate leaving you, Tony. Maybe we should get married and tell them all to go to hell."

Tony concealed the alarm her suggestion instilled

in him. "We'll get into that tomorrow afternoon." He opened the door for her and watched her start down the stairs. Then he closed the door and returned to the drink he had just poured for himself.

CHAPTER THIRTY-SEVEN

The electrifying news that Governor George Wallace had been shot, though he was still alive, reached Brad Kendall late in the day after a long meeting in Ciano's office. He turned on the television set in his office and in minutes a replay of the actual shooting appeared on the screen.

Absorbed, Brad watched the screen and then suddenly stiffened, stood up, leaned across his desk and stared closely at the picture from the Maryland shopping center. The assailant was clearly shown. Even as the telecast continued Brad snatched for his telephone.

"Get me Mr. D'Estang." His voice was shrill and trembling. He continued to watch the screen as the youthful gunman was taken away.

"Mr. D'Estang is in the Star Club having a meeting," he was told.

"Get him out of the meeting," Brad commanded. "This is urgent!" Then, "Forget it. I'll go up there myself." He left his office, walked out to the elevators and took one up to the Star Club on the roof. The headwaiter snapped to attention as Brad purposefully strode toward the entranceway to the roof-top dining room and cocktail lounge.

"Where is Mr. D'Estang?" he asked.

The headwaiter pointed and Brad picked him out sitting with two older men. He started toward them and Maurice looked up and saw him coming. Brad reached the table and before he could say anything Maurice introduced him to Casper Orellian and Judge Michael Rackless. "Did you want to talk to me, Brad?"

"Yes." He smiled apologetically at the two men. "It's quite urgent."

D'Estang shrugged his wide shoulders as he stood up. "Excuse me a moment, gentlemen. I'll make this as quick as possible." D'Estang followed Brad to a secluded corner and they sat down at an empty table.

"Now what's this all about, Brad? You seem unusually shaken up."

"Did you hear the news about Wallace?"

"That he was shot? Of course."

"Have you seen any of the television coverage?"

"No. I haven't had time to look at television this afternoon."

"Well, I looked. The man who shot him was in this hotel."

"A lot of people have been in this hotel."

"But you introduced me to the strange old foreign type this Bremer person was sitting with."

"Yes," D'Estang replied casually, "Dr. Wormsinger."

"What's it all about, Maurice?"

"Sometime I'd be glad to go into it with you, Brad. But I'm in an important meeting. It's a special assignment from C.L."

"What about this Wormsinger? And this gunman sitting right here with him."

D'Estang sighed. "Brad, Brad. No big deal. Wormsinger is a psychologist who travels around looking for likely crazies who can carry out assassinations we require. Has it ever occurred to you how many important people are killed by crazy loners?" D'Estang started to stand up but Brad reached up and grabbed his lapel.

"Wait, you can't just toss off something like that. I'm in, like it or not. I want to know."

"Brad, I'll be glad to tell you all about terminal section later, but this meeting I'm having is really important. Mr. Wallace is one of two likely presidential candidates in 1976 who are impossible for us to influence in any way. Wormsinger must have half a dozen of his nutcakes wandering around after both of them. It could have happened two months ago or a year from now. It was only a matter of time. Now, will you let me get back to something that *is* urgent?"

Brad's fingers loosened and D'Estang pulled away from him, turned on his heel and made his way through the cocktail tables back to the private booth where he had been sitting.

"Sorry, Casper, Judge, I guess we shouldn't have tried to meet in my own hotel. There's always something coming up."

"Maurice," Orellian said, adjusting his pince-nez which hung around his neck on a black ribbon, "the judge and I were just looking at the list of defendants."

"This Jorge Ramirez shouldn't be a problem," Judge Rackless said, clearing his throat. "He can be deported."

"Just what we had in mind for him," D'Estang agreed.

"The problem cases, of course, are Joseph Sterrato, this Karl Echeverrea Brandt from the Caribbean, and the two Frenchmen. Fortunately, Congressman Adams did not see fit to include an assistant district attorney in planning his dramatic roundup or the prosecution would have had an ironbound conspiracy case against all of them. However, by not having secured any heroin in Sterrato's possession, even though the chain of its movement was well documented, it may be possible for the defense to successfully move for dismissal of the case. The key, of course, is to make a motion for suppression of evidence. There are a number of grounds, the best one being that it was seized with no search warrant."

The old judge smiled wryly. "I might say this investigation was conducted in a sloppy way. An ADA would have had a State Supreme Court justice like myself ready to write out a search warrant the instant location was established and then hit Sterrato while he was in possession. That way everyone who came to the room later could be convicted of conspiracy to illegally import heroin into the country."

"They'd never have got the nigger," D'Estang pointed out.

"Yes, and there's little doubt that this Permagon Antilles and his people will be convicted and receive heavy sentences."

"That's what we wanted," D'Estang said. "And we wouldn't be unhappy to see Falconi go up too."

"Now you come to an interesting point. This Anthony Falconi, A K A Tony Falcon, could be very helpful. He was found in possession and even though there was no search warrant the chances are he'll be convicted and receive a long sentence unless special steps are taken. However, if he said that he did not receive the heroin from Sterrato, that could further help the defense in the conspiracy case."

"We'll have to talk about what we want to do to help Falconi," D'Estang answered. "Mainly, we're interested in helping Sterrato, Echeverrea and the two Frenchmen."

"What about the men that were picked up in Chicago and Detroit?" the judge asked. "I have friends on the bench in both places."

"Forget them."

"They could be useful in a successful motion by Echeverrea's lawyer to suppress evidence," Judge Rackless pointed out.

D'Estang looked across the table at Orellian. "Look, you know everybody's lawyers, they're all good. You handle everything."

"Of course, Maurice. I just wanted you to understand the complexities of the case and what the judge is going to have to do. Because of his seniority Judge Rackless was able to get assigned to Part 30 of the State Supreme Court where all motions are heard and assignments to other judges made."

"I understand perfectly." Maurice pulled a thick brown envelope from his pocket and handed it to

Orellian. "Here is what you need from us, Casper. If all works out there will be a bonus." He turned to the judge. "Always nice to see you again, Judge."

"Same on this side, Maurice. Whatever happens, this Congressman Adams certainly made a national name for himself. It certainly is interesting how the gaping holes in his apparently extraordinary victory over the narcotics syndicate have not been publicized."

"Not so strange, Judge," D'Estang replied. "You saw what happened to the head of the House Crime Committee when he started complaining about a junior member of the committee running an investigation without bringing him in on it." D'Estang chuckled. "He tried to say some of the things you just brought out and where is he? Fighting for his political life, accused of taking bribes—which he took—from us." Maurice stood up. "Enjoy your dinner, Judge, Casper. See you again."

D'Estang turned and left a thoughtful Judge Rackless and a satisfied Casper Orellian slapping the heavy envelope against the palm of his hand.

CHAPTER THIRTY-EIGHT

Rose, who was now as much a secretary to Pat Kenney as she was to Representative Fred Black, laid the current *New York Law Journal* down on the detective's empty desk. He looked up from the issue of *True Detective* magazine he was reading and let his eyes wander over Rose's ample bosom. In all the time they had been working together he had been unable to escalate their relationship to something physical although she was always pleasant and now even sympathetic with him.

"I hate to give you this, Pat. But I knew you were anxious to find out what Judge Rackless' decision would be on Sterrato's motion to suppress."

Kenney took the *Journal* and read the judge's decision on the front page. Motion to suppress granted. "Well, I guess that blows our case, Rose," he said quietly. Then his anger erupted. "Goddamn, except for the nigger, they're all going to get off. Strega Joe is going to walk. If they can't use the heroin for evidence they got no case."

"I'm sorry, Pat," Rose said sincerely.

"You know, there's a hell of a lot more to this whole thing than we realize—or than I realize." He looked at her suspiciously.

"Well, Mr. Black's friend Congressman Adams sure did just fine no matter what happens," Rose declared.

"He must be one of the most famous congressmen in the House all of a sudden. Did you read they're talking about making a movie out of the case?"

"Sure. And they're going to let me play the part of myself," Pat replied. Then, his anger temporarily abating, he read through the decision carefully. "You know, Rose, I remember thinking about it at the time, but there was no ADA involved in either the investigation or that big show for the press at the end."

"So what?"

"So maybe if a prosecutor had been with us all the way through we'd have gotten a conviction."

"Mr. Adams is a lawyer."

"Yes, he is. And he knows criminal law. And come to think about it, he wanted to hit Sterrato while he still had the evidence in his possession but for some reason—" Pat's forehead wrinkled up as he thought back to the night in the communications room—"it was Brad Kendall who talked him out of it. At the time I didn't know what to do and I guess I was more concerned about getting the big nigger than anything else."

"Well, you got him all right. No way he's going to miss going to jail for a good long time," Rose said proudly.

"Son of a bitch deserves it. I hope they throw the key away. But Strega Joe. It's funny, you know. I've known him for a long time. He was always involved but we could never prove anything. But for him to be the big juice in narcotics?" Pat Kenney shook his head. "You know, Rose?" Kenney suddenly catapulted from the chair in which he'd been leaning back and grabbed his hat off the rack beside his desk. "I'm beginning to think maybe old Pat Kenney has been had. And that doesn't happen too often. And when it does old Pat doesn't take it lying down."

"What are you talking about, Pat?"

"Tell you all about it later. So long." He started to walk out of the office, then turned. "Look, Rose, do me a favor and don't say anything about this to Representative Black just yet, OK? I'll talk to him later."

"OK, Pat. The poor man has more than he can take care of now anyway. Between here and Washington he is really busy."

Pat Kenney had discovered that he did his best thinking, sometimes accomplishing prodigious feats of deductive reasoning, in a bar. And to his favorite bar in the neighborhood he repaired to think things out. It was almost lunchtime anyway.

At two-thirty in the afternoon Brad Kendall's secretary came into his office in the Spire Building to tell him that Detective Kenney was waiting to see him. Surprised, Brad told her to send Kenney in and cancel the appointment he had made over at the hotel.

As the familiar figure of the broad-shouldered, red-headed, beefy-faced detective appeared in the doorway to his office, Brad stood up to welcome him.

"Hi ya, Pat. Long time no see. They keeping you busy following up that investigation?"

"You should know better than that, Brad," Kenney replied. Brad gestured at a chair and Kenney sprawled into it. "The day after Adams hit in all the papers and TV stations my funds were cut off. I couldn't even investigate why there's no toilet paper in the men's room of the office, for Christ's sake."

"What's on your mind, Pat?"

"What's it all about, Brad? That's what's on my mind. Somehow, I don't completely understand it, but I think this whole Adams thing was a setup. He sure got a lot of political mileage out of it. He'll probably run for the Senate, he might even make it to Vice President. From nowhere he's suddenly the country's leading expert on crime in Congress." Kenney slapped the *Law Journal* down on Brad's desk. "Did you see this? Sterrato is going to get off. We aren't going to get convictions on any of the big guys. They'll be back at their old stands bringing shit into the country."

"We're going to get some convictions, Pat," Brad replied defensively. "And look at the large amounts of heroin that didn't make it to the street."

"There's plenty more to take its place. The big guys haven't even been touched."

"Well, in any case I'm a hotelman not a detective so none of this really is in my area of competence."

"You sure had a lot of competence that night," Kenney retorted. "You kept Adams from hitting when he could have picked up evidence, grabbed Sterrato in possession."

"Pat," Brad replied wearily, "I had nothing to do with the law enforcement aspects of the case. I am acting as a political adviser to Adams. Naturally, I was interested in seeing as many criminals apprehended as possible and as much heroin confiscated. And I must say Adams was responsible for by far the largest heroin haul ever made. Half a billion dollars' worth."

"That's a lot of bullshit, we all know how those figures work. And why wasn't a prosecutor brought in at the beginning of the investigation? How come no ADA was around that night when Adams was directing the big roundup?"

Brad smiled patronizingly. "I seem to recall you saying on several occasions, as you were getting ready to tighten the noose, that you didn't want the DA's office in on the investigation. You were afraid of a security leak, as I understand."

"But who the hell am I to tell you and Adams what to do? I'm just a detective first grade, a patrolman in plainclothes. Adams should have brought in an ADA if he wanted to get convictions, which I am beginning to doubt. But I guess he got what he wanted."

"Why not have a word with Adams?" Brad suggested.

Kenney shook his head. "He doesn't know bird turd. I worked with him long enough to realize that he has no more to do with what William Fortune Adams does with his political future than I do. In fact, maybe I have more to say about his political career than he does. He's what you call a puppet. And for who? You?" Again Kenney shook his head. "Not you, Brad. But I've been doing a little detective work in the last few hours. Who owns you? Who pulls your strings? Whitehall associates, right? I found out a hell of a lot about Whitehall I didn't know. I read all about the investigations made into Whitehall and Ciano and Hyman Steinert. They always came out smelling like a rose legally, but they smell like something else not so good to me."

"I have very little contact with the hierarchy at Whitehall," Brad replied. "It's true that because of my experience in political campaigns I frequently take on a political assignment if I believe in the candidate and it's true Adams is receiving some support from the parent company." Brad paused. "But I don't see what that has to do with your dark suspicions."

"What would you say if I told you I want to see Ciano?"

Brad felt a sudden tear in his stomach but his expression didn't change. "Mr. Ciano is a very busy man, even I see him very rarely."

"Well then, how about Steinert?"

"I've never heard of anybody seeing Steinert. I don't think even Mr. Ciano gets to see him. In any case, Mr. Ciano is the acting head of state in Whitehall."

"So I'll go see Ciano."

"Why, Pat?" Brad tried to hide his concern.

"Because I don't want him to think he's fooling Pat Kenney."

"Nobody's trying to fool you, Pat. Come on."

"Ciano is right in this building, isn't he?"

Brad nodded. "Now look, come off it, Pat. Seeing Ciano won't accomplish anything. He probably doesn't even know what's been going on in this Adams investigation."

"For a long time things didn't add up. Now suddenly they do. I may only be a high school graduate and I may look like a dumb cop, but there's such a thing as street sense and you only get it out in the jungle with the animals. But when you have it you get to know a lot about life and the people who manipulate us. I just want to tell Ciano that he doesn't manipulate me. That's a word I learned from Adams and he doesn't know it's being done to him." Kenney laughed. Then he stood up. "I'm going up to see Ciano."

"He'll never see you, Pat. Don't waste your time."

Pat Kenney gave Brad a long look. "By the way, Brad, there is something I guess you should know especially now that the investigation is off. How much do you know about this Tony Falcon?"

Now Brad felt a real stab of concern. "Not much," he answered cautiously. "Why?" He tried to keep his tone even.

"Did you know he's seeing your daughter?"

"I knew she had a dinner date or two with him sometime ago. Andrea tells me she hasn't seen him for a long time."

"What's a long time?"

"Since long before this Adams case hit the papers."

"She was seeing him right up to the day we broke the case. And, even though I've suspended most of my investigations, I personally followed up on Falconi. Your daughter saw him as recently as yesterday afternoon. And she was seeing him steadily, every day or two right up to the night he was arrested. She was at his apartment to greet him when he came out of jail." Kenney saw the anguished contortions that came to Brad's face. "I'm sorry, Brad. I thought you ought to know. Too bad we can't get him back in jail where he belongs. I hoped to catch him making a sale but I can't, all by myself, keep a twenty-four-hour surveillance on him."

"How long have you known this, Pat?" Brad asked quietly.

"Like I said, since long before we busted the operation. I didn't tell you because I didn't want Tony to find out we were on him. If any one subject had figured out he was being tailed it would have blown the whole case in France and the United States."

"I see your point. I would have considered the well-being of my daughter more important than the case," Brad replied dryly.

"Something like that, I guess. I'm a cop first. Everything else comes second." Looking down at Brad, who seemed to have withered behind the desk, he went on. "Like I said, I'm sorry, Brad. If you want me to go over to Tony's and rough him up a bit, tell him to stop seeing your daughter or else he goes back to jail the next time he so much as spits in the street, I'll be glad to do it."

Brad shook his head. "No, that would only make it worse. At least I can talk to my daughter now. You know how these kids are. If they think you're trying to force something on them it's the end of all dialogue."

"Dialogue I don't know. But these kids today are getting away with murder, literally murder. Some day someone is going to have to change things, make them behave or else."

"I appreciate your thoughts, Pat. Now, may I suggest that you give up trying to see Mr. Ciano. He's a very, very busy man and doesn't like to be disturbed."

"I'll wait around his office until he has a few minutes. See you later, Brad." The big detective held up a hand palm toward Brad and then turned and left the office.

Brad was picking up his telephone as Kenney walked out. "Get me Mr. Ciano," he ordered.

"C.L.," he said as Ciano answered, "I've just had a disturbing talk with Detective Kenney. He seems to feel that the whole narcotics bust was some sort of a hoax and he was the victim."

"Sorry to hear that," Ciano replied.

"Somehow he's gotten it into his head that you planned and carried out the whole thing and he's on his way up to try and see you now. I told him you were too busy to listen to his gripes."

There was silence on the phone a few moments. Then Ciano said, "It's possible that Kenney could be of further use to us. I'll see him."

"You will?" Brad was startled. "In his present frame of mind I can't see him being any use to anyone."

"Let's see what happens after I've had a chance to talk to him. I think there's a great deal we could do for him that he would appreciate."

"I'll be interested to hear what happens, C.L.," Brad said.

"I'll let you know. I don't think Detective Kenney will be so difficult to deal with."

Brad hung up the phone wishing he had some of Julius' devices planted in Ciano's office so he could actually witness the confrontation. Then he thought of Andrea and Tony Falcon and nothing else seemed important.

CHAPTER THIRTY-NINE

Detective Kenney was greatly taken by surprise when the security guard at the elevator on C. L. Ciano's floor was not only cordial to him but seemed to be expecting him. He was ushered into the main office complex from the elevator foyer and from there an attractive secretary escorted him down the hallway to Ciano's office. The door was closed and the secretary outside smiled pleasantly at Kenney and said that Mr. Ciano wouldn't keep him waiting long.

"How did you know I was coming?" Kenney asked. "I wasn't so sure myself."

"Mr. Kendall called up to us. Mr. Ciano was delighted to hear that you were in the building. I know he's looking forward to meeting you. We all have read so much about you and how you worked with Mr. Adams to break up that big dope syndicate."

In spite of himself Kenney couldn't help but be pleased at the cordial reception and flattery. "I was only one small part of the whole team," he said modestly.

The buzzer on the secretary's intercom sounded and she said into it, "Mr. Kenney is here to see you, Mr. Ciano."

Kenney heard Ciano's voice. "That's fine. Please bring him right in." The secretary stood up and walked around her desk to Ciano's office door and opened it.

This just goes to show how much Brad knew about things at the top, Kenney said to himself as he walked into the large office, almost intimidating with its splendid view of the city and its elegant appointments. Ciano walked across the wide space between the large, uncluttered desk and the door holding out his hand.

"Detective Kenney, this is a privilege. I'm so pleased you thought of calling on me. I suppose you are very busy pulling together all the loose ends of the big investigation." Ciano gestured at the arrangement of furniture beside the fireplace over which hung the large map of the world. Kenney looked at the array of colored pins in the map, surmising they represented operations in which Whitehall was involved throughout the world. "Come, let's sit down and talk. I've asked my secretary not to disturb us with telephone calls."

Kenney followed Ciano over to the intimate conversation area of the office and sat down on the sofa. Ciano sat across from him. "Well, Mr. Kenney, I am most interested to hear whatever it is that you wish to discuss with me. I have followed your exploits and from Congressman Adams and Brad Kendall I heard about the meticulous piece of detective work you did during the heroin investigation."

Kenney replied, "I expect you know all about the operation."

"On the contrary. Even though I have loaned Brad Kendall to advise Congressman Adams on his campaign strategy and authorized a campaign contribution to Adams I have not had the time to be personally active in his efforts for re-election."

"I understand he's running for senator," Kenney said.

"Yes, so I heard. And after the remarkable attack you two engineered on the narcotics syndicate I would hope he would be nominated and elected to the Senate."

There was a long pause in the conversation as Kenney tried to marshal his thoughts and figure out how to begin. Ciano broke the silence. "Now, Mr. Kenney,

don't keep me in suspense. Tell me what's on your mind."

"Well, in the first place, Mr. Ciano," Kenney plunged in, "I figured you were the man who really made the investigation for Adams happen."

"Me?" Ciano asked, surprised.

"I know from Adams that the Spire Building which you own gives him all that valuable office space for very little cash outlay. And that communications room, even the feds don't have anything like it."

"We feel that showing prospective tenants the Adams layout helps make them decide to lease space here. The way competition is we have to do something extra. Sell the sizzle, not the steak, the old adage goes." Ciano chuckled.

"Right, sir. Anyway, I'm sure Brad Kendall isn't the final authority on the Adams campaign or on this investigation. Let me tell you what the facts are and then you can tell me what you think should be done."

"I'm anxious to hear the facts, Detective Kenney, though truthfully there isn't much I can do one way or another about the follow-through."

"Well, sir, in the first place, no matter what came out in the newspapers and on television we came nowhere near touching the top levels of this drug syndicate. Joe Sterrato, Strega Joe as he's known, isn't anywhere near the top of any New York crime family. And it doesn't look like Adams is going to get a single meaningful conviction out of this except for the Big Nig, as they call Permagon Antilles. We'll probably make something stick on Falconi even though we didn't have a search warrant when we hit him."

"This is all most interesting, Mr. Kenney, but I don't see where it really concerns Whitehall."

"I will make the connection as I go along, Mr. Ciano, if you'll let me lay the whole thing out for you."

"Certainly, go ahead," Ciano allowed.

"Everything in this investigation revolved around Sterrato. As I said, I've known Strega Joe for many

years. He's nothing more than a good button man, a stand-up guy that can be trusted. If he really was the Mr. Big of the narcotics syndicate, do you think he would have sat all night in a suite at the Pierre Hotel waiting for us to come and get him? Sure we caught a lot of people going in and out of that suite like a Marx Brothers movie, but all it added up to in the long run was a big show for the press and TV. And, like I said earlier, we never even established a case against Strega Joe."

Kenney held a hand up against Ciano's impatience and continued talking, perhaps a bit faster. "Another thing, sir. Five cars from the federal Bureau of Narcotics managed to lose Jorge Ramirez who was being driven in from JFK. Then he was found by a new man, Dan Gason, right at the Pierre Hotel where he was going although the Bureau didn't know that. I did a little checking on Gason. He's been with the Bureau only a month and he got his job through political influence used by Representative Fred Black of the House Appropriations Committee which funds such outfits as the FBI and the federal Bureau of Narcotics and Dangerous Drugs."

"You work for Black. Why don't you ask him about it?"

"I haven't been able to talk to Representative Black since the day after we broke this case. What I'm trying to tell you is that the moment the newspapers and TV came out all over the country, the world I guess, with the story of Adams' big bust there has been no follow-through and my usefulness has been cut off."

"That seems a shame after all that brilliant investigative work you did, Kenney," Ciano commented.

The detective shrugged depreciatingly. "Now, that I have had the chance to evaluate what I did and didn't do, the whole case starts to add up to something far different from what the press made it sound. I am aware of the invaluable use to which informers can be put. Almost every case I have broken has been done with stools. But in my fifteen years as a detective first grade on the New York Narcotics Bureau I have never seen

a network of informers all coming to me over a two-month period and all of them helping me piece together the same case. Things just don't fall in place so neatly, at least not in two months. I had a good thing started when I went to Representative Black, but I never in my wildest dreams expected to put together a bust of the magnitude this one looks like—to those who don't know," Kenney added.

Then before Ciano could interrupt him Kenney pushed on. "At the time I was so busy and excited I didn't bother to take an overall view of the case. In the Virgin Islands the right informers were looking for me to tell me all about Echeverrea Brandt. The same thing happened in Marseilles and Paris. In two days I knew everything I needed to know, and I can't even speak French. Then in Switzerland right to my hotel comes a guy who tells me that the courier I need to find is a United Nations diplomat with a beautiful blond girl friend who travels with him, and the two of them are in the hotel right now. Sure enough there is a Mr. and Mrs. Jorge Ramirez listed. I get a look at them, put a tail on them and find out he brings a satchel into a Swiss bank and then goes home via Marseilles where he picks up a suitcase and takes it home. Like I said, Mr. Ciano, informers are great but this is ridiculous."

"I think I understand what you're trying to say, Mr. Kenney, but I still don't quite see where it fits in with Whitehall."

As Ciano stood up to signify that the meeting was over, as far as he was concerned, Kenney quickly shot out, "It fits right into your private life, sir, or your daughter's."

Ciano paused in midstep toward the door, frozen. "Through stools," Kenney pursued, "new ones and some of my old reliable guys, I found out that this character I was having tailed, Anthony Falconi, known as Tony Falcon, had once gone out with the daughter of a big businessman from Westchester County named Ciano. From observation I saw that he was going out with the daughter of the president of one of your companies, Ascot Hotels. He still sees her. What Falcon has been doing is to build up a society business for pills, pot, cocaine and heroin." Kenney stood up also. "May I finish? This is important to both of us."

"Go ahead, Mr. Kenney."

Kenney tried to choose his words carefully. For his own mental well-being he wanted to make Ciano perfectly aware that nobody had fooled Detective Kenney. "This Falconi is still trying to expand his business even though he is out on bail. However, he is one of the two men of some importance who we will probably convict and send to jail. The other is the Big Nig in Harlem, Permagon Antilles who, I understand from my stools, has recently been trying to muscle out of Harlem an operation long run by the Italian-organized groups."

The mention of Tony Falcon and the fact that Kenney was able to make a connection between Falcon and himself gave Ciano one of the few shocks he had experienced in years. He listened now, wondering what else this tough cop might reveal.

"Now, sir, I had all the heroin we intercepted analyzed. The junk Ramirez brought in, the load Echeverrea brought to Miami that went up to Detroit and Chicago was the lowest grade, cheapest heroin we've seen in a long time. If it was cut the way the usual high-quality shit is cut the pushers would all be beaten up by their addict customers for selling them worthless white powder. All the stuff came from the same batch. Under 50 per cent pure as opposed to the 88 or 89 per cent quality of most of what comes in. So whoever planned this caper probably paid not much more than a thousand dollars a pound at the laboratories in Marseilles. Thus at the most two hundred thousand dollars was laid out for the heroin. As for the thousand pounds of morphine base that was confiscated from the trawler, that was pretty cheap stuff at its best. Sure, if it had reached Marseilles and had been turned into a thousand pounds of pure heroin and it had somehow reached the streets of New York, and the stuff that we picked up had been pure, then perhaps its street sale value, after having been cut and packaged into five-dollar pops, might reach the half billion dollars so widely quoted.

"So what I'm saying, Mr. Ciano," Kenney pressed, "is that for an outlay of perhaps a quarter of a million dollars' total, the greatest advertising campaign in the history of the United States was launched for an unknown political candidate. And nobody of consequence was hurt. Also two very unmanageable characters have been put out of the way.

"Very good, but Pat Kenney was used and didn't like it. I'm sure that you'll get good results out of Adams and that when he becomes a senator he will be very useful to you. But don't think Pat Kenney was fooled. I know who you are, Mr. Ciano, I know what Whitehall is, and I know that no matter how many times Whitehall is investigated you'll always come up smelling like a rose. You can buy most everybody you want, the Brad Kendalls, but not me. I just wanted you to know that I at least wasn't fooled. Also I thought it would interest you to know how close, even to you, these mob guys on your lowest levels still come to the boss. I'm not sure about your daughter Elda, but Andrea Kendall and thousands of others like her are being hooked and destroyed at the cash generating level of your outfit. So, I guess I've said it, Mr. Ciano. There are a few of us you can't buy and mostly we're on too low a level to do you any real harm anyway. It will be interesting to watch the political fortunes of William Fortune Adams." He paused to draw a deep breath. "Thanks for letting me get off my spiel." Kenney started for the door.

"Mr. Kenney." Ciano's cold voice cut through to him. "You have given your little speech for what it's worth. Now let me have my say. It might be interesting, you might even learn something."

"Of course, Mr. Ciano," Kenney said, turning. "Standing up or sitting down?"

"This is fine." Ciano walked over to the mantelpiece above the interior decorator's fireplace and leaned on it, glancing up at the map of the United States.

"Mr. Kenney, I'm a businessman although certainly not a traditional or conventional businessman. In building my corporate structure I found it convenient to make use of monies which I knew had been accrued through criminal activity. I put it into building American industry and business, creating more jobs, more housing, and more consumer goods, increasing the Gross National Product if you will. Crime is going to go on regardless of whether or not I showed what you would call the Mafia families how to legitimize their money."

Ciano glanced at Kenney and since the detective showed no reaction he went on. "There are and have always been many direct ties between so-called organized crime and organized labor. Because of our connections with labor we do not have strikes. You may recall the elevator strike of a few years ago. Not one elevator operator went on strike in Whitehall buildings. And by the same token, if it is advantageous we can stop or start strikes all over the country."

"And you still work closely with the mob."

"President Nixon pardoned a proven mobster and union chief, Jimmy Hoffa, earlier this year. That means the President will get the Teamsters Union endorsement for his re-election campaign in the fall. So who is working with who?"

"What about narcotics?" Kenney asked. "You know who is bringing the big loads of shit into the country. You are taking narcotics money into your laundry."

"Perhaps," Ciano conceded. "But I can assure you that I am as anxious as anyone in this country to stop the importation of narcotics into America. But it can't be done under present operating rules."

"I gotta admit you're right there, Mr. Ciano. The way Warren's Supreme Court had us tied up we still can't arrest and convict anyone."

"You can't even make a proper investigation without getting into trouble," Ciano taunted. "You can't use as evidence any material gained through electronic surveillance. Congressman Adams' big bust cannot, as you have finally come to realize, do any real harm. In fact, there is nothing that you or any law enforcement agency can do to really cripple the narcotics trade, is there? Every year the narcotics traffickers become more successful and the liberal legislators and interpreters of existing legislation make the heroin shippers richer and safer. Right?"

"Right!" Kenney agreed.

"So what do you think is going to happen, Mr. Kenney?" Ciano let the question hang out for a long silence as he waited for Kenney to answer.

Finally Kenney admitted, "I don't know."

"But I do know, Mr. Kenney. And since even if you wished to thwart me you are powerless to do so, as you yourself observed a few moments ago, I'll tell you what my plan is. And perhaps you will decide that my alternative is a better one than the present impotent methodology of the United States Government."

"I'm listening," Kenney replied, trying to impart a belligerence to his tone of voice that he didn't really feel.

"As you suspected, the Adams investigation was planned from our side months ago. It was even planned that you would head up the investigation and we would subtly feed you the information you needed. And yes, we did it to get the important publicity needed to make a serious candidate out of a comparative unknown figure. All that is true. And where do we go from here? We elect the President of the United States in 1976. Maybe it will be Adams; it could be any one of a dozen or more candidates we are grooming. We then take over the entire governing process of the country with the aid of the military. And then we clean up the country fast. At this point every arrest you make for street crime and narcotics addiction results in the total banishment of that individual from our society. How would you like to never have to arrest the same man twice?"

Kenney couldn't help nodding in approval.

"But, Mr. Kenney, we go much further than that. As you suggest, we know every method and every route used to import drugs into this country. We also know all the individuals involved. And I might add, few if any of these individuals are known to the people on your side. And those who are known can't be touched under today's laws. However, when we take over the country we will not play by those rules. We will round up and execute every drug trafficker operating in this country and abroad. And we won't hesitate to assassinate all those involved, even if they happen to be the president or premier in their own country. In a few weeks there will be no more dangerous drugs coming into this country."

"You'll have hundreds of thousands of crazed addicts in the streets murdering everyone they see," Kenney countered.

"And the police of every major city will have open season on them. You can destroy them with impunity. Knowing your background this should appeal to you, Detective Kenney."

"You mean just knock off every addict and pusher in town?" The concept was too paralyzing for Kenney to digest.

"Do you know how mainland China cured its narcotics problem? China had more addicts than all the rest of the world put together up to the nineteen forties."

"I heard something about the Chinese solution," Kenney replied.

"It is estimated that Mao had approximately three million people killed. And the problem was solved."

"If we could get rid of a million niggers we could end the dope problem and crime in the streets," Kenney exclaimed, being swept up in the concept. "And life would be good for the black people left in this country."

"That's what I'm getting at, Kenney."

"But in the meantime you sit on top of the biggest web of organized crime in the world."

"That is true, Kenney."

"You're some kind of a super Don."

Ciano shook his head. "No. Intellectually, I am at

the opposite end of the pole from a Mafia family head if you want to use that outdated word. I control crime in order to destroy it. But then some things now considered to be crime would no longer be so under the new rules."

"Crime is crime no matter how you look at it," Kenney said dogmatically.

Ciano shrugged. "In New York State there are now legitimate and highly patronized chain-operated abortion clinics. Just three years ago such a business operation would be termed an infamous criminal abortion ring run by a warped evil doctor who desecrated his profession." Ciano smiled at a perplexed Pat Kenney. "See what I mean?"

"I gotta be honest, you mix me up real good, Mr. Ciano."

"Then why don't you come to work for us? You've been working for us unknowingly since I arranged for you to be transferred from the eight-one and assigned to Representative Black."

"You did that?"

"Of course. And a few years ago I arranged for you and a number of your colleagues to be transferred out of the Narcotics Bureau. It's never functioned properly since."

Kenney shook his head. "I'll be a son of a bitch. We always figured something like that happened."

"In the long run my methods will end crime in the streets and once again America will be the safest nation in the world to walk in at anytime of the day or night. The power and respect that the cop on the beat once knew will be restored to him." Ciano fixed Kenney with a long stare. "How about it, Kenney? Are you ready to work my side of the street?"

Kenney seemed to wilt before Ciano's logic. He was silent for a long moment. Ciano walked from the mantel back to his desk and looked down at a sheet of paper on his otherwise clear desk. He made no other move to hurry Kenney's deliberations.

After the long, agonizing thought process had ground out a decision Kenney began to talk. "Mr. Ciano, I'd be a liar if I said I wouldn't like to see everything you've said come true. But I'm not any kind of an intellectual, I can only live by my instincts, my street sense. And everything that I've lived by tells me that you are as crazy as a shit-house mouse, sir."

Ciano looked up, startled.

"Yes, sir," Kenney went on, "intellectual arguments are wasted on me. I can see how they'd work just fine on a man like Brad Kendall. But I go by gut. And my gut tells me to get the hell out of here. You can use your power as you will but there's no way you can buy me or convince me. Have me killed or transferred or fired, whatever. Fortunately, I don't have a wife and children to consider. May I go now, Mr. Ciano?"

Ciano nodded in reply. Kenney turned, walked to the door, opened it and walked out. Ciano sat down, stunned.

CHAPTER FORTY

No candidate seeking delegate and press support at the Democratic National Convention in Miami had a more lavish and efficiently designed base of operations, Brad Kendall thought proudly. He strolled through the penthouse suite of the Ascot Surf Hotel, the company's third house in Greater Miami, where the well-organized Whitehall group was rallied behind William Fortune Adams.

Brad recalled C. L. Ciano's frequently expressed determination to control the press. This suite at the Ascot Surf was as close as it was possible to come to buying an important segment of the press. It was Sunday afternoon with the convention officially starting the next evening. In one of the two main living rooms of the penthouse Luciana was talking animatedly with a famous television newscaster. Mrs. Adams was acting as hostess and a number of beautiful girls brought down from New York State were entertaining the newsmen and delegates fortunate enough to have been invited to the suite.

The west living room was plate glass on four sides. Three sides looked north and south, up and down Miami Beach, and west over the city of Miami. The fourth side was a window into the lower regions of the swimming pool. Several girls and their male companions were swimming, diving down from the roof-top pool, and waving to the people drinking cocktails on the other side of the transparent wall.

The east living room was designed the same way facing out over the ocean. Both rooms were full but not crowded. Brad had made this the most prestigious press hospitality facility at the convention. Special badges with the media representative's name on it had been issued to the invitees. The suite was reserved for New York State news representatives and New York State delegates to the convention only. Of course, all the major television newscasters were from New York and all the major newspapers in the country had a New York bureau. Thus, Ascot Hotels were entertaining the national press, and still the smaller New York State newspaper and radio and television outlets, upon whom Brad would be depending so heavily to keep Adams before the New York voters when he started campaigning for the Senate, could have the feeling that they were an exclusive fraternity at the convention.

With the Sunday reception in full swing Brad moved about checking on how his headquarters was functioning. He walked down the stairs to the full floor of facilities below. At one end of the floor was the Adams private suite. Brad had his own suite and the rest of the Whitehall staff had bedrooms on the floor with several guest rooms available when needed.

At the opposite end of the floor from where the Adams and Whitehall people were staying was the real heart of the operation. At the west end of the floor was a large suite with a direct line of sight up and down Miami Beach to all the other hotels and on the ocean and across Biscayne Bay to the hotels in Miami including the Tropic Plaza, Ascot's first hotel in the area. It was in this suite that Julius the Genius had been setting up his monitoring equipment for the past six weeks.

Brad Kendall had arranged to be chosen by the Miami Beach Hotel Association as the head of the liaison committee with the Democratic and Republican Convention housing bureaus. Ascot had acquired three major hotels in Miami and Miami Beach and naturally had a big interest in the two conventions. As head of the housing committee Brad had been active in placing the key contenders for the presidential nomination in appropriate facilities in the various hotels. He had reserved a floor in the hotel for the candidate he considered most likely to get the nomination, the floor below his own headquarters here in the Ascot Surf. How the political scene had changed in the five weeks since he had been instrumental in making the room assignments. Now the most likely candidate was one he had felt had little chance at the time. However, he had been able, as chief of housing, to make it possible for Julius to install his virtually undetectable electronic surveillance apparatus in all the headquarters suites. Fortunately, all the really important people at the convention wanted their suites to be placed as high in the hotel as possible, which gave Julius a line of sight to almost every candidate's rooms.

By 1976, Ascot would have completed its newest hotel in Miami Beach, the tallest building in Greater Miami, ideal for Julius' operations.

Brad passed the security guard he had posted outside Julius' suite and with a special key let himself in. The large four-room suite was a jungle of directional antennas. Julius and two junior geniuses were busy with the large electronic devices they were operating as Brad walked in. "Everything under control?" Brad asked.

Julius, a beautiful smile on his face, turned from monitoring a bank of video tubes. "It's gorgeous," he said. "The greatest job of my life. In the history of my business nobody has come close to this setup. Nobody important can take a crap without us knowing about it."

"Maybe at last we'll get the lowdown on sex at a national convention." Brad chuckled.

"If there's any interesting sex going on we'll know about it, maybe even see it. We've got girls and a couple of boys too in four different hotels besides this one on the tube now." He tapped one of the video monitors on the bank in front of him.

"Anything more you need from me?"

"I don't think so. I'm sorry I couldn't tap all the special lines the candidates put in their headquarters but I have every house phone tapped and we can hear at least one side of most of the conversations through the mikes I installed in the rooms. As a matter of fact, I didn't tell you but in the key hotels I can switch calls on the house phones to any room I want. If some candidate wants to call an aide in his room we can have the call diverted to another room. I figured this could be useful."

"It sure can, Julius. Every trick you've got we'll probably use before this show is over. And, remember, this is really a rehearsal for 1976."

Brad left Julius' surveillance center, walked past the security guard and down the hall to his own control room. Inside, with telephones ringing, two secretaries taking messages, a man listening to a radio receiver for walkie-talkie transmissions from intelligence agents scattered about the hotels, Maurice D'Estang and Representative Fred Black were discussing strategy.

"Everything all right here?" Brad asked. His nose wrinkled at the strong smell of D'Estang's French cigarette.

"Great," Black answered. "What a setup. Peabody, a vice-presidential candidate, is out at the airport now greeting the delegation leaders as they come in on their flights. This minute he's talking to the Pennsylvania delegates." The man at the radio receiver took his headset off, stood up and handed a message to D'Estang who read it. "Another vice-presidential hopeful just went up to see Senator Humphrey."

"Intelsec is right on the ball," Brad replied. "I still haven't figured out how we're going to get Adams mentioned as a possible vice-presidential candidate by whoever is nominated to run for president. But before this convention is over we'll do it."

"We should be able to get a lot of insurance out of this convention on a lot of people," D'Estang chortled. "That setup of Julius' is sweet."

"Just remember," Brad said commandingly, "we all keep careful records of what we did, what our mistakes were, where we could have been more efficient, where we were successful. Because come '76, our operation has got to make the CIA look like amateurs." Brad started for the door. "If you need me, I've got my beeper on at all times."

"We're OK, Brad," Fred Black said.

In the middle of the floor, where the stairs came down from the penthouse above, Brad stopped at a function room which had been turned into a press-information suite. Three TV sets were turned to the three major networks. News tickers from AP and UPI chattered away spewing out the latest news. Newspapers from every major city in the United States plus the leading papers from London and Paris were displayed. Each morning these daily papers would be flown in for the four days of the convention.

An attractive girl acted as hostess for the room, dispensing information and keys to rooms which newsmen could use to type their stories and phone their editors. An attendant served cocktails and sandwiches.

"Is everything going all right here, Linda?" he asked the girl. "Let me know if you need help on anything."

"Everything is just fine, Mr. Kendall."

"Good girl," he replied. She was about Andrea's age, he thought. A sadness welled up in him as he thought of his daughter. Leaving the press lounge he walked down the hall to his own suite and let himself in. He poured himself a drink and sat down in an easy chair. How great it would have been if Andrea had accepted his invitation to come down for the convention and help out, he thought. But Andrea, using Gwen as an excuse, had refused. Her mother wasn't well and needed her.

He thought back to the confrontation he had gone through with Andrea after Pat Kenney had told him that Andrea was still seeing Tony Falcon. He hadn't been able to get her on the telephone for several days. Gwen wouldn't let him speak to her and she didn't call him. Finally, Elda Ciano had arranged a meeting, unknown to Andrea, who thought just she and Elda would be having lunch together.

Andrea had been frightened when she found Brad with Elda, but the two of them had tried to reassure her and then Elda left Brad and his daughter alone. As gently as possible he had broached the subject of Tony Falcon and expressed his disappointment that she was still seeing him.

Andrea had suddenly burst into a passionate defense of her relationship with Tony. She loved him, she declared, and she wouldn't stop seeing him. In vain Brad tried to reason with her and suggested she spend a week or two with him in Miami. She refused to leave New York and declared that she had definitely decided on going to Hunter College right in New York City. That was what her mother wanted and that was what she was going to do.

Brad had suggested that her mother would be extremely upset if she knew Andrea was seeing Tony Falcon. In that case, Andrea had replied, she would leave home and go live with Tony.

"Until he went to jail?" Brad asked.

Andrea was convinced that Tony would be exonerated. And then Brad had made the mistake he knew he must guard against. He could and would have Tony put away, he told his daughter. Either he'd go to jail or otherwise be eliminated from her life. From her long talks with Elda, Andrea realized her father could do what he threatened and in an embarrassing outburst of tears and invective she declared that if anything happened to Tony, if he went to jail or disappeared, she would never forgive her father, and never talk to or see him again. With that she had run weeping from the restaurant in which they had met and he hadn't seen her again.

Brad finished the drink and stood up to make another. He had tried to get Elda to come to Miami and persuade Andrea to come with her. But when C. L. Ciano heard that his daughter was considering going to the convention he flatly told her she couldn't go.

Elda was twenty-two but she still respected her father's wishes. Later C.L. explained to Brad that he had only one cardinal rule as far as Elda was concerned. She was never, in any way, no matter how indirect, to become involved in Whitehall projects.

It was odd, he thought, here he was, with all the power he had dreamed of and all the money he needed to properly engineer a political coup. He was now probably the most important man in his industry, and he wasn't happy. In fact, these days he was actively unhappy. The only thing to do was to lose himself in his work. So, when he had finished his second drink he put the glass down and left his suite.

Back in the penthouse the party was picking up momentum. Brad walked up behind Luciana and possessively placed a hand around her waist. "Hi, Brad," she greeted him cheerfully. "Great bash, no?"

Brad nodded. "How is Mrs. A doing?"

"She's great. The problem is her husband. He just doesn't seem to know how to relax but he's very popular with the newsmen anyway. They want to know what the next big crime ring he's going to bust is all about."

"I told him to attack police corruption. That makes him anti crime but a little more palatable to the liberals who hate cops."

"He'll do all right. He is an attractive young man, physically."

Brad tightened his grip on Luciana. "Concentrate on me, love, not the candidates. You saw what happened to our last prospect you involved yourself with intimately."

"What a bastard you are to bring it up," Luciana hissed. "It wasn't my fault Ev Jamison and his wife broke up."

"You just might have awakened him to how good sex can really be and he decided his political career wasn't as important as finding the right woman which his wife apparently was not," Brad whispered back. Then, "Everything is going fine. Why don't you come down to my suite for a while."

"Are you suggesting that I leave my post?"

"I'm asking you to come and give the mission chief here in Miami some personal attention."

"Oh, Brad." Luciana laughed. "Every time you get near me you want me to leap into bed."

"I'm awful, I know. How about it?"

"Not now," she replied decisively. "I take my work here very seriously. And Terry Adams needs help. Remember, you yourself said that this year's delegates will be back again in four years for the big one."

Brad shrugged and took his hand off her. "OK. See you later." Looking around the party Brad saw Maurice D'Estang enter, take a glass of champagne from a waiter and start to sip it. Brad walked over to him.

"Got tired of reading intel reports, Maurice?"

"Yeah. As a matter of fact, I came up here to find you. There's not much more you can do now. How'd you like to watch something interesting?"

"What's on your mind?"

"Remember how upset you got about the man who shot Wallace?"

"Of course, Maurice," Brad replied sharply. "I just wanted to know what the hell he was doing in my hotel."

"OK. Doctor Wormsinger is here in Miami. You kept asking me about him and his nutcakes. How'd you like to see him in action?"

"Doing what?"

"Recruiting."

"You mean finding crackpots to shoot people?"

"First he finds them, then he conditions them. Want to go?"

"I might as well know as much about us as I can learn."

"The doctor is in his room waiting for me to call him."

Brad looked over at Luciana in animated conversation with a group of youthful male delegates. "Sure, let's go."

A rented chauffeur-driven sedan pulled up in front of the Ascot Surf Hotel and Brad, D'Estang and Dr.

Wormsinger got in. The air conditioning felt refreshing after the few minutes they'd waited for the car in the hot, humid air. Wormsinger was in high spirits; his eyes magnified behind his thick glasses seemed to radiate good humor. Your cheerful family psychiatrist, Brad thought ironically.

"Now this will be very interesting," Wormsinger said. "My usual method has been to volunteer my time at YMCAs and youth rehabilitation centers around the country. Not often do I have a chance to observe such a situation as you will soon see at Flamingo Park. These young people, many of them seriously disturbed, all camped out together, have only the intention to make trouble for whatever they consider to be the establishment."

"The doctor has been out there and already made some acquaintances," D'Estang explained.

"Yes, this will be my third day. There should be many new non-delegates, as they call themselves, coming in today."

The drive down Alton Road to Flamingo Park took about fifteen minutes and the driver stopped half a block from the entrance. "We walk from here, it is better. They get upset seeing older people arrive in chauffeur-driven cars."

"How about their reaction to older people in general?" Brad asked. The doctor certainly looked like an older establishment type, wearing a dark suit and tie. His thin, gray-white hair was neatly combed back from his forehead.

"They take you as you are. If you ask them friendly questions they will answer the same way. Now here we are."

They turned into the gate of the wire-mesh fencing that surrounded the park and pushed through a crowd of long-haired young men wearing headbands and stringy-haired, bad-complexioned girls wearing light T-shirts without bras underneath.

"Now," Wormsinger said happily, "we will see the entire spectrum of disaffected young people arrayed before us. Follow me and here you see the blacks who hate everybody sitting in their decrepit Freedom City the second. They don't even know what they want to be free from. By and large, they are completely undependable and either fail to respond to conditioning or fail to stay conditioned."

"You had quite a success with one of your blacks, Ulric," D'Estang commented.

"Yes, of course. But, unfortunately, I never had an opportunity to observe how he would react to the post-assassination pressures put upon him. They killed him within seconds of the time he hit his target."

Wandering away from the blacks sitting around their area they approached long rows of army pup tents with young people standing around or napping in their tents. Several young couples in their tents were unconcernedly going through the preliminaries to all-out sexual intercourse. Beyond the small tent village was a larger canopy around which were groups of young men laughing and talking. Across the large tent stretched a banner bearing the legend "Gay Power."

A leader suddenly decided it was time to shake the lethargy out of his group and shouted, "Give me a G!"

The homosexuals shouted back a "G." "Give me an A!" The "A" was lustily returned. "Give me a Y!" The group shouted, "Y."

"What are we?" cried the leader.

"Gay!" his followers yelled back. "Gay power!"

"You can never trust a homosexual to stay conditioned," Wormsinger observed. "I once worked with one a long time, building up his hostility toward the target, instilling in him a desire to kill the subject even if it meant his life too. And what happened? When he got his big chance the target was wearing a suit, tie and shirt combination that so captivated my gay boy that he never did shoot."

As they walked along it was impossible not to notice the heavy, musky smell of a hundred marijuana joints burning constantly throughout the park.

"Pot is only a more distinctive smelling stuff than what you smoke, Maurice," Brad observed. D'Estang grunted and puffed out a stream of smoke.

Approaching a spreading mangrove tree the air was even more saturated. Perched throughout the branches of the tree like a flight of molting, shaggy-headed birds, some half hidden by the foliage, were two dozen or more young people smoking and surveying the area. Another two dozen youths sat about the tangled roots of the tree.

"I see that the Miami police have suspended any laws against marijuana," Brad observed, reading the sign hanging from one branch proclaiming "Pot People's Party" and adorned with various esoteric sun signs.

"A wise decision on their part," Dr. Wormsinger said. "I would say that these young people are not apt to cause any real trouble unless they are stirred up. As long as they are sitting about idly smoking pot they will stay peaceful, but it is dangerous to disturb young people as they smoke their joints, much like kicking a bowl of food out from under a hungry dog's mouth."

As they walked about, the smell of pot wrenched Brad's thoughts back to the scene at the pot party in New York. He kept trying, as they walked through the groups of young people, to keep from thinking of Andrea and Tony Falcon and Gwen's sick determination to keep Andrea in New York City with her.

Brad found himself peering at the young girls, wondering if they had nice homes someplace and had been seduced away by a Tony Falcon type. Again he became aware of how really unattractive these girls were. He had yet to see the first nice-looking, cheerful, wholesome girl in this large crowd of youths. What a contrast to the sparkling, happy, interested, well-groomed girls who were taking part in the convention in some official capacity, he thought. Those girls seemed happy to be in Miami whereas the Flamingo Park young people seemed listless, aimless, even despondent, waiting for leaders to focus their emotions on some issue of dissent or protest.

Side-by-side a knot of Jesus freaks singing hymns coexisted with a group whose sign proclaimed them to be Satanists and were mumbling incantations against the leaders of the government of the United States.

"Now there are a couple of studs with the right idea." D'Estang chuckled. Near an entrance to the park a camper utility truck looked especially luxurious in the mass of tents and bedrolls. A sign on the truck identified its occupants as being observers for student newspapers. It was obvious that some of the girls had quickly tired of the crude living conditions to which they had been subjected since their arrival. They appreciated the luxury of resting in the air-conditioned camper. The boys with the camper had their pick of the birds.

Beyond the camper and ring of girls surrounding it was another tent complex. "Vietnam Veterans Against the War" read the sign. "How about those types for your purposes, Ulric?" D'Estang asked. "They must have the experience to be effective."

Wormsinger shrugged. "Experience? What experience does it take to spray six shots out of an automatic pistol into a target at point-blank range. It's the mind that's everything. These veterans as a group are not good prospects.

"They might bomb a building if they get mad," Wormsinger continued, "but basically they aren't suited to be conditioned against a particular target. They think too much, they aren't really dissidents. They have drawn their conclusions from personal experience, not from hotheaded rabble rousers manipulating immature minds."

Wormsinger gestured at the veterans sitting or standing about their tents. "Look at them, they aren't smoking, some are reading books, others talking together in an orderly manner. These do not lend themselves to my operations. Let's go on."

In a corner of the park a mixed group of blacks, Puerto Ricans, and what looked to be American Indians and Mexicans were standing listening to a black orator demanding more liberal welfare payments to minority groups. "They aren't interested in working at anything," Wormsinger commented.

"What *are* you looking for?" Brad asked in curiosity.

"Come, I'll show you." Against the hibiscus-covered cyclone fence in the direction Wormsinger was headed was a somewhat different-looking group of young men. A neatly printed sign said they were "Students for Greater Understanding." Most of the young men were wearing pressed slacks and sport shirts and their hair was not obtrusively long. The two or three girls with them were cleaner and better dressed than the others in the park. Even the blacks seemed less disheveled than their brothers at Freedom City, their Afros not quite as long and unsanitary-looking.

"Despite their appearance, these youngsters are real misfits, misfits among misfits, you might say. Almost every one of them has been expelled from school and college. There isn't one of them who does not frequently consider suicide. I picked them out the first time I came through the park," Wormsinger added proudly.

"What is this understanding they refer to?" Brad asked.

"They don't really know. Most of them have some deep-seated resentment within them they don't really understand. Unlike the rest of the youngsters out here who are basically uninhibited and sure of their role in the country's social structure, these people have inferiority complexes which they compensate for by trying to dress better than the hippies and yippies and defiant minority groups out here. Every one of them would like to be in the Convention Hall instead of being part of this ragged protest regiment. But in actuality they are neither well-enough educated nor psychologically capable of rising above their feelings of being inferior to the establishment-oriented young people on the inside of this convention. Most of all, they are a group of loners. This is a sort of contradiction in terms, I realize, loners in groups. Yet they do seem to find each other. You'll notice there is very little rapping between them, and almost total exclusion between them and any other young people here."

"They seem kind of sad," Brad remarked. "Certainly not dangerous types."

"Any one of them is capable and ready to quietly walk in and shoot the president of the college which has expelled them. They grovel and suffer in their own anonymity, yet are helpless to make singular strides to rise in station and respect in life. Since it is impossible for them to recognize their own inadequacies they conveniently blame their problems on someone or something outside them. With a little conditioning any one of these boys and girls can be made to believe their whole problem lies with the selected target. If the target is a famous person, a political leader in particular, this loner, this inferior being in his own mind, not only strikes a noble blow for the people of the world who like himself are oppressed, but at last the attention of the world will be focused on him, he will receive adulation from his own, he will have risen from the obscurity imposed upon him and made an immortal mark in world history."

"I should think they would be very unreliable with a background of losing at everything, unable to concentrate enough to stay in school or college or in a job." Brad threw a troubled glance at the youths they were approaching.

"On the contrary, Mr. Kendall. Their problem in part is that no guidance counselor or parent took the trouble to motivate them toward positive goals at an early age, or even give them corrective therapy at the schizophrenic stage at which they are now. But when I have the opportunity to take one of these lads, talk to him, spend time with him, implant the seed in his mind that the target should be eliminated after making him reason it out for himself that the target is responsible for his miseries, it is fantastic to watch the process of motivation set in."

They had almost reached the Students for Greater Understanding area as Wormsinger finished his dissertation. "Once my subject has been motivated to devote his life to assassinating a target he changes completely. No longer is he morose and withdrawn. He plans, he studies, he dreams of nothing but the assassination. He keeps a diary and for the first time in his fragmented-thought pattern everything falls together, his life has a purpose. Where as before the subject was shy about meeting people he almost becomes an extro-vert if it is in the interests of his goal. It may take him months to achieve it but he will doggedly, fanatically pursue his quarry. His planning invariably ends with an assault on the target. That is why so few of these people succeed in getting away after their deed. Their mind is incapable of projecting a plan of action to fol-low after the ultimate objective has been achieved."

Brad disguised a shudder by turning his body as though to look about the park.

"Well, here we are," Wormsinger said merrily. "I won't introduce you to any of these fellows. I'll just chat with them a bit. I have invited one lad for supper tonight. I'll just make sure he has cab fare."

"Aren't you afraid that when they're caught they'll compromise you?" Brad asked in morbid fascination.

"You don't seem to understand. They don't know that I am conditioning them. I am merely an older person who is interested in them and can talk to them unpatronizingly."

As Brad and D'Estang watched, a young man with the pigmentless white skin and hair of an albino came over to Dr. Wormsinger. The youth's eyes were similar to Wormsinger's in that they were magnified behind thick lenses and had a pink tint to them. The two talked for a few minutes as Brad and D'Estang looked at the other Students for Greater Understanding. It was certainly the quietest of the compounds. One of the girls was playing chess with a young man.

"It's surprising that they could get a group like this together," Brad remarked after studying the students who were so uncommunicative.

"You've got to hand it to Wormsinger for finding them," D'Estang said. "Personally, I think he's as crazy as the nuts he digs up. Probably that's why they all relate to each other."

Brad looked at the albino and shuddered again. "I suppose we'll see him on TV and in the newspapers someday."

"He does look promising from the doc's point of view," D'Estang agreed.

Brad studied one of the girls. In a wistful way she made him think of Andrea. He was tempted to try and open a conversation with her but she seemed so withdrawn that he didn't try. It occurred to him that if Wormsinger could motivate this type of individual to kill a famous political personality why couldn't a competent psychiatrist motivate the same person to some positive action that would be beneficial to himself and society?

Wormsinger seemed to be finishing up his conversation with the albino and Brad and D'Estang edged away from the circle of Students for Understanding. Soon the psychologist joined them and they headed for the gate.

"What is it that these kids are after?" Brad asked. "What do they want the Democratic Party to put in its platform for them?"

"They feel that the academic establishment doesn't understand them. They seem to sense that they have problems they themselves don't understand. The whites here believe that while militant blacks and other minority groups are pampered on campuses, white students with problems are ignored and expelled. They say that the colleges they have attended never expel blacks for any reason, yet let them get into any trouble, academic or behavioral, they are fired out."

Wormsinger chuckled. "Now the blacks in this group believe the opposite is true. Yet they band together, blacks and whites, looking for the understanding that is impossible for ordinary teachers and parents to give them."

"But I don't know what the Democratic Party can do to help them," Brad said.

"As far as I can see, as a man who doesn't take much interest in politics," Wormsinger said, "none of these protesters or non-delegates have anything to gain except a big get-together in Miami."

"You're not having that white-haired kid meet you at the Ascot Surf Hotel, are you?" Brad asked. "I mean someday, if two or three of these nuts all turned out to have had meetings at Ascot Hotels, someone might start thinking. You know what I mean?"

"The boy is going to meet me at a restaurant across the street from the Ascot Towers. I anticipated your fears, though I think they're groundless. You see psychologically——"

Brad held up a restraining hand. "No more theory today, please, Doctor Wormsinger."

"Very well. But it is not theory."

"Right. So I know all too well."

They walked out of the Flamingo Park gate and had to wait only a few minutes for the driver of their car to pull up and pick them up.

Settled back in the air-conditioned comfort of the sedan Brad felt as though he had been dreaming all the casual psychological discussion of creating self-sacrificing assassins. His mind still couldn't accept the concept. He didn't want to believe it was really happening, sponsored by the organization for which he worked. What he wanted was to get back to the penthouse for a drink, maybe several drinks.

Wormsinger was humming contentedly to himself.

CHAPTER FORTY-ONE

It wasn't often any more that Brad Kendall woke up in the morning with Luciana beside him, but on Monday morning, the opening day of the convention, the strident ringing of the telephone disturbed him at a most inopportune moment.

"The hell with it, darling," he whispered. "I'm not going to answer it."

"Oh, Brad, you'd better take it. I'll still be right here when you finish talking."

Reluctantly Brad drew himself away from Luciana who emitted an involuntary sigh of disappointment. At that he almost abandoned the phone to take her again. Luciana giggled. Then she pushed him toward the phone. He rolled over, his back to her, and snatched the telephone from its cradle.

"Kendall here."

"Good morning, Brad," the familiar voice said smoothly. "I hope I didn't wake you up."

"Hell no, C.L. I've been up an hour or more trying to figure strategy on Adams."

"Guess the morning *Times* hasn't reached you yet. Very nice story on Adams and his wife. Will she be Mrs. Vee Pee sort of thing. Just what we're looking for."

"Glad to hear it, C.L. We'll be following up with plenty more." Brad reached behind him with his free hand and stroked Luciana's thigh.

"Brad, I have an assignment for you down there. You'll be getting a call from some friends who have the big muscle with the unions. Here's what I want you to do. Our friend Flannerty, the old sneaker of the house, and Casper Orellian are having a little trouble with the Democratic Committee. Something to do with the new reforms involved in delegate selection and seating. I don't think they're going to get what they want but we've got to give them a club, let them show that they can make life inconvenient if they so desire. You understand what I mean?"

"I think so. What kind of a club are you talking about?"

"What can the unions do that would directly affect the convention, something that the television viewers would notice, something that will really upset the Democratic National Committee?"

"That's one tall order, C.L." Brad glanced at his bedside clock. It was 8 A.M. "Let me give it some thought, C.L., and I'll get back to you."

"I'll be in my office by nine, Brad. I'll be waiting for your call."

"As soon as I work something out I'll call you." Brad hung up and rolled over to Luciana.

"What was that all about?" Luciana asked. "What did Ciano want?"

"I'll tell you later."

"Nope. Now. No tell, no love."

Brad sighed, feeling his desire for Luciana welling up strong against her. He kissed her smiling lips. "OK. Ciano wants me to do something that will embarrass the convention, something that will be visible to the television audience. I get all the help I need from the unions down here. Great. But what do I do?"

"Well, let's think about it," Luciana said.

"I'm thinking about something else right now. I'll solve Ciano's problem after you and I have taken care of our immediate needs." Brad buried his face in her breasts and then kissed her throat and the little hollows between her neck and shoulders. Luciana stirred and pulled him against her.

"I love you, Luciana," Brad said passionately.

"Make love to me, baby," she whispered back throatily.

At nine o'clock Brad came awake again with a start. Luciana was still sleeping. He slipped out of bed and went into the bathroom. Fifteen minutes later, bathed, brushed, and wide-awake he came back into the bedroom and began dressing.

"So what exciting mischief are you going to work for the good of the cause?" Luciana asked from the bed.

Brad smiled back at her. She looked so appealing propped up on two pillows, holding the bed sheets to her bosom. "I'm beginning to get some ideas. We've got to do something that will affect the three thousand delegates. What inconveniences them inconveniences the convention. If you were a delegate what would be foremost on your mind right now?"

"Getting to the convention and finding my seat," she replied after a moment's thought. "By the way, how do the delegates get to Convention Hall. They can't all have rented cars and limos like we do."

"They'll be taken by bus." Brad snapped his fingers. "Bus. That's it. We'll get a bus strike going tonight. All the delegates will be waiting at their hotels to pile into buses at seven o'clock and the drivers will be on strike. With the networks having canceled all other programming from 8 P.M. on, when the gavel is scheduled to fall, there'll be nothing for the anchormen to do but speculate on why the delegates were all late. How about that?" He grinned triumphantly at Luciana.

"Magnífico." She clapped her hands and the sheet fell away revealing her taut, full breasts.

Brad walked over to the bed and bent over, kissing the nipples and starting to take off the shirt he had just put on. "Hey." Luciana laughed. "C.L. is sitting in that office waiting to hear from you. Haven't you had enough? You'll get a heart attack."

"I got a heart attack the first moment I saw you and never recovered." He stood up and tucked his shirt into his pants. "Big day today. You're right, my darling."

The phone rang and Brad snatched it up. It was

D'Estang. "Brad, I'm with some gentlemen who would like to see us."

"On the union matter?"

"Yes. Shall we come to your suite?"

Brad glanced at Luciana. "No. Let's meet in the headquarters suite in the penthouse."

"We'll see you there, Brad. Shall I order some breakfast sent up?"

"Good idea." He hung up and put his hands on Luciana's shoulders. "Shall we try to have lunch?"

"Let's see what happens. I think I'm supposed to do something with Mrs. Adams."

"Let's keep in touch through the commo room. Don't forget to keep your beeper with you at all times."

"I never forget important things. Go to your meeting."

Upstairs in the penthouse suite Brad found Maurice D'Estang and three hard-looking, deeply tanned men standing around the room. Maurice was reading the paper.

"Looks like your party yesterday was a success. Here's the Miami *Herald* with a story on the party, describing Adams' suite, the one we're in, and the story says Adams is a leading choice for the vice-presidential nomination."

Brad took the story from Maurice, scanned it and put the paper down in satisfaction. Maurice introduced him to the three men and they sat down to talk.

At about eleven in the morning, with the bus drivers' strike breaking out like a flash flood to the dismay of the delegation leaders and the organizing committee, Brad reported to Ciano who was pleased with the strike concept. Ciano told Brad he would be informed when Flannerty was ready to settle the strike.

Shortly after his conversation with Ciano Brad's beeper signaled that someone wanted to reach him. He called the commo room and found that Congressman Adams wanted to see him in his suite. Brad walked down the corridor to the end suite and pressed the bell. Terry Adams opened the door.

"Brad, I'm glad you could come so quickly. Bill is very anxious to talk to you."

"What's it about, Terry?" Brad inquired.

"I'll let him tell you." She closed the door and led the way back to the parlor. To Brad's immense surprise he found Adams conversing intently with big, beefy Pat Kenney. Adams looked up when Brad came in and gestured at the empty chair beside him facing Kenney.

"Well, Pat Kenney," Brad said genially. "What brings you so far from home turf?"

"I'm working down here," Kenney replied. "I resigned from the Department a few days after my talk with Ciano. I figured that was better than what he would probably have arranged for me."

"I don't know why Ciano would want to harass you, Pat," Brad replied.

"Didn't he ever tell you about our meet?" Pat asked.

"Not much. Just that he saw you, you made some accusations, he tried to explain things to you and offered you a position with us and you turned him down."

"Brad," Adams broke in, "Pat has a security job through the detective agency he works for. He saw the story in the paper this morning and decided to come up and say hello. He also told me some very disturbing things about my heroin investigation."

"Speaking of your investigation, the New York *Times* had a big story about you being a vice-presidential candidate."

"I saw it," Adams replied. "Now to get back to what Pat was telling me. I am most upset. If what he says is true I have been grievously used and made a fool of."

"Being considered for the vice-presidential nomination this year and maybe the top spot in 1976 is making a fool of you, Bill?" Brad snapped.

"I don't feel I'm running my own campaign. You seem to be making all the decisions," Adams complained. "I'm the member of the House of Representatives, I'm the one who's working toward the nomination to run for the Senate, not you, Brad. I'm the one who makes decisions."

"So make them. Nobody's stopping you. Make a decision," Brad challenged.

"First I want to hear your reply to what Pat's been telling me."

"Which was?"

"My whole investigation, the big heroin roundup was a put-up job."

"It was your operation, nobody else's. Was it a put-up job, Bill?"

"Goddamn it, Brad. Don't play games with me. You know whether or not it was a setup."

"I know you were responsible for the seizure of half a billion dollars' worth of heroin."

"That's just a meaningless number, goddamn it."

Brad noticed a copy of the New York *Times* on a coffee table. He stood up and went over to the coffee table, brought the paper back to Adams and dropped it in his lap. "Is that front-page story about you meaningless?"

Adams stared at the headline. "Of course not, but—"

"But that seizure and those numbers are why you are being mentioned for the vice presidency. Right?"

"I guess so. Now what about Kenney's story?"

Brad turned his attention to Kenney who seemed somewhat bemused at the byplay between the congressman and his political adviser. "What's he talking about, Pat?"

"He's talking about the fact that Ciano and the mob fixed the whole thing to make it look good for Adams. I told Adams that Ciano takes off into the stratosphere where the Mafia or Cosa Nostra or whatever you want to call the mob leaves off. They used to call me super cop. I call Ciano super Don."

"My God, Brad, if this is so I must make an immediate public disclosure."

"What are you going to say? That poor Bill Adams was used by the mob, brainwashed into thinking he had really accomplished a big victory against narcotics traffickers? Not only would that destroy you politically, but it would destroy your law firm and your partners. You couldn't get a job as a lawyer, you might even be disbarred. You know who owns the interior decorating company that did a one-hundred-thousand-dollar job on your offices for two thousand dollars? One Joseph Sterrato, Strega Joe, the big narcotics syndicate man who you exposed."

Kenney jumped to his feet. "You bastards, you really framed this man. I ought to——"

"Oh, calm down, Pat," Brad said. "Nobody can ever prove that Sterrato owned the company. That was just a bit of what is called insurance around here. In fact, nobody can ever, under any circumstances, prove that the investigation was a frame-up because a lot of it wasn't. You started it yourself, Pat. And you didn't have to quit the cops. Ciano wouldn't pay any more attention to your accusations than an elephant would to a flea climbing up his ass with intentions to rape."

Brad took a long breath, decided to change his tactics, and smiled pleasantly. "OK, Bill. Sure the investigation received a little help from unexpected sources, which will never be revealed, but you did a great job. You truly are responsible for shutting down the poppy path from Turkey to Harlem and the other ghettos of America. If Kenney hadn't started the investigation on his own this never would have been accomplished. You deserve the acclaim you're getting. You deserve the vice-presidential nomination, which of course you won't accept. So quit feeling bad because some people who believe in you gave you an additional boost."

"This was a legitimate investigation started by you, wasn't it, Pat?" Adams asked, his tone pleading for some modicum of reassurance.

"That's right," Kenney replied gruffly.

"And the heroin traffic from Europe was severely curtailed by our findings, wasn't it?"

"Sure, but you should see the stuff coming in from Asia now." Pat Kenney stood up. "I did what I could for Adams and I guess I'm too late. But there's a couple of things you better remember, Brad. That shit coming in from Asia is the purest stuff that's ever hit New York. Until they figure out how to use it there's going to be a lot of deaths from heroin overdose coming up. More than ever before."

Kenney started for the door. "There's nothing I can really do alone to stop or even slow down what Ciano is doing. Both of you have been bought, paid for and are owned for life. But, Brad, even though I'm just a cop I can see some things better than you. Someday you are going to need me bad. Someday you are going to wonder who in this whole world isn't owned by Ciano or someone like him. I don't envy you the hell you are going to go through. But here's my card. When, to use a Ciano bit, you want to walk across the street again with some slight chance of keeping a whole skin, call me. I'll help you."

Kenney strode through the parlor, into the foyer and let himself out the door.

"Now you see why Pat was known to his fellow cops as The Actor," Brad said with a derision he didn't entirely feel. Adams seemed in a comatose state, hardly breathing. Brad dropped a hand on the seated congressman's shoulder. "Bill, if we just keep fighting ahead you'll be the next senator New York sends to Washington and we'll win the nomination for you in 1976. So stick with it, old man."

Adams still sat staring stonily ahead. He might end up a politician yet, Brad thought, once he gets over his shock at some of the realities of the game. Terry Adams came into the living room. "The meeting is still going on?" she asked brightly.

"I think it's over, Terry," Brad replied. "Bill is thinking over alternatives. I think I'll let him digest what he's heard and get back to him later. You and he can go all the way, it's up to Bill. I think if Abigail up there is watching, she would be pleased to see another Adams, Teresa Adams, as first lady."

Terry's eyes sparkled. "We'll do our part."

"Good. Why don't you spike a hot coffee with some brandy and give it to Bill. He seems to need a little perking up."

"Fine idea. I'll go back to the kitchen. Are you staying?"

Brad threw a glance at the motionless, reactionless congressman. "No, Terry. But I'll be back later. Oh, tell Bill that he doesn't have to worry about being ready to take the bus at seven o'clock with the delegation. The buses will be running at least an hour late." Brad left the suite and headed down the hall toward the communication room.

At seven-thirty Brad let himself into the electronic surveillance suite, locking the door behind him. He made his way through the antenna farm which this suite had become and found Julius at his console tuning in to different conversations and scenes throughout Miami Beach.

"I just thought of a good code name for you, Julius, Asmodeus."

"What's that?" Julius asked without turning around.

"Asmodeus, the devil on two sticks. He could strip the walls from the houses in Madrid and see everything that went on inside."

"What did he use? TV?" Julius asked.

"No, magic. He was a mythical character."

"Well, I'm no myth, but if I ever wrote a book I'd sure become a legend."

"We have a little rule about that, Julius," Brad said severely.

"Yeah, I know."

A short, ferret-faced man, black hair combed straight back from his forehead, sidled up to the console.

"Getting any nourishment, Irv?" Brad asked Irving Lanzer, the director of Defamesec.

"The greatest. I'm keeping two secretaries busy filing reports, pictures, video tape references, tape recordings, rumors—the works. You never know who is going to be where in a month or a year or in 1976, right?"

Brad nodded. "Anything interesting?"

Julius hit a button and on the main monitor above him appeared a picture of a man and young woman, nude. The girl was caressing him as he sipped on a highball. "There's a delegation leader waiting for word about the bus strike. I'll bet he hopes it isn't settled for another hour," Julius chortled.

Lanzer made some notations. "Anything with our two handsome boys yet?" he asked.

"Not yet, but the convention is just starting, or will if they get the buses moving." For a moment Julius did turn from his console. "Sorry about one thing, Brad. I couldn't bug the trailers where campaign floor managers work out strategy and send orders onto the floor to their whips."

"I know all about them."

"There's gotta be a way," Julius went on with determination. "Jesus, what a bunch of amateur meatheads those guys doing the bugging job on Democratic headquarters in Washington turned out to be. Makes my job here twice as hard. Everybody is worried about electronic surveillance. At least you can be sure that nobody else at the convention has a setup like ours."

"OK fellows, carry on," Brad said cheerfully. "If anything of real interest develops give me a call on my beeper." He surveyed the busy room a moment and then left it, Intelsec and Defamesec of Whitehall cramming their files with useful information.

It was quarter to eight when Brad slipped into the communications room. Maurice D'Estang was pacing about behind the secretaries on the telephone and the radio operators receiving and transmitting information. D'Estang looked up with a grin as Brad entered.

"This strike is driving them all bughouse." He chuckled. "The Democratic Committee doesn't want to alienate labor so it's being cautious about muscling the union boys."

"I suppose the mayor and probably the governor are putting on a lot of pressure. Are our guys holding out?"

"They love it," D'Estang commented. "These local labor guys in Florida hate the national leaders giving them orders. They're having a ball showing their independence. What really pisses them off is when the national leaders try and tell them how to vote. They figure this little show just proves nobody owns them.

They're all for Wallace and they know the convention is going to shaft him anyway." Maurice put his hand on the red telephone beside him. "This is a direct line to our guys in the negotiating room. All we have to do is give them the word and the buses roll."

The radio operator turned to D'Estang. "Our people at the hotels report everybody is mad as hell. There aren't enough cabs and the cabs are too expensive anyway. What a mess." He laughed. "Our people in Convention Hall say that the networks are really worried what they're going to do when they go on at eight and things haven't started yet."

The white telephone beside D'Estang rang and he picked it up and answered it. "Right here," he said. Looking over at Brad he said, "Ciano."

D'Estang listened intently. He nodded. "Yes, Brad's right here." He handed the phone to Brad. "Flannerty got what he wanted. Strike's over." He handed the white phone to Brad and reached for the red instrument.

"Yes, C.L.," Brad said.

"Your idea on the buses was brilliant, Brad. Brilliant."

"Thanks. By the way, what was it Flannerty wanted?"

"I don't know. Doesn't make any difference anyway. We're going to be needing the sneaker. And he is delighted. I just talked to him. How is Adams behaving?"

"Is your line secure, C.L.? This one is."

"We're both on scramble. Go ahead."

"It may be that Detective Kenney, ex-Detective Kenney I should say, has done us a favor. He's down here as a security officer."

"Interesting," Ciano said. "I knew he'd retired."

"He told Adams the whole thing. Of course it was too late for Adams to do anything. I put the pressure on him, told him who his decorator was, I hope that's all right, C.L."

"Do what you have to do, Brad," Ciano replied.

"Well, of course, old straight-arrow Bill Adams went into a coma but I saw him late this afternoon and he seemed pretty cheerful. In fact, he's looking forward to campaigning this fall for the Senate. I think he did a lot of thinking about the realities of political life and today he became a politician."

"Good, Brad, but watch him."

"Of course. I'm going to see him now and send him off to the Convention Hall with his delegation."

"OK, great, Brad. And, again, the bus strike was superb. I've got the television on and they haven't mentioned it, just that the gavel will fall about an hour late."

"Right. Just about an hour. Well, I see Maurice hanging up. The buses are rolling. The action is under way. So long, C.L."

Brad hung up and grinned at D'Estang. "OK, I'm going to see Adams off and then I'll be back. I wish it was '76 already."

CHAPTER FORTY-TWO

In the early hours of Tuesday morning as the opening session of the convention began to produce significant results, the first serious discussions about vice-presidential candidates began to come over the various devices Julius the Genius was monitoring.

Brad was wearily sipping black coffee in the control room when one of Julius' minions came in with a message. Brad read it and turned to Maurice D'Estang beside him. "The leading candidates for the nomination are saying that in no way do they want the vice-presidential candidate to be picked by the convention. Each one wants to make the choice himself."

"How does that affect us with Adams?"

"Well, it kills one ploy. We could have had him proposed as a candidate, built up a lot of publicity, and then he could have called a press conference here and announced that he could not accept the candidacy if it was offered him because he feels New York and the nation need him as a crime buster."

"That's the speech he's got to make," D'Estang approved.

"Sure, but we've got to work out a new and plausible motive for him to make it. And this is going to be tough because the presidential candidate is not going to put Adams on his list of prospective running mates. Seventy-two is the year of the liberals, they're going to get badly licked, but this week they're trying to appease liberals. And liberals are against law and order, crime busters in particular."

"This isn't my bag, Brad. You'll have to figure it out."

"I will. With the help of Julius and his assortment of electronic tricks we should be able to at least make it appear to the press that Adams is a possible choice for the number-two spot."

"Good luck to you, Brad," D'Estang said. "I think I'll get some sleep."

"I guess we'd all better," Brad agreed. He thought of Luciana and hoped she was waiting in his suite, which triggered another thought. "I hope Defamesec is alert. About now there should be a lot of cross-bedding being planned and executed."

"I'll stop in and make sure all systems are being manned," D'Estang replied. "Good thought, Brad."

When he returned to his room Brad found that Luciana was not there. He decided against calling her and he was so tired it didn't make much difference anyway.

After five hours' sleep Brad was up, showered and dressed. He had a Continental breakfast in his room and then walked down the corridor to the surveillance suite to check on what was happening in the hotels.

Julius the Genius, his eyes red rimmed, was moving about the forest of antennas checking on all the receiving instruments and their operators. Irving Lanzer had arrived moments before Brad and was checking on all the information that had accrued which could build up his files for defamation of individuals who might become obstacles to Whitehall objectives.

"Brad, it's definite that the vice-presidential candidate will not be chosen by the convention at large," Julius said. "The Peabodys and Gravels might as well go home although they don't know it yet."

"That's good to know, Julius. Now let's discuss my chief problem here. I think the solution to it lies in this room."

That afternoon for two hours Brad, Luciana, the Adamses and a group of New York newspaper reporters sunned and swam at the roof-top swimming pool. Luciana helped keep the female reporters coming to Mrs. Adams and sending back stories to the newspapers around New York State about the possibilities of Terry Adams becoming the nation's second lady. Bill Adams, sitting in the air-conditioned splendor of the penthouse suite, gave informative background talks to the reporters interested in his views on the Democratic platform which would be adopted that night at the convention.

Brad and Adams had spent a long luncheon discussing what Adams' views and opinions would be. Now, as he talked to the press, Adams sounded far more conservative than the probable presidential candidate. But Adams, as he pointed out, was running for the Senate from New York. He was not a candidate for the vice presidency despite rumors to the contrary.

The press suite was always full and all the facilities were in full swing as reporters filed their stories through the two teletype machines instead of having to fight their way to their press cubicles in the basement of the Fountainebleau Hotel or at Convention Hall. It was difficult for the reporters not to have a constant subliminal image of Adams as they wrote their stories in the comfortable Ascot Hotel's hospitality suite. There was no overt Adams propaganda, no Adams position papers, not even a picture of him. He was just another New York delegate enjoying the New York-based Ascot Hotel company hospitality suite. But his presence was always felt.

That evening at eight o'clock Brad left the hotel to drive over to Convention Hall. Luciana had decided to stay in the hotel and watch the proceedings on television and oversee the functioning of the penthouse. It was almost nine o'clock by the time Brad had parked his car and, showing his credentials, entered the enormous Convention Hall complex.

Through the Democratic Committee he had been able to secure floor passes for all the Ascot and Whitehall crew. At least five of the men walking around among the delegates with walkie-talkies and hand-held television cameras were reporting back to the communications suite at the Ascot Surf Hotel via their communications trailer in the Convention Hall, which stood out back with many other trailers representing the press and potential Democratic presidential candidates.

Julius had hoped by having his own trailer at the convention he could find a way to bug the other key trailers of candidates and he was still experimenting. In the meantime, the trailer acted as a relay station for the signals coming from his men on the floor to the control suite at the hotel. Many of the preparations this year were in rehearsal for 1976 when the fifth estate would dominate both the Democratic and Republican conventions.

Since Brad had the highest credentials and badges he was free to walk wherever he wanted through the hall. He even had the requisite card with his picture on it which permitted him to go back to the special lounge behind the speakers' podium where the hierarchy of the party committee and those addressing the convention waited for developments to unfold. He decided to check into this exclusive lounge for a few moments just to get the feel of how the convention was being managed. The security guards passed him through.

Inside he met several of the party officials with whom he had worked to set up hotel accommodations for the convention. Then a flurry of excitement swept through the small lounge. George Wallace had just arrived to address the convention. His wheel chair was being pushed along the ramp now.

Brad stood off to the side as the governor of Alabama was wheeled into the room to await his turn to address the convention. A clutch of remorse, regret, fear and horror lanced through the pit of his stomach. The governor looked so haggard close up, so thin, such a shadow of the man he had been. What a cruel turn of fate for this man who could have played such an important part in the American political scene but for the insanity of one lone psychopathic youth.

A shudder wracked Brad's shoulders as he thought of Dr. Wormsinger turning a dozen twisted psychotic youths out into the United States to fanatically track down and assassinate those figures whose presence on earth interfered with the aims of C. L. Ciano.

Brad decided to stick it out at the Convention Hall until the governor made his speech, so he spent the next half hour talking to prominent Democrats, wondering why the convention committee did not put Governor Wallace on immediately. It was obviously distressing to him, sitting here indefinitely in his wheel chair, unable to have a drink of water because of the lack of control of his bladder and bowels the grievous wounds had caused. Yet the committee unmercifully made him wait. After the governor had been waiting an hour to deliver his address and still hadn't been called Brad decided to go back to the floor and await the speech. He unobtrusively made his exit and for a while wandered among the delegates, halfheartedly listening to the speakers discussing the planks to be included in the platform. Everyone was obviously waiting for Governor Wallace to make his entrance.

Finally Brad walked up to the press section and found a place from which he could get a good view of the podium. It was another half an hour before Governor Wallace was carried up to the podium in his wheel chair and set down behind the microphones. After a mixed welcome of cheers and applause Wallace delivered his address on the platform he felt the party should adopt. Most of it was precisely what Ciano himself would have approved, Brad thought. The problem was, of course, that there was no way whatsoever that Ciano or anyone else could buy or influence Governor Wallace. His ideals were firm and until his wounding there was every reason to believe he could and would carry them out precisely as he saw fit.

Brad didn't have to ask Ciano to know who at least one of the other targets of Wormsinger's gaggle of psychos was. He listened attentively to the governor finish his speech and watched the reaction, 50 per cent adverse, to Wallace's conservative, hard-hitting speech.

Obviously, there was no chance at all of the presidential candidate even considering Adams as a vice-presidential candidate when the convention repudiated Wallace's rather basic plea to stop crime in the street.

Watching Wallace in his wheel chair giving everything he had to articulate his views, the whole political process and especially the part he was playing in it disgusted him. He left the hall after the finish of Wallace's speech, not wanting to watch the four strong young aides lift the chair from the podium.

Brad walked out of the hall, went over to the parking garage, picked up his car and drove himself moodily back to the hotel. He didn't even go upstairs, preferring to have a drink by himself at the crowded bar downstairs with the television blaring out the convention proceedings.

After two solitary drinks Brad left the bar and took the elevator up to the top floor of the hotel. He headed straight for the control room and after being admitted checked over all the information that had emanated from the surveillance over the past few hours.

"Julius," Brad said decisively, "by tomorrow we have to put our plan into effect. Put one of your best men onto the console tonight and get some sleep. I'll get my actors primed. There's nothing more to do tonight."

"Thanks, Brad. And if you want a little X-rated video tape fare tonight, look at some of the stuff we picked up this afternoon."

"I'll leave that to Irv Lanzer. As I've said many times, I don't consider sex a spectator sport."

In the penthouse Luciana was entertaining the remnants of the press group and various social friends and connections whose only business at the convention was the behind-the-scenes hotel lobbying that went on between the sessions at Convention Hall.

"You're working hard," Brad said softly as he came up behind her. "Now that things are quiet why don't you let one of the girls take over and enjoy yourself."

"I'm enjoying this, Brad," Luciana said. "And I'm picking up all sorts of interesting information."

"Why don't you come down to my suite and we'll

have a nightcap and you can tell me what you've been doing all day."

"Maybe later, Brad," she said noncommittally. "Would you like something here?"

Brad shook his head. "I guess I'll go down and try and figure some way to pull off what I came here to do."

"Good luck. If there is anything I can do, that's why I'm here."

"You're doing fine. But in this case I'm afraid a woman's wiles are not the answer. See you later, I hope. I'll be home all night." Brad took her hand a moment and then, letting go of it, he left the penthouse party and walked down the stairs to the floor below and his suite.

In the suite he made himself a weak highball for a nightcap and wandered about looking out over Miami. He had no interest in turning on the convention. There was only one thing left for him to do and tomorrow was the day.

A restlessness came over Brad. He felt like talking to someone he was really close to, yet how few people there were these days with whom he enjoyed a truly warm relationship. When he allowed himself to dwell on what was really between himself and Luciana he had to admit that her interest in him now seemed rather superficial.

Looking at the telephone Brad thought of Elda Ciano. What was she doing, he wondered? Probably at home looking at the convention on TV. It wasn't midnight yet. Why not call her, he thought, just to say hello. She had her own private number. If she wasn't there nobody would answer. He could call to ask her if she had seen Andrea lately.

Brad strode to the phone and sat down at the desk. He gave the long-distance operator the number and then waited to hear the familiar contralto voice. He hoped very much all of a sudden that she would be there to take his call.

On the third ring Elda answered. She sounded as pleased as she was surprised when she heard Brad's voice. Brad was about to open the conversation asking about Andrea when he recalled Elda's admonition not to say what wasn't really on his mind.

"I just wanted to hear you say something," Brad began honestly.

"Anything in particular?" Elda asked.

"No. Too bad you couldn't make it down here. Lots of excitement."

"I've been looking on television. I thought maybe I'd see you wandering around the floor or in the gallery or something."

"I was over there for a while."

"You must be very tired."

"Yes. I guess everyone is."

"Is everything coming along all right?"

"I think so, Elda. If you hear a lot about Adams tomorrow evening and Thursday morning you'll know we've been successful."

"I'll be watching, Brad. You haven't asked about Andrea," Elda noted.

"No. I wanted to talk to you. I figured if there was anything special on Andrea you'd tell me. There's so little I can do except to be available when she realizes she needs help."

"I haven't seen much of her. I guess she's still living at home or I would have heard from Mrs. Connor."

"I'll be back in town on Friday at the latest. I might even be able to pull up stakes here Thursday. Any chance of seeing you?"

"There's always that chance, Brad. What did you have in mind?" The lilt in her voice when she was happy about something always delighted Brad.

"Oh, dinner or something like that?"

"Call me when you know when you're going to be back and I'll be available. I'll try and reach Andrea and give you some news of her also."

"Thanks, Elda. I'd appreciate that too."

"And don't get too worn out down there, Brad," Elda cautioned.

"I'll try not to."

"I'll be waiting to hear."

After talking to Elda, Brad felt relaxed and right with the world. He undressed, pulled on his pajamas, washed and brushed his teeth and, turning out the light, sank into bed for a restful sleep. For once, the only time he could remember, he almost hoped Luciana wouldn't come to him.

Wednesday morning he awoke refreshed and ready to pull the rabbit out of the hat. Luciana had not come in during the night.

At ten Brad was in the surveillance room with Julius monitoring all channels of communication originating with the probable Democratic presidential nominee. "Not much activity yet," Julius commented. "If the pattern of yesterday is repeated there should be a lot of telephoning beginning about eleven-thirty."

"Right. Can you hear what most of the aides are saying in the suite?"

"I get his suite clearly. Both through the bug I put in last month and my line of sight directional focusing microphone on the top floor of the hotel next door."

"So there's nothing to do but sit here and wait," Brad said. "OK. Let's start thinking about how we can do an even better job in four years. And we may not have as convenient and open a location to work as Miami."

"In four years, with the backing I get from your outfit, I will have developed the coolest surveillance devices you ever imagined! I'll have sensors the size of a half a dollar that can be dropped onto a beach and pick up the conversation of people who meet in the nude to talk, figuring that's the only way that nobody can bug themselves. I'll have invisible suction cups that can be slapped onto the side of a trailer parked outside the Convention Hall that will transmit to me everything said in the trailer and all the radio and telephone transmissions coming out of the trailer. I'm working on a gun that can shoot a suction cup sensor three hundred yards and when it sticks it will bring me every word. I should be able to bug any room anywhere with a TV-transmitting device the size of the head of a stickpin. My

TV transmitters now are the size of a pack of cigarettes."

"We'll need it all, Julius," Brad encouraged.

The voice of a campaign aide from the candidate's suite came over very clearly ordering coffee, orange juice and muffins. "That was coming from the main suite," Julius said. "That means that they'll be having a meeting pretty quick. Now let's just hope that our man himself calls his financial adviser, Bobby Marmelstein, the way he has the past few days in the morning. Is your end set up?"

"Right. I put a great mimic into the controlled hotel room."

"Then all we have to do is wait for the man to make the call," Julius said. "It should come anytime now."

"My actor is ready."

Julius turned up the volume on the conversation in the candidate's command hotel suite. "In four years I'll be able to bug the hot lines they have put in to avoid the hotel switchboard. Sorry I couldn't do it this year."

"This year it doesn't make that much difference. Everything is pretty cut and dried. But in '76 both parties will be fighting it out to the last roll call for the nomination."

Then the unmistakable voice of the candidate came over the bug. "Guess it's time to call Marmelstein and get a reading on what the contributors are saying about the platform we adopted last night. I'll probably wake him up. He was romancing money people most of the night."

Julius picked up a microphone beside him. "Get ready. The call is about to go through." Julius turned to Brad. "My guy has the control lines of the switchboard going right through his own board set up in his room. Was that ever a tough job. Good thing you could get to the manager and convince him we were just making a security check when we set that one up last month."

"I just hope I can control all the hotels in whatever city is picked for '76," Brad replied.

"Well, like I said I'll have much more sophisticated devices by then. We may not need all the co-operation we got this time."

"Alert my actor to expect the call," Brad ordered.

Julius turned the transmitter to a different channel and reaching for the microphone and pressing the transmitting button he said, "Call from the senator to Marmelstein coming through. We're taping it here."

Julius turned down all the other listening devices in the surveillance suite and sat back. They heard the senator's voice say to the hotel operator, "Get me Mr. Robert Marmelstein in suite 1160, please."

The ringing of the phone in the room being used by the spurious financial adviser came over the tapped line. The actor who had been practicing imitating Marmelstein's voice and peculiar New York accent softened by many years of living in Texas answered.

"How did your potential contributors react to the platform the party adopted last night, Bobby?" the senator asked.

"Not too damn good, Senator," the actor impersonating Marmelstein replied. "I told you many times my big money people are worried about your tax reforms."

"They won't get hurt, Bobby."

"What they want to know, Senator, is who you're going to put on the ticket to run with you."

"I am seriously considering several men but I'm certainly not ready to discuss my choices before I've even been nominated myself."

"There's speculation out of New York that you might put Adams on. Our potential contributors like Adams. Middle America likes Adams. You can't please businessmen with your tax reform program but at least you could please them on law and order."

"I'm not trying to satisfy middle America this week."

"Adams has a lot of support among prospective campaign contributors. Do you like Adams?"

"I have a lot of respect for him, of course. But he'd give the ticket just enough of a conservative, law-and-order look to alienate my supporters here at the convention. To them law and order means oppression of minority groups, you know."

Julius turned to Brad. "Damnit, can't he make the senator at least say Adams' full name?"

"I told him it was of the utmost importance," Brad replied. "Give him a chance."

"Who will the big contributors go for, Bobby, other than Adams?"

"I'm feeling them out. By the way, I didn't even hear them talking about Adams until two days ago. What the hell is his whole name? He's got some funny middle name."

"Fortune," the Senator replied. "But much as I admire what William Fortune Adams did to break up the heroin smuggling operation out of France I just can't consider him as a running mate. I can't understand what's causing his name to suddenly start coming up."

"I understand, Senator," the actor, satisfied with his performance, replied. "But if you get a chance to say something nice about Adams, it wouldn't hurt you any with the people we're trying to promote for the big contributions."

"Clear, Bobby. Anything else to report?"

"No. Just don't move too fast when you pick your number two."

"I'll keep you informed. See you this afternoon at the meeting."

"I'll be there, Senator."

One hour later Brad played the edited tape he and Julius had created. The senator's voice clearly and forcefully made a statement.

"I am seriously considering William Fortune Adams as my running mate. He'd give the ticket just enough of a conservative law-and-order look to satisfy middle America. I have a lot of respect for him and I admire what Adams did to break up the heroin smuggling operation out of France."

"Beautiful," Brad exclaimed. "Now to leak it to the right sources and get it on the air. By 1976 we're going to have to own or control some key radio and television stations."

By two-thirty in the afternoon the announcement in the senator's own words had been played on a New York City radio news station which had only with the greatest reluctance gone to the expense of sending a reporter to the Miami convention. The reporter had wisely spent all his time at the Ascot Hotel's hospitality suite. He was rewarded by having had leaked to him the tape of the Democrats' most likely candidate, discussing his vice-presidential choice, a New Yorker.

Within minutes on the tape being played over the station in New York the networks and wire services were dispatching their reporters to Adams' hotel. He greeted them in the penthouse suite. All was ready for the battery of TV cameras to be quickly and efficiently installed. Private interviews for New York media representatives were arranged for the rest of the afternoon and evening.

William Fortune Adams and his wife, Terry, made a gracious entrance into the penthouse suite. The cameras immediately began whirring and the still photographers were popping their flash bulbs. In his mind, Adams had all the salient points he and Brad Kendall had worked out firmly fixed. This was his chance, at last, to address the nation and dramatically reach his state constituency. He would not blow this chance.

"May I first say," Adams began, looking relaxed and tan in an open sport shirt and slacks, "that I am as much surprised as all of you at the generous endorsement given me by the man who will be elected this fall to the office of the President of the United States. I had no idea he had ever considered me as a prospective running mate. I am grateful for the confidence he has expressed in me."

Adams paused dramatically, smiling into the cameras. Then, "However, I have pledged my faith to the people of my home state of New York. Our state, more than any other in the United States, suffers from the hideous and gratuitous street crime which is a direct result of the narcotics and dangerous drugs being brought illegally into this country. As our next President mentioned, I was able to score a major upset victory over the crime lords who profit in the human misery caused by heroin. I believe it is my duty to remain in a position where I can concentrate on fighting crime and working for new legislation to tighten the noose of the law around the neck of this scourge of all America and particularly of my home state. If the Democratic Party in New York nominates me to run for the Senate I will happily accept because I believe that in the upper house I could do even more to end the crime and narcotics problem that threatens the very fiber of America.

"I would like to take this opportunity to do something politicians avoid whenever possible and that is express my views on crime and the sort of legislation I will be working for. I notice that none of the presidential hopefuls have made a positive statement on abortion. I believe that the nation should follow the lead of the great state of New York and allow any woman who feels she must, to have a legal abortion. I think women will have to rise above all other considerations and support such legislation if it is what they want."

A spontaneous burst of applause from the women journalists greeted this statement. Brad Kendall, standing inconspicuously at the back of the room, smiled appreciatively. Adams had not wanted to commit himself on this issue or any of the others he was now bringing forth.

"It is absurd to allow the graft and payoffs to continue that rot away the integrity of the big city police forces as a result of victimless crime. I believe that prostitution, for instance, should be legalized and controlled as it is in the state of Nevada. Making unenforceable laws is absurd." Adams paused again and looked the cameras straight in the lens. "I have gone on record in both rhetoric and in action as an effective opponent of drug abuse in our nation. I will continue to fight narcotics trafficking with all the vigor and persistence within me. But I feel that marijuana should be made legal and like tobacco and liquor controlled strictly by government agencies. I notice that the Miami police have wisely refrained from making any effort to enforce the laws against marijuana during this convention."

Great, Brad thought to himself. He's appealing to women, youth and the law-and-order people. As for the Catholics, the women will neutralize the screaming priests. You're doing just fine, William Fortune, just fine.

"And so I look forward," Adams continued, "to working with the new Democratic President in Washington next fall in my present capacity as a legislator backing new, tough anti-crime laws. I will give him and his running mate, whoever he picks, all the support I can. My position here in Miami is not and it never was anything more than a delegate from New York State, that's why I am so surprised, happily surprised of course, at our future President's expression of confidence in my work. I thank you."

But there was no escaping the news hungry press. There was a tremendous gap between available hard news and the enormous amount of time and energy allocated by the news media of the United States to the convention.

After half an hour of questioning, a journalist returned from phoning in his story to report to Adams that the senator denied ever making such a statement and in fact had never considered Congressman Adams as a prospective number-two man on the ticket. The senator did express admiration for Adams, the reporter hastened to add.

Adams smiled depreciatingly. "As I said at the beginning of this press conference I was surprised, astonished would be a better word, at the senator's mentioning me as a possible candidate. However, I heard him make his statement personally over the radio as did all of you and that is the only knowledge I have concerning the statement."

In the back of the room Brad smiled to himself at the position in which the Democratic candidate for

President had been placed. He was aware that it would be a great mistake to attack Adams in any way. What the spurious Marmelstein had told him certainly was true and undoubtedly the real Marmelstein was telling him that the ultra-liberal cast of his supporters was harming fund-raising efforts. After all, when a liberal gets rich he generally ceases to be a liberal.

Brad congratulated himself at the way he had managed to get away with an audacious tactic. From now on it was downhill in the shade. Famous as Adams had become through the heroin episode, turning down the vice presidency, whether or not in fact it had been offered, had generated for him a whole new wave of the finest kind of national prominence.

So that's it, Brad said to himself. Mission accomplished. Let Wormsinger, Defamesec, Intelsec, and Julius the Genius do their things. He had accomplished his mission. Now he was going to relax and have a drink. Somewhere, deep in the back of his consciousness, and becoming more suppressed every day, was the nagging backache of a realized and discarded notion that he was fast approaching total desecration of the soul with which he had entered this earth, a soul once bent on service and self-improvement, now dedicated to quite something else.

He headed for the bar in the press hospitality suite where he could drink and listen to the results of the tactical victory he had scored. How happy he was that he didn't have to do something similar at the Republican Convention next month. That job was strictly in the hands of Defamesec.

CHAPTER FORTY-THREE

Salvatore Di Siccerone, resplendent in a navy-blue blazer with brass buttons, under which he wore a white turtle-neck sweater, stood on the landing float at the Seventy-ninth Street Pier staring down the Hudson River. His white captain's cap sat squarely on his head and the white duck pants and white shoes bestowed an expensive maritime appearance on the *capo di capiri*.

To his left and right in less successful nautical garb stood his bodyguards and on his arm, in a filmy summer dress, hung a garishly decorative blond girl. A gray-haired, salesmanlike man in a seersucker suit hovered about the retinue. He looked down the river, straightened up, smiled confidently and said, "Here they are now, Mr. Di Siccerone. The yacht will be dockside in a few minutes."

Sal the Hand squinted his eyes against the mid-afternoon sun glinting off the polluted brown river. The trim, white cruiser was headed directly at the dock. "She's a beauty," Sal growled. "How long is it, did you say?" he asked the man who had pointed out the boat.

"Sixty-five foot over-all. The largest model we manufacture," the salesman replied.

"You think it could make it to Miami OK?" Sal asked.

, "Certainly. You could go anywhere in the hemisphere with her. She's built to cruise in comfort."

"Well, we'll give her a little test this afternoon." He turned to the blonde. "You ever been out boating, baby?"

"No, Sal. I'd rather fly. Who wants to be all junked into a boat. You go to Newark and two and a half hours later you're in Miami on the way to the hotel. You know?"

"What's the matter you ain't got no sportsmanship."

"I'll fly, Sal."

"Someday I gotta bang you on a boat. They say it's romantic."

The boat approached the dock and a crewman standing on the bow tossed a line to an attendant. The cabin cruiser was soon secured.

"Have a nice cruise, Mr. Di Siccerone," the salesman said. "You'll contact me later and tell me how you liked the boat?"

"Sure, I will. How do you get on this thing?"

As Sal asked the question a set of three steps was placed on the dock beside the boat. One bodyguard went first, then the girl followed by Sal, and finally the second bodyguard. The crew member pulled up the steps and the captain maneuvered the craft away from the dock and into the mainstream of the river.

Sal and his party went to the afterdeck and sat down. A steward took orders for drinks and left them alone. Sal sighed contentedly. "This is the life, huh? Out on the sea, away from all the shit on shore. Yeah."

After the ship had been out in the river five minutes cruising north toward the George Washington Bridge, Sal stood up. "Guess I'll take a look down below." The blonde nodded, sipping the drink the steward had brought her. Sal descended the companionway into the large, luxuriously appointed main salon.

"Hi ya, Charlie," Sal greeted C. L. Ciano. "This was a good idea."

Ciano looked up from a sheaf of papers spread out on the table in front of him. "Good afternoon, Sal.

This is about as secure a place for us to talk on a hot summer day as I could come up with. We should be successfully confusing your friends who keep track of where you go and who you see."

"Yeah. I thought the broad would give them something else to think about beside who I might be meeting. So what's up, Charlie?"

"What's the story on Strega Joe and the other boys?"

"They're all doing great. What the hell, they're on bail, all the judges are so busy or on vacation that nobody's been called up. They're not worried. Except for Augie Falconi. He thinks his boy isn't being taken care of."

"He'll be taken care of," Ciano replied darkly. "Now we don't want anyone connected with the case to come up for trial before the elections. We've got things fixed nicely with the judges but we don't want to get a lot of news stories saying everyone in the big Adams bust got off. That wouldn't help his campaign at all."

"I get you, Charlie. We won't have any trouble. Echeverrea don't know he was set up, of course, but he's all right. I told him not to worry, he's getting the best legal guys."

"Ramirez has already been deported," Ciano remarked. "It was in the papers and helped remind everyone what a big deal Adams pulled off."

"He sure got the headlines at the convention," Sal said approvingly. "How's his chances to get elected?"

"He'll make it to the Senate big this fall, you'll see. And, Sal, don't worry about Adams. He's mine. All the way. And he knows it now. I understand it took him a day or so to get used to being owned but he's all right now."

"How many boys have you got in the race for the President in '76? I still don't think that Adams can make it."

"I'll have plenty on both sides. But don't worry about Adams. He's picking up a lot of popularity. A lot of kids who were afraid of him are with him now that he's come out for legal pot."

"Some of my boys were pretty cut up about that. Pot becomes legal and they're out of business."

"Tell them not to worry. I've got something bigger for them, which is why we had to get together today." Ciano handed Sal the Hand an envelope which brightly denoted it contained sales material for the yacht.

"In here, after you've read all the good stuff about this boat, you'll find further information about a company I bought based in California that sells audio-video teaching aids to community colleges west of the Rocky Mountains."

"Teaching aids?" Sal exclaimed. "Our only interest in colleges is that's where we're selling half the snow we bring in. Coke and horse."

"That's my point, Sal. We replace all the salesmen with your own guys. They'll be able to walk on any campus anytime to supply the student pushers. Pretty quick this company will be supplying all the community colleges in the country and moving in on the big colleges too."

The magnitude of the concept suddenly hit Sal. He pushed his yachting cap back on his head and smote his forehead with the palm of his hand. "Jeezus!" he exclaimed. "What a fucking big idea. We can get into every college in the country, all innocent and respectable. You're some brain, Charlie."

"The name of the new manager of the company is on the literature. I put him in a couple of months ago. Already the stuff we're getting in from Asia is going into this pipeline. It's working great. What you want to do now is put your best younger men into this company and let them take over the college market. You understand?"

"Just leave it to me. Can we cover the whole country?"

"Make this operation in the West pay off and we'll be into every college in the country in six months."

Sal the Hand reached across the table and took the envelope from Ciano. "I'll get the right boys together," he promised. "By the way, I hear that stuff coming in from China is the purest we've ever seen. The wholesalers can cut it an extra round. They have to. It would be too strong if they didn't."

"Sal," Ciano went on in a crisp, businesslike tone, "the Super-Save stores could use more merchandise. We haven't seen as much as usual from you."

"Yeah, I know. The security at the airports has tightened up bad in the last six months. Over at Kennedy where we used to get ten or fifteen truckloads of stuff a month we're lucky to take out two trucks, maybe three a month. Even our union contacts can't help us any more. The feds got two of our inside men at Kennedy, one at Newark, and one at Chicago in the last two months."

"The best thing is to lay back and pretty soon the heat will be off," Ciano counseled. "I'll see what I can do."

"Talking about security reminds me. What happened to that detective, Kenney, the one you took off the street for our people out in Brooklyn? He got a lot of publicity with Adams."

Ciano frowned, thinking of Kenney. For several moments he did not answer. Then he said, "Kenney figured out what really happened on the Adams bust. He's not as dumb as I thought."

Sal the Hand looked concerned. "Anything he can do?"

Ciano shook his head. "Don't worry about him. I tried to hire him but he wouldn't come. He quit the cops figuring I could get to him and took a job in a private security guard company." Ciano chuckled mirthlessly. "I happen to own the company that hired him. That way I can watch him. He was assigned to a job in Miami during the convention. I didn't know it or I would have stopped the assignment. While he was there he saw Adams and told him the whole story."

"Jeezus, Charlie, that could bring us trouble," Sal exclaimed. He stood up and prowled around the yacht's main salon.

"Turned out to be good for us," Ciano replied. "One of my best men, a straight guy even though he knows what we do, worked Adams over pretty good. Mentally, of course. Told him he was through if he didn't stick with us. Fortunately, we had him well insured and each day now that he goes along with us makes him better insured."

"If you say everything's OK, it's OK," Sal said doubtfully.

"If any problems come up you'll hear about them. Now, one more little thing. How many more hits are going to happen?"

Sal shrugged and grinned. "I don't know. The boys are a little restless."

"I think you should try to put an end to it," Ciano said seriously. "Every time there's a hit the newspapers get on it and the cops have to do something about it which makes them mad. You should try to keep the spotlight off you. Just when people are beginning to believe your organization doesn't really exist any more there's another theatrical execution. And now Tommy Ryan in all the papers. Why the hell did he have to get hit?"

"He thought he was bigger than the commission. He was very bad for discipline. I couldn't do what you ask me to do if I didn't have discipline, from every man on the commission and all their soldiers, you understand?"

Ciano sighed. "I suppose so. But couldn't they just disappear? Not be seen around any more?"

"It's better for discipline if there's a little publicity. A nice picture in the *Daily News* of blood on the street. They all gotta have a little fear in them all the time."

"Did it ever occur to you that you could be hit?"

"Sure. I'm *capo di capiri,* boss of bosses, but if I got out of line, sure, the others would have a meet and vote to hit me. But I've been around too long. I've got what you call seniority. And I don't make mistakes. I don't muscle in on another guy's thing, ever. I'm more like a judge."

"Well, if you could hand out a few less death sentences it would be better for all of us. All you need is for one of your buttons to hit some straight businessman by accident and you'll have heat like you never felt. I promise you, Sal, you don't need that kind of publicity. Even though you just kill each other it's gotta bring you heat you don't need."

Sal the Hand let out a horse chuckle. "You never did like that part of our thing, did you, Charlie? But you never hesitated to ask me for a hit when you needed one."

"I try to handle that myself nowadays," Ciano said quietly. "Anything you need from me?"

"Well, there's always pressure to get some of the other boys sprung since we did the thing for Sam the Stick. But I wouldn't even bother you with a job like that unless it was real urgent, like something that the entire commission asked me to do."

"Just stick with me, Sal. In four years we'll have no trouble springing any worthy member of your organization."

"Oh, I'm with you, all the way, Charlie."

"Right. We'll set up another meet in a couple of weeks through the same channels. Meantime, enjoy what's left of your yachting afternoon. I'll tell the captain to turn around and head back down to the Hudson. So long, Sal."

Ciano watched Sal walk up the companionway to the afterdeck and then turned back to the stack of reports before him.

CHAPTER FORTY-FOUR

Brad Kendall glanced at his wrist watch. Seven in the evening. He decided to make himself a drink alone. Elda was half an hour late. He switched on the television set to the evening news to check the progress of the Adams-for-Senator campaign. Then he walked across the living room of the small but comfortable apartment he had rented recently as an escape hatch from his own lavish quarters, which with good reason he was convinced were under electronic surveillance.

It was increasingly a source of uneasiness to have to be careful of everything he said to visitors. And now that he and Elda saw each other almost every week, a private place was a necessity.

He was just stirring a martini when he heard the key inserted in the lock. Elda let herself in. He added another measure of gin and continued to stir.

"My God, it's hot for October," Elda commented. "This air conditioning feels good." She put down a shopping bag from Bloomingdale's.

"Late Indian summer," Brad commented. "What kept you?"

"I wanted to get something special for Andrea's new apartment. I looked around forever before finding what I thought she would like."

Brad poured them each an ice-cold martini. "This will cool you off."

Gratefully Elda took the drink and sat down on the sofa. Brad sat on a chair opposite her. He held up the drink. "Here's to Andrea's new life, if she has the guts to carry it off."

Elda held her own glass up. "I think she's got what it takes. Cheers."

"She's a funny girl. I can't understand the rationale of these young girls today. She's made up her mind to leave her mother and stepfather now that she's nineteen and they can't force her to come back. So why doesn't she move into the big, comfortable apartment with me? She could even walk to Hunter College from my place. But no, she'd rather have a little dump down in Greenwich Village."

Brad looked up at Elda. "Did I tell you what she said?" he went on. "She told me that it would hurt her mother less for her to be living alone in the Village than living with me."

"I guess she just wants complete independence."

"But you're in your twenties and you are happy to live in your father's home."

"Yes. But I'm as independent as I want to be. It's almost like having my own home, living in the wing of Dad's house. My own door, my own garage, my own telephone, my own parlor, my own kitchenette. I'm very happy there."

"Andrea could have most of that here." Brad lifted his glass and took another long sip. "It's going to be quite something when Andrea walks out of that house. They'll hear Gwen and Ed shouting and wailing all over the city." Brad could not help the pleasurable sensation it gave him to contemplate Gwen's vain ire.

"When is she actually moving in?" Elda asked. "I thought from what she said to me a few days ago she'd be there now."

"I refused to let her move in until she has a telephone. I'd rather have her with Gwen and Ed a few more days than down in that apartment with no outside communication."

"You're right, Brad. I'm looking forward to seeing what she picked out for herself."

"We'll go down and take a look, if you like, before she actually gets moved in. I expect it will be another few days before her phone is installed. I insisted on having a key to the place although," he grinned wryly, "I promised her faithfully no surprise calls."

"She'll probably have the lock changed when she's in."

Brad shrugged. "I can only do my best to make sure she's reasonably well looked after. She still doesn't seem well. I don't know why she's so pale and thin. Young girls today are too worried about being thin. I like girls that give you something to hold onto."

"Like me?" Elda asked smiling.

"From what I can determine when we are dancing, you are perfection."

"Thank you, sir. And I agree about Andrea. Maybe when she has her own place, starts cooking for friends and is more content she'll eat more."

"Friends?" Brad picked up bleakly. "I think she's still seeing that Tony Falcon. I don't know why they haven't jailed him yet. Here it is October, six months since he was arrested, and he hasn't been brought to trial yet."

"There's not much you can do about her seeing him if she's made up her mind—without resorting to something drastic, like asking my father to have him hit."

"Oh, Elda, stop that talk. You know better than to keep thinking your father is some sort of a Mafia overlord."

"I know what he is. And I love him. He's Dad. For that matter I know what you are, or what you are becoming—" she paused.

"And?"

"And—" suddenly with resolution, "and I love you, Brad. There, I've said it. And I'm not sorry. In spite of Luciana."

"Luciana doesn't seem to be in love with me. She's so busy with Whitehall I hardly get to see her any more." He thought a moment. "And you're not really in love with an old guy like me. What would your father think if he heard you say such a thing? It's a good thing I found this place."

"Is the bugging and spying really that bad?"

"From what I know, what I've seen, yes. When I think of what I don't know, it scares me. But I made my choice." He took a long drink of his martini.

"I've never tried to make a secret of the fact that you and I see each other," Elda said. "My father believes it's because of Andrea which of course it was—once."

The phone rang through the room startling them. "My God, he's got this place bugged too and he's already after us," Brad said only half in jest.

"Who has your number here?" Elda asked mildly alarmed.

"I have a line into here from my main apartment phone. I can't be completely isolated on weekdays, unfortunately." He picked up the telephone. "Brad Kendall here."

"Brad," the shrewish voice shrieked, "you've got Andrea there, I know it. If you don't send her back immediately I'll have Ed call the police."

"Andrea is old enough to do what she wants," Brad retorted in deep annoyance, "and when she wants and there is nothing you can do to stop her. She's old enough to vote, get married without your consent and live where she chooses."

"We'll see about that. If you don't send her back this instant you'll be in jail. How will that sound? The president of the Ascot Hotel chain in jail for kidnapping."

Now Brad was worried. Not about Gwen's threats but about Andrea. She should have been home by now. She had promised not to make the break until she had a telephone. Was she out with Tony?

"Gwen," Brad replied evenly, "Andrea isn't here. I haven't seen her for two days."

"You're a liar. She's there. Let me talk to her."

"I told you, Gwen, she isn't here. Now I'm not going to talk to you unless you speak and think rationally."

There was a long pause. Then Gwen said in calmer tones, "Do you have any idea of where she is?"

Brad disliked lying but he couldn't give away Andrea's plan prematurely. "No, Gwen. I have no idea. But it's only seven-thirty. That's hardly a late hour."

"She promised to be back no later than six to give me a back rub. She knew we were having some people in at seven and she was going to make tea and little sandwiches."

"Well, Gwen, if I hear from her I'll certainly call you right away. But I can assure you that she is not here and I haven't seen her for two days."

"What were you seeing her about two days ago?" Gwen asked suspiciously.

"She's my daughter, she's a woman now. If she wants to see me she has the right."

"Not without asking me," Gwen's voice shrilled. "She's in my custody." The sound was not dissimilar to a nail breaking off on a blackboard. It made him wince and then get angry.

"She came to see me for some money to keep you and your misfit unemployed husband, who I understand is now making passes at Andrea, eating and paying the rent."

"My husband!" Gwen screamed. "You goddamned drunk. All you do is drink and you insult my husband."

"Tell him I drink Tanqueray gin in the summer and Old Fitzgerald Bourbon in the winter. Maybe if he drank my stuff he'd become half as successful. I'll send him over a mixed case. It would be cheaper than supporting you both."

"Now I know you are a liar," Gwen shrieked. "Andrea hasn't given us any money, from you or anyone else, in the last six months. I'm sending the police over to get you now."

"Lots of luck." But Gwen had already slammed her telephone down. Brad turned to Elda. "I'm sorry you had to listen to all that."

"She is a real bitch. Poor Andrea. I don't know how she has stood it all this time."

"I don't either. But I am worried about her now. It isn't like her to get home late, much as she must dread going back to that apartment. But more than that, Gwen claimed that none of the money I gave Andrea got to her."

"I know, I could hear her clear across the room."

"If she's telling the truth Andrea had a lot of money to do something with." He thought a few moments. "Elda, I think I'll drop down at her apartment."

"I'll go with you, Brad."

"Thanks. I'd appreciate it." They both finished off their martinis. "Sorry I don't have the car. We'll have to take a cab."

"That doesn't bother me. Let's go."

The apartment Andrea had picked out in Greenwich Village had a vestibule and a locked door leading into the building which was opened by pressing a button to the apartment. Brad pressed the button to apartment 3A which had no name tag on it. He and Elda waited but there was no answering buzz. Once again Brad rang Andrea's apartment and still no answer.

Brad reached in his pocket for his keys and opened the front door. Elda followed him up the three flights of stairs. "Andrea will keep her legs in shape this way," Elda observed.

Brad stopped outside 3A and knocked. Then he called Andrea's name. There was no answer. With a burgeoning sense of dread closing around him he put the key in the lock and turned it, pushing the door open into the one-room studio apartment.

Brad walked into the small foyer of the back apartment, followed by Elda who closed the door behind her. Then he turned left into the rectangular-shaped room with the barred window at the back. At the other end of the sparsely furnished room was a gaily colored chintz-covered sofa. Brad's stomach knotted and churned, his face contorting as he saw his daughter lying sprawled on the floor, as though she had fallen off the sofa.

"Andrea!" he cried.

"Oh, no! No!" An anguished sob tore from Elda.

Brad strode across the room to Andrea and looked down at her. His throat constricted, his eyes closed to shut out the sight. But when they opened again Andrea was still lying there. Her short skirt was above her waist, and just below her panties, high up inside her left thigh, a hypodermic needle hung imbedded in her flesh. Her hair was an auburn swirl partially covering her face, fanning out on the floor behind her. Her arms were straight down, both hands close to the needle. They must have been holding it as she died from the overdose, he realized.

"Oh, Brad," Elda sobbed. "I didn't know she was into this. I didn't know." She put her arms around his neck as though to hold herself up. "I didn't know."

"Of course you didn't," Brad said gently trying to control the quaver in his throat. He patted Elda. "I guess—I'm afraid we have to get the police." For a moment Gwen's threat of half an hour ago ran through his mind. Elda continued to stare down at Andrea's body.

"Come on, Elda." He led her weeping back across the room and out the door, closing it after them.

CHAPTER FORTY-FIVE

Pat Kenney lurked across the street from Tony Falcon's West Side apartment, the *Daily News* under his arm. Since the moment he had seen the headline, waves of anguish had rolled over him. So unnecessary. If only he had immediately reported that Andrea was being seduced onto dope by Tony Falcon this young girl's death might have been avoided. But no, the investigation he had decided, a meaningless piece of pap as it had turned out, had to be considered before the girl's best interests.

He stalked across the street, into the apartment-house foyer and soon found the right skeleton key on his chain to admit him into the building.

He walked up the steps to Tony's floor and paused outside the door. There was no sound inside. If Tony was not there he would let himself into the apartment and wait for him. But first he had to make sure Tony was indeed absent. If he was true to type he would be still sleeping. It wasn't noon yet.

Kenney pressed the buzzer and waited. His heart beat faster as he heard a stirring inside and then voices. Tony wasn't alone. Listening at the door he recognized a female voice. OK, no problem then. He buzzed again. Then he heard through the door Tony calling, "Who's there?"

"It's the super," Kenney replied. "There's a leak in

the gas lines. We're checking all the apartments to make sure there's no danger. You wanna let me in and have a look?"

"Can't you come back later?"

"Later could be too late."

"Wait a minute."

Pat heard more whispering and then bare feet padding across the floor and a door, probably the bathroom door, being shut. Now the door opened cautiously, still on the chain. When the door was open as far as the chain would permit, Tony wearing a tightly tied bathrobe peered out and saw Kenney.

"You aren't the super!" He started to slam the door but with one deft movement Kenney jammed a steel hook through the crack, caught the chain and pulled it tight into the crack in the door. Now Tony could not close it.

"You're right. I'm not the super. Police. We want to ask you some questions."

"You have no right—" Tony began.

"Open up the door or you and your broad won't ever see again." Kenney squirted a whiff of tear gas into the apartment from an aerosol can. "That's just a sample. Get this door open or I'll fill the place with tear gas and you'll either open it yourself or jump out the window. And it's a long fall."

"I'm going to call the police," Tony cried.

"I am the police," Kenney replied. "Get this door open now!" He squirted another short cloud of gas into the apartment and heard Tony cry out and start coughing.

"OK, OK, I'll open it. This is a hell of a way for a cop to come into someone's place." He started to work at the chain. "I've got to close the door to get it open," he cried.

"Yeah? Well, you better figure some other way of getting it open because I'm not taking this hook out of the door."

"But there's no way," Tony cried.

Kenney squeezed off another cloud of gas. "You better figure a way to get the door open."

"At least let go of the chain. You can keep the rod in the door."

"Now you're getting smart." Kenney pushed the rod with the hook on the end further through the crack. The chain dropped loose but the door was still open the width of the rod, enough room to put the nozzle of the can through and fill the room with tear gas.

Kenney heard the rattling of the chain as Tony struggled to release it. Finally he succeeded and the door swung open. "All right, officer, identify yourself," Tony began.

"Sure I will." In one sudden, practiced movement Kenney swung a hard fist into the side of Tony's head, slamming him to the floor. "That's my identification, you fuckin' punk. I've been watching you for a long time. I made you for Adams."

"I have no narcotics here," Tony cried. "Search the place. And don't think you won't be reported for assault."

"For a guy who committed a murder last night that's pretty big talk. And we know where you keep the shit. In the apartment of that girl you killed with an overdose last night."

"Killed?" Tony shrieked. "Whaddya talking about? I didn't kill no one."

Kenney pulled Falcon to his feet, turned him around and smashed a fist into his face sending him reeling back against the bathroom door with a crash. "What about the girl you got up here with you? You getting her hooked too? You going to let her kill herself with your shit?"

From the bathroom a loud scream emitted. "Tony, what's happening?"

"Some maniac broke in here. Keep yourself locked in."

"He'll get me too," she shrieked.

"Just shut up and sit there and you won't get hurt," Kenney yelled through the door. "It's the police."

"What murder you talking about?" Tony asked trembling.

Kenney pulled the rolled-up newspaper from his hip pocket and threw it at Tony's face. "This murder. Andrea Kendall. I watched you get her hooked."

"Andrea dead?" Tony cried.

"Read it, you punk."

Tony opened the paper, still sprawled on the floor against the bathroom door, and looked at the headline and Andrea's picture. Then he dropped the paper. "She was alive when I last saw her," he groaned.

"When was that?"

"Five o'clock yesterday afternoon, maybe five-thirty. She was on her way home."

"Where did you see her?"

"Her new apartment. She was getting ready to move in."

"Did you help her shoot up?"

"No, I swear I didn't." He tried to pull himself to a standing position, leaning against the door. "She doesn't need any help there. She shoots pretty good all by herself."

With the flat of his hand Kenney knocked the smirking young man to the floor again. "She does, huh? Who taught her? Who sells her the shit? How come she's dead if she shoots pretty good herself?"

Kenney leaned over and dragged Tony to his feet. "We found your shit all over the apartment. Read it in the paper. You kept maybe five or six ounces at her place."

Tony remained silent. Kenney, holding him by the bathrobe he was wearing, twisting the collar into his neck with a huge hand, shook him viciously, slapping him first with the heel of his palm then with the back of his hand.

"You want to talk or walk out of here shopping for false teeth? I'm not going to knock them out, I'm going to shake them out, your head against the wall."

"I only told her where to buy the stuff!"

Kenney backhanded Falcon in the mouth. A trickle of blood started to ooze out of the corner of his lips. "This girl was going into the ounce business, you trying to tell me?" Kenney continued shaking Falcon in a white, cold fury. "This college girl was coming back to her apartment in the evening and cutting and bagging that six ounces of pure shit you were hiding in her place? That what you telling me?" Blood was coming from both sides of Falcon's mouth.

"No, no. Let me tell you, for crissake."

Kenney dropped Falcon into a heap on the floor and stood over him, legs apart, both huge hands ready to continue the punishment. "I'm listening."

"OK. I told her not to shoot without me cutting the stuff we bought. It's the new stuff coming in from the West Coast and China or wherever over there. It's more pure than what we seen before here. God sakes, I told her not to shoot. I swear."

"But you left your stash in her apartment. Enough, according to the newspaper, to cut and sell for ten thousand bucks or better on the street."

"You can't prove I left it."

"I don't have to prove it. I know it."

"You get out of here," Tony blustered. "I don't believe you're a cop anyway."

"You're right. I was a cop but I'm private now." He reached for Tony with both hands, jerked him to his feet and holding the young man's limp form in front of him, Kenney charged into a wall of the apartment. Tony's back and head hit the wall with a sickening thud and he slid unconscious to the floor.

Kenney stared down contemptuously at the young hood, kicked him in the ribs and then went to the bathroom. "You can come out now. Your boy friend probably needs you. But don't never forget, he is responsible for the death of a girl last night. No reason you shouldn't be next."

There was no response from the bathroom and Kenney turned on his heel and stalked out of the apartment.

In the street Kenney hailed a cab. "Etoile apartments," he directed the driver. In fifteen minutes the doorman was letting him into the building. "Mr. Kendall says for you to come right up. You're the only person he's seen this morning." Pat had been to Brad's place several times during the investigation and immediately after it.

Brad Kendall's haggard, totally devastated countenance and carriage cut to the marrow of Pat's emotions. He could never recall, in a long police career, feeling so sad for another person.

"Come in, Pat." Brad's tone was so subdued Kenney feared he might not be able to converse with him. "Sit down," he invited, gesturing at the wide living room with its view of the East River.

"Thanks, Brad."

"I'm glad you're here. But why?"

"I had to come see you, Brad. I feel responsible for this tragedy. I had to talk to you."

"Why should you feel responsible?" Brad asked.

"Because I was all cop, not a human, during the investigation. I knew Andrea was seeing that bum. And I didn't want him tipped off I was tailing him so I didn't tell you."

"I understand, Pat. You did what you had to do."

"I should of told you," Kenney went on miserably. "And the whole lousy investigation amounted to what? A publicity stunt for Adams. He gets elected and Andrea dies. What kind of a world is this?"

"The world of the fifth estate, Pat."

"I don't know that. What is it?"

"Sometime I'll tell you all about it, Pat."

The detective nodded. "You know who did it all, Brad? Who got her onto drugs?"

Brad nodded. "Tony Falcon."

"That's right. Yesterday afternoon she was shooting that high-grade, pure stuff that's coming in from Asia. Tony Falcon got it through his connections and stashed it in Andrea's apartment. He wouldn't take a chance keeping it at his place while his trial is pending."

"Would you like a drink, Pat?" Brad asked.

Kenney shook his head. "I just had a talk with Tony Falcon. That's how I know what happened. And what the hell happens to him? The way the law is, he's totally protected. And he'll probably get off on the charges from the investigation."

"I suppose."

"Well, I gave Tony a working over. I wish you could have seen it, Brad."

"In the long run, the wide view, I, not Tony Falcon, am the one responsible for what happened to Andrea."

Kenney shook his head. "I've seen it happen over and over again in narcotics cases. A nice girl from a good family gets in with a Tony Falcon type. She can't help herself. First he becomes the habit, then he gets her onto the deadly habit. And there's nothing the family can do. You just have to catch it at the beginning, the very beginning and put a stop to it. But half the time you don't know. That's why I feel so bad, Brad. There might have been time if I'd thought more about Andrea's future than the stinking investigation. I'll never forgive myself."

"I told you, Pat. Don't feel that way. I am the one really responsible and I know it." For a moment Kenney thought Brad was going to cry. "That's why this is so goddamned bad for me. I guess I deserve to suffer. But not Andrea. She should have lived. She was just getting ready to take life by the hand and live."

Pat stood up. "Brad, if there's ever anything I can do for you, any way I can help you, the offer I made you in Miami is still open. You're going to need help someday."

"Thank you, Pat." Brad managed a businesslike tone. "By the way, it might be of interest to you that last week I received a memo to use the security service you work for exclusively in all Ascot Hotels. So maybe I'll be seeing you again."

Pat's face suddenly reddened, and from sympathy his look became one of anger. Brad put a finger to his lips and pointed about the room. The anger welling up in the beefy Irishman immediately subsided as he let out a long breath. Kenney nodded in understanding. He took out a card and wrote something on the back of it.

"That's good news, Brad. I'm writing my home number down for you on the back of my card. Call me anytime."

"I will. Give me a few weeks. So long, Pat."

CHAPTER FORTY-SIX

The memorial services for Andrea had been, at Gwen's insistence, a Catholic funeral Mass in the city. Gwen, a converted and almost fanatical Catholic, had called for the old-fashioned Mass of the Resurrection to be celebrated. What difference did it make now? Brad thought. Nothing was going to bring Andrea back. He had avoided going to the wake at the funeral home the night before, knowing that Gwen would throw an emotional scene.

Outside the church on the sidewalk the priest and three altar boys greeted the coffin. It seemed comforting to Brad that the priest wore white robes and it was a white pall placed on the coffin, not a black one. One of the altar boys carried a large white candle and the priest sprinkled holy water on the casket and then it was carried up the steps and rolled down the aisle of the church up to the altar.

Instead of walking down the aisle to the family section in front Brad sat at the rear of the church, not wanting to see any more of Gwen than was necessary. Around him were many people from Whitehall. Although C. L. Ciano did not come, Elda sat on one side of Brad and Luciana sat on the other. Detective Kenney had come to the church and was sitting away from the small cluster of Ascot and Whitehall people. Maurice D'Estang sat stolidly beside Fred Black and for once the cigarette was missing from his lips.

Congressman William Fortune Adams and his wife, Terry, sat on the aisle and Brad's secretary sat in the same row with them. Brad felt a moment's uneasiness. With less than two weeks to elections he should be out campaigning with Adams. All in all, Brad realized, as he looked around, he had very few real friends. The service seemed to go on interminably and rather than let his thoughts roam freely, stimulating strong emotions, he strained to listen to each word and phrase intoned by the priest. Elda had explained to him that at a funeral Mass there was no eulogy. For this he was thankful. He preferred to have his own thoughts on Andrea's short life.

When the service was about half through Brad heard the priest intone, "Let us pray for ourselves and for all Christians who are living witness to the risen Christ and of all mankind's victory over sin and death."

Well might he pray for himself, he thought. He had scored no victory over sin and death. Far from it, he had contributed to the proliferation of both. How do you pray for yourself? He started to ask for guidance in silent prayer and immediately realized that it wasn't guidance he needed, it was courage to change the course of his life drastically. This was something he would have to consider later. Not now.

Outside the church in the bright autumn afternoon the people climbed into the waiting cars and limousines to drive to the impersonal Catholic cemetery on Long Island that Gwen had picked for the interment. In vain Brad had begged Gwen to have Andrea buried in the small New England graveyard where his family rested. But Gwen, the hardened convert to Catholicism she was, refused to have Andrea buried in a Protestant cemetery. Everything was handled by the priests and the undertaker and paid for by Brad.

Brad, Elda and Luciana rode together in his limousine to the interment site. Williams, the driver, who had become well acquainted with Andrea and driven her around town on many occasions had attended the service. There was little conversation on the drive to the cemetery. Brad's thoughts came in jerky, unconnected bursts. Rafe Leighton had sent him a long telegram of condolence from his home in Texas. C. L. Ciano had sent him a beautifully composed handwritten note. He found his right hand reaching out for Elda's. Strange, he thought, that the unconscious gesture had not been in Luciana's direction. Then crazily he remembered the time he found himself with two dates at the movies and had held hands with both of them simultaneously.

Brad wondered what pleasure Gwen received out of this long torturous trip to the cemetery. Everything could have been made so much easier. Finally, after almost an hour's drive, the hearse up front slid to a halt beside the iron rail fence that separated the cemetery from the street. The other cars in the procession parked behind the undertaker's limousines and the mourners left their cars and walked through the gates to the cemetery.

It was a substantial walk through the slate jungle of headstones to the flower-decked mound of earth beside the neat rectangular hole in the ground. The casket was just being placed on the supports over the grave as Brad arrived with Luciana and Elda. Pat Kenney came up and stood beside them along with Congressman Adams and his wife. Maurice D'Estang and Fred Black joined the Whitehall group. At a right angle to Brad's friends Gwen and Ed Connor and a number of their people stood at the foot of the grave. Brad's glance met Gwen's for an instant, they were standing quite close together, and even the black veil she was wearing failed to hide the venomous expression on her face. Ed Connor's wide features were also contorted into a look of hate. Brad shrugged. It was easier for them of course to blame Andrea's death on him rather than to accept the fact that they were responsible for the state of mind that caused Andrea to seek escape in drugs and a hoodlum like Tony Falcon.

The priest standing at the head of the grave, a simple white stole around his neck, began the interment service and Brad bowed his head. His eyes were dry. He was utterly devastated by Andrea's needless death and the part he had played in it. He knew that other overdose deaths like hers were yet to come, partially as a result of his trip to the Orient and the poppy fields of the Golden Triangle. So overwhelmed was he by the tragedy that ordinary emotion escaped him.

The priest's words and stock phrases washed over him and eddied away with no effect. It was almost as if he was loooking down at this scene, watching the body he knew to be his own standing with the others beside the grave. His soul would have much to pay for. He longed for another rationalization session with C. L. Ciano. Somehow Ciano would make him feel that all that had happened, including Andrea's death, was in some way contributing to America's and mankind's eventual greater good. And maybe it was.

Brad looked up as the priest's verbiage seemed to be coming to a climax even as a symphony orchestra unmistakably signals that the end of a great movement is near.

"We pray now," the priest concluded, "that Andrea Kendall be freed from every sin so that she may share with all your saints the everlasting joy of your presence through Christ our Lord."

The undertaker's assistants removed the supports which held the casket and slowly lowered the box into the ground as the priest sprinkled holy water and Andrea's sorrowing friends and family threw the white carnations they had been handed into the grave on top of the casket. The finality of the ceremony descended upon the silent mourners.

The shriek was piercing. "You bastard!" Brad looked up as Gwen lunged at him across the corner of the grave. Mortified, Brad stood there as Gwen struck and scratched at his face. The heavy diamond princess ring, a pyramid of small stones capped with a one-carat diamond, bit into his forehead and then his upper lip. He had given the ring to Gwen twenty years before and it was the one good piece of jewelry she had left. Blood spattered on his white shirt and tie.

Elda watched horrified and then reacted, pushing Gwen away with all the strength of a young, strong woman. Gwen fell back into the grave on top of the casket, screaming, scrambling to her feet and clawing at the earth trying to climb out. Ed Connor rushed at Brad, throwing a wild punch which grazed his cheek. Brad suddenly snapped into reality and countered Ed's next blow and drove a pistonlike right jab to the beefy ex-athlete's gut, crossing with a left to the jowl. Bent and staggered, Ed Connor covered with the blood which spattered from Brad's face tumbled groaning into the grave, knocking Gwen, screaming and sprawling, back onto the casket.

Now Ed Connor's brother, a replica of the overweight, oafish ruddy-complexioned, wide-eyed Irishman moved in on Brad, cocking a fist. And suddenly Pat Kenney was standing between them. Ed's brother stopped short in the face of the menacing detective. Meanwhile, the undertaker's assistants hauled first Ed and then Gwen, screaming profane imprecations at Brad, out of the grave. Brad pulled a handkerchief from his pocket and with as much dignity as he could muster held it to his torn upper lip, which was bleeding profusely.

"Are you all right, Brad?" Elda asked. "I'm sorry, I had to push her away from you. I didn't mean to shove her into the hole."

"I'm all right. And you did the right thing. I'd have had that ring in my eye next."

The priest surveyed the scene in helpless consternation. The undertaker was wringing his hands in dismay. Ed Connor, still recovering from the sharp blow to his stomach, was panting and making retching sounds and

Gwen, being restrained now by some of her friends, was still screaming at Brad.

"Let's get out of here, Brad," Elda cried.

Maurice D'Estang came up to him. "What do you want done, Brad?"

"Let's all of us leave. As fast as possible."

"Brad, I'll ride back with Maurice," Luciana said. "You take Elda in your car."

Brad nodded. He watched Maurice lead Luciana away from the group at the grave and turned as Pat Kenney, having discouraged Ed Connor's brother from further tendency toward violence, came up to him.

"Did you ever think that all you have to do is drop a word to your associate there," he nodded at Maurice's retreating figure, "and you'll never have another problem with your ex-wife again?"

Brad, holding his handkerchief to the bleeding upper lip, considered what Kenney had just said.

"Come on, Brad, let's go," Elda said urgently.

He looked at Kenney and nodded somberly. It was true. A word to D'Estang or Ciano and he could have almost anyone eliminated. The thought made him shudder. He had never before entertained the notion that he had the power to order the execution of a human being if he so chose.

"I'll walk to your car with you, Brad," Kenney volunteered. "Just to make sure nobody gets any more crazy ideas."

"Thanks, Pat," Elda said and took Brad's arm as they walked from the cemetery, Pat alertly watching the group around Gwen and Ed Connor. It was with great relief that Brad settled back in his limousine beside Elda, and Pat Kenney pushed the door closed.

"Would you like to drive out to Rye for the rest of the afternoon?" Elda asked. "I don't think it would be good for you to sit alone in the apartment."

"I don't feel like going anywhere, Elda," Brad replied. "Besides, I'd like to clean up the mess." He looked down at his blood-spattered shirt ruefully.

"Maybe I'll go back to the retreat and have a drink."

"Do you want to be alone or can I come too?"

"I wish you would keep me company. It's funny at a time like this how you realize who you have in the world that you are really close to. Neither my mother nor my father are alive and I have no sisters or brothers."

Elda put her hand on his. "I'd love to sit with you in our little retreat. Tell your driver to take you to the Etoile and we'll take a cab from there."

"You are as careful as I have to be," Brad said admiringly. He lowered his voice. "I don't doubt that Williams reports to someone on everything he sees me do and every place he takes me."

The ride back to the city seemed much shorter than it had out to the cemetery. Brad dismissed the driver at the front door of the Place d'Etoile and they walked into the apartment house.

At home Brad washed the dried blood from his lip and forehead, changed out of his blood-flecked clothes and he and Elda quickly left the place. They walked back out to the street, hailed a cab and went to the retreat. Brad made them each a drink and then sat back in an armchair, staring morosely at the floor.

"I think Andrea would be happy to know that we are together a lot," Elda said to break the silence. "She loved you very much even though she found it hard to communicate with you."

"It was difficult. For a while I thought we had broken through but then she got involved with Falconi and things just deteriorated."

Brad and Elda continued to talk and as they did he began to feel less shattered. An hour after they had arrived at the small apartment the telephone rang. Brad looked at it reproachfully.

"Do you want me to answer it for you?" Elda asked.

"I'll get it." Reluctantly Brad stood up and walked to the phone.

"Maurice here, Brad."

"Yes, Maurice," Brad replied wearily.

"I'd like to come over to the Etoile and pick you up. There's something I want you to see."

"Can't it wait a day or so?"

"I don't think so. This is something C.L. personally asked me to show you."

Brad glanced at Elda who looked back sympathetically and shook her head. "It's really important, Maurice?"

"C.L. thinks so."

"OK, in front of the Etoile in one hour."

Elda spread her hands in resignation.

"See you then, Brad," D'Estang said.

Brad hung up. "Something must be important for them to need me now," Brad remarked.

"I think it's dreadful," Elda said. "I worry about you, Brad. I don't think this whole business with my father is right for you. It's something you have to be born to, brought up with. You aren't like the other people around my father."

"Maybe that's why he needs me. It takes all kinds to make a big organization work."

"Even after what happened you don't have second thoughts about staying in this thing of my father's?"

"Once you're in you stay in," Brad replied. "You should know that."

Elda nodded seriously. "Yes, I told you I know a lot. But if you really wanted to you could get out."

Brad did not answer. He swallowed the last of his drink and put it down. "I guess I'd better start back to the Etoile. I wouldn't want Maurice finding out I have another apartment."

"I don't suppose you know how long you'll be, Brad."

He shook his head. "I have no idea what they have in mind or how long it will take."

"I'm going to tell my father how dreadful I think it is for the company to call you out right after Andrea's funeral."

"No, I wish you wouldn't, Elda. That's part of the game. We're all well compensated for what we do."

"Shall I wait for you?"

"I'm afraid it's going to be a long wait. And there's no way I can telephone you to tell you how long I'll be."

Elda stood up. "I'll leave with you then and go home to Rye. Will you call me when you get home?"

"Of course I will. And Elda, being with you does make me feel much better."

"I'm glad. I felt so badly myself and so responsible I introduced her to Tony."

"And you tried in every way you could to stop her from seeing him." He put an arm around her shoulder. "Come on, dear."

Brad and Maurice sat together in the back seat of the black limousine as it snaked its way westward through midtown traffic. It seemed to Brad that they were making an unusual number of twists and turns, as though to throw off a tail.

"Can you give me some idea of what this is all about?" Brad asked.

"You'll see," Maurice replied. "In our organization, or society, we do have certain laws or rules of conduct. One of them is not to hurt another member of his family in any way."

Was he being taken for a ride? Brad wondered. For seeing Elda? It was the only lapse of adherence to the rules he could think of. Well, so be it, he thought. This was the only way you got out of the fifth estate once you were in. Brad realized with a start that he really didn't care whether he lived or died. And, furthermore, he realized that he did not want to be in the fifth estate any longer.

"When a member breaks the rules he is punished in proportion to the seriousness of his offense," D'Estang continued. "One of the worst offenses is to make an addict out of someone in the family of a member."

"Falconi?" Brad asked.

"Yes."

There was no conversation as the car reached the

West Side Highway, proceeded up to the George Washington Bridge, crossed the bridge into New Jersey and after a twenty-minute drive on the parkway wound its way through streets and alleyways in a dismal industrial section. Brad had no idea where they were. Finally the limousine came to a stop in front of a warehouse. The driver hit his horn and a large door opened. The limousine drove in and the door closed behind them.

"OK, we get out here," D'Estang said.

Once again Brad had the feeling of being taken for a gangland-style ride. However, he felt reasonably confident that it wasn't his bones that were going to be made by some aspiring young mobster striving for advancement in his chosen field. Not that he wouldn't be terminated with extreme severity should he contravene the rules of his establishment, Brad realized.

At the side of the large, bare warehouse store D'Estang led Brad to an iron spiral staircase which they descended. On the floor below, lit by a dim light bulb burning in a ceiling plug, Brad found himself walking down a dank corridor. D'Estang halted before a heavy iron door. He banged on it with a fist and moments later it grated open. D'Estang gestured Brad inside.

The room was a long one, windowless, lit by several light bulbs hanging from the high ceiling. In the gloom at the far end of the room, groaning and whimpering, Brad saw that a man was spread-eagled against the wall, his legs and arms handcuffed to bolts in the wall. He looked somewhat like a decorative animal skin hung against a cold wall to give warmth to a room.

"Take a good look," D'Estang said gruffly.

Brad walked forward and suddenly recoiled in distaste. It was Tony Falcon pinioned to the far side of the room. Two young hoods stood on either side of him. As Brad approached, one of them removed a cigar from his mouth and calmly applied it to Tony's naked belly. In fact, Brad realized, Tony was totally naked. The hood held the cigar against the quivering skin and as though a button had been pressed Tony let out a long shriek of pain. The other hood, an ice pick in his hand, grinned foolishly.

"Usually a straight hit will do the trick but in Tony's case we go a little harsher," D'Estang commented.

"I didn't do nothing," Tony cried.

D'Estang nodded grimly to the goon with the ice pick in his hand. Immediately the grin on the young hood's face widened and his eyes lit up. He reached for Tony's limp penis which he held in his left hand. With his right hand he inserted the point of the ice pick into the canal and pushed it in.

The screams reverberated through the cement room as Tony seemed to vibrate on the wall against the chains holding his wrists and ankles. The more he struggled the further the point of the ice pick penetrated. Brad could imagine no more excruciating pain. Sweat poured from Tony's face.

"Stop!" Brad shouted. "Stop it!"

The torturer obligingly pulled the ice pick from the head of Tony's penis. D'Estang gave Brad a puzzled look. "This is the guy who hooked your daughter and killed her. We have our own law and this punk kid thought he could break it. Never, ever bother the family of one of our own."

"I didn't know her old man was in," Tony screamed.

"You know where you met them both."

"I never thought he was in," Tony shrieked.

"You know now," D'Estang said grimly and nodded to the ice pick.

This time the point was swiftly pushed into Tony's ear and a sudden jab sent it into the eardrum. The screams were so loud and shrill Brad wanted to put his hands to his ears but resisted the urge. For a moment one incongruous thought brought a brief smile to his face. Tony could give Gwen competition in a shrieking contest. D'Estang caught the fleeting smile and misinterpreted it.

"Enjoy," he rasped. "The little son of a bitch has it coming to him. If it had been my daughter I would personally do his eyes, ears, nose, tongue and take a couple of days working the rest of the way down."

The hood with the ice pick pulled it out of Tony's ear and reached again for his penis and the other torturer, puffing on the cigar to get it glowing, carelessly applied the burning end to Tony's scrotum.

The screams sounded as though they would tear Tony's vocal cords apart as half-formed religious blasphemies and appeals to God, other deities and his mother poured forth.

"How long has he been here?" Brad asked.

"He was picked up last night. C.L. personally ordered it."

"Does C.L. know what's happening to Tony? What they're doing to him?"

"Of course," D'Estang replied matter-of-factly.

Brad shook his head against the shrieking. "Can you let the law take its course?"

"The straight law?" D'Estang shook his head. "Their law doesn't work. You ought to know that."

"How long does this go on?"

D'Estang peered at the writhing, sweating, screaming Tony. "He should be good for a couple of days. He'll end up on the meat hook." D'Estang gestured at the high ceiling. Brad had not noticed it before but a scimitarlike hook hung from the ceiling on a chain. He couldn't repress the shudder which racked him.

D'Estang seemed to be amused at Brad's squeamishness. "I've seen 'em last a day and a half hanging with the hook through their guts. It's an old Italian device."

"Jesus, Maurice, can't you make it fast for him?"

"Fast?" Maurice exclaimed as though Brad was crazy. "After what he did to your daughter?"

"This isn't going to bring her back. Just shoot him."

D'Estang shrugged. "If that's what you want. You are the aggrieved party. He's yours."

"Then let the law take care of him."

"That we can't do, Brad. He's broken our law and he'll pay."

Brad turned his back to the thrashing, screaming Tony Falcon. "Then just shoot him and let's go."

D'Estang shouted a command and the two hoods ceased their torture of Tony who hung whimpering and moaning from his fetters, his eyeballs turned up so that his eyes showed mostly whites. The tall Corsican made a quick gesture, drawing a hand across his throat and turned from the scene. Brad had already reached the heavy door and was waiting for Maurice to open it. D'Estang slipped the bolt and gave the door a push with his shoulder. It opened noisily.

"The boys were disappointed, they had looked forward to a long night."

A shot and then another rang out behind them as Brad walked through the door and headed for the spiral staircase.

CHAPTER FORTY-SEVEN

Maurice D'Estang dropped Brad off at his apartment building with a cheerful "See you when you feel like getting back." As far as Maurice and probably the rest of them were concerned, Brad thought, the incident was closed. Andrea's death had been avenged and things could go along as before.

Brad let himself into the luxurious apartment and headed straight for the telephone. He dialed Luciana's office in the Ascot Towers Hotel. It was five-thirty and Luciana usually worked until six. He let the phone ring long after he knew that Luciana wasn't there to answer. Then he dialed her apartment. The answering service picked up.

"Please tell Mrs. Blore to telephone Mr. Kendall at home. It's very urgent." He hung up and went to the bar and made himself a strong Bourbon and soda, which he rapidly drank as he paced about the six tastefully furnished rooms high up in the Etoile. He fixed a second drink, Bourbon on the rocks. He wanted badly not to think. Probably what he needed was electric shock treatment. There had been a great deal about shock treatment written in the papers and news magazines over the summer as a result of the Democratic vice-presidential candidate having withdrawn because of his history of such treatments. However, the way things were, if the booze didn't do it for him temporarily nothing was going to.

Then he tried to telephone Luciana again. He needed her now. If she would just stay with him tonight and spend the following day with him he could get through, he thought. She was one of the few people in his life he could talk to, she and Elda. He thought of Ciano's daughter and for a moment his desire to find Luciana abated. But Elda, mature and beautiful though she was, couldn't, or at any rate shouldn't, be interested in a middle-aged man, somewhat emotionally burned out. Luciana was more prepared by life for a serious affair, marriage even, with someone like Brad.

Brad telephoned the Ascot Towers Hotel and methodically tried to track Luciana down through all the other executives' offices. Maurice D'Estang had not returned to his office, he was told. Luciana hadn't been seen in any of the cocktail lounges, the Star Club or the lobby. He left word with everyone from the bell captain and desk clerk to the assistant manager and the resident manager to have Luciana call him. Then he telephoned her apartment again and once more found himself talking to her answering service. He left a second urgent message and hung up.

He told himself that Luciana was out for the night and he might as well forget her and started to pour another drink. Then he wondered how thorough the surveillance in his apartment really was. God knows what sort of a setup Julius the Genius had on his place. He decided to go back to the retreat but he didn't want to stop drinking. He poured his drink from the cut crystal glass into a plastic cup and, carrying it in his hand, he walked out of the apartment, closing the door after him.

On the street he walked half a block and hailed a cab. Inside he settled back, gave the address of the retreat, and sipped on the Bourbon in the cup.

Brad finished the drink just as the cab stopped in front of the building in which he kept the hideaway apartment. He paid the driver and dropped the empty cup in the gutter. Then he made his way into the vestibule of the building, fumbled for the key in his pocket and let himself inside. He walked up the two flights of stairs to his door and once again turned the key in the lock and stepped into the cozy living room. He went immediately to the phone and called his answering service. No calls.

Already the mental pictures were assaulting him. Andrea lying dead in the Greenwich Village flat, the horrible telephone calls to Gwen informing her that Andrea had died, making funeral arrangements, and the events of today. He still couldn't believe that the melee had really occurred beside the grave. Brad recalled the look of shock on Bill Adams' face as Ed Connor fell sprawling into the grave on top of Gwen. Actually he couldn't help but chuckle now that it was over. He had to admit to a certain sense of satisfaction at the two punches he had given Ed. Andrea's pompous, hypocritical, bullying stepfather certainly had it coming to him. Then the picture, complete with sound, flashed through his mind of Tony Falcon's torturous death. This of course made him start thinking about his own future.

Brad headed for the liquor cabinet and pulled out an unopened bottle of the best hundred-proof Bourbon. Hands trembling, he twisted the cap off the bottle and poured himself a generous shot. He did not even wait to get ice cubes out of the refrigerator before starting to drink the mind-numbing elixir. It was not long before the horror the past few days faded from his memory. After another slug of Bourbon he darted around the room shadow-boxing and chuckling, re-creating the moment when he had scored two sharp hits on Ed Connor and knocked him into the open grave.

He felt in the mood for some music and turned on the radio. Patiently he turned the dials until he found a station he liked and let it play softly. Things weren't so bad now. Tomorrow or the next day or the next he'd sort his life out and resolve his position with Luciana and Ciano's fifth estate once and for all. But meantime—he went to the refrigerator and took out a tray of ice cubes. No point not drinking in a civilized manner.

Brad awakened slowly. What had happened? Where was he? He was lying in bed. He was completely undressed he realized and quite comfortable except for a fierce thirst. He rolled over and saw a glass of water on the bedside table and shakily reached for it. He was in the retreat. He seldom slept here. Small snatches of remembrance began to come through. His hand was finding it difficult to close on the glass of water.

"Need some help, baby?" the warm, throaty voice asked. Brad blinked and shook his head. He turned his head and saw Elda Ciano sitting in the armchair near his bed. He nodded. She stood up, walked around the bed, picked up the glass of water and held it close to him. With her left hand she raised his head and gently poured the water into his mouth. He gulped it eagerly and then sat up under his own power, took the glass in his hands and drank the rest of the water.

"Thanks, Elda," he said at last. "Thanks for everything." He was aware of his nakedness under the sheets. "Did you put me to bed?"

"I couldn't let you sleep fully dressed sprawled all over your sofa. You would have had a neck ache as well as a headache in the position I found you."

"You're a good nurse," he said looking up at her.

"I even made you swallow some Bufferin so you wouldn't have quite such a bad hangover."

"What have you been doing all the time I was passed out?"

"I did some shopping, got us some food and for you a big bottle of mouthwash."

"Hungry I'm not but the other, I guess I need it. What time is it? How long have I been sleeping?"

"It's almost noon. I came over about midnight when you didn't answer your telephone." The affectionate look on her face melted him. "I was worried about you, Brad. It's a good thing I came around."

"You've been here all night?"

Elda nodded. "The sofa in the living room is very comfortable."

"Won't they be worried about you at home? Your father?"

"I called to say I wouldn't be home for a couple of days, staying with a sick friend."

"Do you think you can find a bathrobe in the closet so I can get up and brush my teeth and all the good stuff?"

"Here." Elda reached down, picked a bathrobe up from the foot of the bed and handed it to him. "Go make yourself fresh."

Sitting in bed Brad tucked the robe around him and then swung his feet onto the floor and stood up, swaying slightly. Elda steadied him. "Hey," he said. "What was it you told them at home? A couple of days with your sick friend?"

Elda nodded. "I think it may take a couple of days to get the friend well."

"The friend may never get well if that's what it takes to keep you around." He headed toward the bathroom. "See you later, in much better condition, I hope."

Half an hour later Brad emerged looking fresh and fit. "At least I can breathe near you now," he said walking over to the chair in which Elda was again sitting. He leaned over and kissed her. "I don't know how to thank you for coming when I needed help, so I won't try."

Elda stood up and he held her to him, feeling her firm supple body from thighs to breasts pressed against him.

He kissed her and tried to hold the passion he felt for her in check. It just wasn't appropriate. Elda was only a few years older than Andrea. What would he have thought if his daughter had an affair with a man in his forties. A lot happier than he had been about Tony Falcon he answered himself.

"You seem so stiff, Brad," Elda said.

"I can't help wondering what your father would say if he knew I was physically attracted to you. What would he do if he knew you had undressed me and put me to bed?"

"Is there any reason why he should know?" Elda smiled up at him impudently. "There's no reason for him to know there's anything between us."

"Except that you've been one of the few friends that either Andrea or I have made."

"It's a beautiful fall day outside. Why don't we go for a walk? We could even do something corny like going for a buggy ride in Central Park. Then we could go to a concert or the theatre. The main thing is not to brood. You know?"

Brad nodded seriously and then tried to smile. "You are being very good to stick by me, Elda. It's a lot more than someone who is supposed to be very close to me is doing."

"Come on. Get dressed and we'll go out. OK?"

"Of course. If you'll wait in the other room I'll put on some fresh clothes."

Elda giggled. "After last night I have to go in the next room when you dress?"

Brad chuckled to cover up the desire for her he felt. He wanted to take her and make vigorous love to her. He knew she wanted him too. But he couldn't ignore the voice of conscience within him, so long stilled, telling him it would be wrong. "But last night I was *non compos mentis*," he explained. "Today I am in perfect control of all faculties—I think," he added, his eyes straying over her face, neck and the revealing cashmere sweater she was wearing, the two taut nipples protruding, urgently telling him she was ready for love.

"OK, I'll get ready," Brad said too loudly, making himself stop thinking of her sexually. He opened the closet door, took out a pair of slacks and a sport jacket and laying them on the bed he pulled open a drawer and took out a pair of undershorts which he pulled on.

"It was more fun taking them off," Elda remarked, smiling mischievously. Brad pulled on his shorts, dropped his robe and taking a shirt from the drawer pulled it on. Soon he was completely dressed.

"My, you look smart," Elda said approvingly. "We'll have to go somewhere and be seen."

"Lunch at '21'?" he suggested gaily. Then his face darkened.

"I know what you're thinking, Brad."

He shrugged. "Those of us who are left have to eat," he replied philosophically. "But maybe we will let '21' wait. Anyway, let's get outdoors."

Just walking in the crisp autumn sunlight with no place to go and someone he was very fond of beside him was a pleasure Brad had not experienced for a long time. They found a quiet restaurant on one of the few tree-lined side streets and went inside and sat at a small table in the rear.

"Martini," Brad replied to the waiter's first question.

"What if we split half a bottle of wine?" Elda suggested.

"Good idea. I don't really need a drink with you beside me."

Late in the afternoon they did clop through the park in a horse and carriage and Brad couldn't help but remember that it was almost exactly a year ago that he and Luciana had done the buggy-ride scene through the park. A lifetime, it seemed, had passed by in this one year. Occasionally he thought of the hard-fought Adams-for-Senator campaign. But his heart was no longer in C. L. Ciano's political ambitions.

The concert at Carnegie Hall had been inspirational. He was glad that Elda had suggested the concert rather than the theatre. Afterward they had a light supper at the Russian Tea Room and then took a taxi back to Brad's retreat.

Since waking up that morning Brad had forgotten to check his answering service to find out if Luciana had telephoned; it had not seemed so important. Now, as soon as they stepped into the apartment, Brad picked up the phone and dialed the service.

"I'm sure there were many calls," Brad said to the service operator. "Don't give them to me. Just see if Mrs. Blore called." There was a long pause. In a disappointed tone he said, "Thank you," and put down the phone.

"You're still hung up on her, aren't you, Brad?"

"I don't know. Kind of silly to stay interested in someone who isn't interested in you."

"It's also kind of silly not to realize when someone is very much interested in you." Elda gave him a long look from under half-lowered eyelids.

"Are you trying to tell me something, Elda?" Brad asked gently.

"I just did."

"What would a beautiful young woman with the world out there in front of her see in some old guy like me who's well over the hill."

"You're not over the hill. You are a youthful, glamorous man to me."

It seemed incredible to Brad that a girl like Elda could see him in that light.

Elda looked at him speculatively. "Brad, you have to realize I am a woman and if I find the man I want I go after him. It really hurts me to see you still hung up on Luciana. Do you know where she's been since the funeral?"

Brad shook his head. "I've tried to locate her."

"Well, if she really loved you, even cared for you, she would be here with you now. She wouldn't have left you yesterday when you needed her."

Brad felt almost a physical stab in the stomach. "I guess you're right," he admitted.

Brad went over to his bar and started to make a drink. Elda came up behind him. "Don't you want to feel fresh and rested tomorrow?" she asked.

"I suppose so. But one nightcap won't hurt." He continued fixing a Bourbon and soda. "Tomorrow I'll have to get back on the Adams campaign trail."

"Then make a weak one for me. We'll both have just one together. And stop worrying about Adams. My father says he'll make it easily."

Seated on the sofa in the living room Brad and Elda chatted comfortably together as they sipped their drinks. Then Elda gave him a superior look. "I know all about my father's plan to elect a man he owns as President of the United States."

"Just don't talk about it," Brad cautioned.

"Only to you. I want you to know everything because you picked a very tough, ruthless and totally pragmatic man to work for."

"He picked me. But you're right, Elda." He wondered how she would react to a description of Tony Falcon's death. He took a long swallow of his drink.

"I could help you a lot if we were a couple," Elda suddenly interjected.

Brad looked up surprised. Then he replied, "Yes, but would you be helping yourself?"

"I think so, Brad, or I wouldn't have mentioned it. And do you know how I would help you first?"

"No."

"I'd help you get out of my father's cobweb."

Brad shook his head alarmed. "You know that nobody leaves the fifth estate."

"He can be pompous with his phrases, can't he?" Elda chuckled.

"Maybe so, but don't let's ever suggest in front of anyone me pulling out."

"Of course not."

They sat quietly and Brad wondered what to do next. Elda seemed to care truly for him. For an instant the thought of settling down and marrying her occurred to him. He felt that she wanted this now. But he couldn't allow her to so disrupt her life. C. L. Ciano would never agree, he was sure. What would happen if she openly defied her father? Among other things Ciano would have him hit. The thought flitted through his mind that he and Elda could draw all his money out of the various accounts and start running. They might have a month together, even a year, but nobody could elude the fifth estate permanently. Not that he wouldn't enjoy having Elda completely. He had to actively fight with himself to keep from falling in love with her. But he had obliterated one young woman's life. What sort of an evil soul was he to allow Elda to destroy herself.

Elda, snuggling up to him, made his resolve more difficult. He couldn't resist kissing her upturned lips. Here was the girl he really could be happy with for the rest of his life. She was an innocent, possessed of the full knowledge of the evil around her, a remarkable state.

"Elda," Brad said quietly, "I love you, I want you to know it. I love you too much to hurt you or let you hurt yourself. Do you understand?"

"Sure. But why don't you let me be the judge of what's going to hurt me and what's going to make my life mean something to me?"

How was he going to answer that one? he asked himself. He couldn't. And suddenly he felt debilitated emotionally and physically.

"Elda, would you forgive the old man if he said he's got to drag his bones to bed?"

Elda looked into Brad's face anxiously. "Are you all right?"

"Sure I am. Just exhausted."

"Would you like it if I stayed with you? I don't think you should be alone." She patted the sofa. "As I said, it's very comfortable."

The thought of Elda staying in the apartment with him now that his mind was clear and he could sense her presence gave him a feeling of tranquillity. "You don't know how much I would like that, Elda."

"Good. I'll make us a nice breakfast and we can have another relaxing day. You need it."

"It will be the last one for a while. First, the final days of the campaign and then your father presides over his favorite institution, the Conference of National Leadership. All of us are expected to be on deck for that."

"I know. For the first time he's allowing me to actually see some of his activities. I wonder how he uses the leaders of all walks of life in our country to his own advantage?"

"I guess we'll get a firsthand look. Well," Brad stood up, "tomorrow's another day. Would you like to use the bathroom first?"

"You go ahead. I'm going to sit in here and think for a while. I'll be very quiet and won't wake you up when I go."

Brad bent over and kissed Elda, stroking her cheek and forehead. Then he straightened up. "Good night, dearest girl."

Elda watched him go into the bedroom. She shook her head, smiling to herself. When he was well again she knew that she would find a way to convince him of what was right for both of them in this life.

CHAPTER FORTY-EIGHT

A week after President Nixon won his landslide re-election victory across the nation the Conference of National Leadership assembled in New York City. William Fortune Adams had been an outstanding exception to the general Democratic debacle. Already a member of the CNL, Adams was now being proposed by C. L. Ciano to sit on the steering committee of the Conference. It had become traditional to convene the Conference within a few weeks following national elections for the purpose of discussing results and planning for the future.

It was an august group that met in the Ascot Towers' polished oak-paneled Governor's Club the evening before the opening sessions of the CNL. The Conference had become one of the most fruitful results of Ciano's long-range planning, which had begun in the late fifties, to gain the immense national power he now so anonymously enjoyed.

Ciano had reasoned that if the leaders in the four other estates of American life could be brought together physically once a year, and between these conferences contact regularly maintained with them, Ciano's own ideas and opinions could be subtly, almost subliminally imposed upon them and he could influence the molding of public opinion in America.

In 1961, Bryant Beddington had been a respected

young investment banker with strong social and financial connections. With C. L. Ciano's financial backing he had formed the Conference of National Leadership. Now, in 1972, important leaders in labor, business, government, church, education, communications and the ethnic and racial minorities were represented in the Conference.

As the prestige of the Conference grew it became an honor of considerable proportion to be elected a member. Recommendations of the Conference were considered with great attention by decision makers in all areas of American life. The last three Presidents of the nation were known to have read, undigested by aides, the yearly reports of the Conference.

Although always the power behind the scenes, C. L. Ciano had not had himself made a member of the Conference for the first five years of its existence, but when it had become an established fact of national expression of opinion, he had allowed himself to be elected. Once a member Ciano had moved rapidly upward to first sit on and then chair the Steering Committee which planned the agenda of the yearly Conference and controlled the correspondence that went out to the membership and the national prime movers the members wished to influence.

Twenty-three members of he CNL Steering Committee sat around the large coffin-shaped table at the head of which sat Bryant Beddington. C. L. Ciano occupied the chair next to him. General Alton Mac-Farland, representing the military, sat at the foot of the table resplendent in campaign ribbons and decorations. William Fortune Adams, senator-elect, was also at the table, proposed for election to the self-perpetuating committee by C. L. Ciano and Bryant Beddington. A long-time member, Francis X. Flannerty, sat beside Adams. Brad Kendall sat on the other side of Adams.

Imposing, the nation's most powerful cardinal sat at the end of the table, as though he was chairing the meeting. The cardinal and C. L. Ciano had exceedingly close business ties, Brad knew.

With great satisfaction Ciano looked around the table

of important and influential leaders and then proposed Brad Kendall to membership on the Steering Committee to replace Rafe Leighton. He also gave a short presentation on Adams' qualifications and both men were unanimously accepted.

Brad watched the proceedings, fascinated by the way Ciano played on the minds of these prestigious decision makers and their expressions of opinion as if he were playing the organ. The chairman of one of America's most influential news magazines listened intently as Ciano talked. One of the country's most effective law-enforcement officers turned to the president of the largest news wire service, both of them nodding assent. The chancellor of one of the world's great universities handed a note to George Washington Jefferson, the Negro leader, sitting across the table from him. The union president was also nodding his agreement with Ciano's thesis.

"Although we can look forward to a solid and progressive Administration for the next four years," Ciano was saying, "it is none too soon to start planning for 1976 and trying to shape America to be ready for the type of new leadership that will be required. Our biggest issue by then will be the rise of crime in direct proportion to the rise of unproductive population. All other problems, domestic and foreign, will seem minor in comparison to crime and overpopulation. The nation, the voters are just beginning to realize this and I think it's the job of the Conference this year to concentrate on creating solutions to this problem and then using our combined influence to see that they are put into effect. I see our nation destroying itself from within, financially and spiritually, if Draconian methods are not taken to eliminate casual street crime and the soaring overpopulation in the ghetto areas."

Brad expected to see Jefferson, the Negro leader, take exception to Ciano's statements but the black sat quietly listening.

"Obviously, this is politically an undesirable area in which to make meaningful efforts and I do not expect to see anything but more crime and more racial problems bursting out across the nation. However, it is possible to be optimistic about the success of candidates who pledge themselves wholeheartedly to the extermination of crime and of course narcotics." Ciano paused and gestured at William Fortune Adams. "The election here in New York of Bill Adams to the Senate is a good indication of how the voters in this reputedly liberal state feel about the social disorders, crime and drug abuse which Senator Adams has pledged himself to combat."

The men around the table broke into an impulsive burst of applause. Ciano smiled and continued. "Our President for the next four years, while certainly far and away the best choice we had to lead the nation, is nevertheless, as we all know from personal experience, a partisan politician. The answer to the nation's ills lies in highly unpopular political action. Reports financed by the CLN have concurred with government reports, which were never released, and support the writings of America's foremost criminologists. There is no possible way of curing our problems if we must continue to labor under the restrictions imposed by the constitutional rights given the population of America. Our Constitution is, in effect, obsolete. Did the framers of the Constitution anticipate today's ghettos and drug abuse? Did they visualize the overpopulation of the nation? George Washington said that it would take a thousand years to develop America, yet less than two hundred years after he made that remark we are overdeveloped."

Ciano paused and looked around the table. "We are running out of time, gentlemen. If by 1976 our national leadership is unwilling to adopt the harsh measures that must be undertaken to prevent the destruction of America from within it will be too late. We are approaching the complete breakdown of the country when packs of armed wild men will overrun the cities, suburbs and even rural areas looting, destroying, killing. A national state of guerrilla warfare is on the horizon. We must prevent it."

This was strong fare and the black leader was becoming restive.

"One solution to the drug problem," Ciano went on, "is to legalize heroin. Let it be sold cheaply or given away. This will take the profit out of dope and prevent the shocking monthly rise in muggings and street crime."

The black leader could no longer remain silent "That's genocide, Mr. Ciano."

Ciano smiled bleakly. "That, of course, is the answer of the black community, George. You take the position that the majority of Negroes in America will get hooked if they can get dope. But that makes as much sense as the Prohibitionists who said if liquor was made legal the Irish population of America would drink itself to death."

George Washington Jefferson shifted uneasily in his seat, but before he could come up with an answer Ciano was continuing his dissertation, "George is right, of course. Making heroin legal, while certainly one solution, would be too unpalatable politically for any presidential candidate to advocate. Nevertheless, the biggest problem in the minds of the solid-core American people in 1976 is going to be the enormous and constantly expanding worthless population of America that lives off them through welfare and preys on them through street crime."

Ciano paused and stared at the black leader. "What I say, George, is merely realistic, not some form of racial prejudice. The easiest way to win a national election is to tell people what they think, what they fear, and what they either cannot or are afraid to express themselves. The candidate who expresses their innermost thoughts and fears is the man they're going to vote for. Laying it on the line, in 1976, whoever promises to cure the black problem, at least from the white point of view, will be elected."

Clearly, Brad thought, Ciano was expressing the secret point of view of those at the table. The black leader looked across the table at Ciano thoughtfully. "You speak in a frightening way, Mr. Ciano."

"If what is real and true is frightening, you are right." He turned to the chancellor of the large university. "Chancellor, you have had several murders, shootings and stabbings on or near your campus. In every case they were the result of unreasoned black hatred or blacks' need of drugs. One of your professors was shot by a black student. What solutions do you see that this conference can recommend?"

The chancellor looked stricken and cleared his throat. Finally he managed an answer.

"That is a problem, sir, for which America's greatest conglomeration of thinkers has been unable to even approach a solution. Somehow we must help the underprivileged to help themselves and turn their thoughts from violence."

Ciano allowed a ten-second silence to follow the chancellor's statement. Then he said in quiet tones, "I am convinced that this conference must bring about the election of a man to the presidency in 1976 who is willing to suspend such constitutional rights as are necessary and without fear of political consequences take whatever drastic measures he and his advisers see fit to save this country. To curb drug abuse we can only turn to Mao for inspiration. No longer should a search warrant be required. Anyone apprehended selling drugs or illegally carrying a weapon will be permanently separated from society. We must institute separation societies into which every person guilty of an anti-social act will be sent to exist. They have their choice of making the desert or wilderness in which they are settled bloom, or they can die. Only in this way can we protect our society, our strong, free multiracial, multiethnic society from its own excrement."

Brad had heard Ciano's proposals several times before and now the words did not have the impact they once had on him. He was more interested in the reaction of the men around the table to Ciano's speech. They seemed as hypnotized by the ultraistic concepts Ciano so eloquently presented as he himself had been when first exposed to them. As Ciano continued it was obvious that the Steering Committee including the black leader was sympathetic to his advocacy. But Brad knew what Ciano's basic aim was. To use money and fear, the tools that had served him so expediently all his life, to take over control of the United States.

Brad tried to keep an alert expressiveness about him as Ciano went on with his comments, but the words no longer reached him. He had set a quiet dinner date with Luciana after the Steering Committee meeting and he was thinking of little else. Brad realized that he had come to the end of the line with Ascot and Whitehall and it was just a matter of time and circumstance before he made his escape attempt. He was under no illusion that he could just take his leave and say good-by to Ciano. He felt he could elude pursuit, and he thought of how for the past two weeks he had been converting all his assets into cash, which he had placed in a safe-deposit box. There were places in the Middle East, Latin America and Malaysia where he could buy control of a small hotel and with a changed identity operate it. It was the immediate escape that needed extensive planning. The question was, would Luciana go with him?

Finally, after hours it seemed, the Steering Committee adjourned to the following day, having resolved to put Ciano's ideas before the entire Conference for discussion. Unanimously, the members of the committee resolved to gain the support of the entire Conference behind a concrete proposal embodying the Ciano plan. As the members stood up, Brad unobtrusively detached himself from the group and sidled out the door before Ciano, engaged in earnest conversation with the black leader, could catch his eye and summon him.

Out on the mezzanine of the hotel Brad walked along the corridor, beyond the various function rooms to the public relations department where Luciana had a comfortable, femininely decorated office. Brad found her seated on the sofa, looking through photographs spread out on the coffee table in front of her.

"I thought C.L. would never stop talking and let us out," Brad greeted her. "Shall we get out of the Ascot influence and find us a nice little restaurant?"

He glanced at his watch. "It's nine o'clock and I'm hungry as a bear in March."

"Better tempered, I hope?" Luciana quipped back.

"With you? I'm almost always good tempered."

Luciana stood up. "OK, let's find that secluded little restaurant and eat." Brad took her arm, feeling the old desire and infatuation coming back stronger than ever. He kissed her but there was no response and he led her from the office.

The East Side Italian restaurant they sat down in was one he had been patronizing over the past few months. He was always given the rear booth where he could talk freely, with no other patrons able to overhear his conversations. He and Luciana ordered cocktails and leisurely glanced over the menu.

"I don't seem to see you much," Brad said tentatively.

"Well, you know how busy we all are."

"I had hoped to see more of you after Andrea's funeral," he pursued. "This is the first time we've had a chance to talk since then."

"I know, and I'm sorry, Brad."

"Are you really so busy? Or is it something else?"

"It's work, Brad." Luciana sighed. "There just never seems to be a break."

"You've got to make your own breaks." He swallowed the last of his drink and plunged on. "I'm making the big break soon. I want you to come with me."

Luciana looked up at him in surprise, her eyes widening. "I don't think I understand you, Brad. What are you saying?"

"I'm leaving Ascot, Whitehall, the fifth estate, that's what I'm saying."

"Have you told C.L. yet?"

"Of course not. Now look, I've got a good cash stake. We can buy a lovely little hotel in South America or someplace and run it together. We could have a happy, peaceful life. No more of this involvement with the crime lords of the world."

"You're crazy."

"I was. I'm not now."

"You'll never get away with it, Brad. Do you think

I want to be on the run the rest of my life? I'm happy at Whitehall, don't you understand?"

"Don't you understand? We're criminals. We're responsible for overdose deaths like Andrea's among many other criminal acts. My God, have you come across Dr. Wormsinger?"

"What a funny name." Luciana laughed.

"Let's stop before it's too late."

"In the first place, it *is* too late."

"Luciana, I try not to love you because you are too involved to love. But if you quit, came away with me, it could be the way it was with us in the beginning. We're basically right for each other."

"In the second place, I don't love you and we're not right for each other. I like what I'm doing. Now, Brad," Luciana reached across the table and put her hand on his arm, staring at him searchingly, almost pityingly, "you've had a miserable thing happen to you. I'm sorry, we're all terribly, terribly sorry about Andrea, but you mustn't let that tragedy derange you."

"I'm not deranged. I may be thinking straight for the first time since I listened to Ciano's mesmerizing grand plan more than a year ago."

Brad stared at her intently. "He can sell any idea to anyone. I don't know how I fell for it. Sure, you can say I was perfectly happy to get the big money, have my jet, be a political kingmaker, start my own airline to smuggle narcotics and generally be a big man around the world and act as Ciano's WASP flunky. You can say that it took the death of my daughter to make me face up to my own weaknesses. Well, I am absolutely alone in the world now and yes, it did take Andrea's death, and the realization that I personally share in the responsibility for her and the many other deaths and destroyed lives that have and will occur as a result of the new narcotics routes I helped set up from Asia to this country. And the worst thing is that if I confronted Ciano with all this he would convince me that everything I was doing was in a good cause and in the long run save the nation. And he'd have me back on his team again. You can't argue with him, you can't dispute him, he has all the answers, all you can do is follow his orders. And you do this in the firm conviction that he is right, he is the genius who will make the country and the world right again." Brad shook his head. "No, I'm through. I watched him sway the thinking of some of our country's leading opinion makers. I personally think he's the one who's deranged, the way Hitler was. And I'm frankly afraid of him, afraid for the country, for the world. And I'm afraid to ever see him again because I know he'd convince me I'm all wrong and have me back under his influence again."

Luciana tightened her grip on his arm. "Brad, listen to me, please. I know you're lonely and upset but you're not being rational. You're part of the family. You must know that Elda Ciano is in love with you. I happen to know that C.L. would not be unhappy if Elda married you." She chuckled. "You take Elda, I'll take C.L., and we'll be one big happy, monumentally rich family. We'll make Charles Blore look impoverished."

Brad felt shock tremors in the stomach. So his vague suspicions about Luciana and Ciano were correct. He had her completely in his power as a snake hypnotizes a bird. He felt compelled to make one last effort to bring Luciana back to him, futile though he knew it would be.

"Luciana, Elda and I aren't right for each other. She is too young to hook up with a man almost as old as her father. Whatever I might think of C.L., he certainly did everything to bring Elda up to be a lovely and good young lady. You and I are right for each other. And don't be taken in by the money Ciano spreads all over the place. He's going to destroy himself and everyone around him one day. Come on away with me, while there's time."

Luciana's voice was hard, her eyes narrowed. "Time's run out for you, Brad, if you do what you're talking about. I don't want to be around you." She suddenly stood up. "I've lost my appetite. Good-by, Brad."

Brad stood up also. "I wish you wouldn't leave like this. I'd like us to keep talking."

"We simply have nothing to talk about. Nothing."

As she turned to leave, Brad called after her, "I'll be here awhile. Call me or come back. Please think about it."

He watched Luciana walk out of the restaurant and discovered that he was still hungry. He felt as if some gigantic force that had been enslaving him had suddenly weakened and loosed its hold on him. He sat down, ordered an Old Fitz manhattan and planned his supper from the menu.

CHAPTER FORTY-NINE

Elda Ciano seldom stayed at the New York town house if she could help it. But tonight, the opening of the Conference of National Leadership, her father had asked her to stay in the city and help him host an informal supper for the most important members of the Conference.

As the party progressed Ciano couldn't help noticing the way Elda kept herself close to the head of the stairs and her anxious glances as new people arrived. Finally he drifted to his daughter's side. "Brad will be here later, I think. So will Luciana. She told me he was anxious to have dinner with her alone and discuss some personal matters that couldn't wait. After what he's been through I excused them, of course."

"I wonder what problems they are," Elda mused.

"I suppose the biggest one is that he still has some strong feelings for her, fancies himself in love with her." He shook his head. "Luciana is in love with her present life style and nothing more."

"Poor Brad," Elda said sympathetically.

"He'll get over it and soon be working harder than ever," Ciano replied confidently. "During the Conference I'll have a private meeting with Brad. He'll quickly be back to his old self and, better, he'll be cured of his romantic interest in Luciana."

"I hope so." Elda's tone reflected doubt. Without

joy she went back to being a good hostess to the arriving notables and tried to keep from thinking about Brad and Luciana but jealousy uncontrollably pervaded her thoughts.

Then Luciana arrived alone. Elda saw her come up the stairs and wondered where Brad was. Luciana seemed agitated, Elda noticed, as the beautiful woman brushed past her with a nod, looked around the room impatiently and headed for C. L. Ciano. She waited for him to finish the conversation in which he was engaged and then she and Ciano left the main salon, for Ciano's private den, Elda surmised.

She tried to put what she had seen and knew into perspective. What was going on? Luciana and Brad were to have had supper together and now Luciana, obviously distraught, was here needing urgently to see her father. Somehow, she sensed, Brad was involved. She wished she could hear what was being said but she knew that eavesdropping on her father when he was in the den was futile. He had gone to great lengths to make it secure. Still instinctively she felt that whatever was being discussed boded no good for Brad. If anything the effect of whatever information Luciana was passing on to her father would bring about results detrimental to Brad.

Suddenly an idea raced through her mind. She left the reception and hurried up the stairs to the next floor on which her father's bedroom was located. She entered the room, closing the door after her and sat on the edge of the bed. There was a telephone on the cabinet beside the bed. She reached down and pulled the cabinet door open. Here was another instrument, red, with a small light on its base. This was her father's special, secure telephone with two extensions, one in the bedroom and one in the den.

Elda gingerly lifted the telephone out of the cabinet and placed it on her lap, staring at the light bulb. If it went on her father would be making a call out. She waited and watched the bulb until she felt herself going into a sort of trance. She blinked her eyes, shook her head and took a deep breath as the vigil continued. Suddenly she started. The light glowed in a blinking orange. Her father was dialing a number. Then the bulb glowed constantly. The number was ringing. Carefully, holding her breath, she lifted the telephone off the cradle and placed her hand tightly across the mouth piece, putting the instrument to her ear. She could hear deep breathing on the other end and then Luciana's voice in the den below asking, "Are you sure this is the only way?"

There was no reply. Then the deep, coarse, slightly accented voice she recognized as Maurice D'Estang's answered. No names were exchanged. Ciano merely said, "It's as we feared. Kendall was unable to be one of us. He's come apart. He has left us. He was last seen at Mama Louise's on East Fifty-third. He may still be there. At this point we cannot have him walking around talking about us."

There was a short pause. "I understand. The problem will be taken care of immediately."

"Good. Call me back when you have been successful." There was an abrupt, sharp click. Elda hung up the phone and placed it back in the cabinet closing the door. Stealthily she left her father's room and walked across the hall to her own bedroom.

Elda reached for her private telephone and dialed information. Moments later Mama Louise restaurant answered. She asked for Brad Kendall and breathed a sigh of relief when she was informed he was there. Then she heard his voice cheerfully say, "You did change your mind, darling."

She swallowed hard. "Brad, this is Elda. Get out of there this instant. Don't go back to your table even. Just start walking downtown on the east side of Second Avenue. I'll pick you up soon."

"Elda, what's this all about?" Brad asked.

"Darling," she bit out the word sarcastically, "has just fingered you, to use the vernacular. You know what happens to bad boys in Italian restaurants?" Elda heard the sharp intake of breath on the other end of the line.

"You're lucky I still love you or the *Daily News* would have another mob shooting decorating its front pages. Now, out! I'll pick you up as quick as I can."

"But Elda—"

She hung up and began to think out the next step. At least she had sent him away from the first place they would look for him. She glanced around the room. What would she take with her? Fortunately, it was a mild November so far. She didn't dare try to get her fur coat out of the house. That would have given everything away. She went to her dresser, opened her top bureau drawer, dumped all the jewelry in her jewelry box into her pocketbook, and decided to let it go at that. There were at least fifty thousand dollars' worth of hockable gems, she figured. She'd buy whatever else she needed. Now to dissolve from the party.

She pulled herself to her full height and with her bag carelessly under her arm, albeit unusually fat for a young lady entertaining in her own home, she sauntered down the stairs and was quickly caught up in the swirl of CNL members and their wives talking excitedly to one another. She moved through the small groups of guests toward the staircase to the grand floor, keeping her eye to the rear of the large room beyond which was the den from which her father and Luciana should emerge at any moment. Sure enough, her father, smiling as if nothing had happened, entered the salon, Luciana beside him. She at least had some vestige of a troubled look on her face. However, her forced smile, as Ciano introduced her to a cruising notable, chased the concern from her visage. Elda caught her father's eye across the room and gaily waved to him. He smiled and waved back, satisfied that she was working the guests for him with her usual flair. Ciano continued his own lobbying, Luciana brilliantly complementing his compelling presence.

Good-by, you two, Elda thought to herself as she slipped down the stairs. At the bottom she walked back into the kitchen where a chef and a female assistant were working. "Everything is beautiful, Karl," she said as the chef looked up. With that she went out the kitchen door into the delivery pantry and from there into the two-car garage where her Aston-Martin was parked. Inside her car she took the electronic cartridge that opened the garage doors from the dashboard compartment and pressed it. The doors rumbled open and she started the car and scooted out even before the doors reached full up.

Elda turned east, drove toward Second Avenue and reaching it she turned south, hugging the east side of the street. She was in the sixties and by now Brad should be walking south somewhere in the forties. The traffic was medium and moving well downtown. She reached the fifties, wondering what she and Brad would do once she picked him up. This was the sort of operation you just had to take carefully one step at a time. She hit Forty-ninth Street and kept an alert watch along the sidewalk. Down the forties she searched in vain for him and then she was in the thirties. Had he failed to take her advice? Was he at this moment lying in a pool of blood on the floor of Mama Louise? And then, between Thirty-fifth and Thirty-fourth she saw him striding along.

She drew the sports car up alongside of him and leaned her head out the window. "Can I give you a lift, sir?" Brad turned his head, saw her and quickly ducked around the back of the car, pulled the passenger seat open and jumped in.

"My lord, you walk fast," Elda greeted him, "nineteen blocks, practically a mile, in fifteen minutes."

Brad leaned over and kissed her cheek. "Somehow your telephone call made me want very much to live." He pulled the door shut. "So Luciana is truly one of them."

"What do we do now, Brad?"

"Run, I guess. But where?"

"Let's go to the retreat first. We can decide what to do from there."

"It should be safe. Luciana doesn't know about it."

"We could get some sleep, make some telephone calls and when we're ready move out smartly," Elda said turning west off Second. In ten minutes she had parked her car on the sidewalk in front of the walk-up apartment building. Brad pushed his door open, stepped out onto the sidewalk, walked around to the street and helped Elda get out of the traffic-side door. Brad escorted Elda around her sports car and across the sidewalk to the front door of the building.

"Shall we use your key or mine?" Elda asked, smiling now that they were approaching comparative safety.

Brad pulled his key out and opened the door. Holding her hand and going ahead, Brad let Elda up first one, then the second flight of stairs and started down the short hallway. Suddenly he came to a halt, his nerves tautening. Elda looked at him and opened her mouth to say something. Instantly Brad put his hand over her lips. He stood there, sniffing. Then, letting go of Elda, cautioning her with a hand signal, he tiptoed down the hall to the door to his apartment. Again he sniffed, nostrils twitching. It was unmistakable, the acrid, almost sour smell of French tobacco, the kind Maurice D'Estang smoked. How often had Brad had to restrain himself from asking Maurice not to smoke his noxious cigarettes indoors.

Brad turned and silently trod his way back to Elda, pointing down the steps which they descended. In the vestibule he whispered to her.

"They're onto this place. D'Estang is waiting inside." He whispered some instructions into her ear and then she nonchalantly walked out of the apartment, crossed the sidewalk and entered her car, slamming the door and starting the engine. Abruptly she threw the passenger door open and started ahead.

Brad suddenly burst from the apartment door, dashed after the moving sports car and rolled into it as three wild shots came from the darkness behind them. He pulled the door shut and Elda gunned the car forward. They looked at each other a moment but said nothing. Elda concentrated on driving through the streets as Brad looked out the rear. Elda sped through a red light just as Brad spotted the car that had been parked behind them starting after them. "They must have waited for Maurice D'Estang to run down the stairs," he conjectured.

"Get off this street, take your next left or right," he called out. Elda skillfully cornered right with the traffic and wove her way in and out of the cars.

"Why are all these people driving around the city at night?" she asked in frustration.

"That's New York," Brad answered. "And here come those bastards. They've got a much bigger car fortunately. We should be happy about the traffic. You're doing great."

As Elda twisted through the traffic, cornering wherever she could, she asked, "Where do you want to go eventually?"

"I don't know. Let's shake D'Estang first, then we'll figure a plan."

"I'm doing my best." Again she wheeled around a corner, leaving angry, horn-honking motorists behind her. "Do you want me to head for a police station?"

"I don't think so. They'll come in too and if nothing else figure a way to separate us. We just have to lose them and try not to get arrested for speeding, running lights or reckless driving." Elda twisted through the traffic in the streets but was unable to lose the big sedan that stayed unrelentingly behind them. "Try to stay in the traffic, they won't try anything in the middle of so many people," Brad advised.

Elda made a turn onto Sixth Avenue and started uptown. They passed Radio City Music Hall, the traffic moving along well. Elda stayed as far over to the right as she could so that the pursuing car could only overtake her on one side. She wanted to make a right turn but at Fiftieth Street, Fifty-second Street and again on Fifty-fourth Street the traffic was so heavy she didn't dare turn and get stuck. Then just beyond a badly clogged Fifty-sixth Street all traffic came to a dead stop. The heavy traffic proceeding in both directions on Fifty-seventh Street completely jammed up the flow of the cars and the frustrated motorists sat, hands on horns, vainly trying to blow the congestion away with their honking. Brad made sure that both doors of the little sports car were securely locked.

Then, out of the traffic, his right hand in a paper bag, walked Maurice D'Estang. He approached the driver's side of the car and raised the bag menacingly. "He's got a gun," Brad said hoarsely. "Nothing we can do. You did your best, Elda."

D'Estang reached out and tried to pull the door open. Realizing it was locked he placed the concealed gun close to the window and bent down to look inside.

"I love you, Elda," Brad said. "I'm so sorry I got you in this mess."

"I love you too, Brad. I'd never forgive myself if you were alone when my father's hired killers found you."

D'Estang's face leered into the car and then suddenly he recognized Elda and recoiled. His lips said, "What are you doing here?" There was no mistaking the shock and confusion the sight of Elda instilled in him. For a moment he lowered the hand in the brown bag and studied the situation. Then the traffic began to inch ahead and Elda gunned the engine slightly. D'Estang stared coldly at Brad, measuring his chances of getting a shot at him without hitting Elda. He raised the concealed gun and aimed through the window. Elda threw herself forward putting her head between the pistol and Brad. D'Estang shifted position and trained the gun on Brad from behind Elda. She leaned back, once again blocking the shot. Angrily he turned from Elda's window and started toward the rear of the car.

"He's going to come around to my side," Brad said. "Maybe I can get out and run."

"Don't move!" Elda commanded as she turned in her seat and watched out the back window as the form of D'Estang reached the rear of the car and started around.

She waited another moment and then jammed the stick shift into reverse and stepped on the gas. The car shot back smashing D'Estang's legs against the bumper of the car behind. Even with the windows closed and the high noise level outside D'Estang's screams of anguish could be heard. His crushed legs were now pinned between the two bumpers and his upper body was hunched over the rear of the Aston-Martin, blocking out the view through the rear window. Ahead the traffic was moving, and Elda shoved the gear shift into forward and the car jumped forward, dropping a crippled D'Estang sliding to the street. Through a break in the traffic Elda streaked across Fifty-seventh Street and into the clear beyond. Wordlessly she drove on to Fifty-ninth Street, crossed it and plunged into the Central Park drive.

Brad took a deep breath as Elda, free of the traffic behind them, sped through the west side of the park. "My God, what a woman," he managed.

"Now we are going to need some help, some professional help," Elda said quietly. "Is there anyone you can trust?"

Brad thought a moment and then reached for his wallet. "Only one man I know of can help us. Pat Kenney."

"He's your friend? You can trust him?"

Opening his wallet Brad took out the card with Kenney's name and address on it. "I can trust him. I hope he's my friend. Let's find a place where we can make some phone calls and I'll try to locate him."

"I'll head across the park and come out on the East Side. We'll find a bar where you can call and I think we could both use a drink."

"Amen."

"Hold on," Elda warned gaily. "I'm going to make sure no one follows us."

CHAPTER FIFTY

"Are you sure you weren't followed?" Pat Kenney asked Brad over the telephone.

"Elda did some fancy driving. I think we would have spotted a tail," Brad replied.

"Maybe. Anyway, I'll be right over. You picked the right place, a crowded singles bar." Kenney chuckled. "You're goddamn lucky I scored early tonight or I wouldn't be home. I'm going to have a mad little chick on my hands when she hears that I'm leaving her in five minutes."

"We'll be waiting anxiously, Pat." Brad hung up. He turned from the phone and his heart threatened to leap into his mouth. A dark man in a blue pin-stripe suit wearing a yellow tie was coming up behind Elda. Brad saw him place a hand on her shoulder.

As Brad shoved his way through the crowd to her, Elda, a startled look of fear on her face, turned sharply. Singles trying to become couples blocked his way as he made for her.

Surely they wouldn't shoot in a crowded bar, he thought. Somehow he would manage to get himself and Elda out of here. Just as he reached Elda's side he heard her warm, contralto laugh.

"Sorry, Don," she was saying, "here's my boy friend now."

The interloper looked Brad up and down and then

his eyes went back to Elda. He was obviously wondering what such a beautiful young bird was doing with a character so much older than herself. Brad placed a possessive arm around Elda, and Don moved off.

"Pat's on his way over. Ready for that drink?"

Elda leaned against him, drawing security from their closeness. "Good idea."

Brad ordered drinks and paid for them and he and Elda, free arms entwined, sipped their drinks, nestled together. "So this is what a dating bar is like," she said. "Never seen one before."

"You never needed one."

"I don't any more. From this moment on I'll never be single again." Their arms tightened on each other.

Brad put his drink down on the bar, pulled a pretzel from the bowl and reduced it to one ring. "Put your drink down a moment and give me your left hand," he said.

Elda complied and held her hand out. Brad took the pretzel ring and slid it over the third finger. "With this ring I thee wed, to have and to hold, for richer or poorer, in sickness and health, until C.L. doth us part."

Elda shivered. Brad kissed her. "Don't worry. We'll keep away from him. It just seemed the appropriate phrase in our little ceremony. It's something we can never afford to forget."

Elda put her lips to Brad's ear as the throng jostled against them. "I, Elda, take thee, Brad, for my lawful wedded husband from this day forward and will let nothing part us."

They kissed again, a long one. Uncoupled singles glanced at them enviously and redoubled their efforts to find a mate for the rest of the night.

"And that is probably the only ceremony we'll have for a long time," Brad whispered as their lips came apart and they reached for their drinks.

They had just ordered a second drink when Pat Kenney lumbered into the bar. Singles bounced off him as he strode toward Brad and Elda. Brad looked up. "Boy, are we glad to see you."

"So you finally did it!" the detective exclaimed. "Congratulations." The cynical expression on his ruddy, wide face softened as he turned to Elda. "This has got to be the toughest thing you ever made up your mind to do."

Elda shook her head. "It all happened so naturally I didn't have to come to any decision, I just did what I needed to do."

"Tell me a little more of what happened while I get a drink down," Kenney said.

While he ordered and consumed a rye and ginger ale Elda and Brad told Kenney everything that had happened. When they came to Elda's maiming of D'Estang the chunky detective laughed into his drink, blowing it up around his eyes. "I hope that son of a bitch never walks again," he declared.

"Shall we go somewhere and decide what to do?" Brad suggested.

Kenney worked his drink thoughtfully. Then, "I think we're better off right here. D'Estang's pals will be combing the city looking for you two. Even if D'Estang didn't want the cops in, leaving the scene of an accident is a serious offense." Kenney looked around the crowded, rowdy bar. "We'll get more privacy here than anyplace else."

"I agree, Pat. Here's the way I see the situation. Some way or other Elda and I have to get out of New York, out of the country." He turned to Elda. "Do you have a passport?"

"It's at home. I'm sorry, Brad."

"Don't worry, darling. As a matter of fact, we'd probably be better off not using our own passports. Anyway, we'll figure that one out later. Let's talk long-range strategy. Pat, do you want to do something about destroying this fifth estate as Ciano calls his power structure?"

Pat's grin bordered on insolence. "Didn't I tell you, when you were riding high down there in Miami, that someday you'd need me? That someday you'd work my side of the street?" Brad nodded. "Of course, I'm ready to crack Ciano and his thing wide open. But, Jesus, we're going to need help."

"We'll get it somehow. We've got the person who knows him best in the world with us." He tightened his arm around Elda's shoulder. She nodded silently. "Here's what we do. Elda and I will drive out to Connecticut. I know a little place in Southport, the Pequot Inn. We'll check in there under the name of," he paused, "O'Brien. Mr. and Mrs. John O'Brien." Brad reached into his pocket and pulled out a key chain. He selected one key. "Here's the key to my safe-deposit box. You take it and clean it out. There's over a hundred thousand dollars in cash I've managed to put by. I'll call the bank manager to expect you. He's a close personal friend."

"While you're at it," Elda added, "would you mind hocking my jewelry, Pat?"

"Glad to do it, Elda, You have it with you?"

Elda patted her purse. "You ought to be able to get fifty thousand dollars for all this."

"I'll do the best I can," Kenney promised.

"You'll meet us at the Pequot Inn tomorrow after you've got the money. That's off Exit 19 on the New England thruway. Out there we'll figure what to do next. My thinking is that you should try to make contact with the Attorney General. I doubt that Ciano reaches that high yet, and set up an appointment for Elda, myself and you."

"I don't know the Attorney General."

"I'm sure he's heard of you. By tomorrow I'll give you a list of names of the highest government officials I know personally, and know to be untouched." Brad smiled and clapped Kenney on the shoulder. "You're just going to have to learn to walk and talk with high-level people."

"I'll do what I can, Brad."

"We'll talk about it some more tomorrow. Elda and I are going to have to find a safe place to live, a place we can operate out of, and then we'll be ready to start an aggressive offensive against the fifth estate. It's got to be done in the next year. By '74 Ciano will have won another set of elections and we'll never know who has been subverted. It's now or never."

"That's right," Kenney asserted.

"But how to get out of town now is the question." Brad looked apprehensively toward the door. "The cops will probably have a description of Elda's car and be out looking for it. I feel sure that D'Estang would not tell them about Elda and me. He'll have to say it was a simple hit and run."

"OK, here's what you do," Kenney offered. "My car is parked out in front. You take it and drive out to Connecticut. I'll take Elda's car to a garage I know not far from here and have them store it. Then tomorrow I'll rent a car and drive out to you and pick up my own car. You turn the rental car in somewhere when you're ready."

"Good plan," Brad approved.

Kenney handed him the keys to his car. "Now, let me have Elda's keys." Elda gave them to him. "OK, let's not waste any more time. I want to get that sports car hidden right now. Anything in it you need?"

Elda shook her head. "We'll start in with all new things."

Brad took her arm. "We're on our way. Don't forget to be at the bank at nine in the morning. I'll be on the phone to the manager."

"I'll be there."

Brad and Elda pushed their way out of the teeming bar behind Pat Kenney and followed him up First Avenue to his car a block away. "Elda is parked right around the corner," Brad said. "It's the Aston-Martin."

"I'll find it and have it off the street in fifteen minutes. Take care."

Brad helped Elda into Kenney's tired Ford and walked around and climbed into the driver's seat. The traffic was still heavy but they were soon on the East Side Highway heading north and finally when Brad had flipped fifty cents into the toll machine and they were driving along the approaches to the New England thruway he began to relax. He reached out and took Elda's hand in his.

"We're driving into a whole new world, dearest," he said.

"I'm ready for it." She laughed happily. "I never thought I'd start my honeymoon out at the Pequot Inn in Connecticut."

"We don't have to actually consummate our little ceremony until you are sure you're ready."

"Brad!" she exclaimed, shocked. "What are you saying? Do you have any idea how long I've been ready? I wish the inn was closer so we could start consummating sooner."

Brad laughed, the last of the tension draining from him. He squeezed her hand. "I'm ready too, darling. And tomorrow let come what may. I love you."

"I love you too, Brad. I've never been happier." She leaned her head on his shoulder, watching the exit signs flash past them.

CHAPTER FIFTY-ONE

C. L. Ciano stood at the foot of the hospital bed. He looked down at the pale haggard face of his chief lieutenant. "They're only giving me three minutes," Ciano said, "so we'll make it fast. Are you sure that my daughter was acting strictly under her own volition?"

"Yeah," D'Estang replied weakly.

"Kendall in no way seemed to be influencing her?"

"Naw, C.L.," D'Estang croaked. "I tried to get the gun on him but she kept putting herself in my line of fire." The effort of getting the sentence out seemed to exhaust him.

"She backed down on you herself?" C.L. probed. "Kendall didn't grab the gear shift and step on the gas?"

D'Estang gathered his strength for another answer. Finally, "I saw it coming when she looked back at me. I saw it in her face. But—too late, nothing I could do. She's like you, C.L. But Kendall? Naw. His shit is weak."

"I'm sorry, Maurice. I'll see that this is made up to you."

"In the wheel chair?" D'Estang asked hoarsely, a hopeless look in his eyes.

"We'll get you the best doctors, the best care there

496

is. You'll be up and about and you'll be in charge of finding them. I want them alive, both of them. I want to take care of Kendall personally." Ciano's dark eyes glittered. "It's been many years since I've done the job myself but this time . . ." his voice trailed off.

"Right, C.L." Then D'Estang seemed to lapse back into a coma. Ciano stared down at him a moment, turned on his heel and left the hospital room.

Luciana was waiting for Ciano in his office at the Spire Building when he returned from seeing D'Estang. He paced about the office, looking from the city outside, resplendent in the clear November morning sunlight, to Luciana. "I should have known better than to trust him. He was a straight businessman too long to be converted. I thought because of Beddington I could trust a WASP."

"Bryant Beddington like so many Wall Street operators was born with a criminal mind," Luciana analyzed. "And you got him at an impressionable age. Brad was different. His business career was devoted to building up something, not manipulating pure money."

"He and Elda can't hide from me. It's been," he looked at his watch, "twelve hours since Maurice almost caught them. I won't permit them twenty-four hours. The entire fifth estate is looking for them. They can't get away."

The buzzer on the intercom sounded. "Yes," Ciano said in the direction of the speaker.

"Mr. Beddington is here with Mr. Loring Gardiner," the neutral voice announced.

"Send them in," Ciano commanded. "Another WASP, this Gardiner," he muttered to Luciana. "But you have to have a certain type to front an organization like Ascot."

Beddington walked in with Loring Gardiner, the epitome of the upper-class, well-connected businessman. Luciana gave him an appraising look. He was young, in his late thirties, with attractive prematurely graying hair. He was tall and the double-vent gray suit, the softly striped shirt and conservative tie gave him the look of a suave actor cast as the young president of an important corporation.

Ciano shook hands with Gardiner and introduced him to Luciana. He wasted no time in coming to the point. "Bryant has been talking to me for some time about you joining our organization here. Actually I had a specific situation in mind for you, but just today the office of the presidency of Ascot Hotels has become open."

Ciano paused to see what effect the announcement would have on Gardiner. Beddington spoke up. "Loring is the type of executive who could take on the presidency of any corporation, C.L." He turned to his companion. "You have some background in hotels, don't you, Loring?"

"Certainly. I've been in real estate for the past ten years. A company I founded bought and operated several hotels for a few years before selling out at an unconscionable profit." His forehead wrinkled slightly, a philosophical expression came to his face. "But that's what it's all about. Yes, I know hotels."

"We've done some research on you, Gardiner," Ciano said. "I assume you've done the same."

"I have, Mr. Ciano," Gardiner said forthrightly.

"Any questions in your mind about us?"

"I wouldn't be here if I had any qualms about allying myself with Whitehall. I am an expansionist, the history of Whitehall, or such history as is available," he allowed himself a tight smile, "indicates that Whitehall has expanded faster than any corporate structure in America. I am aware that your methods are unorthodox but that is the only way to build fast."

Ciano looked over at Luciana, a satisfied smile on his face. Then to Gardiner he said, "We do try to give our people all the tools they need. You will have our jets to help with transportation and, if you will direct your attention over here," Ciano walked over to the map of the world and pointed at the myriad-colored pins adorning all the continents, "I can give you some ideas on our international expansion programs."

About an hour later Luciana watched the door close on Loring Gardiner's back. "C.L., did you know that you may be the world's most powerful hypnotist?"

A pleased smile came over Ciano's face. "Yes, I think Mr. Gardiner will make a fine and, in the long run, far more reliable president of Ascot than did Brad Kendall. And once Gardiner is completely indoctrinated and insured he should be a valuable asset to us on the political front."

"Pity he's married," Luciana pouted.

"On the contrary. Had Brad been married and bringing up children he would not have left us. And I'm sure that Loring Gardiner and you will form a fine business and personal relationship which will benefit Ascot and Whitehall."

"That won't be too unpleasant an assignment, C.L."

"I thought not." He paused as though in thought. "Replacing Maurice D'Estang will be somewhat more difficult. He'll be able to direct operations, I suppose, but the doctors told me he'll never walk again. I wonder how his brother would work out?" Ciano mused.

Luciana shook her head. "No class, C.L. He really is a Corsican pirate."

"Yes, I suppose that's right." Ciano's face hardened. "Kendall has damaged us. And Elda," his shoulders sagged. "I don't understand. I was always a good and understanding father. We communicated, we knew each other, we loved each other."

"Perhaps when you find her and Brad you can re-indoctrinate her, C.L. I think I can help. Surely her infatuation with him will wear away when they find themselves always on the run, always afraid of people, never able to relax. Just you wait and see. One day she'll call you and ask to come home, that is unless you find them first."

"We'll find them. We can't afford not to find them. They can hurt us more than any two people alive." Morosely he stared out at the city. "They're out there, somewhere, Luciana." After a few moments he pulled his gaze away from the window, wandered back to his desk and pressed a button.

The wall panel slid away and Ciano walked into the music room. He sat down at the electric organ, switched it on and poised his hands over the keys, his feet positioning themselves over the foot bars. Then he brought his hands down in a crescendo opening of the final movement of Beethoven's Choral Symphony, Song of Joy.

ABOUT THE AUTHOR

ROBIN MOORE was born in Boston and graduated from Harvard in 1949. He was a European correspondent for the Boston GLOBE in 1947 and worked as a television producer in New York City from 1949 to 1952 and, in 1956, developed a closed circuit TV network for the Sheraton Hotel chain. Mr. Moore is best known for his adventure novels, *The Green Berets* and *The French Connection*, which were both made into extremely popular motion pictures, and for his most recent book, *The Fifth Estate*.

RELAX!
SIT DOWN
and Catch Up On Your Reading!

We Deliver!
And So Do These Bestsellers.

FREE!
Bantam Book Catalog

It lists over a thousand money-saving best-sellers originally priced from $3.75 to $15.00 —bestsellers that are yours now for as little as 50¢ to $2.25!

The catalog gives you a great opportunity to build your own private library at huge savings!

So don't delay any longer—send for your catalog TODAY! It's absolutely FREE!